Best Knight Ever

A Kinda Fairytale

Cassandra Gannon

Text copyright © 2019 Cassandra Gannon
Cover Image copyright © 2019 Cassandra Gannon
All Rights Reserved

Published by Star Turtle Publishing

Visit Cassandra Gannon and Star Turtle Publishing at
www.starturtlepublishing.com

For news on upcoming books and promotions you can also check us out on Facebook!

Or email Star Turtle Publishing directly:
starturtlepublishing@gmail.com

We'd love to hear from you!

Also by Cassandra Gannon

The Elemental Phases Series
Warrior from the Shadowland
Guardian of the Earth House
Exile in the Water Kingdom
Treasure of the Fire Kingdom
Queen of the Magnetland
Magic of the Wood House
Coming Soon: *Destiny of the Time House*

A Kinda Fairytale Series
Wicked Ugly Bad
Beast in Shining Armor
The Kingpin of Camelot
Best Knight Ever
Coming Soon: *Happily Ever Witch*

Other Books
Love in the Time of Zombies
Not Another Vampire Book
Vampire Charming
Cowboy from the Future
Once Upon a Caveman
Ghost Walk

If you enjoy Cassandra's books, you may also enjoy books by her sister, Elizabeth Gannon.

<u>The Consortium of Chaos series</u>
Yesterday's Heroes
The Son of Sun and Sand
The Guy Your Friends Warned You About
Electrical Hazard
The Only Fish in the Sea
Not Currently Evil

The Mad Scientist's Guide to Dating
Broke and Famous

<u>Other books</u>
The Snow Queen
Travels with a Fairytale Monster
Everyone Hates Fairytale Pirates
Captive of a Fairytale Barbarian

This book is dedicated to the many thoughtful fans who wrote me over the course of two years and asked me one or more of the following questions:

>Will Trystan have a book?
>Will Galahad have a book?
>Will Trystan and Galahad have a book together?

>>Yes.
>>And I hope you like it.

Prologue

Look, everyone knows that the First Looking Glass Campaign was a direct response to the gryphons' violent natures. King Uther had no choice but to prevent the winged devils' inevitable attack on Camelot, by attacking them *first*.

And their attack *was* coming. Make no mistake, listeners. If not for Uther marching into Lyonesse, we would all be speaking that heathen gryphon dialect right now.

They were monsters and we needed to kill them all!

"Stopping the Savages" Podcast
Sir Dragonet of Camelot- Former Troubadour of King Uther and Host of the Program

---

During the last days of the Meliodas Cycle, the wingless came from the east and invaded our lands. Their knights carried godless weapons. Their numbers shook the ground as they marched. They killed every living thing that crossed their path, simply for crossing their path. Within days, all gryphons knew that these men were not warriors, at all.

They were nothing but monsters. And so it was just that we kill them all.

How the Wingless War Happened
Skylyn Welkyn- Gryphon Storyteller

Thirteen Days Ago
Camelot

"People say Galahad is perfect." Guinevere Skycast, Queen of Camelot, explained in a very serious tone. "I've said it myself. But, really he's just a sweet, humble, regular guy."

Trystan glanced at the woman he considered his sister, remaining quiet.

"Sure, he's a gorgeous, successful, famous knight, who had a couple of highly-rated TV shows and who invented those candy-coated potato chip thingies." She nodded earnestly. "But, if you focus on his sweet, humble, *non-perfect* qualities and see him as just a regular guy, I think you'll really like him."

Trystan said nothing.

That was apparently enough.

"Yes, I know. You're right." Gwen held up her hands, like Trystan had won her over with his argument. "Galahad was on the wrong side of the Looking Glass Campaigns. Everyone in Camelot was wrong for what happened to the gryphons and I will do *everything* I can to fix it. I swear."

She would try. Trystan knew that. His honorary sister was small and wingless, but she was mighty in her determination. Gwen was a great queen, who would do all she could to help his people. But she was too late. The gryphons were all but gone, now. Camelot could pour its unlimited resources into helping the small group of Trystan's people who remained, but no one could buy them a future. No one could undo the past.

A past that Sir Galahad was at least partially responsible for destroying.

Trystan zipped up his bag, ready to begin his idiotic journey. His bedroom in Camelot's castle was bare and free from gaudy furnishings, just as he preferred. His clan was gathered around pestering him, just as he preferred. Leaving it all to go questing after some asshole knight was *not* what he preferred, but he would do it for Gwen.

He would do *anything* for his clan.

Trystan had lost two clans in the War, so he knew what the world was like when you were alone in it. Having people to care for was a blessing that he did not take for granted.

"Gal is a Good man. He was with me when I was completely alone and scared." Gwen rushed on, unconsciously matching his thoughts. "He wanted to leave the King's Men, after Uther died, but he stayed to protect me and Avalon. His banishment was all my fault. No other knight would've sided with me over Arthur."

Galahad's devotion to Gwen and Avi was the main reason Trystan didn't plan to kill him on sight. The knight had protected them, long before Midas had married Gwen and Trystan knew she and Avalon even existed. He owed the man something for that, regardless of Galahad's soulless nature.

"Gal will always do what he thinks is right, no matter the consequences." Gwen insisted. "He's my *family* and I want him home. All of Camelot does."

That was also true. Galahad had been banished for treason and still won every popularity poll in the land. How the hell was that even possible? Who put his name on the ballots?

In Camelot's eyes, their favorite son was exceptional at *everything*. Galahad had done it first, done it best, starred in a successful movie *about* himself doing it, and gave all the profits *from* doing it to wild rhino preservation. Then he cheerfully went on to do something *else* that no one had ever dreamed possible, all the while staying modest and generous and disgustingly handsome.

It was... unnatural.

The knight might be the Golden Child in Camelot, but outside the walls of the kingdom, people knew better. *Trystan* knew better. The knight's beautiful face and charity work were all a façade. The mass graves at Legion spoke for themselves.

Gwen sighed again, as if she completely understood Trystan's continued silence. She probably did. Trystan and Guinevere understood each other in most things. "The point is... I know you don't like knights and I don't blame you. I know you're only finding Galahad for me." She nodded, her blue eyes on his. "Thank you, Trystan. Thank you so much."

She gave him a smile that made this entire enterprise worth the wasted effort.

Trystan grunted.

"Fucking hell, did Galahad really invent those potato-chips with the sugary stuff on them?" Midas complained from the doorway. He was a huge wingless man, with an unhandsome face, abysmal fashion sense, and an unparalleled intellect. There was no one Trystan trusted more. "I *love* those things."

"Everyone loves Gala-Chips." Gwen turned to arch a teasing

brow at her husband. "Galahad concocted them on a whim one day, in between teaching Avi to finger paint, protecting Camelot from that octopus-monster, and becoming the world's foremost expert on antique firearms. Then, he donated the recipe to a non-profit that benefits underprivileged children interested in STEM subjects."

"Jesus." Midas pinched the bridge of his nose, like he was tired.

"Focus on his non-perfect qualities." Gwen stressed again. "He's always collecting random junk that he wants to fix, but he rarely has the time to actually do it. And he can be a little bit boring and beige, because he's so unrelentingly Good, all the time. Oh! And he loses all his hats and sunglasses. It's crazy how many he manages to misplace."

Lyrssa save him…

"His Good and Bad qualities do not matter to me." Trystan told Gwen, not wanting to hear any more stories about the jackass' brilliance, philanthropy, or daring deeds. "You and Midas asked me to locate this man. I have taken on the duty of caring for you all, no matter how pointless your wishes. So, I will retrieve Galahad for you. That is the end of it."

"If anyone can find Gal, I'm sure it's you." Gwen sounded confident in Trystan's abilities, which was appropriate given his skills. "I'm just worried that Galahad's in some kind of trouble. He doesn't usually get into trouble, because he's so capable at… *everything*."

Midas and Trystan rolled their eyes in perfect unison.

"It's true!" Gwen insisted. "But, now no one has seen him in *such* a long time. I'm really worried. Something must have happened to him."

"Probably." Trystan agreed. The wingless were a dim bunch and knights were particularly stupid.

"I want you to be very careful." Gwen straightened Trystan's jacket and gazed up at him worriedly. "Okay? Don't take any unnecessary risks. I don't want *two* brothers lost."

"I will be fine." What could possibly befall him that he couldn't handle? Trystan was the best at all he tried. "I always avoid unnecessary risk. You know this."

Gwen frowned. "Do I? Because I've seen you do some pretty risky things when you're angry, Trystan. You killed half the population of Celliwig to protect me that time."

"That was necessary." What else could he have done? Allow those bastards to harm his sister? No. They needed to die. It was very clear to him. "My behavior was justified and logical. Feelings never sway me. Gryphons are generally born without emotions."

"Generally." Midas chimed in and his tone was… amused?

Trystan glanced at him sharply.

Midas arched a brow in contrived innocence.

Trystan's eyes narrowed and he decided to end this pointless discussion. "Gwen, you will be in charge in my absence. Try to keep everything running smoothly and I will sort out whatever problems you create, once I return." He emphatically pointed a finger at her and then Midas. "*Do nothing dangerous*. I mean it."

Midas made a rueful face at that, because he was technically the king. He didn't argue, though, because how could he? The man was helpless. It was good that Midas had originally hired Trystan as a bodyguard, because the former gangster never would have survived on his own. Trystan was uneasy leaving him even now.

Trystan looked back a Gwen. "I entrust you with our clan." He warned, slinging the satchel over his shoulder. "Protect Midas and the child."

"Always."

"I'll be *fine*, Trystan." Midas sounded amused. "Stop worrying."

"Gryphons do not worry." He muttered, wondering what else he could do to secure his clan before he left. They seemed very vulnerable. The three reasons for his existence were all terrifyingly helpless and utterly ridiculous most of the time. If he knew how to worry, that would certainly worry him. "Perhaps we should hire more guards."

Midas had had enough. "Stop obsessing, *j'ha.*" He slapped a hand on Trystan's shoulder, calling him "brother" in the gryphon dialect. Midas had been raised by a gryphon, so he spoke the language fluently. "Attempt to consider this a vacation."

"Gryphons do not *obsess*, either. Or vacation." Seeing no logical way to put the hellish trip off any longer, Trystan stalked out the door, starting down the hallway. "Fine. I will return with the knight in a few weeks. I do not promise he will be in one piece."

"Try not to kill everyone you meet along the way." Midas sounded amused, again. "And remember to call."

"Hang on. A few weeks?" Gwen blinked and hurried after Trystan, blonde hair bouncing as she tried to keep up with his long strides. "You really think you can find Gal that fast, Trystan? No one else has been able to track down even a trace and Midas has hired every detective in a dozen kingdoms."

Trystan snorted, unsurprised. Why was everybody else so

incompetent? "A month at maximum." He predicted, stalking down the stairs. "The man is probably passed out in a bar, somewhere."

It wasn't like he could go unnoticed, looking as he did. In photos and on television, the knight seemed to glow with some kind of magical glow-y light. It remained a mystery how Galahad accomplished the trick, again and again, but it was always there. Trystan often found himself staring at the images, baffled and irritated by the pull of the man. Galahad had to be relying on makeup and fakery. *Had* to be. No one was that golden and shiny and... *bright*.

Maybe some kind of magic was involved.

"You know, you really do remind me of Galahad sometimes." Gwen told him, hurrying down the stairs in his wake. The woman liked to talk. Trystan kept an eye on her to make sure she didn't fall in her rush to continue haranguing him. "You both like children... You both do crazy things for the people you care about... You're both heroes..."

"All the heroes died in the War."

Gwen ignored that grim truth, undeterred from her ridiculous lecture. "You're both very honorable. Very handsome. Very protective. Very sweet. If you think about it, you and Galahad have a lot in common."

"This conversation is ludicrous." He told Gwen in a very reasonable way, because he was conscientious of her strange feelings. The wingless were such an emotional species. "And do not rush down the steps. Why must I continually tell you this?" He reached the landing and paused for a second, so she could safely catch up.

While he waited, his gaze fell on the wall of the stairwell and a giant gilded painting of an angel battling demons. It was the one piece of art in the world he didn't detest. He wasn't sure why but he found himself looking at it often.

"Just give Gal a chance, before you decide to be your most Trystan-ish, okay?" Gwen reached his side. "Galahad was going through a lot, even before he was banished. And it can take a while for him to connect with people. It was years before he'd call me 'Gwen' and not 'your majesty.' Gal is *so* sensitive."

"The man starred in a film about himself. I doubt he is shy."

"That movie was before the last Looking Glass Campaign. He changed after that."

"Burning peaceful villages can change a person."

"I *promise* you, he wasn't a part of that, Trystan. I would never ask you to do this, if I thought he was involved in any of those atrocities. Uther, yes. My ex-father-in-law was a monster. Arthur, too. But Gal would *never* hurt innocent people. He doesn't talk about the War, but I know in my heart he acted honorably."

Trystan grunted and continued down the steps, unwilling to disillusion her.

Gwen had no idea what men at war were capable of. He hoped she never knew. Trystan still dreamed images that he wished he could forget. Flashes of violence and screaming and death. Felt his mother's hands grasping for him as soldiers ripped him from her arms. Heard the sound a wooden stick made when you ran it back and forth against the bars of the zoo. Smelled the acrid scent of decaying bodies in the sun.

He wanted none of those memories for his new clan. Wanted none of the horrors of battle to ever touch them. There was no reason in the world to try and explain to Gwen what the Looking Glass Campaigns had truly been like.

"You can make your own judgement, once you get to know Galahad." Gwen insisted innocently. "You'll see I'm right. Just be nice to him, okay?"

"No. Why would I do such a pointless thing?"

"Well... he really is *very* handsome." She offered *very* casually.

Trystan sent her a sideways look, caught off guard by that remark.

His sister enjoyed strong-arming those around her. Currently, she was intent on finding Trystan a mate, whether he wished for one or not. She often pointed out how attractive women were, hoping to entice him. This was the first time she'd ever mentioned a *male's* appearance, but the new tactic was only to be expected. Midas must have told her that gryphons weren't strictly binary in their choice of partners. Gwen was no doubt thrilled to have more options to choose from in her matchmaking campaign.

It was surprising that she would consider a man for *Galahad's* potential partner, though. The wingless tended to be far more puritanical than the gryphon. They typically preferred one gender, usually the opposite of their own. Nothing in Trystan's research had indicated that Galahad favored males. That trait would have gotten him kicked out of the King's Men, in fact. ...Which was probably why Gwen hadn't mentioned it before. If she suspected that Galahad wanted to keep his private life a secret, she'd guard it too. It was her nature to protect.

Except now she was telling Trystan.
Why?
"I do not care what the knight looks like." He told her,

unsettled by this turn in the conversation. ...And his assertion was almost true. He certainly didn't *want* to care what the knight looked like. "I judge the worthiness of a potential mate based only on their *actions*."

"I totally agree." Gwen bobbed her head. "That's very fair."

"The knight's actions do not speak well of him." Trystan persisted and it was a vast understatement. "Choose someone else -- *anyone* else, of *any* gender-- and I will consider sleeping with them, if it makes you content."

There. Maybe that would satisfy her.

"I don't want you to sleep with somebody to make me happy, dummy! Ew!" She batted his arm. "I want you to have a *relationship*."

"A relationship?" That seemed to be the wingless word for claiming a mate. "This is a very serious thing."

"Yes! It's also a very *great* thing, if you don't want to die alone."

"We all die alone."

"God, you're morbid." Gwen waved that aside. "Anyway, I've put lots of perfectly wonderful romantic prospects in front of you and you just run them right over. At least three have cried."

"You choose weak prospects. That is not my fault."

Since boyhood, Trystan had always wanted a hero for a mate. They were all gone, now, but he would still accept no less. He remembered Lunette and Ban too clearly. He would have no one at all, before he had less than that example.

"Can you just keep an open mind about Galahad? Please?"

"No. My mind is stubbornly blocked by facts." He paused. "And I cannot choose my mate, at this time. Soon, I have to journey many places, killing all the men on my list. That will take all my time and focus."

Gwen glowered up at him. "You're still stuck on that vendetta thing? Really?"

Trystan braced himself against the accusation in her eyes. "I will bring Galahad back to you, but then I must leave Camelot to hunt down my enemies. It will take months. Possibly longer. I have *told* you this."

Gwen was a warrior. She accepted nothing but victory, so she shook her head and ignored his plans completely. "Just... be *nice* about bringing Galahad home and see what happens. That's all I ask. Don't --like-- put Gal in a sack, or knock him unconscious, or tie him up, or anything."

"And if the knight doesn't wish to come home?" He challenged. "If he wants to *stay* lost?"

Gwen's mouth thinned in determination. "Oh, he's *coming* home." She declared righteously. "Put him in a sack, knock him unconscious, and tie him up if you have to."

Trystan so enjoyed the woman's ruthlessness. His expression softened, his eyes finding hers. "It's done, *j'aha*. I promise you."

She beamed up at him again and wrapped her arms around him in a hug. "I love you, brother."

If he knew how to say it back, he would have.

Instead, Trystan ran his thumb down the center of her face, from her forehead to the bridge of her nose. Keeping his clan content in his care was worth anything. Even a senseless mission to save a monster.

"Do not die while I'm gone." He warned and went striding into the palace's inner courtyard.

The rest of the castle had developed into a mix of influences from three very different people. Midas was focused on maximizing the garish aesthetics of the place, and Gwen was focused on preserving some traditions, and Trystan was focused on defenses. Somehow they made it all work, with tacky furniture being placed around heirloom vases and intricate security systems. Trystan thought the effect very pleasing.

But, the inner courtyard where Avalon played was positively fortified. Trystan didn't give a shit about aesthetics or tradition. The child was his goddamn heartbeat. Nothing and no one came near Avi until Trystan was sure they weren't a threat. He was insistent on that and nobody argued. She was the heartbeat of all of them.

"Avalon." He called, treading across the grass. "I am leaving, now."

There was a maudlin sculpture in the center of the yard, featuring a young soldier, courageously holding his sword aloft. The plaque at the bottom declared it a commemoration to "Bedivere the Brave. Knight of Camelot and Martyr of Legion. Who Died Saving Children From the Flames of War." Bedivere was the only King's Man who'd ever acted heroically, so Trystan did not overly mind the man being remembered.

He just minded *how* he was remembered.

Art served no purpose. How was that not obvious? Surely, if Bedivere gave his life for such a noble reason, he would've preferred his memorial to be something more worthwhile. Food for hungry families or arms for living soldiers. Yet this dead hunk of metal, in a walled garden, was how his people chose to tell his story. If he lived in Camelot forever, Trystan would never understand the wingless.

He spared the hideous bronze monstrosity a dismissive look, his attention on Avalon. "Do nothing overly cute while I'm gone, yes? I do not wish to miss it."

"'kay, Trystan."

The little girl was wearing a vividly pink, glittery dress and playing with sidewalk chalk. She'd drawn a vast map on the cobblestones, using lavender and yellow lines to form a checkerboard pattern. Trystan studied it for a beat and felt the hair on the back of his neck rise. "What is that?"

Her big eyes blinked up at him. There was a fuzzy cat-ear headband on her head. He had no idea why. "It's Legion, of course. The gone-away gryphons was talking to me about it."

P'don.

The florid gryphon oath filtered through his head.

"Cursing is a no-no." Avi said, easily reading his mind. "Mommy says so."

Avalon Skycast was an Enchantress. She might be a child, but she already saw the future, the past, and all possibilities in between. The dead gryphons often spoke to people burdened with an important destiny, helping to guide them. Since Avalon Skycast would one day change the world, they communicated with her regularly. Trystan easily accepted that. But, while he honored his ancestors, *no one* was allowed to frighten his niece.

"Avi," he knelt down so they were at eyelevel, "I told you to ignore the gryphons, if they told you anything scary, didn't I?"

Avi wrinkled her nose at him. "The gone-away gryphons aren't scary, Trystan. We's friends. They like me." She grinned and threw her arms wide. "Everybody likes me!"

He ignored her mind-blowing cuteness, but it was hard. "If you wish to know about Legion, I will tell you."

Her head tilted in curiosity. "Do you know what really happened?"

"Yes. It was the last day of the Looking Glass Campaigns." He pointed to Bedivere's tragic statue. "Where he died."

Her blue gaze flicked to the bronze eyesore with a small frown.

"Uther, King of Camelot, attacked a peaceful gryphon village with his villainous knights." Trystan continued, giving her a sanitized version of events. "Lyrssa Highstorm, queen of my people, rightfully killed him for it. But too much damage had been done to the town of Legion. It burned and many people died. The gryphons lost that fight and the War was finally over."

King Uther had been Avalon's grandfather, but he'd also been an evil bastard. There was no use in pretending the man's death hadn't been just. Trystan always believed in telling the young the truth. It was the only way they'd learn.

Avalon's eyes went back to her chalk map and then she looked up at Trystan. "I think Galahad should tell us what really happened." She decided. "He'll know. He was there."

Yes. Galahad of Camelot certainly *had been* there.

The son of a bitch had led the troops that massacred the town.

Trystan had often tried to kill Galahad during the War. They had been on opposites sides, after all. And it occurred to him, not for the first time, that he could simply kill Galahad, *now*. It would save him no end of trouble. Trystan had promised to find Galahad and bring him back to Camelot, but he'd never said the man would be *alive*. Producing a body for Gwen to bury would, in theory, fulfil his vow. It really was the simplest solution.

Except Avalon and Gwen loved Galahad.

Trystan met Avi's blue gaze.

She smiled back at him with warmth, and purity, and total trust.

Trystan sighed. "How *much* do you love the knight?" He asked, wanting to be sure he couldn't solve this problem the easy way.

"A *lot*." She clapped her hands together. "He's the best knight ever!"

"He's not." Trystan assured her, because the man obviously wasn't.

Trystan had been in prison during Legion, so he hadn't seen that battle firsthand. But he witnessed what Uther's knights had done in countless others. The gryphons had been nearly exterminated in Camelot's relentless genocide. Trystan had known it was impossible to stop the sheer numbers of knights that came for his people, but he'd still stood against the onslaught. It had cost him years on battlefields and locked in cells, but he would do everything again, if he had to. Make all the same choices. He might have lost the War, but he'd been on the right side.

Galahad had chosen a much darker path.

"Gal's my third best friend in the whole world." Avi continued cheerily, believing in the man's Goodness, when she really should know better. "You's going to love him, too!"

"I wouldn't count on it." Trystan resigned himself to returning with a breathing knight. "While I am gone, remember I am your *second* best friend, yes?"

"I know." She bounced forward to hug him goodbye. "I'll miss you! Tell Gal to bring me back a magic carpet, 'kay? He said he would, before he left."

Trystan closed his eyes briefly, his chin resting on her curly-cue curls. "He's probably forgotten your gift." No knight had ever kept a promise. Being lying dickheads was part of their nature. "I will remind him, though."

And then beat the shit out of him until he bought Avalon exactly what she wanted.

Avi pulled back to look into his eyes, again. "You don't need to worry so much." She said quietly and he knew she saw every thought in his head. "We'll all be okay."

"Gryphons do not worry. I told your father this. I just don't like to let this clan out of my sight. I do not trust any of you to survive without me."

She tilted her head. "But you want to go find all those mean guys on your list, don't you? If you did that, you'd be gone for a loooooong time."

Trystan hesitated, because that was true. He did plan to hunt down the men on his list. He'd never mentioned that to Avalon, obviously, but it didn't matter. She could read his intentions. Killing them would take Trystan from his clan, which was the last thing he wanted. But what choice did he have?

Those traitors *had* to die.

"I do not know where those men are, so I will not be going off to kill them anytime soon." He temporized, unsure how else to respond.

"Oh, I know where they are!" Avalon's hand shot up like she was eager to be called on in her kindergarten class. "The meanest one is in St Ives."

"Marcus is in St. Ives?" Trystan's heart leapt in anticipation and frustration.

St. Ives was a pit of brothels and casinos on the edge of hell. The last city before the Moaning Sea, St. Ives was situated on territory so inhospitable that no one else wanted to claim it. It was also surrounded by a forty foot magical wall that not even gryphons could fly over. The only people welcomed inside were Bad folk and, occasionally, their abducted hostages. How the hell was he going to get to Marcus, if the jackass was hidden in a locked city?

"You should be careful if you go there, Trystan. There's other Galahads in St. Ives." Avi nodded, as if that was common knowledge. "But, I just want mine, okay?"

He had no idea what that meant, which was typical of many of his interactions with Avalon. It was difficult to untangle all the threads that were woven into her visions. Perhaps she was telling him the city was filled with knights.

Shit. He hoped it wasn't filled with knights. He hated knights.

"I will only return with *one* knight." He assured her. "Even that is too many."

Avi's small palms cupped either side of his face, smearing chalk all over his skin. "Galahad is *supposed* to be with us." She assured him sweetly. "You'll see. Be nice to him."

Avalon was always right.

Trystan accepted that, even when he wished she was wrong.

"Fine." He could not stand against her *and* Gwen on the matter. Besides, Trystan could be "nice" to anyone. Even asshole knights. He was nothing if not gracious and fair. He'd be the first to tell anyone that fact and then fight them to the death if they disagreed. He ran his thumb down the center of Avi's face. "I will do my best and return home soon, yes?"

"'Kay. Bye-bye! I love you. Bring me back a present!"

Trystan's heart melted in some unexplained way. He watched her go skipping back to her sidewalk art. "What kind of present do you want?"

"The big glass bubble. It's pretty. And big! We need it *a lot!*"

"Uh-huh." Trystan had no idea what that meant, either. It didn't matter. He'd figure it out. Whatever Avi wanted, he'd provide. "I'll get it for you, then." He rose to his feet, prepared to go. The sooner he left, the sooner he could return to his clan.

"Hey, Trystan?" Avalon called after him. "When you get back, can you tell me about *ya'lahs?* Like Elaine used to tell you?"

Trystan stopped dead in his tracks, his head snapping back to gape at her. "You know of the *ya'lah*?" He had told Avalon nearly all of Elaine's stories, just as the woman would have wished, but he had never told her *that* legend. "You've seen this person in your visions?"

"Sure." She didn't look up from the drawing, cheerfully humming an ancient gryphon hymn. Trystan's mother used to sing him the same song. "That's how the curse breaks."

Trystan stood there for a long moment, his mind spinning and his heart pounding in his chest. He had not heard anyone mention a *ya'lah* since the zoo. Now, Avi spoke of one in the same conversation where she claimed Galahad of Camelot was the best knight ever?

Knowing Avalon, that was no coincidence.

The child saw everything and the dead gryphons were always whispering to her. Trystan's ancestors would want the curse lifted as much as anyone. If they saw a path where it could happen, they would help to guide...

No.

Trystan shook his head, unable to believe he was thinking what he was suddenly thinking. *No.* Avalon Skycast was always right, but not this time.

No way was the Butcher of Legion the *ya'lah*.

No fucking way.

Chapter One

Camelot and the gryphons once lived in peace with one another. But then Uther came to power and he was jealous of all we had. Our freedom. Our lands. Our knowledge.

And especially our graal.

The graal is the greatest treasure of the gryphon people. No one alive has ever seen it. Some even think it to be a myth, but I believe the old stories. I believe that the graal is not of this world. I believe that its powers surpass even level six magic. I believe it can do things that are beyond our understanding.

And I believe that our ancestors knew such an object could easily be used for ill purposes.

That is why it had to be hidden away.

How the Wingless War Happened
Skylyn Welkyn- Gryphon Storyteller

Lyonesse Desert- East of the Umberland Plains

Through the smoke came an angel.

Galahad's stinging eyes widened in amazement when he saw the man striding through the squalid desert town. Large and tanned, with white wings and golden hair, he looked like he had stepped right off of an old master's canvas.

Galahad loved art. His favorite painting had always been a century-old, thickly-varnished masterpiece that hung in the stairwell of

Camelot's palace. It depicted a heavenly warrior battling demons and protecting the innocent. Galahad had stared up at it when he was younger and thought that angel was the most beautiful thing in the world.

But the two-dimensional image was *nothing* compared to this man.

"I've come for the knight." The angel said very distinctly. His accent sounded out of time in the modern world, but there was no mistaking his words, even over the growing roar of the flames.

The beautiful angel was there for him?

Uh-oh...

For the first time, it occurred to Galahad that he might die in this place. Why else would an angel be appearing? Shit. How was that possible? He hadn't expected to die, even as they lit the pyre beneath him.

But he also hadn't expected an angel to show up at his death. That was a triumph, by any measure. Galahad always tried to see the bright side of things, even when being roasted to death. If he died today, at least he was on the right side. The angel's appearance proved it. It proved that Galahad had been right to trust in a bigger purpose to the universe. In a greater plan. He'd been *right*.

He'd always believed in God, which was so much harder than not believing. When you'd seen what Galahad had seen and done what Galahad had done, holding onto faith sometimes seemed next to impossible. But he'd clung to it by his bloody, ragged fingernails, even though he always --*always*-- feared what divine judgment would mean for someone who'd fallen so short of his noble ideals. Someone who felt hidden darkness inside of himself, every single day.

Someone who was damned.

But God was still with him. Galahad might be dying in a pyre, far from home, but he wasn't alone. An angel was here for him, so he wasn't alone, after all.

"The knight has trespassed on our land." Wilbur, the leader of the pigs, bellowed.

The entire village was filled with humanoid hogs, who didn't take kindly to outsiders visiting their primitive sticks-and-straw village. Galahad knew that better than most. One minute he was refilling his canteen by the thin trickle of a nearby river. The next, a horde of angry hogs had attacked him and dragged Galahad into the center of town

Galahad no longer killed people. He had too much blood on his hands, as it was. Instead, he'd attempted to reason with the pigmen. He *always* tried to reason with people.

...Usually with this exact amount of success.

Instead of listening to his very logical explanations, they'd tied his hands behind a huge post, piled logs beneath his feet, and set the bonfire ablaze. Obviously, Galahad had a lot to learn about diplomacy. His attempts invariably ended with people trying to murder him.

"And this is not just *any* knight." Wilbur continued, his voice rising in exaltation and malice. "This is Galahad. The Captain of the King's Men, who savaged our lands when we were powerless to stop the foreign invaders. Well, now *we* are the ones with the power!"

Wilbur's armed followers roared in approval at that statement. All the soldiers in the village were gathered around to watch Galahad die. Galahad really did try to view everything that happened to him in the most positive light he could, so he was looking at the exuberant throng surrounding the bonfire as him having a well-attended funeral.

The angel crossed his arms over his chest. "You're going to be a pain in the ass about this, aren't you, Wilbur?" He sighed out in apparent exasperation.

Wilbur smirked, bolstered by his men's cheering. "I'd think you'd appreciate our little barbeque, gryphon, given what the knights did to your kind." He waved a hooved-hand towards Galahad, as the flames grew bigger and bigger. "They wiped out most of your people like bugs."

"I'm still here." The beautiful voice stayed calm. "And that particular knight has been placed in my care. So, I'll be taking him back."

Gryphon? Galahad focused on the winged-man, straining to see him clearer through the smoke. It was thick and suffocating, burning into Galahad's lungs. It must have been messing with his mind, too, because he was apparently hearing things. No gryphon would ever help him.

Ever.

The "angel" explanation made way more sense.

Except, Galahad finally noticed that the man's tawny-colored hair was pulled back in the intricate braid of a gryphon warrior and his clothes possessed the simple lines they favored. He *was* a gryphon. Shit. Now, Galahad was *sure* he was going to die.

"Taking him?" Wilbur scoffed, not understanding it, either. "You must be joking."

"Do I look like someone who jokes a lot?"

No, he really didn't. Especially not if he was a gryphon. They were born without emotions. Cut way down on the comedy. Galahad squinted, trying to figure this out and coming up with... nothing. Not one explanation explained it.

"If you're not joking, then you must be out of your mind." Wilbur snapped. "We're burning that dumbass knight at the stake, in case you missed it. We already lit the wood! You think we're just going to hand over our prisoner before he fries?"

"I think my niece and sister want that knight back." The angel-who-was-really-a-gryphon retorted in an even tone. "So, I *know* you will give me that knight back... one way or another."

Whoever this man's sister and niece wanted him to save, it certainly wasn't Galahad. What the hell was going on?

Wilbur puffed himself up, refusing to back down to the gryphon's threats. "Well, my men might have a little something to say about that." He sneered. "What will it be, boys? Shall we give the gryphon our knight... or shall we have a second roast tonight?"

More shouting ensued, none of it in support of the "letting Galahad go free" plan. Several of the nasty little porkers raced forward, weapons drawn, ready to kill the angel for interrupting their fun. If Galahad had any oxygen available, he would have shouted a warning.

The gryphon sighed, again. "Why is everyone so fucking stupid?"

Then, somehow, a double-bladed axe was in the man's hand, swinging out like a part of him. After that it was all... art. Unexplainable and undeniable, as with all genuine masterpieces. Galahad had given up killing, but he'd trained at it for years. He knew what it was to see a true artist at work.

It was as if everyone else in the village was stuck at a lower speed. Their movements slow and clumsy and doomed before they even made them. The gryphon knew just where to step. Just when to spin. Just how to hit. He struck one pig with the axe, even while shifting sideways to avoid a second pig's attack, and slamming a fist into a third pig's face. And it was all effortless. All perfect and precise with no extra motions or false moves.

A thick, powerful mist developed over the gryphon's face, resembling an eagle. His kind summoned the masks in battle. The shifting veil would obscure their regular features, making them seem... otherworldly. Galahad had always been fascinated by the magic of it.

More pigs ran at the gryphon and they fell. One dozen. Two. Impossible odds, for anyone else. But the odds were meaningless now, because this man was an unmatched talent. All of Wilbur's forces could have charged at once and the gryphon would still win.

The gryphon used his wings to propel himself backwards, avoiding an unavoidable bevy of spears, and Galahad knew what it was to be awed. The man flipped a pig ten feet in the air, sending him crashing into three others, while simultaneously stabbing another through the torso with his own sword. This gryphon was performing a symphony, while the rest of them were picking out random keys on a piano.

Flames burned the edges of Galahad's clothes, the fire scalding the bottom of his boots. And *still* he was grateful to be standing there, seeing something so beautiful.

Galahad had been the Captain of the King's Men. The top knight ever to graduate the Knights' Academy. He was always the best at everything he did. *Always*. But Galahad was now living a life of truth. And looking at the gryphon with clear eyes, he realized that this man was the only person in the world who just might be able to beat him in a fight. And oddly that idea didn't bother him, at all. How could anyone resent witnessing true artistry?

The gryphon was so... beautiful.

Wilbur let out a squealing yell of panic, seeing that his position was absolutely hopeless. "Take him! Take the knight!" He screamed before all of his soldiers became hams. "Take him if you want him so much!"

Bones crunched as the gryphon dropped his final attacker to the ground. "As if I need your permission, at this point. Goddamn waste of my time." His features back to normal, now, he stalked towards the pyre, jabbing his axe-blade at Wilbur for emphasis. "Pray to all your gods that the knight isn't scorched beyond repair. If he is damaged, and it upsets the females of my clan, I will hold *you* responsible."

Wilbur paled beneath his piggy-pink skin.

Muttering to himself in his own language, the gryphon knocked some of the larger logs away with his axe, so he could reach the pole. "Knight? Do you live?"

Galahad tried to answer, but it resulted in a coughing fit. The fire wasn't singeing him, but smoke filled his lungs and made it impossible to breathe. He should have thought about that. In another moment, he'd pass out. There was no getting around it. Still, that wheezing hack seemed to be enough for the gryphon.

"Good. You're alive. Attempt to stay that way." There was a heavy vibration through the wooden post and Galahad realized that the gryphon was trying to cut him loose with the axe.

...Which was *not* going to work, because the ropes were enspelled and unbreakable. Galahad would have told him so, except he was blacking out.

"*P'don.*" The man muttered. "Hold on."

The gryphon was clearly a problem solver by nature. He stopped hacking at the ropes and attacked the wooden pole, instead. His axe slammed into the post, again and again. And then suddenly it toppled over and Galahad was free of it. Without the support of the pole, he began to fall. The flames seemed to rise up to meet him. He would have collapsed face-first into them, except the gryphon was already lugging him upwards again.

"You weigh a ton." The gryphon complained, but he didn't let him go. "Two weeks tracking you and you've not made one second of it easy, I swear to Lyrssa." There was the brief sensation of flight and then Galahad was being laid down on damp ground. "Hold still. Your shirt remains afire."

A sudden flood of water nearly drowned Galahad. He sat bolt upright, gasping and shocked back to full awareness. It took him a second to realize that the gryphon had just opened the town's water tank, which was an elevated wooden barrel that caught and stored rainwater. The gryphon slammed his axe into the side of it, so a waterfall gushed out onto Galahad's head.

Galahad peered up at the gryphon through the torrent, once again struck by the absolute beauty of the man. Not just on the outside, which was flawless. But *inside*, where it actually mattered. This man, who should have been his enemy, had just saved his life. He wasn't exactly an angel, but it seemed as if God had still sent him. He was a gift.

"Thank you." Galahad whispered sincerely.

The gryphon grunted, which was probably supposed to mean "you're welcome." He clearly wasn't the most talkative guy.

"Come on, now." Wilbur whined. "Water is rare in these parts. You can't just waste it on an asshole like him."

"Are you still here?" The gryphon sent him a glare. "Most people would be smart enough to run."

"I know you, now." Wilbur continued, heedless of the danger. "You're Trystan Airbourne. They said the old king sent you away to die in a hole, because of the attack on the Mynyw Garrison."

"That was one reason."

This was Trystan Airbourne? Galahad blinked against the pouring water. The gryphon most knights had called a demon for his constant surprise attacks? The one who'd waged such a relentless war against Camelot that they'd been forced to stop their advance in the west?

Trystan had used the mountain's maze-like passes as traps, bottlenecking the soldiers and nullifying their vast numbers. Even when he'd been the one trapped and nullified, Galahad had been forced to silently acknowledge the superior planning of his enemy.

If Trystan Airbourne had been on the winning side of the Looking Glass Campaigns, his strategies would have been taught at the Knights' Academy as works of military genius. Instead, he'd been locked in prison for years. For a gryphon, being confined was worse than death, which was probably why Uther had selected it as punishment. The old king had been an evil bastard.

Wilbur looked betrayed. "You killed hundreds of knights, Trystan, and now you protect their leader? Do you know who this man truly *is*?"

"He is Galahad, the Butcher of Legion."

Galahad cringed at that nickname.

"*Exactly.* Have you forgotten what his kind did to everyone they deemed 'inferior' races? The lives they took and the lands they destroyed. Your entire clan was wiped out!"

"I now have a new clan and they claim this man. No one will harm him."

Wilbur spat on the ground in disgust, but he didn't push his luck. "Then you'd best get him the hell out of here. Everyone within a hundred miles is going to try and kill that man. Folks in Camelot might think he's hot shit, but this will look like a goddamn birthday celebration compared to what the Welkyn Clan will have in mind for him around here." He waved a hand toward the still raging bonfire.

"Luckily, we're headed east."

"No." Galahad gave another cough, tossing his hair back from his face. "I have to go west." He struggled to his feet, which wasn't easy given his hands were still tied.

Trystan Airbourne sent him a quick dismissive look, then seemed to do a double-take. Fathomless brown eyes stayed locked on Galahad for several beats, like something had surprised him. His gaze skimmed over Galahad's features, not saying a word.

Galahad smiled at him. "I was on TV." He explained, thinking that Trystan recognized him. That happened a lot. They'd never met in battle, (Galahad would remember that, since he probably wouldn't have survived,) so television was the most likely place for the gryphon to have seen him before.

His two TV shows had been family programs, which taught that violence wasn't the best answer. One had been for smaller children and featured lovable puppets. The other was for older children and took a more action-adventure tone. Both series had focused on Galahad traveling around, meeting new friends and spreading the most vital part of the Knights' Code:

A knight protects those weaker than himself.

Trystan gave his head a clearing shake and looked back at Wilbur. "We're going east," he repeated, like Galahad hadn't even spoken, "with two of your horses and a week's worth of supplies. Which *you* are about to give me."

Wilbur gasped in outrage. "And if I say 'no?'"

Trystan arched a brow.

"Son of a *bitch*." Wilbur went stomping off to gather up everything Trystan wanted.

"I have to go west." Galahad said again, because it seemed like Trystan wasn't understanding. Gryphons had their own language, so maybe there was a translational issue. He didn't speak Trystan's native dialect, so he jerked his head off to the left, thinking that might help clear up the confusion. "*That* direction. I certainly appreciate all of your help, though."

Trystan flicked him another glance. For someone "born without emotions" he looked kind of pissed about this whole situation. "Helping *you* is not my aim here, knight."

"Well, I still appreciate it." He pointedly moved his hands, which were still bound behind his back with the enspelled ropes. "Can you get these off of me? Then, I'll get out of your way and you'll never have to see me again."

Trystan disregarded the request. Instead he sighed like he was about to perform a particularly arduous task. "Our way is the same. I was sent to collect you. For some reason, it seems you are missed."

Galahad forgot about the glowing ropes wrapped around his wrists, his face breaking into a wide, happy grin. "Really?"

Trystan blinked again at his excited expression.

"Queen Guinevere sent you?" Galahad persisted. In the whole world, there was only one person who'd care enough to look for him, so it really wasn't a question.

Trystan answered it anyway. "Yes."

Joy filled Galahad. It had been so long since he'd seen Gwen and Avalon. Galahad missed his homeland, but he missed his best friend and her daughter far more. "Is she alright? She and Avi are well?"

"They are perfect." Trystan studied Galahad for a long moment, his expression less hostile. "Arthur is dead. Guinevere is now married to the man I claim as my *j'ha*. My... uh..." He waved a hand, as if trying to come up with a suitable translation of the word. "Brother."

Galahad's jaw sagged open. "The king is dead?"

"No. *Arthur* is dead. Midas is king, now. He is Guinevere's True Love."

Galahad blinked at that insane recap. Everyone was born with a True Love, but only the lucky ones found theirs. Bad folk tended to know their destined mate just by looking at them. Good folk needed to actually sleep with the person to know about the bond.

Either way, Galahad had never felt anything approaching that kind of soul-deep connection. He doubted he ever would, given his inability to relate to people. Still, it was wonderful that Gwen had finally found her True Love, after years of suffering through a marriage to Arthur. She deserved to be happy. Even if her one-and-only, fated-from-God, perfect-match was a huge, badly-dressed gangster.

And if he was married to Gwen, then Midas really *was* the king, now. Galahad almost laughed. Uther would roll over in his grave, assuming he had one. It all seemed so delightfully impossible it occurred to Galahad that maybe Trystan was tricking him.

"Is this a joke?"

"Why does everyone persist in thinking I have a sense of humor?" Trystan shook his head in bafflement. "Pay attention: Guinevere and Avalon wish you home, so I have come to bring you home." He hesitated, looking Galahad over, again. "They say you are their family."

Galahad didn't appreciate that doubtful phrasing. *Nobody* was going to question the depth of his relationship to Avi and Gwen. "They *are* my family. They have been for years."

Brown eyes narrowed at Galahad's possessive tone. "I've now claimed them as *my* clan." He reported and it was a warning. "In my culture, claiming someone is sacred. It means you treasure and protect them, above all else. A piece of you belongs to them. It is irrevocable."

"So, they're you're family, too? That's what you're saying."

"Yes. *My* sister. *My* niece. I will never let them go. Not for anyone or for any reason." Trystan paused. "Do you wish to dispute my claim on them, because I am a gryphon?"

The two of them watched each other, waiting to see if there

would be a battle.

"No." Galahad finally decided. Gwen and Avi were the only things he was still willing to fight for, but this man didn't seem like a threat to them. "Not if you treat them well." He arched a brow. "Do you wish to dispute my claim on them, because I'm a knight?"

Another, much longer, pause. "Yes. But I am refraining. ...For now."

That wasn't very reassuring. "We have no quarrel anymore. The wars are over."

"Only because your side killed or imprisoned everyone who opposed them."

"I'm done with killing forever." Galahad's voice was certain. "I am focused on the best parts of our world now and Gwen and Avi are among them. If you want to share them with me, that's fine. But I claim them, too. I claimed them *first*."

Brown eyes flicked to Galahad's face and stayed there.

"Unless I'm dead, you can't keep me from them and you know it." Galahad went on. "The innocent belong to all who would care for them."

Trystan's head tilted slightly.

That was a gryphon saying. The baseline belief of their culture. They protected the innocents of the world. Galahad had understood far too late that no people who lived by such a code could be savages. It wasn't until his banishment that he'd been able to break completely free of the lies he'd once believed. To think for himself and set aside the prejudices that had been instilled in him since he was a small boy. To fully comprehend that the Knights' Academy justified injustice by demonizing everyone who stood against them.

To admit that most everything he'd learned since childhood was bullshit.

Galahad took a deep breath. "I don't blame you for disliking me. Really. I just want you to know that I'm sorry. I'm sorry for what happened at Legion. I'm sorry for being on the wrong side of the War."

Trystan remained quiet.

"I'm going to do *everything* I can now to balance the scales." Galahad continued. "I want to live peacefully, now. I want to be someone that Avalon can grow up respecting. I'm committed to living a life of truth." He nodded earnestly. "It's why I've given up my sword."

Once he'd left Camelot, Galahad's sword had slowly become the symbol of his old life. The more days that passed in exile, the more it reminded him of things he wanted to forget. He became almost phobic about the blade. Worried about what he might do, if he lost control. It wasn't safe. *He* wasn't safe. It worried him, constantly.

Once, the sword had brought Galahad comfort. He liked the red hilt and unique scabbard and everything else about it. King Uther himself had presented it to him, when Galahad graduated the Knights' Academy. Those memories added to its weight and carrying the sword soon became impossible. Galahad had felt safer ever since he threw it away. Secure in the knowledge that he couldn't hurt anyone with the blade, ever again.

Trystan squinted, like giving up your sword was crazy. "Are you crazy?" He demanded.

"No, I'm on a mission to make things right. I don't kill anymore. Not ever again."

"For Lyrssa's sake…" Trystan rolled his eyes so hard it was a wonder they didn't circle around in his skull. "Your idiotic 'mission' will get *you* killed, knight."

"Maybe. But I'll die on the right side." And being on the right side was all that mattered to him now.

Trystan gave another grunt, this one conveying his skepticism. "Well, I am on a mission, as well. Guinevere and Avalon want you retrieved and sent me to do it. Gwen has placed you in my care, until I return you to Camelot." He pointed to the right. "Which is east."

"I'm banished from Camelot, though. There was a trial. Arthur found me guilty of treason, because I helped Gwen burn down a Dark Science lab. I can never return."

"Arthur is dead. Midas is now king and he welcomes you back. Congratulations."

Galahad blinked at that flat summation, finally processing what all this meant. "So… I'm allowed to go home?" He hadn't expected to ever see Camelot, again. He'd expected to die forgotten in exile. He was fairly certain he deserved it. "Really?"

"Yes." Trystan nodded as if it was settled. "Now, do you wish to pack anything?"

"I don't really have anything *to* pack, but that's not…"

Trystan interrupted him. "Nothing? No fancy shampoos or face… things?"

"Face things?"

Trystan seemed agitated, again. "I don't know what they're called. The jars of magic creams that make your features look more pleasant. You must use those."

"Like makeup?" He shook his head. "I only wore that on TV. You have to for the cameras. Otherwise you look shiny."

Brown eyes narrowed. "You just *naturally* look like this?"

"What else would I look like?" Galahad retorted. "Usually, I'm not soaking wet, but otherwise this is me." He lifted his shoulders in a self-deprecating shrug. "Ta-da."

"*P'don*." Trystan stared up at the sky like he was seeking guidance.

Galahad decided to interpret the foreign swearing in the best way possible. In his new life, he tried hard to only see the Good around him. Optimism. *That* was the key to achieving peace. That and not carrying a sword. At least that was his working theory.

So, in a glass-is-half-full kind of way, maybe Trystan's annoyed muttering was actually a *compliment*. Gryphons didn't worry about genders when it came to relationships. As a people, they rejected most labels and barriers.

So maybe Trystan found him attractive.

The idea was far-fetched, but kind of awesome. Galahad was good-looking, in a very blond and wholesome kind of way. People usually responded favorably to his golden hair and blue eyes. He constantly got "Sexiest Man in Camelot" internet awards, which baffled him since his features were kind of... boring.

Gwen sometimes teased him about being "beige" and Galahad had to agree. When he looked in a mirror, he was always disappointed with how un-interesting his features were. Honestly, *everything* about Galahad was boring. He tried to do his very best to be his very best. Always. That was it. His entire secret to success. Completely expected and not at all mysterious. He would never be exotic or rebellious or extraordinary.

Not like Trystan.

Part of Galahad living a life of truth meant not worrying about who knew that he preferred men. Before he'd kept it a secret. He imagined that Gwen suspected it, but she'd never pushed him about it, and no one else had ever guessed. At least not out loud. Under Uther and Arthur, having a relationship with a man would have meant being kicked out of the Knights' Academy.

He should have done it, anyway. Obviously. An actual hero would have.

Instead, he'd been beige, and lonely, and followed the rules. Being a knight had been his entire identity. He couldn't give it up, even if it meant living a lie. And, in the end, what had that gotten him? He'd *still* been banished and stripped of his knighthood.

So now Galahad just worried about being accountable to himself, and being answerable for himself, and being honest with himself. And *honestly* Trystan was the most beautiful man he'd ever seen. When Galahad looked at him, it felt *true*. He was very drawn to anything true.

"A lot of men think I'm handsome." He offered, testing the waters.

Shit. That sounded like boasting, but it was the best he could come up with. He'd always struggled to connect with people. They never seemed to get close to him.

Trystan grunted, unimpressed with Galahad's claim. "Perhaps most men don't notice you're an idiot."

Yeah. That hadn't gone well. Huge surprise. Galahad made a face. "I'm not an idiot. You just don't understand my mission."

"You are a hated man who has given up his sword to aimlessly wander a foreign land. I understand enough to see that your 'mission' is stupid."

Galahad mentally counted to ten. "If you would just untie me, we could sit down and have a real conversation."

"I'm not going to untie you." Trystan scoffed, like that was the insane babbling of a lunatic. "You could run away and I would have to spend days hunting you down, again." He shook his head. "No, I am keeping you safely contained until I can give you back to Guinevere."

"You can't do that."

Trystan gave a dismissive sound that clearly meant, "Sure, I can" without really saying the words. It was astonishing how much the man could convey with nothing but a grunt.

Wilbur came back over, leading the horses that Trystan had ordered. "You want anything *else?*" He snapped, looking pissed.

Trystan flashed him a bored glance. "Not unless you know a way I can get into St. Ives." He casually stole the hat off of Wilbur's shaggy pink hair and the pig didn't even bother to argue about it. He knew better.

"No one Good can get into St. Ives. It's locked up like a fortress, unless you're born Bad." Wilbur muttered. "It's an oasis of debauchery, so Good folk would just screw up the fun."

Everyone was born either Good or Bad. It was part of your DNA and you had no control over it. For some reason, Bad folk were still blamed for their Badness, though. They were kept from certain jobs and faced laws designed to keep them oppressed. That meant that many of them became criminals, just to make a living. And *that* perpetuated the belief that Bad folk were all lawless monsters.

It was completely unfair. Good folk's actions could be horrible, but they were still protected by the system. Bad folk could live honorably, but they were still seen as rotten to the core. Galahad had spent a lot of time lobbying for villains' rights legislation, trying to correct the obviously flawed system, but most people still saw Bad folk as... less.

St. Ives was a town that had reversed the status quo. Bad folk ran it and Good folk were kept out. Trystan wanted to get past the city walls, but, if his muttered cursing was anything to go by, he couldn't get in. Which could only mean that he'd been born Good. So had Galahad. Technically.

But he was also pretty damn talented at improvising strategies.

Galahad's mind made a jackpot sound, seeing an opening. "Trystan? I think we can use reason and come to an agreement that satisfies us both here." Reason was always the answer. Reason and optimism and not carrying a sword.

Trystan sighed. Loudly. "I am not untying you, knight." He dropped the stolen hat onto Galahad's head. "Left to your own devices, you make terrible choices, like throwing away your weapons and standing in the desert sun without a hat."

"I don't like hats. I never wear them, because I always lose them."

"But, that's *my* hat." Wilbur whined.

Trystan looked over at him, again.

"Which, obviously, I'm happy to share with the knight." Wilbur continued. "He needs it more than I do, for sure. They're a frail race."

Trystan grunted in agreement and adjusted the brim so it covered most of Galahad's face. "Gwen put you in my care, knight." He repeated. "It is my duty to see you safely returned to Camelot, before you do yourself irreparable harm. That is the end of it."

"I don't need a bodyguard, though. I'm fine on my own."

"Ten minutes ago, you were nearly burned alive by pigs."

"That was a cultural misunderstanding."

"That was turning into a luau."

"I was working on a plan."

"It was clearly a very bad one."

"My plans sort of evolve as I go along. But, they usually work. I wasn't going to die. Believe me. And anyway keeping me tied up is still completely..."

"Enough." Trystan waved a hand. "You stay restrained. I swear to Lyrssa, if you don't stop talking, I will gag you, as well. We are stuck together for the duration of this journey. I will not listen to you nag about your bindings or this 'mission' of yours for the next…"

It was Galahad's turn to interrupt. "I can get you into St. Ives."

Trystan stopped talking and turned to stare at him.

Galahad smirked, seeing he finally had the gryphon's full attention. He tipped the hat back on his head and knew he'd won. "It's to the west."

Chapter Two

I'm not saying *allllll* the gryphons are evil. People keep saying that I'm saying that, but I'm not saying that. I'm sure *some* of them aren't malicious monsters. They're just too stupid to know that their backwards ideas are relics of the past.

That's why the War happened, right? They wouldn't give Uther the graal, because of old legends or some shit. They weren't even *doing* anything with it, but their oggity-boogity 'gods' told them to hide it away, anyhow.

Think about how many people died because of the gryphons' ancient superstitions. Because of their greed and stupidity and barbaric beliefs.

That's what I'm saying.

"Stopping the Savages" Podcast
Sir Dragonet of Camelot- Former Troubadour of King Uther and Host of the Program

Lyonesse Desert- Umberland Plains

This was the stupidest thing he had ever done.

Trystan knew it was stupid, even as he did it. Which was stupider than doing the stupid thing, in the first place. And yet he kept going, which was the stupidest part of all.

He should drag Galahad back to Camelot, no matter what the man wished. Did he really believe this wingless moron could gain entrance to St. Ives? You had to be Bad to get invited into the city and the knight was indisputably Good. Galahad claimed he "knew someone" inside the town who'd open the gate for them, but he was probably lying.

Knights were all liars. Trystan *knew* that.

So why had they been heading west for two days?

The thought of finally finding Marcus had temporarily clouded Trystan's better judgment. If the knight *wasn't* lying, this could be Trystan's chance to finally have his revenge. Even when he knew it was stupid, he'd still been swept along in the man's vortex of lousy ideas. And it *really* hadn't helped his brainpower that the knight was so damn handsome. ...For an idiot. The golden strands of the man's golden hair turned all rational thought into white noise.

Stupid, stupid, *stupid*.

"I'd be more comfortable if you untied me." Galahad volunteered for the hundredth time.

Trystan grunted. He wasn't *that* stupid. "You will stay tied, until I return you to Gwen."

He'd moved the man's bindings to the front of his body. That was comfortable enough. It also allowed Trystan to tie him to the saddle, just in case he began to list off the horse. No one ever did well betting on the wingless to be capable riders, or swordsmen, or... well... *anything*.

"You know, it doesn't make sense for us to be at odds, when we can be allies, Trystan."

"Allies?" The desert sun must be affecting the man's brain. "You and me?"

"Sure." Galahad looked more cheerful than anyone tied to a horse had ever looked. Possibly because Trystan was finally bored enough to respond to his inane chatter. Thus far, he'd mostly been ignoring him. "Why not?

"For starters, I find you irritating, most of the time."

"We'll focus on the times you *don't* find me irritating, then."

Trystan gave a skeptical grunt. Most of those times involved picturing the knight in various sexual positions, so that was probably a bad idea. "And I certainly do not wish to hear about your 'mission,' if that is what you're plotting, now."

"You don't even feel a little bit curious?"

"Gryphons do not 'feel' anything. We are generally born without emotions."

"Curiosity isn't an emotion. It's more like an intellectual curiosity to..." Galahad squinted. "Wait. Okay. How do you describe 'curiosity' without using the word 'curiosity?'"

"In your language, curiosity is defined as a drive to know and understand something better." Trystan sent him a put upon look.

"Were you truly called upon to teach children?"

"Mother Goose's show focuses on building vocabulary and learning the alphabet." Galahad told him defensively. "Mine taught values and ethics."

"The Butcher of Legion imparts 'values' to the young." Trystan shook his head in disgust. "That's even worse. No wonder your culture is so fucked up."

Galahad flinched and didn't respond to that.

Trystan eyed the man from the corner of his gaze, displeased by his subdued expression. Why did his own words seem unnecessarily harsh, when they were so obviously true?

After a long moment, Galahad frowned. "Did you ever wonder why 'phonetics' isn't spelled the way it sounds? It should obviously be spelled phonetically, right? That's a good example of why I couldn't teach kids reading skills. The rules don't make any sense."

Trystan's squinted, baffled by every word of that statement. "What?"

"Sometimes I wonder why things are the way they are." Galahad shrugged. "Especially, since I was banished and *really* started thinking it all through." The knight was apparently ready to continue his harangue. "Anyway, untying me wouldn't do any harm. That's what I'm saying. This is a dangerous road we're traveling on. If we're attacked, what good can I do tied to a saddle?"

Trystan gave his head a clearing shake, slightly dizzy from the knight's conversational tangents. "You refuse to fight, so what good could you do even if I freed you?" He retorted. "If I unbound your hands, you could only *wave* at our assassins before they slayed us."

Since this was the only road through the desert, it was the one Trystan was using, no matter its reputation. If Galahad could fly, the trip would be easier, but he couldn't and Trystan wasn't going to carry him. He was larger than average, for his species, so it would strain even Trystan to hold him aloft for long. Besides, touching the man's perfect body would be a *very* stupid idea. He already knew that.

"I live a life of peace." The knight argued. "That doesn't mean I'm useless, though. I just don't rely on a sword. I use *other* methods to diffuse situations now."

"For instance, you allow pigs to set you afire. Very effective."

"That usually doesn't happen." Galahad was quiet for another beat and then he sighed. "Actually, no. I don't want to lie to you. I'm bad at making friends, so this kind of thing happens more than you'd think. Not with the pigs before, but, in general, people try to kill me *a lot*. I don't know why."

"Perhaps they have seen your terrible television program."

The knight looked genuinely offended. "What's wrong with my TV show?"

"You would like a list?" Excellent. Trystan was eager to provide one. He took storytelling seriously and Galahad's program was an affront on all levels. "The narrative is filled with holes. Direction is lacking. Themes are muddled. Fight sequences all look fake..."

Galahad cut him off, refusing to see his own failings. "I'm fighting puppets!"

"They are poorly trained puppets." Trystan retorted, appalled all over again by the memory of their incompetence. "They hold their weapons incorrectly. When they even *have* weapons. Mostly they just sing. How can you win a battle with songs?" He considered his own words for a beat. "Unless all the puppets are secretly sirens, which the text does not support."

"It's a *kids' show* and kids remember things better when it's put into song."

"All I remember is how bad the puppets are at singing. And fighting. Sometimes you lose to them. How can you possibly lose to a puppet?" He shot Galahad an irritated look. "Well, perhaps *you* could. You lose to pigs."

"Not killing the pigs was a *choice*. I was trying to reason with them."

"Next time, reason with a sword."

"I don't carry a sword! I told you..." Galahad stopped short and took a deep breath, like he was trying to quell his temper. "You know what? I don't want to argue with you."

"Because I am winning."

"Because I want us to get along. You and I are stuck together for a while. Tying me up is pointless. Arguing is pointless. I just don't see the *point* in being enemies."

Trystan turned to give him a flat look. That last remark deserved no response.

"Yes, I know. The Looking Glass Campaigns had us on opposing sides. But that was a different world and we were different men."

"I am the same man whose villages were burned and whose people were slaughtered."

"Well, *I'm* different," said the poster boy for Uther's campaign of death and despair. "And you have to know that, if you know Gwen. She loves me. She would *never* love me if I was a heartless killer. She would never trust me with Avalon." He met Trystan's eyes, willing him to believe. "That has to mean something, right?"

Stupidly, Trystan found himself actually considering that point. Gwen was one of the few people he respected and she favored this man. Perhaps, that meant something.

Or perhaps Trystan was just stupid.

"We're both on missions here." Galahad continued. "I won't get in your way and you won't get in mine. Even if you don't want to be allies, you can agree with *that*, right?"

It might be worth the compromise, just to stop the nagging. "It depends on how dangerous and stupid your mission is."

"I found a map that leads to a treasure beyond price. I'm following it."

"Of course you are." Trystan muttered sarcastically, his eyes rolling towards the sky. Gwen and Avi should never question his devotion to them. Not after he willingly suffered through this crazy man's company. "Did this map come in a cereal box or a comic book?"

"The map is *real*, Trystan. And I'm willing to give you half of all the gold I find, if you just let me get to the end. We're riding together, so I think that would be fair."

"Why would I split half of anything with you?" Trystan demanded. "If I believed your nonsense, I could just take your map for myself. How would you stop me without a sword?"

"You can have *half*." Galahad repeated. "I need the rest."

"Your kind always 'needs' gold." Trystan scoffed. The wingless would kill the whole world for a shiny hunk of metal. "How did such a limited people ever defeat my own?"

"We cheated." Galahad said very seriously.

Trystan looked at him sharply. He'd expected some kind of argument or justification.

"I'm sorry." Galahad sounded like he meant it. "I wish we'd lost the War. Truly."

Of *course* this man would be the worst fucking enemy in the world. He couldn't even do that right. No, he just *had* to apologize with sincerity and Good intentions shining out of his big, blue eyes. This *had* to be intentional. He couldn't *possibly* be this irritating by accident.

"Trys? You okay?"

No one had ever shortened his name before. Not even once in his whole life. It should've irritated him. ...Except it didn't. *P'don*, this was stupid.

"I will not untie you." He finally decided. "But we can follow your worthless map, so long as it doesn't take too long, or lead us off the path to St. Ives, or irritate me overly much. And if you happen upon gold on your doomed treasure hunt, I will not stop you from taking it." Against his will, his gaze kept lingering on the knight's incredible hair. It *had* to be under a spell of some kind. "It will no doubt buy you much magical shampoo."

There. Never let it be said that he couldn't be "nice."

"Shampoo?" Galahad squinted. "Why would I need magical shampoo? I've never used that stuff... Oh! You think I'm going to buy --like-- superficial things with the money?"

"Shampoo would not be impractical for you." Trystan allowed, wanting to be fair. "Your hair is... shimmery. Keeping it that way will help you attract and secure a willing mate."

Galahad studied him for a long moment. "You come from the mountains, right?" He asked randomly and nodded off into the distance. "Why aren't you living there with *your* mate?"

Trystan frowned at the strange question and turned to stare off at the horizon. Past the flat desert plain were countless peaks, as far as the eye could see. Within the expanse stood the White Mountains, where the rest of the Airbourne Clan had lived and died... And the Principal Mountains, once the domain of Midas' mother, Corah... And maybe even the fabled Mount Feather, which no one had seen in countless years, but where the most ancient clans supposedly still dwelled in isolation.

On and on, he could see the various traditional territories of his people. Until the mountains were so numerous and so distant that they had no names or clans to claim them.

The jagged stone monoliths of Lyonesse were beautiful to him. His homeland, although they were no longer his home. He could live there again, if he chose. After he killed everyone on his list, he could fly into the endless mountains, finding peace and solitude. He'd once planned on that life. When he was in prison for three long years, that dream had given him the strength to go on.

Why did that future seem so empty now?

Trystan frowned and his eyes flicked over to Galahad. "I am considering many options." He decided, irritated that the knight was confusing what should be very clear.

Galahad didn't look satisfied with that answer. "So... what does your *mate* say about it?"

"Little, as I do not have one."

The knight perked up and he was always fairly perky. "No?"

"No. I have never experienced *ha'na*."

"What's that?"

Trystan shook his head, mystified by the man's ignorance. "You killed so many of my people, yet you know nothing about us."

"It's how I was able to kill so many. The Knights' Academy made sure we knew nothing real about gryphons. Just the hatred and lies. If any of us knew the truth about your people, how could we have done what we were ordered to?"

That was the wisest thing the Trystan had ever heard any knight say.

"*Ha'na* is the bedrock of my culture." He grudgingly told Galahad. "It is a bond shared by a gryphon and their mate. Their *ha'yan*."

The knight tilted his head. Listening.

"It is… looking at your mate and seeing the world they will create with you." Trystan knitted his fingers together, so they were intertwined. "Linking."

"Like True Love?

"It is broader. Gryphons are generally born without emotions, so we do not experience True Love. *Ha'na* is less about feelings, than about finding your light. Your *path*." *P'don*, it was hard to translate the concept into the common tongue. For some reason, he wanted Galahad to fully understand the vastness of it, though, so Trystan tried to find the right words. "*Ha'na* is about the intersection of these paths. Paths are very important, in my culture. You look at your *ha'yan* and see your whole future, stretching before you. The bond touches *everything* in your life. *Ha'na* is… everything."

"Everything?" Galahad sounded worried, again. "But you don't have that?"

"No."

Galahad went back to grinning. "Great!"

"It is *great* that I'm without the greatest gift of my people?"

"No! Not *that* part. It's just… great that you don't have a mate." A cocky, victorious smirk played around the corners of his mouth.

No one should be able to smile like that. It was hot, wicked sex distilled into a facial expression. Trystan felt his jaw sag, awestruck by the brilliance of it. A buzzing sound buzzed in his head, his insides tightening to the point of pain. It was the same sensation he'd had in his stomach the first time he'd flown above the clouds and seen the full breath of the sky.

A whisper of fate flickered through his mind.

From out of nowhere, he remembered the stories Elaine told him as a child. In gryphon legends, there were beings made of moonbeams who slipped between realms. Sometimes, one of them visited this world, bewitching all who saw it with its otherworldly light. But the creature always vanished, just as some poor bastard was about to catch it. Then the gryphon who'd spotted it was doomed, forever after. Fruitlessly searching, high and low, desperate to see its beauty, again. Longing for the brightness.

"I don't have a mate, either."

"Huh?" Trystan had no idea what the knight had just said.

"I don't have a mate, either." Galahad repeated, not noticing Trystan's mesmerized state. "And I'm not going to use the treasure to buy hair products. I'm going to build something."

"A statue?" Trystan guessed, trying to refocus on the multitude of reasons he had to dislike the man. The wingless adored statues. They would slaughter babies in the streets, while they erected ugly monuments to their genocidal leaders.

"No. An art school. It's going to be free and opened to children of any race."

"You will build a school for *art?*" Perhaps there was a more useless idea in the vast, vast world, but Trystan couldn't imagine what it might be. Gryphons hated art. Hated anything that wasn't useful and tangible and real. Honestly, spending money on Galahad's shimmery hair was a far smarter purchase. "Why?

"I love art. I used to stare at the palace paintings for hours." Galahad paused. "You remind me of my favorite. An angel, battling back a hoard of demons to keep the innocent safe."

Trystan hesitated. "In the castle's stairwell?"

"Yes! You've seen it, too?"

"No."

"Yes, you have. And you must like art at least a little bit. You have enough tattoos."

"These are not *art*. These commemorate battles." He lifted an arm so Galahad could see the gruesome depictions more clearly. "Warriors wear them. Why don't you teach the young to be warriors, instead of artists? Give them a useful occupation."

"We already have a school for warriors. The Knights' Academy. It's where I was raised." Galahad's voice was flat. "How useful did you find my occupation, Trystan?"

Trystan turned to look at him, thoughtfully.

"There are enough warriors." Galahad continued in a quiet voice. "Enough nightmares that don't fade in the day. Let's teach the young to do something beautiful, instead. Something that makes the world better, not emptier. I think *that* would be useful."

Shit... That was exactly what a great warrior would say.

"Yes." Trystan agreed softly. "Sparing children from all we've seen is indeed a worthy way to use your riches, knight."

Galahad smiled at him, happy that Trystan understood. Lavender-blue eyes cleared again. "Assuming I find the treasure, that is. Otherwise, I'm broke."

Trystan snorted, unsurprised. "You still have many businesses in Camelot. If you were wiser about your expenditures, you'd surely be rich enough to build an art school already. How much could a few desks and some crayons cost?" He arched a brow at him, slightly interested despite himself. "Or are you searching for something *else* with that map?"

"Honestly, I'm not sure what I'm looking for. It could be gold, but I also think it's something bigger or..." Galahad trailed off with a shrug. "I don't know. I just have to find it."

"And if you don't?"

"I will." Galahad repeated stubbornly. "I've been preparing for this mission for years. I studied and researched it, all the time. Arthur used to make fun of me for it."

"Arthur was an asshole. The world is better since his death."

Uther's son had been nearly as horrible as his father. His only purpose had been to beget Avi. After her conception, he'd been useless to the future. Even King Uther had seemed to favor Galahad over his weak, whiney son.

"Anyway, after I was banished, I had nothing, and no one, and no place to go." Galahad continued. "All I had was this mission. So, I started scouring the most forgotten lands I could find for new clues. At that point, what was the risk in trying something crazy, ya know?"

"Death."

The knight disregarded that obvious danger. "It took a year to find the map. It was on Sarras, by the way. In a library."

Trystan stifled a cringe at that news. Most forgotten realms were forgotten for a reason and Sarras was no exception. No one there believed in anything. It was a point of pride among the denizens that they rejected all gods and laws. How in the hell had Galahad survived there?

Galahad hesitated. "Well, I think it *used* to be a library. A wizard had burned most of it, with all his friends inside." He sighed, recalling the mad creature with pity. "He was troubled."

Trystan prayed for patience. The knight created more chaos than anyone he'd ever met. He should be locked in a padded room, for his own good. ...Or possibly chained to a bed.

Shit. That was *exactly* the kind of thought he didn't want to be thinking.

"I finally got the map from him, by bribing him with my last bag of Gala-Chips." Galahad paused. "Hey, what do you think about a snack that mixes popcorn and chocolate chips?" He asked with his typical lack of focus. "That would be great, right? Like melty and crunchy, at the same time."

"I would sooner devour spiders boiled in arsenic." Unlike the wingless, Trystan didn't eat artificial food, packaged in plastic. It was why he studiously avoided those candy-coated potato chip things Galahad had invented, no matter how enticing they smelled. "More to the point, I think that treasure maps *never* lead to treasure. Why would someone even draw such a thing? Why not simply spend the treasure?"

"I'm not sure of all the details. I just know it's real."

"Well, I will not help you on this hopeless mission. We're riding together, but we are *not* allies. I am going to St. Ives to kill someone and you are my key into the city. That's it."

"Who are you killing?" The knight asked, because of course *that's* what he'd focus on.

"None of your business."

Galahad's eyes narrowed at him, not liking that answer. "Alright. We'll each do our own thing and just stay out of each other's way, then. Just like I suggested to begin with."

"This is satisfactory to me." Trystan grunted. "In St. Ives, you will wait wherever I put you, though. Left to your own devices, you will be dead within minutes in that place."

"That won't work. In exchange for getting into the town, I'm going to need to have dinner with this guy named Mordy. I can almost guarantee it."

Trystan slanted him a glare, not liking that idea. At all. "You have a *date* lined up in St. Ives? Do you have any idea the kind of men who live in that shithole?"

"It's not a date." Galahad rolled his eyes, like that was just silly. The knight was blind to reality. It was the only explanation. "Mordy's just a big fan of my show."

"Is he six years old? Because this is your typical audience, yes?"

"He's an adult, wiseass. Sometimes adults like the show,

too, for various reasons."

"There is only *one* reason." Trystan sneered. "It involves picturing you naked."

"That's not true." The knight assured him, righteously. "A lot of the time, people just want family entertainment. My show provides nostalgia and wholesome values for them."

Trystan's brain might start bleeding from the naivety of that claim. Medically, it was a strong possibility that his mind simply couldn't process it and stay intact.

"Now, I haven't actually met Mordy, but he seems very nice in his letters." The knight assured him. "Almost all my fans are incredible. He just wants to hang out."

Trystan's teeth ground together. "*No.*" He decided and didn't even question why the very idea of the knight consorting with this man pissed him off so much. "You are not 'hanging out' with a total stranger, who writes you letters. He will probably drug you, rape you, kill you, and post pictures of your mangled corpse on the internet."

The wingless loved posting pictures as much as they loved statues.

"Do you want to get into St. Ives?" Galahad challenged. "Because Mordy is the one who's going to open the gate for us."

Son of a *bitch*.

"Mordy's invited me to visit him a thousand times." Galahad continued. "He seems great. Besides, I think he can help me with my mission. He knows that area really well."

Trystan's temper ignited so quickly that even he was surprised by the force of it. "Are you *out of your mind?*"

Galahad frowned a bit, bafflingly unintimidated by a gryphon bellowing at him. "You really do yell a lot for someone without emotions. Has anyone ever told you that?"

Trystan stabbed a finger at him. "You will not discuss this ludicrous treasure map with *anyone*. Understand? If they are dumb enough to believe it's real, they will want to kill you and take it for themselves. It isn't safe."

Silence.

Trystan turned to look at Galahad. "Understand?" He demanded again.

"Well, about that…" Galahad began in a cautious tone.

"Lyrssa save me." Trystan pinched the bridge of his nose. "You already told someone."

"Well, before you came along, I had met these five ex-knights from Camelot. It seemed like such a lucky break. They'd never gone home after the War. They said they were exploring Lyonesse, just like me."

No. *Not* like him. "Exploring Lyonesse" clearly meant "looting and killing" to those not gazing at the world through a prism of eternal optimism.

"And they had supplies for a journey in the desert. I didn't have supplies, because I was --like I said before-- broke. So we made a deal. I would lead them to the treasure and they would share their supplies and we'd split the gold." Galahad shifted uncomfortably. "But then we had a difference of opinion and I left them. I never showed them the whole map, though, so..."

Trystan cut him off. "Explain the difference of opinion."

Galahad hesitated.

"Recall that you live a life of *truth*." Trystan reminded him pointedly.

Galahad made a face and relented. "A few days later, another guy showed up. I didn't know that he was the leader of the group. He was one of my former soldiers, before he deserted."

Trystan snorted at that. "Disloyalty is the worse offense a warrior can commit."

"You think so?" Galahad asked quietly.

"One of them, anyway." Trystan believed that like holy truth. "So this failed soldier returned to the group of wingless and remembered you? I take it they weren't fond memories?"

"No, they weren't." The knight cleared his throat. "Things ended on bad terms. And now he's apparently become a dealer in consumer magic, so there was *that* issue..."

"He and his friends tried to murder you." Trystan translated. It wasn't a question.

Galahad winced slightly.

Trystan could feel the foggy mask of the eagle begin to form over his features, the gryphon in him wanting to hunt down and destroy his new enemies. He didn't question the force of his anger. It was simply there and he embraced it.

"I'm okay." Galahad assured him. "For a few minutes, though, I was afraid I would have to kill them. I don't want to kill anyone else, Trystan. Not ever again." Wide blue eyes met his, all sorts of idealistic thoughts reflected in their depths. No one should have eyes like that. "Luckily, I dealt with them nonviolently."

That sounded dubious. "How?"

"They doused me in magic that didn't really work. Then, I

escaped."

Trystan snorted. "This is not "dealing" with anything. This is *delaying* it. These men will be back." It was obvious to anyone with a functioning brainstem. "They did not get the map, so they will return for it. And for *you*."

"No, I don't think…" Galahad stopped talking, which was a sure indication of trouble.

Trystan followed his gaze and spotted the problem. A small being with an ancient gun was hiding in the scrubs along the side of the road, ready to ambush them.

Lyrssa save him from idiots.

"Try it and I will kill you where you stand." Trystan snapped at the creature, in no mood for more stupidity.

The small being ignored that excellent advice. It fumbled its way out of the bushes, the gun weighing down its hand. The would-be robber was a young ogre, with matted blue fur and ragged clothes. "Give me all your money!" It squeaked.

Like all gryphons, Trystan treasured children… but that didn't mean he was putting up with a lot of shit. "Get out of my way, boy."

"I'm a *girl!*" The robber gasped, like he had grievously wounded her. "I'm the most famous highwaywoman in Lyonesse. And I'll shoot you if you don't give me all your money!"

"No, you won't." Trystan kept riding forward, giving the girl no choice but to step aside.

Galahad looked perturbed. Odd things seemed to disturb the man. "We should give the child some money." He whispered at Trystan.

"*No.*" Was the knight insane? Well, obviously he *was*, but still… "I do not like being robbed. Especially, with guns that will not even fire."

"It will so fire!" The ogre cried, hurrying alongside the horses, the broken gun waving around in her hand. "I shoot people with it all the time."

The odds of that were minimal, seeing as how it was a rusted mess. Trystan sent her a skeptical look and then went back to glaring at Galahad. "This is your fault you know." He declared, because it was true.

Galahad was outraged. "How is it my fault?"

"Your men no doubt left that gun here during the War. *This* is the result." The irresponsibility of the wingless was a constant source of consternation to Trystan.

"That gun isn't from the War. At least not *this* war. This is a

Model kf-2802 revolver, most likely from fighting the Harpie Invasion, eighty years ago." Galahad gave it an admiring glance. "It has the original sight too. Really, it's a nice piece."

"Hand over the gold or I'll shoot, right now!" The girl warned, interrupting them.

Trystan's attention flicked back to her. "Then shoot." He challenged testily.

The girl swallowed... and lowered the gun.

Pitiful.

"You are a terrible criminal." Trystan informed her, because she really should know. "If you wish to be a thief, you must practice far more at your craft. Why are you not wearing a mask? You should have a mask on, yes? And use a functional weapon. And this is a horrible spot for a trap, you need far more cover. Did you think of these things?"

The girl hung her head, which meant that she hadn't thought of them.

"Trystan, just give her some gold."

Galahad's commanding tone surprised Trystan enough that he actually paid attention, his face swiveling around. It was the voice of someone used to giving orders and having them obeyed. Interesting that this would be the moment the man pulled it out for use.

"I thought you did not wish to argue, knight?"

"Look at her clothes." Galahad continued quietly, leaning forward on his horse so the girl couldn't overhear. "You know how many orphans the War made. She is hungry and alone. This is all she can do to survive."

"If I give her money, it will encourage her." Trystan stressed. "If she is to succeed as a highwaywoman, she needs to be taught how to do it properly." It was important to educate children. The knight's TV show had done a piss-poor job of imparting useful information, but Trystan was better at building young minds. "Otherwise she will die doing this work."

"She needs *food*, not criminal mentoring lessons. Give her some gold, so she can eat."

Why did the Butcher of Legion care so much about helping a child? What was he plotting? It would be a bad idea to underestimate the knight. Trystan had fought Camelot's forces to a standstill, again and again, but Galahad had never been as predictable as the rest of Uther's men. That made him the most dangerous. Very, very dangerous and very, very...

Gods, his eyes were blue.

"You're a Good man, Trys." Galahad said quietly. "I see it. Help this little girl."

Those damnable eyes met Trystan's, the color of them so saturated they were nearly purple. The intense, vibrant shade of the heavens at twilight, when the pinks of the setting sun met the blues of fading daytime. The result was an illuminated lavender hue that made you believe in the vastness of the sky and the magic of... everything.

Something strange happened inside Trystan's chest. Something that made it hard for him to breathe and robbed him of rational thought. It sent him sliding into stupidity. Muttering a curse, he dug coins out of the pouch on his belt. "I will give you *some* of what I have, girl." He grudgingly decided. "Not all."

"Really?" She blurted out, her lips parting in surprise. Clearly, she wasn't expecting to succeed. Nor should she, considering her abysmal lack of talent.

"Really." Trystan counted out the money and handed it down to the astounded child. "You will use the gold to go that way." He pointed east. "Walk until you reach a phone. Then, you will call the castle at Camelot. Give them your location and tell them Trystan says they should come get you. You will go there and live."

Galahad beamed at him like he'd never been prouder of anyone.

Trystan ignored him.

"Really?" The girl said again and huge eyes began to fill with tears. "You'll help me?"

"Really. Princess Avalon will tell them you speak the truth, if anyone doubts it. My niece knows everything." He impatiently snapped his fingers and held out a palm. "And give me the gun. I do not want you holding up anyone else and getting yourself killed in the process."

She obligingly handed it to him and then stood there like she wasn't sure what to do next.

"Well?" He gestured down the road. "Go. *Now.*"

The girl took him seriously. She ran off at top speed, tripping over her own feet.

"Thank you." Galahad said softly.

Trystan shrugged, irritated at the world. "Caring for the young is the duty of us all."

It would be wrong to leave the ogre girl to fend for herself, considering she seemed dedicated to stupidity. She would do far better in Camelot. Children needed guidance and nurturing. Even the felonious ones. *Especially* the felonious ones. *That* was why he did this. Even if the gryphons had no children of their own, they still had a stake in the future.

"Here." Trystan tossed the useless gun at Galahad. "Hold this, so no other child finds it and gets themselves in trouble."

Galahad caught the broken revolver, absently examining it. "I can fix this, you know."

"For what? So you can *not* shoot it? It already does that."

Galahad shoved the broken gun into his waistband. "Is it really so wrong to think there's a better way than killing each other?"

Trystan's jaw ticked. Galahad had to be tricking him. *Had* to be. Legion had been a smoldering crater when the King's Men were through and Galahad had been in command. Now the same man wanted to talk of peace and help children? No. Something was wrong here.

Trystan reigned in his horse. Determined to prove himself right, once and for all, he turned the animal around, drawing up beside the knight.

Galahad looked baffled. "What's the matter?"

Trystan's hand whipped out, catching hold of Galahad's chin and tilting his head so he could stare directly into his face. The knight automatically tried to jerk away in surprise, but Trystan wouldn't let him go.

He saw the pulse in Galahad's neck increase as he was held in place, but he didn't seem frightened. Any creature with sense in their heads would panic when a gryphon seized them, but the knight stared up at Trystan without even a flicker of genuine alarm. Instead, violet eyes met his, full of curiosity and virtue.

Trystan stared back at him, momentarily hypnotized. Trying to recall what he'd been planning to do. Why wasn't the knight frightened about being captured, and tied to a saddle, and manhandled? Why didn't Galahad see him as a threat? *Everyone* saw Trystan as a threat. Aside from his clan, there was nobody alive who felt safe alone with him. Trystan had never even slept with anyone who wasn't a little wary of him. He'd thought that was normal.

But Galahad didn't seem apprehensive. Instead, he watched Trystan with… interest.

Trystan frowned. There were few beings on the planet he couldn't cow into submission, but Galahad appeared to be one of them. For some reason, the idiot's idiotic fearlessness was arousing to him. It put many thoughts in his head that he did not want to have.

"Explain what happened at Legion." He demanded and he felt Galahad flinch at the unexpected question.

"I don't want to talk about Legion." The tone was quietly and inflexibly stubborn. "*Ever*. Whatever you heard, the reality was worse and I don't want to remember it."

"So, the same man who led troops to slaughter innocent people, throws away his weapons? Allows an ogre girl to rob him? You expect me to believe this?"

"I told you, I'm *not* the same man I was during the War."

"Bullshit." Trystan intoned. "No one changes *that* much. Certainly not a monster who burned children and old people in the grasses at Legion."

Galahad shoved his hand away. "The darkness is still inside of me." He snapped. This subject clearly upset him. "But, I now fight it. Every day. *That*'s what changed in me."

Trystan sat back in his saddle, regarding Galahad thoughtfully. He didn't see any darkness in the knight. No deception in his face or evasions in his tone. Either Trystan was reading him completely wrong or Galahad was telling the truth. And Trystan didn't often read people wrong. What was happening here?

Galahad stared up at him, breathing hard.

Trystan stared back.

Long seconds ticked by.

"When I left Camelot to search for you, Avalon told me you were a great warrior." Trystan said at length. "Why does she think that?

"I don't know. Maybe she watched my television programs too many times."

"It cannot just be because of your lying TV show. She believes you are an *actual* hero."

Galahad sighed, sounding tired. "All the heroes are dead, Trystan. You know that."

Yes. He did. The War took them and nearly everything else. But, Avalon claimed Galahad was the "best knight ever." The ultimate warrior of his people. Worse, Avi had then linked his name to the *ya'lah*.

She didn't fully understand what the word meant, but Trystan did. He knew all of the gryphons' myths. And he knew that connecting this man to any of them was preposterous. Fisher had said no one was the *ya'lah*. Trystan doubted the old man's sanity on many topics, but on that one they agreed. The *ya'lah* was a legend. Nothing more.

And even if the tales *were* somehow true, Galahad of fucking Camelot would certainly not be the *ya'lah*. Anyone else in creation made more sense. Literally anyone.

...Except Avi had insinuated that this man with innocent eyes, who'd slaughtered countless gryphons for his genocidal king and whose smiling face was on a goddamn postage stamp, was the champion Trystan's people had been waiting for.

And Avalon was always right.

Chapter Three

The graal was given to the gryphons' before all history began. Where it came from is lost now, but we have devotedly passed along the two very simple rules for its care:

It can never be used as a weapon.
It can only be used for the Good of all.

If we abide by this, the legends say that the graal will save our people, one day.

And so we followed the rules, year after year, century after century. It was our honor and duty to protect the graal from misuse, until that prophesied time arrived. With this in mind, our ancestors hid it in the most secure location they could imagine

They hid it within the Looking Glass Pool.

How the Wingless War Happened
Skylyn Welkyn- Gryphon Storyteller

Lyonesse Desert- Forbidden Stone Ruins

Trystan leaned against the pommel of his saddle, looking arrogant and unsurprised and maybe a little pleased by Galahad's predicament. "I told you so." He announced with an awful lot of satisfaction for someone born without emotions.

Galahad unfolded his map, ignoring all the negativity aimed his way. Trystan enjoyed saying "I told you so." In the few days they'd been riding together, Galahad had already heard it dozens of times.

He tuned out the newest round of pessimism, like he'd tuned out the others.

"There's nothing here, knight." Trystan reiterated, because he didn't like being ignored. No doubt he wasn't used to it, since he was stunningly beautiful, and carried an axe, and had gigantic wings. All of that tended to draw the eye. "I told you this detour was a waste of time."

"What I'm looking for is here." Galahad squinted down at the map and then up at the aptly named Forbidden Stone Ruins. "Someplace."

Trystan sighed loudly, still not bothering to get off his horse.

Galahad ignored that, too. The map showed a mass of badly drawn circles in rough piles. He was pretty sure that was supposed to represent the Forbidden Stone Ruins. The mountainous sand dunes were dotted with at least six-hundred piles of rocks. Big, small, intricate, simple, made from every color and shape of stone imaginable. It was kinda beautiful. He wished he had the time to study them all. Mazes of cairns were spread out like a spider web all around him.

Yeah... this was going to take a while.

Trystan didn't seem inclined to wait. Uther had called him a demon, but the man looked like an impatient, pissed-off angel, most of the time. "Why can you not admit that your map is wrong? Whatever you are searching for is gone. Probably, it was never here, at all."

Galahad started forward, pushing over the cairns as he went.

Trystan's eyebrows shot up. He didn't say anything, but it was clear from the expression on his face that he wanted to ask what the hell Galahad was doing. He probably thought showing any interest would interfere with his "I hate Galahad," badass, grouchy exterior.

...Or possibly he was just a grouchy badass who hated Galahad.

Galahad continued toppling the rocks, although he felt kinda bad about it. Some of the piles were exquisitely arranged. Destroying small works of art went against his entire worldview. At the moment, he didn't have a choice, though.

"I lived in this land, once." Trystan said after a while. "I know it well. These cairns have been here for centuries."

"Yep." Galahad agreed and knocked down some more.

Trystan's fingers began to drum. Seriously, shouldn't someone without emotions be a little more patient? "So many rocks, from so many places, were brought here. They could only be some sort of offering. This must have been a religious spot, for people long ago."

"It was a temple, I think." Galahad agreed distractedly, checking the map again. He was definitely headed in the right direction. Probably. Jesus, whoever drew it had seriously needed drawing lessons. See, *this* is why art schools were so important. He shoved over a promising cairn that was as large as he was, stepping back as the rocks clattered to the ground around him.

Trystan had apparently had enough. "Perhaps it makes sense to you and your heathen kind to desecrate religious spots, but I do not see the point in it."

Galahad glanced at Trystan in surprise. "You believe in God?"

"Several of them."

Gryphons had a religion? The Knights' Academy had taught that the gryphons were all godless monsters. Galahad should've known they were lying. They'd lied about everything, his whole life. Rage flickered. The dark, bottomless fury that always stirred now, when he thought about the Knights' Academy, and King Uther, and all the bullshit he'd once blindly believed.

"Your men burned all my people's temples." Trystan went on in a flat voice. "Why did you think we built them, if not to pray?"

"I never burned any temples. I didn't even know gryphons *had* temples."

Trystan regarded him with unreadable brown eyes. "Uther burned my people's temples. Systematically and relentlessly, in his quest for the Looking Glass Pool. You led Uther's soldiers. How could you not know about it?"

"Because I'm a fucking idiot." Galahad snapped, his anger at himself and Trystan and Camelot making him sharper than usual. He didn't like to get angry, because he was always afraid he'd lose control. The words were just there on his tongue, though, before he could call them back. "Haven't you said so yourself?"

Trystan tilted his head, watching him silently.

"Uther knew I was an idiot, too." Being away from Camelot, Galahad saw everything so clearly. "He knew he could lie to me and I'd believe it. I *did* believe it. I loved him like a father. I truly did. I believed all of his lies, because there was no one there to tell me the truth. I would have done *anything* Uther wanted. So long as I thought it was honorable, I carried out all the orders he gave. It's why he made sure my assignments always upheld the Knights' Code."

A knight protects those weaker than himself.

Galahad believed in God, but that pledge was his only true

religion. The foundation of his self. Uther had known that and used that against him. Galahad had fought his battles and thought they were just. But behind the scenes, other men slaughtered the innocent in Uther's name. It wasn't until Legion that Galahad had seen...

No.

He squeezed his eyes shut, trying to calm down. What was he doing? He didn't like talking about his time in the War, because it brought back memories he wanted to forget. These days, Galahad only cared about living his own truth, not sharing it with others. No one would believe him anyway. And why the hell was he arguing with Trystan? Did he doubt that temples had been burned? Did he blame Trystan for despising him? Of course not. Galahad despised himself, too. It was why he was on this mission. To make things right, in some small way.

"I'm sorry." He opened his eyes to look at Trystan, his brief spark of temper fading. "You're right. What happened was as much my fault as anyone's. I should have seen and I didn't. There's no excuse."

Trystan still didn't say anything.

"I'm sorry I was swearing at you, too. I try not to do that. Avalon doesn't like it. And she's right. It sets a Bad example for children."

Trystan arched an incredulous brow.

"I'm not destroying these rock formations for fun, though." Galahad went on. "I'm looking for something. I'll be more careful with them, if it matters to you."

Trystan studied him for a long beat. "Fine." That seemed to be his favorite word.

"'Fine' meaning you believe me?"

Trystan sighed. Louder than before. "Why do you struggle with your own language?"

"Because the word 'fine' doesn't really tell me anything."

"Then you are not listening correctly." Trystan looked up to gauge the position of the sun. "It grows late in the day. Hurry and find what you are looking for, so we can be away from this place before nightfall. It is not a spot where I wish to linger in the dark."

Was this some kind of peace offering? Is that what he meant by "fine?" Galahad thought maybe it was and it sent his mood soaring. He was attracted to Trystan when the gryphon was grouchy and uncommunicative. When he was acting semi-pleasant, though, Galahad felt completely dazzled.

Completely.

He stared at Trystan for a long beat, unsure what he should do about the feeling of *rightness* that filled him when he looked at the man. First of all, no one else had ever felt right before, so he'd never felt this pull towards another person. It was a little disconcerting. And secondly because Galahad wasn't all that great with people. They never seemed to want to get close to him. He wasn't sure what he should say to make Trystan like him.

This was going to take some serious thought.

Thinking about giving it thought made him think of other things. His mind had always traveled down multiple paths at the same time, but the solitude of banishment made it easier for him to jump between topics. Galahad now spent a great deal of time thinking about the "why" of everything around him. He no longer blindly accepted other people's rules, traditions, or facts. He needed to figure it all out for himself.

"Do you think God made the universe or the universe made God?" He asked out of the blue, because it was a mystery he pondered a lot and it was the first thing that popped into his head as a conversation starter.

Trystan seemed confused by the non sequitur. "What?"

Galahad winced, because maybe it did sound like a weird question. "I just wonder about stuff." He shrugged self-consciously and pushed at a pile of rocks, careful not to topple them.

Trystan was quiet for a beat. "I think the gods made many universes." He finally said, like he'd thought it over and decided on an answer. "I think each universe then makes many gods, who all represent small parts of the whole."

That was a peace offering.

"That's a good theory." Galahad shot him a beaming smile. "Thank you."

Trystan grunted again, but it seemed less irritated than most of his grunts.

Galahad continued moving through the three-dimensional forest of stones. Each step he took brought him closer to something dangerous and primal. The deities of this place hadn't been forgiving or kind. He could feel their malice seeping through the ground.

Trystan remained at the edge of the cairns, unaware that the evil grew towards the middle of the labyrinth. "You need to keep your hat on, knight." He tilted his head to see around the stone monuments and idly monitored Galahad's progress. "It's why I acquired it for you. Your kind is not made for these temperatures."

Had he lost his hat? Galahad reached up to touch the empty

space above his hair. Shit. He'd lost his hat. He looked around, wondering where it had gone.

"It blew off that way," Trystan gestured to the left, "several minutes ago. I was waiting for you to notice, but it seems clear that you're incapable of caring for yourself."

"You're the only person in the world who believes that I'm incapable at *anything*."

"Yes. I am used to being the sole voice of reason."

Galahad sent a beseeching look towards the sky and headed towards the hat, winding through the graveyard of rocks. If felt like entering a cage, the pillars' shapes twisted in unsettling ways. As he neared the center they began to look almost… alive.

"Do not go far." Trystan called. "Get the hat and come out of there, so I can see you."

"You know, I survived just fine through my whole banishment without your nagging. I wasn't welcomed in any respectable kingdoms and still I did okay. Admit it. Not many people could have done that. Especially since I wasn't carrying a weapon."

"Blind luck should not be mistaken for skill."

"It wasn't luck." People always thought Galahad's whole life was just *lucky*. He didn't know why. Especially since he would've happily traded places with just about anyone. "I knew what I was doing. And when I didn't…? Well, I'm pretty good at improvising."

"Perhaps we should return to our theological debate. In my religion, the gods often allow hapless creatures to survive against insurmountable odds. They think it's amusing." Trystan sounded sardonic. "Your existence seems to validate my belief in their sense of humor, yes?"

"Or maybe I'm just not as helpless as you think I am. I've never failed at anything." Except at being a Good man, and living a life of honor, and every other thing that mattered.

Trystan made an "um" sound of boredom and doubt. "Never failed at anything. Yet you cannot even keep a hat on your head." He checked the sun, again. "I will eat, while I wait for you to fail… for the first time ever." He climbed off his horse and began rooting around in the saddle bags. "Wilbur's idea of supplies seems to be jerky, so dinner tonight will be jerky."

"Is it vegan?"

Trystan's head turned to stare at him through the rocks.

"I try to eat vegan, now." Galahad explained. "Because I like animals and I want to live with them ethically in the world."

Trystan kept staring.

"I can't like animals, now?" Galahad challenged. "What? You don't like animals?"

"I have respect for tigers."

Galahad squinted slightly at that strange answer. "Right, well, I don't like the idea of *any* animal suffering. I wrote a whole cookbook about veganism." It had been on the Best Sellers List for four solid years. It occupied every slot, actually. All one-through-ten. Which was unusual, since it was only one book. They'd finally had to give his cookbook its *own* list, just to keep things fair for the other authors. "Do we have anything non-animal derived I could eat?"

"Of course. Would you prefer sand or rocks?"

Galahad's smile faded at the sarcasm. "Forget it. I'll just find my own food."

"Where?" Trystan gestured to the emptiness around them. "They do not offer vegetarian menu options in the desert. You eat what is available or you starve. And I will not have Gwen blaming me for your wasting death, which means you will *eat the goddamn jerky*."

The two of them eyed each other for a long moment.

"The jerky's not made of tiger, is it?" Galahad finally asked.

"Lyrssa fucking save me." Trystan went back to gathering up the supplies.

Galahad bent down to grab his hat, absently brushing the dust off it with his bound hands. Why did Trystan affect him so much deeper than anyone else? Why did it feel true with him, of all people? There were about a million other men, who wouldn't be so difficult to deal with who he could… His thoughts abruptly stopped, his eyes falling on a mid-sized cairn.

Only it wasn't a cairn. It was a person.

Galahad's eyes widened, his head whipping around to look at the surrounding rocks. There were at least a dozen creatures all frozen in various poses. Some blissful. Some kneeling in prayer. Some screaming, their mouths forever wide. These weren't statues carved by an artist. These were living beings turned to stone. Lawn ornaments for a god.

This wasn't a temple. This was a tomb.

Galahad swallowed hard and edged towards the center of the rough circle their bodies made. A completely average cairn stood there. It was made of smooth river rocks, piled in a deceptively precarious tower. On its side there was a carving of a woman with snakes for hair.

That seemed like a very eerie, probably dangerous, clue.

Galahad laid his palm on the carving and pushed. Rather

than collapse, the rocks moved together. Sliding sideways on their base, they revealed a hole large enough for a person. A long diagonal shaft had been built beneath them, right through the desert floor.

A tunnel.

Now he was getting somewhere. Galahad folded up the map and shoved it in his pocket. "Trys, I'll be right back." He called and started down the hole. It had been lined with mud-baked bricks, which hopefully wouldn't collapse and crush him into paste. Positive thinking assured him everything would be okay.

"What?" Trystan sounded distracted. From his position, he couldn't see Galahad.

"Eat without me. I found what I was looking for."

"You did?" Trystan sounded surprised now, which was a little insulting. "Where?" There was a pause, like he'd suddenly realized that Galahad had completely disappeared from view. "Knight?" His voice grew sharper. "Where are you?"

"I'm okay." Galahad shouted back. "I'll be back before dark."

Unless he died.

The tunnel was sloped at a steep angle, which was going to be hell to get back up again. It was wide, though. That was good. Galahad wasn't claustrophobic, but the larger opening meant more light came in from above and illuminated his path. He half-slid down the passage, trying to keep himself from tumbling headfirst into the darkness at the bottom.

At the very end of the tunnel, a rock blocked his way. Galahad used his feet to push it, bracing his back against the wall for leverage. It slowly moved a few inches to the left, giving him just enough space to squeeze through. He tumbled headfirst onto the hard-packed ground, ineffectively trying to catch himself with his bound hands. Ouch. He reached up to finger his bruised forehead. That could've gone smoother.

"Are you out of your goddamn mind?" Trystan bellowed from the mouth of the tunnel. He must have run through the whole maze of cairns to find where Galahad had gone. That was sweet. "Come back up here, before you get yourself killed!"

"As soon as I find something." Galahad shouted back and his voice endlessly echoed around him. He was in a large chamber. There was some sunlight, coming in from far above, but it wasn't providing much illumination. He should have brought a flashlight. He craned his head back into the hole and looked up towards the top. "Hey, Trys, do you have a flashlight?"

"Get the hell *out of there.*"

Galahad took that as a "no" to the flashlight. He waved a hand in front of his face, dispelling some of the particles floating around. The air felt gritty and thick in his lungs. It was much cooler, underground, though. So, that was a positive. Galahad always tried to see the positives.

This part of the tomb had been built into the sandbank overhead. It seemed like massive pillars had once supported the weight, but over the years, the roof had deteriorated in many spots. Now, streams of sand fell into the cavernous space. Sunlight poured through the holes, glinting off of the gently tumbling grains and making them look like molten gold.

It was lovely, in an ominous and completely unstable way.

Most of the pillars were in pieces on the ground, which meant the ceiling was being held up by... nothing. Galahad stared up at it, his eyes adjusting, impressed that it lasted this long. Even as he thought it, his attention fell on the twenty foot tall deity.

Holy shit...

Galahad moved farther into the room, entranced by the headless ivory statue situated in front of him. Whatever kind of beings built it, they hadn't looked like him. He could tell that, even though the statue had been decapitated at the neck. The snakelike body proportions, and outstretched six- fingered hands, and the remnants of vivid orange paint on its skin all told him this creature wasn't from any land he'd ever heard of.

Looking at it gave him chills.

The massive statue was such a perfect mixture of art and divinity that Galahad suddenly *felt* the malevolent sanctity of it. This is why so many people had come to build the piles of rocks outside as offerings. Because this place really did bring them close to something great and horrible. Something that was still lurking there. Waiting.

"I'm sorry about the cairns." He said out loud, gazing up at the headless god. It seemed like something was looking back. "I'm on a mission, though, and it will help people."

The sense of being watched didn't abate. If anything, it grew stronger. This god didn't give a shit about helping. Whatever dwelled here was even darker than the darkness Galahad fought inside himself on a daily basis.

And was he crazy or was the rubble at his feet... body parts?

"Knight, if you aren't already dead, you're about to be." Trystan had somehow fit his huge wings down the confines of the tunnel, but he couldn't squeeze his way past the rock at the bottom.

He pushed at it, but it was stuck tight. "What the hell are you doing...?" He managed to get part of his head into the main room and his eyes immediately fell on the statue. "Oh shit."

Galahad barely heard him. He moved closer to the god, his attention on the cracked hunks of stone on the floor. They weren't rocks. They were hands and legs and even heads, all solidified into granite and then shattered. There were weapons lying around, which seemed to indicate that some kind of battle had raged here. A battle against the god perhaps?

"Knight," Trystan's tone was now talking-someone-off-a-ledge calm, "this is a Bad place. Come away from it. *Now*."

Galahad reached down to pick up a mirrored shield. It had words on it he couldn't read along with the name "Medusa." Wherever it had come from, it had been enspelled with some powerful magic. Energy made his palm tingle as he held it. A mummified corpse lay next to the shield, the only person here who hadn't been turned to stone. He'd been crushed by a falling pillar and died trapped in place. But he'd won the fight. The shield had to be his.

Years of training allowed Galahad to recreate the battle in his head. These warriors had been attacked by the statue when they entered the tomb. Most had fallen, quickly turned to stone. But one had used the reflective shield to shine the deity's magic back at her. That had destroyed the head of the statue, but also damaged the stability of the chamber and crushed the man in the debris. Had the warriors come to defeat Medusa? Was that what the god was called?

"Galahad!" Trystan's voice rapped out. "Do *not* go any farther."

It was the first time he'd called Galahad by name. The beautifully accented voice made each syllable sound like music. Galahad instinctively turned to look at him, trying to focus. The air in the tomb felt like a drug, hazing his mind. He had no idea how long Trystan had been shouting for him, but he looked desperate.

And Galahad was now directly in front of the statue, close enough to touch it.

He blinked, coming back to his senses.

Trystan watched him steadily through the small opening, seeing he had regained Galahad's attention. "That's it. Return to me. The god's power is still staining this place. It seeks to draw you in. Do not let it."

Galahad gave his head a clearing shake, dispelling the fog from his mind. He had a slight immunity to consumer magic, but this wasn't some cheap secondhand spell, sold on the street. The tomb was filled with the real deal. Had that caught the dead warriors off guard, too? His gaze flicked back to the last man who'd died there. He could now see the black feathers on the remnants of his broad wings.

"There's a gryphon here." Galahad crouched down next to the corpse. "I think he led the fight that destroyed this place."

"There are dead gryphons under every inch of this land. Most died fighting. You should know that better than anyone." Trystan managed to move the rock slightly with his shoulder, but he still couldn't fit through the opening. "*P'don*." He slammed a fist against it in frustration.

Sand poured down, faster and faster, making it hard to see. As if Galahad's very presence had upset the delicate balance of the room. ...Or maybe Medusa was just pissed. He spared the statue a quick look, feeling its growing evil and then looked back to the dead man.

Foreign words echoed in Galahad's head, telling him something in the gryphon dialect. After he was banished, he'd begun to hear voices, which probably meant he was going crazy. Rather than scare him, though, Galahad often found the overlapping whispers comforting.

"I'm on a mission to help your people." Galahad told the skeleton. Insane as it sounded, he found himself talking to dead gryphons a lot these days. He felt compelled to, although he wasn't sure why they'd want to hear from their enemy. "Can you show me the way?" The room seemed to exist between this plane and the next, so maybe the gryphon's spirit was still there.

At least one *living* gryphon certainly had a lot to say. "Knight, if you don't get your ass back over here, I will wring your fucking neck."

Galahad's eyes automatically slipped down to the dead gryphon's neck. Silver glinted in the dim light. A chain. Reaching out with his bound hands, he carefully unclasped it, taking pains not to disturb the parchment dry braid hanging down the gryphon's back. Pulling the necklace free, he held it up and smiled.

Dangling from the silver links was an ornate key, studded with cabochon rubies. It was so easy to find, that he knew he'd been aided in his quest.

His gaze went back to the sunken face of the skeleton, inches from his own. "Thank you." He murmured, bizarrely certain of the dead gryphon's help. "I'll finish this or die trying. I give you my word. You can rest, now." It could have been his imagination, but he swore a sense of peace suddenly filled the air.

Medusa was not nearly so pleased with his promise.

The ground shook. Sand began tumbling down from the ceiling in torrents, as the remaining pillars toppled over. It was like being at the bottom of an hourglass, as time ran out. Whatever force inhabited the tomb was out of patience. It planned to kill him, even if it meant destroying itself in the process.

"*Move!*" Trystan roared.

Galahad was already running for the tunnel. Tons of sand cascaded down in endless waves, ripping the entire roof apart. He could feel the dirt threatening to suffocate him, scratching his eyes, filling his nose, slowing his progress.

"God*dammit*." Trystan heaved the rock another foot to the left, using brute force. "We're about to be trapped down here forever. That counts as *failing*, as you claim to be unfamiliar with the concept."

A horrible sound filled the air. Stone against stone. Galahad looked over his shoulder, towards the statue, just in time to see it crack in two. From its hollow depths, came a swarm of orange snake-creatures. Thousands of them, gliding through the sand like it was water. All of them trying to reach Galahad and stop his escape.

Galahad's eyes went wide. Oh *shit*.

"Shit!" Trystan bellowed. Any sane person would have fled for their life, but Trystan still didn't run. His hand reached out to Galahad, through the larger opening he'd created between the blockading rock and the tunnel wall. "Grab onto me!"

Galahad started for him and then hesitated. The voices in his head were louder, now. Many different people screaming words at him. He didn't speak the gryphons' language, but he still knew what they wanted.

The silver shield.

Galahad raced back for it, leaping over snakes who were trying to strike out at him. He had no idea why the shield mattered, but he knew he needed it. His boots sank into the sand as he waded forward. The floor was disappearing, obscuring everything that lay on it. In another few moments, he'd be buried, too. He began frantically digging in the spot where he'd seen the shield, hoping he could find it in time.

"What are you doing?!" Trystan bellowed.

"I have to find the shield!"

"Are you out of your mind? *Leave it!*"

He couldn't. He wasn't sure why. His fingers finally touched the edge of its smooth surface and he pulled it free of the dirt. The reflective surface shone even in the dim light. Satisfied that he held it,

Galahad looped it over his shoulders and headed for Trystan again. He wasn't certain he was going to be able to climb out of there before the whole tomb collapsed. And if he died, he would take Trystan with him.

No.

"Here, take this and leave me!" His palms reached up towards Trystan's outstretched hand, wanting to give him the key. Wanting to make sure it got out, even if he didn't. "There isn't time. You have to go." Trystan didn't know what to do with the key, but he'd figure it out. The man was the greatest military thinker of the War. Maybe Galahad should give him the shield too, just in case it was important to something...

Trystan's fingers clamped around Galahad's bound wrists. Ignoring the key, he jerked Galahad forward, nearly bending him in half in his hurry to drag him back into the tunnel. Galahad had no idea how Trystan managed it, but he somehow hauled him up and through the opening. Galahad fell on top of him, Trystan's arms locked around him.

The snake creatures slithered into the tunnel after them. Trystan slammed his boot down on the closest serpent, squashing it with his heel. Orange goo exploded out, along with the sickening smell of decay. For once, Galahad was not about to complain about hurting an animal.

"Hold on." Trystan ordered and then they were flying up the tunnel.

Literally *flying*.

Trystan's wings banged against the brick sides as he got them back to the surface in a matter of seconds. Even then it was almost too late. Galahad could hear the tomb collapsing into ruin, taking the tunnel with it. He barely felt the sunlight hit his skin and then Trystan was shoving him face-first into the sand.

"Stay down!"

An unholy shriek of something beyond mortal comprehension sounded from far below and debris rained all around him, but none of it hit Galahad. Trystan's body covered his, as a humongous cloud of dust rushed out of the tunnel behind them. His arms enveloped Galahad's head, his wings coming up to shield him from harm.

Nobody had ever physically protected Galahad before. There was no need, considering he'd spent his life fighting and never lost a battle. It was ridiculous that Trystan would consider him delicate in some way.

And even more ridiculous that Galahad suddenly felt... safe.

He'd never really felt safe before. He'd always been in the initial wave of soldiers wading into combat situations and the first to volunteer for dangerous missions. It was how he'd tried to ensure that everything went the way it was supposed to. That Good triumphed and innocent people were protected. Galahad was the *best* at whatever he did. Always. He made sure of it.

Except, he *wasn't* so sure anymore. Not with Trystan around.

Instead of frustrating him, Galahad found that idea to be a huge relief. Suddenly, he didn't feel like the lone figure standing between victory and defeat. Now, Trystan was there beside him, helping to keep things under control. Between the two of them, they'd win against *anything*. They could save the world, if they had to. And that realization made him feel safer than anything ever had before.

Galahad shifted in Trystan's hold, turning to look at him through the fog of dirt. The man's flawless profile was inches from his face. Despite the chaos around him, Galahad's heart flipped in his chest.

Trystan glanced down at him, their gazes locking. For a timeless second, neither one of them moved. Trystan's weight pressed down on his back, holding him beneath him, and Galahad liked it. Jesus, he *really* liked it. Until that moment, Galahad never would have believed that he could feel anything so strong so *fast*.

He tore his eyes away from Trystan, confused by the strength of the passion coursing through him. This was beyond just finding the man attractive. This was... more. This was *a lot* more. What the hell was happening? Caught a little off guard by the strength of it, he tried to move away.

"Do not." Trystan's palm found his shoulder, pushing him down. His lower body shifted, becoming more aggressive, pinning Galahad's legs with his own.

That did absolutely *nothing* to help the situation.

Galahad's eyes glazed over in lust. "You need to let me up." He demanded in what he hoped sounded like a normal-ish voice.

"It's not safe. Rocks are still falling."

Galahad's only clear thought, through the crazy desire, was that Trystan wouldn't be comfortable if he realized how aroused Galahad was. He didn't want to make Trystan uncomfortable. "You don't understand. When you're on top of me I feel..."

"I won't hurt you." Trystan interrupted. His voice was gruff, like he understood the gist of the problem. "I'm in control of myself, alright?" His head dropped forward to rest in Galahad's hair and he sighed in vexation. "Just give it a minute and we'll both get through this."

Galahad frowned. "Huh?" He tried to find leverage so he could sit up.

Trystan let out a hissing breath as Galahad's hips moved. "For Lyrssa sake, stay *still*."

Galahad froze, realization dawning. Trystan wasn't upset. Trystan was turned on, too.

He hadn't immediately realized that, because it was so unexpected. But now it was kind of impossible to miss. Like *hugely* impossible. His eyes flashed back to Trystan's face in shock.

"It is adrenaline." Trystan assured him, expecting complaints. "It is not my fault."

Galahad slowly grinned, no longer trying to get free. He wasn't imagining their connection. This was real and Trystan felt it, too. Hot damn, that changed everything!

Trystan made a sound somewhere between a groan and a curse. "And do not smile like that, either. It just makes it worse."

"Smiling makes the adrenaline worse?" Galahad clarified, suddenly enjoying this.

Trystan glowered at him, aggravated at everything and everyone, but mostly at Galahad. "You do these things deliberately, don't you?" The air cleared a bit and he leaned back to survey Galahad's body for injuries. "Are you alright?"

"Yeah. Are you?"

"I'm fucking wonderful." Trystan shoved the cairn that marked the entrance to the tunnel back into place with his foot, sealing it up forever.

One of the snake creatures had been right at the entrance, so Trystan ended up slicing it in half. Its decapitated head let out a hiss of fury and hate and then went still. The bright sun seemed to blister its slimy orange skin, causing it to sizzle and smoke right in front of them.

Trystan and Galahad lay on the desert ground, watching it cook for a long moment.

"I think we should camp somewhere else tonight." Galahad finally said.

Trystan snorted. "No shit."

Galahad laughed at the bone dry summation. Trystan blinked in surprise, like he'd never made anyone laugh before. That only made Galahad laugh harder, happy to be alive and with this man.

Trystan's mouth almost seemed to curve slightly in response. Except he was a gryphon and he wasn't supposed to have any emotions. "You're a menace, knight." He decided and rolled all the way off of him. As he left, he dusted a hand through Galahad's hair, shaking it free of sand. "And you lost your hat, again."

In that second, Galahad realized something that reshaped his entire world:

Trystan Airbourne was a knight. A *real* knight. Someone who embodied all the shining principles that Galahad had grown up admiring. The man's arsenal of multi-bladed weapons and litany of sarcastic remarks were just for show. Underneath that, Trystan epitomized all the best traits a knight could possibly have. He was brave, and selfless, and honorable, and kind, and he would willingly die to save a man who should have been his enemy.

No one else had ever quite lived up to the ideals of true knighthood. Certainly not Galahad. He'd come to believe that *nobody* could reach their lofty goals. That *nobody* would be that valiant and Good straight down to their soul. It was exhilarating to see that he'd been wrong. The sensation of finding something *true* washed over him, again.

Trystan's gaze traced over Galahad's face, like he couldn't help himself. "You're sure you're alright?" He asked in a quieter voice. "You weren't hurt?"

"Not a scratch." He gave Trystan a brilliant grin. "I've never been better in my life."

Trystan glanced away from his smile and cleared his throat. "Fine." He stood up, already looking for something to grumble about. "Magical weapons are usually valuable, but going back for that shield was stupid."

"Shields aren't weapons. They protect *from* weapons."

"Shields are defined as *weapons*, because they can be used offensively." Trystan shook his head. "You have a shocking lack of knowledge about your own language."

Galahad made a face. "I just feel like the dead gryphon wanted me to take it, okay?"

"Perhaps it is a cultural difference, but my kind rarely encourages grave robbing."

"I wasn't grave robbing. I just had the very strong impression that the warrior would've been pissed if I left the shield behind." Galahad said, without really thinking about it first. "He thought I needed it. I think his name was... Evalach?"

Trystan looked at him sharply.

Crap. That probably sounded crazy. Galahad winced. "Okay, you have a point. It was probably a dumb thing to do, but I was..."

"Explain this 'strong impression.'" Trystan interrupted, his gaze intense.

"Just a feeling, really. Something told me I should take the shield."

"Voices?" Trystan guessed in a strangely serious tone. "Did voices tell you?"

No way was Galahad admitting that out loud. It sounded like something a crazy person would say and he didn't love the idea of Trystan thinking he was crazy. "I should have forgotten about the shield." He said instead. "You're right. It was dumb to go back."

Trystan tilted his head, like he noticed the non-answer. "Evalach was a fabled *ya'lah*, from long ago." He said after a beat. He seemed to expect that Galahad would have a big response to that news, but Galahad wasn't sure what it should be.

"What's a *ya'lah*?" That word sounded... familiar.

Trystan made a face, like the question annoyed him and he went back to his normal frowning. "A *ya'lah* is someone who has never designed a "body positive" clothing line for magazine covers. *That's* for fucking certain."

"I didn't design that collection. I just modeled it. It sends a really relevant message about expanding the fashion industry to everyone."

"Fine." Trystan grunted, like he didn't want to talk about dead gryphons or society's unrealistic beauty standards. "I am just amazed that you managed to survive the afternoon." He dusted off his clothes like the task took all of his attention. "As I said, the gods like to waste their miracles on helpless beings."

The casual insults didn't faze Galahad a bit. He doubted they ever would again, because now he'd seen behind the curtain. "Thank you for helping me."

"I did it for my sister." Trystan headed back towards the horses. "You will not disappoint her by dying, so you'd better smarten the hell up." He shook his head in exasperation. "I do see the foundation of your bond with Gwen more clearly, though. She's a lunatic, too. It's no wonder you get along so well." He slanted Galahad a look over his shoulder, grudgingly curious. "What is that key you found?"

"I'm not sure, yet."

"You risked your life for a key and you have no idea if it is even important?"

"I'm going on faith."

"I will not call you an idiot, because it seems to upset you. ...But that is exactly what an idiot would say." Trystan grabbed the reins of his horse. "If you try something like this again, I will take you straight back to Camelot. I'll find another way into St. Ives, before I have Gwen's chosen brother dying in my care."

Maybe it was the lingering magic in his head at work, but, in that moment, Galahad knew he was at a crossroads. He could continue on his own path... or he could step onto Trystan's.

Rationally, there wasn't much of a choice. Trystan couldn't feel emotions, and saw him as an enemy, and had kind of kidnapped Galahad. There were probably sixty reasons why it wouldn't work out between them. He should obviously slip away from the man and continue west on his own. Choosing Trystan would almost certainly leave Galahad broken in the end.

...But what if it didn't?

"I'll get you into St. Ives." He said, optimism winning over logic. "We'll go together."

"And we need a new approach to this treasure hunt madness, yes?" Trystan persisted. "You will not risk yourself searching for it, again. When we get back to Camelot, I will select some trusted men for you to hire. *They* can follow the map and prove there is nothing there. That will satiate your desire to know where it leads and also be far less dangerous for you."

"That's a nice offer." Galahad said, not agreeing to a damn thing. He got to his feet and looped the chain around his neck, so the key fell against his chest.

One step closer to Atlantis.

"So... ready to keep heading west, then?" He asked, hoping Trystan didn't notice his evasion. "Unless you feel like you're on the verge of another adrenaline attack and need to rest."

"Shut up, knight." Trystan muttered without any heat. "I am..." His attention jerked upward suddenly. "*P'don*." He whispered.

"What's wrong?" Galahad tilted his head back to scan the sky and instantly saw the problem. Any King's Man who'd fought in the Looking Glass Campaigns would've known who was closing in on them. "Gryphons." He said softly.

Chapter Four

Battle of Pen Rhionydd
Start of the Second Looking Glass Campaign

By the time he was ten years old, Trystan had become used to life in a cage. He had lived in the zoo for four years and it became normal for him. The wingless races came to stare and laugh and it was normal. The zookeepers' assistants fed the gryphons scraps of food in buckets and it was normal. The people around him constantly died of homesickness and neglect.

And it was all normal.

Trystan spent his days playing games around the enclosure. It was easy for him to picture faraway places and adventures in his head. The adults in the cage encouraged his daydreams, wanting to keep him occupied and content. So long as Trystan didn't endanger himself and he took time to eat and learn, they allowed him to do as he wished.

Trystan was the only child in the zoo. One of the youngest gryphons left in the world.

He was consequently cherished by the other prisoners.

None of them had known Trystan before their confinement. But, it didn't matter. The innocent belonged to all who would care for them. Once he was with them, he became *their* child. Because of the curse, none of them could adopt Trystan through the gryphons' rituals, but they *all* claimed him. They *all* needed him. Having Trystan there gave the adults a sense of purpose. Gave them something meaningful to focus on. They taught him skills, listened to his concerns, and let him sleep safely covered by their wings.

For the rest of his life, Trystan would say that there were far worse places to be a boy.

And he meant that. By and large, the memories of his childhood were not unpleasant. He never forgot the gryphons who cared for him in the zoo. He considered them his second clan. He carried their faces and their teachings with him always.

He remembered watching the night sky through the glass dome of the enclosure, while Ban told him the names of all the stars. He remembered Cador showing him how to move silently, when stalking your enemies in the dark. He remembered Ywain, who barely spoke, stepping in front of Trystan whenever the assistant zookeepers shouted curses at them. He remembered Fisher teaching him about gemstones, and Olwen strange eyes brightening when Trystan finally learned to multiply numbers, and Lunette using sticks as makeshift weapons to show him fighting techniques.

And he remembered every single story Elaine told him.

Elaine Cloudbearer was kind, beautiful, and the best storyteller Trystan would ever know. It wasn't so much the words she chose, but how she said them. All her tales sounded like music. Elaine would braid his hair each night, using the intricate knots of gryphon warriors, and tell him the myths of their people in her lyrical voice. Trystan would struggle to stay awake for as long as he could, so he didn't miss a single word.

She told him of giant rocking-horseflies who came down from the sky and beings on moonbeams who no one could ever catch. She told him of gods and heroes, and why the seasons existed, and who made the sun.

Her favorite story, though, and the one she repeated the most, was about the *ya'lah*. The champion of the gryphons and the hero who would lift the curse that had doomed them all. She told that tale to Trystan on the night the city was attacked by the gryphons.

On the night that she died.

The zoo was located in Pen Rhionyyd, which sat in the northwest of Camelot, bordering Lyonesse. It was the very edge of Uther's domain and so it was the most vulnerable spot in the kingdom. The gryphons caged there had been all but forgotten by both sides, as Lyrssa and Uther focused on plotting their next moves.

The First Looking Glass Campaign had ended with Lyrssa Highstorm escaping Uther's captivity and regrouping with her people. After that, the fighting had died down for a few years, as each side entrenched and took stock.

...But neither of them was ready to quit.

Uther's curse still plagued the gryphons and he still wanted the Looking Glass Pool, so more warring was assured. Since the king still possessed large portions of Lyonesse, the queen decided to match his invasion with one of her own. Like pieces on a catur board, they acted and reacted. Uther had marched his troops into Lyonesse, so

Lyrssa flew hers into Pen Rhionyyd.

It was a shocking move and one that launched the next phase of the decades-long conflict between the wingless and the gryphons. No matter the reasons for it, thousands would die in the middle Looking Glass Campaign.

Beginning that very night.

The gryphons in the zoo watched the fighting through the glass dome of their enclosure, none of them saying a word. The sky was orange with flames and the air filled with screaming. Even Fisher seemed subdued. He had lost his mind, they said, which was why he now spent his days pacing around the cage with his cane, talking nonsense about ghosts. As the battle raged outside, though, he sat under one of the enclosure's trees, finally silent.

It wasn't until much later that Trystan understood why they'd all become so quiet. At the time, he'd found it all exciting. Hopeful, even. They were about to be rescued!

He'd told Elaine so, as she brushed his hair. The two of them sat on the floor of the cage, as she prepared Trystan for bed. Everyone else was aloft, staring out of the unbreakable glass, except for Fisher, who was in the corner.

"The gryphons fighting outside do not know we are here, Trystan. We will not be rescued by anyone. That has never been our path." She gently steered his thoughts from the battle raging. "Did I ever tell you about the *ya'lah*?"

"Yes. But you can tell me, again. I don't mind."

Fisher's head came up, like he was interested in the tale, as well.

Outside, sounds of the conflict grew louder.

Trystan frowned. Gryphons did not worry, but he felt his heartbeat increasing. The noises did not seem entirely safe to him. The fighting was closer, now. Some of the zoo's animals were already roaring out in alarm. Trystan had spent years listening to the elephants and lions. He had never heard them sound so furious and scared before.

Not ever.

Elaine made a soothing sound. "All will be well."

Trystan recalled his mother saying the same thing, as Camelot's soldiers approached their home. And he blamed the Yellow Boots for making her comforting words a lie. In his mind, the traitorous gryphons who'd chosen to work for Uther were all faceless and interchangeably evil. He had no idea which Yellow Boots had been in his village that day and so he despised them all.

The Yellow Boots helped Uther to round up and defeat their own kind. In return for betraying their people, the Yellow Boots were not even made knights. They were treated as less. They *were* less. Knights at least fought for their own kind. The Yellow Boots fought for a man who hated them. They were given *different* uniforms than the wingless soldiers, marking them as non-warriors. Instead, they wore yellow boots that earned them their nickname and the derision of the other gryphons. Maybe they hoped to offset their own peoples' scorn with rewards from the wingless society, but that would never come to pass.

Their choices meant that they would never be accepted by either culture.

Trystan would've liked to see them all dead. They had led the wingless king to the Airbourne Clan and now there was no more Airbourne Clan. It was very clear to him who was to blame for the loss.

Trystan alone was spared from the slaughter, because the zoo had needed children for the exhibit. His mother had fought to stop the King's Men from ripping him away. Trying to protect him. She had died thinking only of his safety, beaten to death before his eyes. He saw it all again, as Elaine held him. Elaine reminded him so much of his mother.

Suddenly, that gave him a chill.

"You're not going to die, are you?" He asked her, even though a part of him suddenly understood what was really happening.

"Listen to the story, Trystan." Elaine ran a hand over his hair, not answering. "It is important that you know these things. Stories are what we leave behind."

Above them, the other gryphons began talking in low voices. Casting glances Trystan's way, as if they were discussing him and did not want him to overhear. Orange light was reflected off the glass of the dome in a way it hadn't been before. Like the fire was moving nearer to them.

"King Uther enlisted a witch named Igraine to curse Lyrssa. You know this."

Trystan nodded, trying to focus on the story. "Her spell made it so no gryphons could have children."

"Yes, it was a cruel plan to try and break our people. Through our queen, Igraine's spell would slowly infect us all. Soon *no* gryphons will be able to have young. We cannot even adopt them. Uther and Igraine stole our future."

An explosion *boomed* from somewhere in the distance.

Trystan jolted, instinctively leaning back into Elaine's hold.

"All curses have a way to break them." He said, trying to sound brave. "We just need to find it."

Elaine's dove-gray wings came forward to gently encircle him. "This is true. But Igraine was clever. To ensure that the curse could not be lifted easily, she made it so only someone from the wingless race can find the cure. Without wingless blood, they will never locate it."

"The wingless will never help anyone but themselves." Even at a young age, Trystan knew their true nature.

"Some of them may yet prove themselves." Elaine murmured. Trystan wasn't sure how Elaine could possibly retain her faith in *any* of the wingless, after seeing her clan butchered before her eyes, but she never condemned the entirety of their race. "Judge everyone on their *best* day, Trystan, not their worst."

"I think we should capture a wingless, once we escape. We can *make* him help us lift the curse." To Trystan, it seemed like the only possibility.

"If we were able to escape, that would be a sound idea." Elaine praised. "In fact, Uther also feared that a wingless might be willing to assist us, for one reason or another. So Igraine, who knew something of gryphon culture, added another stipulation to her spell: A *ya'lah* must lift the curse. No one else."

"And a wingless cannot be a *ya'lah*." Trystan finished, brooding, as he always did, over the paradox Igraine had created with her spell. "None of them are brave enough or strong enough. So the spell can't be broken."

Fisher's attention was on Elaine and Trystan, looking more focused than he'd been in months.

"There has not yet been a wingless *ya'lah*." Elaine agreed. "But I would not say such a thing could *never* happen. The longer I live, the more I believe all things are possible."

"So you think a *ya'lah* is really coming to fight for us?"

"I do not know." Elaine shook her head, the cadence of her voice like music. "Uther certainly thought we would not find a champion. But then he also thought that we would have no option but surrender. And he was *very* wrong in that. Our people fight on, Trystan."

Trystan glanced up at the enclosure's dome. There was not much room in the cage to fly, so the adults were jockeying for position by the glass. Whatever they were staring at must have been really horrible or really great, because they couldn't seem to look away.

And Trystan doubted it was really great.

"Why do you favor this story?" He asked Elaine in agitation, because it suddenly made no sense. "Lyrssa is *still* cursed. The gryphons *still* cannot have children. The *ya'lah* is *still* not here to help us. The end is not satisfying, at all."

"The end has not been written, yet."

"Then why not tell a tale that *is* finished. One of our victories, instead of our losses? Or maybe tell the tale of the moonbeam creatures, again." The moonbeam creatures fascinated him.

"This is not a tale of our loss. It is a tale of our *strength*." Elaine explained, finishing his braid. "Each gryphon will stand alone against a thousand foes, if we must. No matter what comes, we do not bow to our enemies. We protect those in our care. And if we are *right*, we do not say we are wrong. Remember this as you grow."

"Yes." He looked at Elaine over his shoulder, his expression serious. "But I'd still rather hear of the moonbeam creatures."

"The next time you hear either tale, you will have to be the one who tells it." She ran her thumb down the center of his face, from his forehead to the bridge of his nose. "It has been the greatest honor of my life to care for you, Trystan. Carry my stories into the future. Ensure that my path stretches on."

And that's when he knew for sure that Elaine was going to die.

That they probably all would.

The backs of Trystan's eyes burned, but he didn't let the tears fall. Gryphons didn't cry. Instead, he nodded at her, unable to speak for fear of his voice breaking.

"Elaine." Lunette called from up above. "Come here. We think we have a plan."

Elaine rose to her feet and flew up to join them, leaving Trystan and Fisher on the floor.

Fisher arched a brow and made a show of checking right and then left, like someone might be lurking around trying to overhear. After ensuring they were alone, he leaned closer to Trystan, his milky gaze intent. "I know the ending to that story she told you." He whispered, loudly.

Trystan blinked hard against the sting in his eyes. "You do?" He swallowed. "But, Elaine said it was still being written."

"That's because she's never been to Atlantis."

Chapter Five

Uther is the real victim in all of this.

That's the part that makes me sick. Everyone wants to wring their hands about him "starting the War" --boo-fucking-hoo-- but let's all take a second to *really* remember our fallen king. Murdered by that winged bitch Lyrssa. Castrated by some asshole, who was probably a gryphon. Has to search the world, hoping for some way to give the kingdom another heir.

I mean... No disrespect to Arthur, but some time has passed since he died. We can look at him a little clearer, right? If you were Uther, wouldn't you think *maybe* you could give us a better future king than *that* guy?
Of course you would! Let's be real here, people. The graal was never something Uther wanted for *himself*.

He wanted it for the Good of Camelot.

"Stopping the Savages" Podcast
Sir Dragonet of Camelot- Former Troubadour of King

Uther and Host of the Program

Lyonesse Desert- ~~Sparrowhawk~~ Welkyn Pass

Galahad had never been inside a gryphon village before.
Not when it was still thriving and filled with people and *alive*.
This village was so different from what he'd seen in the War.
He found himself looking around with deep interest as the gryphons

dragged him to the center of their small town. It was shocking to see living beings in the organically-shaped wooden buildings. To witness them walking the streets and staring back at him with living eyes. He'd never imagined the day he would see a living village full of living gryphon.

He'd thought they were all gone, thanks to him.

For a moment, Galahad's mind played tricks on him. Black ash against the blue sky, and hot blood coating his hands, and the Rath's horrible green power lashing out. The images were suddenly superimposed over the thriving town before him, now. Bodies in the checkered grass. Raging fire. Screaming and laughter. It was so real that he could smell the smoke, again.

Shit.

He squeezed his eyes shut and inhaled deeply, forcing the memories away.

Trying to center himself, he looked over at Trystan who was being herded along next to him. The man hadn't stabbed anyone, yet, which was a minor miracle. He'd grudgingly allowed the gryphon scouts to... well... abduct them really.

Apparently, this stretch of desert had been claimed by the Welkyn Clan, but how was anyone supposed to *know* that? Galahad had pointed out that there weren't any trespassing warnings posted, but no one seemed to care for that logic. Instead, there had been a lot of shouting in the gryphons' language that Galahad hadn't fully understood. From what he could tell, the gryphon scouts wanted to slaughter Galahad and Trystan was against the idea. After some debate and unmistakable death threats, the scouts had settled on taking them both back to this village to face their leader.

And so here they were, surrounded by a dozen or so living gryphon in their living town, awaiting a ruling on their future from someone named Ayren.

Galahad already knew he *wouldn't* be living by the end. No way would the gryphons let a knight walk away from this place. Why would they? And if they realized he was the Butcher of Legion, the death would be slow and painful and involve a lot of screaming.

It was probably justice that the gryphons would kill him, considering who he was and what he'd done. Still, it kind of pissed him off to die *now*. Before he'd finished his mission or saw Gwen and Avi, again.

Or slept with Trystan.

Yeah, that was a big one. Galahad was not looking forward to dying a virgin.

He'd had chances for sex before, with both men and women, and he'd always had to say "no." Galahad couldn't sleep with the women, because it would have been totally unfair and untrue. With men, it was less cut and dry. Occasionally, some good-looking guy would offer a night together and Galahad would be tempted. In the end, though, he always had to refuse their advances, because it just felt wrong when they touched him. It felt... false.

Gwen had always been talking about finding the "right man" and, somewhere along the line, Galahad internalized her logic. Living a life of truth wasn't just about sleeping with men. It was about sleeping with the *right* man.

And Trystan was the right man.

The longer Galahad was with him, the truer their connection felt. Trystan was stubborn, and unfriendly, and mostly communicated through grunts, but Galahad had never wanted anyone more. If he somehow survived this, he was going to suggest they have sex. No doubt about it.

Unfortunately, he wasn't going to survive this.

"They're going to kill me." Galahad told Trystan seriously. "Let them."

Trystan shot him a scowl, unhappy even by Trystan standards.

"I mean it." Galahad pressed, seeing the other man wasn't eager to agree. "There's no sense in both of us dying. Just let them have me." Everything inside of him told him to protect Trystan. The instinct was strong, and swift, and inexplicably true. "You live and take care of Gwen and Avi. They're all that's important."

Trystan squinted down at him for a moment. "This isn't an act, is it?" It wasn't a question, so much as an exasperated realization. "You're really just *like* this, aren't you?"

Galahad frowned. "Are you feeling okay?"

"Gryphons generally 'feel' nothing, as I have explained." Trystan shook his head in aggravation, pitching his voice low. "Look. You are supposed to be a great warrior. If I untie you and get you a weapon, how many of the gryphons would you be able to kill?"

Galahad was still bound with that enchanted rope, so technically he was a prisoner of Trystan *and* the gryphon. No one had even *tried* to tie Trystan, of course. They were too intimidated by all the Trystan-ness. It was a little bit annoying that no one ever seemed intimidated by *him*, but Galahad was rising above it.

"I'm not killing anyone. Ever. I told you, I don't do that, anymore."

Trystan shot him a glare. "You need to kill at least six." He declared in a dark tone.

"No."

"Five, then. Pick some smallish ones. I will kill the others."

"*No*." Galahad repeated. "I'm living a peaceful, truthful, useful life, now. I no longer fight. Besides, there's too few gryphons left, as it is. Better they survive then me."

Trystan's jaw ticked. "A shame you did not take that stance at Legion."

"Well, I'm taking it now."

"Very laudable. Perhaps your people will give you another medal. Posthumously."

"They probably will. They love to hand out awards for death." Galahad had won the Camelot Medal of Honor six times. He'd destroyed all those gleaming citations long before he was banished, unable to stand the sight of them. "When I'm gone, I'm sure I'll get some ugly statues, too. Calling me a martyr and a hero. Just like the rest of the monsters."

Trystan let out a long breath, like he was struggling to keep from bellowing. "This is the Welkyn Clan." He explained in an overly calm voice. "They are among the few gryphons who still live in these mountains, because they are willing to endure unimaginable hardships. They will be *merciless*."

Galahad nodded. "Just… Don't let me hurt anyone, okay? No matter what."

Trystan glanced down at him, skepticism all over his face. "If you believe you're the threat here, you're misunderstanding the situation."

"I'm *always* the threat, everywhere I go. And this town is bringing back memories for me, and I'm not exactly right in the head, and I don't want to hurt anyone. Especially not gryphons. So don't let me, alright? If something happens, you stop me."

Trystan stared at him.

Galahad stared back.

"Fine." Trystan looked back at the other gryphons, who were forming a loose circle around them. "Fuck it. I'll just kill them all myself."

He no doubt could. The man could wage war on an army and come out the victor in battle after battle. He'd proven that in the Looking Glass Campaigns. On their separate sides of the War, Trystan and Galahad had kept their armies in play and each other in check for years. They were the only ones who'd been able to rival each other's tactics. If they worked together, imagine what they could accomplish.

Such a shame Galahad was going to die before he found out.

"Don't fight your own people." Galahad said again. "Their blood will be harder for you to wash away. Trust me. If we can't reason with them, just let them kill me."

Galahad didn't have much success with convincing people not to murder him, but it was always worth a try.

"I can't let them kill you." Trystan sounded disgusted, but resolute. "I'd like to. Believe me. But, it's my duty to care for you, no matter how irritating you are. Stand there silently and do not interfere."

Galahad sighed. The man wasn't going to see reason, so Galahad would just have to save Trystan before Galahad was executed. That was completely doable. Galahad was nothing if not optimistic, even in the face of certain doom.

The gryphons gathered around them shouted questions and insults. Galahad's grasp of their dialect was minimal, but he knew most of the curse words. They'd been bellowed at him for years. Hatred came through loud and clear in any language.

Trystan's jaw clenched, his eyes flicking from one angry face to another. Galahad figured they had about thirty seconds before someone got dead. Luckily, before the mental countdown to Trystan's explosion reached zero, a woman appeared. The shouting stopped and the crowd parted as she approached, leaving little doubt that she was Ayren Welkyn, the leader of the group.

"Trystan Airbourne." Ayren stood in the middle of the group, wearing the gryphon's traditional garb and a wary expression. "I have heard many tales of your exploits, since we last met."

"Only the worst ones are true."

Galahad nearly snorted. It truly was a pity the man had so little confidence.

"Why are you trespassing on our territory, Trystan?" Ayren spoke the common tongue, probably so she could more effectively threaten Galahad.

"This is not Welkyn land." Trystan argued. "The Sparrowhawk Pass is open to all."

"The wingless destroyed the water source in Welkyn territory, so the Welkyn have moved to *this* territory. It was either that or fruitlessly wander the mountains, searching for the lost clans on Mount Feather to take us in. Which would you have chosen?"

Trystan didn't reply.

"What's Mount Feather?" Galahad asked him.

"The mythic home of the old clans." Ayren told him, overhearing the question. "The gryphons who have avoided the wingless and stayed free of your taint." She arched a brow at Trystan. "You, on the other hand, live with the wingless now, yes? Claiming kinship to the new king, who's taken the Skycast name."

"The name belongs to Midas." Trystan stepped in front of Galahad and braced his feet apart, his arms crossed over his chest.

Galahad felt his mouth curve. Trystan was protecting him, again. That was so cute.

He stared at Trystan's broad back, his gaze tracing over the scarred wings and his heart melted. Jesus, this went far beyond just wanting to sleep with the guy. This was the feeling he'd been waiting for all his life. He couldn't explain it and didn't even want to. What he felt was all-consuming, and sudden, and beyond any question.

It was simply *true*.

"Midas has taken nothing." Trystan continued. "Corrah Skycast claimed him as a son. Her clan is his clan. The name is his name, by right."

Ayren considered that. "There are rumors that our kind is now welcomed in Camelot." She finally said. "That this new king favors the gryphons. That he's giving us sanctuary."

"Corrah was his mother." Trystan reiterated, as if that explained everything. "Do you doubt that she raised him well?"

Ayren nodded, accepting that. "Corrah was a great queen." She agreed. "A great warrior. I am pleased that her clan survives with her son, even if he is wingless. We have no quarrel with Midas Skycast."

"Then you have no quarrel with me."

"Don't I?" She asked softly. Her eyes flicked to Galahad, who was partially blocked behind Trystan's massive wings. "My scouts have been tracking this knight." She made the word "knight" sound like "worm." "I was satisfied he would die in the desert without my help and was content to watch his suffering. But you are now protecting him." She seemed confused by that. She could join the club.

"I *am* protecting him."

Ayren digested that vow for a long beat. "Why are you here, Trystan?"

"I am going to St. Ives to kill Marcus Sunchase."

The other gryphon murmured amongst themselves.

Ayren's head tilted. "You are still on your quest to kill Yellow Boots?"

Trystan shrugged. "Of course. Many are still alive."

"I would think that growing up with Fisher would have taught you something of the price of obsession. He was an uncle of mine, you recall. This is one reason I keep you alive, now. You once brought news of how Fisher said the death prayer, before the end came, and thus found eternal peace. This meant much to the Welkyn Clan."

"Fisher will always have my honor and esteem." Trystan said very formally.

"That old man drove himself crazy chasing gemstones and the nonsense in his head. Others warned him to stop, but he could not. And look what it wrought him at the zoo. Do you wish to follow this example, Trystan?"

Zoo?

Galahad squinted at the back of Trystan's head. "Why were you visiting a zoo, with an old man?" He whispered. "I thought you said you only liked tigers."

"I said I *respect* tigers, not that I liked them." Trystan corrected, not looking his way. His attention stayed on Ayren. "Perhaps Fisher just valued seeing things through. As do I." He told her in a louder tone.

"Regardless," Ayren waved a hand, "it doesn't explain why you help a King's Man, now. They are our *enemies*. ...Or have you forgotten your dead clan, last of the Airbourne?"

Galahad winced, knowing *that* remark wasn't going to go down well. He instinctively grabbed the back of Trystan's shirt. Keeping him in place, when the other man would have started forward, ready to fight.

Was he the only one who noticed this particular gryphon wasn't emotionless?

Like *at all*.

"Don't." Galahad urged quietly. "Find a way besides death. You'll thank me for it later."

He heard Trystan muttering curses under his breath, but there wasn't a multiple homicide. That was a positive sign. "Midas' wife claims this knight as her brother." He ground out, angry eyes on Ayren. "He is part of the Skycast Clan."

"So?"

"So, the Skycast Clan is *my* clan, now."

Several gryphons in the crowd exchanged looks, as if realizing that this wasn't going to be an easy day at the office.

"*Mine*." Trystan reiterated harshly. "Midas and Guinevere and their child are in *my* care. I give them what they want. So, if they want this knight alive, then I will fight to keep him alive for-fucking-*ever*." Each syllable was a snarl.

See? That didn't sound like someone born without emotions.

"You side with the wingless, then?" Ayren challenged. "Over your own people?"

"For my clan, I would do *anything*." Trystan arched a brow. "You saw what I did when I lost my last two clans, Ayren. I leveled a mountain. Literally. It was over there." He pointed into the distance. "So what do you think I'll do to guard my *new* clan? Where I have a baby niece who runs into my arms, and a sister who nags me about finding a mate, and a brother who saved my life. What do you think I would do to keep that light?"

Everything.

There wasn't a doubt in Galahad's mind that this man would give *everything* for his family. To keep them happy and protected, he would bleed his last drop of blood. Jesus, Avalon and Gwen were the safest two people on the planet. It was such a relief.

Ayren began talking to Trystan in the gryphons' language, still arguing that Galahad should be killed. Galahad was only picking up every fourth word, but some of the reasoning actually seemed pretty compelling.

Trystan was unmoved. "I will slaughter you all and die myself, before I surrender the knight." The words were flat. "Let us pass or arm yourselves and try to stop me. The choice is yours."

Ayren was not pleased with the options. "*You* can go." She swept a hand towards the edge of the town and the barren desert beyond. "We have no quarrel with the Airbourne or Skycast clans. But the knight will stay and die for the crimes of his people."

Trystan's eyes narrowed.

"That's fair." Galahad interjected before Trystan's diplomatic skills got the other man killed. Galahad would figure out some way to survive. Probably. More importantly, though, the fierce pull he felt towards Trystan was screaming that Galahad *had* to protect him, no matter the cost. "Trystan's leaving." He bumped him with his shoulder, trying to get him moving. "Bye, Trystan."

It was a miracle Trystan's glare didn't eviscerate him right there.

Galahad kept his eyes on Ayren. "I was burned at the stake a couple days ago. You could try *that* to kill me, if you're looking for inspiration." Fire would be the best chance he had, even though the smoke had kinda sucked. Optimism promised there was a way.

Trystan let out a hiss of frustration. "Knight, I will gut you myself if you don't..."

Ayren cut him off. "We don't burn our prisoners to death. Not even your kind. You will be given a fair chance, against a worthy opponent. If you survive it, we will let you live. Vallon!" She turned to the crowd. "You will have the honor of killing this wingless being."

The other gryphons cheered as a man with black wings stepped forward. Covered in scars and ceremonial paint, he was bigger than Trystan. ...And Trystan was massive.

Galahad blinked.

"*P'don.*" Trystan muttered.

Vallon tilted his head to crack his neck, his gigantic shoulders rippling. He fitted a dented knight's helmet over his skull, which he could only have acquired on the battlefield. "I am ready." He declared in a heavily-accented voice and pulled a gigantic pole from a holster on his back. An iron ball hung from it, covered in spikes.

Vallon fought with a Camelot chain-mace?

Galahad's head tilted.

That wasn't a traditional gryphon weapon. The heavy flail was flashy as hell when you spun it around and it did crushing damage if you hit your enemy with it. Vallon must have taken it is a souvenir after killing a mounted knight and now used it to show off in these ritualized fights. He seemed like a guy who enjoyed the trophies of war.

Trystan squinted down at Galahad, trying to interpret his small smirk. "The expression on your face gives me chills. Whatever you are plotting... *stop.*"

Galahad shot him an arch look. "I have an idea."

"Lyrssa help us all..."

Galahad didn't get a chance to respond to that negativity. A dozen hands grabbed at him, dragging him away from Trystan and towards a ring of red painted stones. "Don't worry! I'll be right back!"

"Gryphons do not worry. We *cause* worry."

"No, don't 'cause' *anything*." Galahad insisted. "I can handle this with no one dying."

Trystan looked like he was holding onto sanity by his fingernails. "I have never before met anyone who is so confident, with so little reason."

Yeah, that was a fair point. Galahad was unceremoniously dumped in the middle of the ring, while everyone else gathered around. He was pretty self-assured, but he hadn't been having the best run of luck lately. This would be a turning point, though.

He was sure of it.

"Bring the knight a sword." Ayren ordered, standing back so there would be room for Vallon to kill Galahad without blood splashing onto her white clothing.

"I don't need a weapon." Galahad got to his feet and dusted himself off, as best he could. Okay. Bad luck aside, he could do this. He just had to stay calm and positive. "I don't use swords anymore." He tilted his head. "Hey, do you ever wonder why people have invented so many ways to kill each other? Wouldn't just *one* kind of weapon have been enough?"

Trystan cursed in three languages. It was impossible to tell if he was more frustrated with Galahad or the other gryphons.

Probably Galahad.

"Why don't you stay tied, while you're at it?" He snapped, as if reaching the end of his never-very-long patience. "I am always eager to teach stupid beings something worthwhile. You think you are the 'best knight ever?' *Fine*."

Galahad blinked. Huh? "I never said I was the..."

Trystan cut him off, pointing at Vallon. "Fight this jackass with no sword and ropes on your hands, while you ask questions without answers. See if you can't then figure out why listening to me *might* be a good idea, in the future."

Yeah, he was *definitely* most frustrated at Galahad.

"You don't want a sword?" Ayren repeated like the words made no sense. She looked over at Trystan. "Why doesn't he want a sword?"

"The man is a raving lunatic." Trystan gave an elaborate shrug. "He enjoys losing to puppets and pigs."

"I live a life of peace now." Galahad explained, because his non-violent stance made a lot of sense when Trystan wasn't confusing it. "I've given up killing."

"I haven't." Trystan intoned. "Have your fight without a sword, knight. I will stand here and watch you get the shit kicked out of you, hoping you gain some wisdom from it." He looked over at Vallon. "But, if the knight dies... *you* die." It was a flat statement of fact.

Vallon's lips thinned at the challenge. He very obviously planned to kill Galahad *a lot* and then Trystan, too.

Trystan must have sensed the same thing, because he seemed to hesitate. Galahad could see his un-gryphon-like temper receding, as he rethought this whole idea. Questioning whether or not Galahad was capable of surviving long enough to learn the "lesson"

Trystan was trying to teach.

Galahad wasn't worried. He smiled at Vallon. Stay calm and positive. That was his new mantra. Calm and positive. "We can come to an agreement without bloodshed. We don't have to do this."

Vallon let out another bellow of impending destruction.

...Or maybe they did.

Chapter Six

The beginning of everything was an accident.

One day, while hunting with King Uther, a wingless man shot an arrow that went astray.

Instead of killing the deer he'd been aiming at, he struck Uther in the groin.

The deer escaped into the woods.

The man was executed.

The king nearly died.

In order to save Uther, the doctors had to remove most of the flesh between his legs. When the king awoke, they were executed, too. But, their deaths did nothing to restore what Uther had lost.

How the Wingless War Happened
Skylyn Welkyn- Gryphon Storyteller

Lyonesse Desert- Welkyn Pass

"I know that you hate my people." Galahad told Vallon sincerely, feeling sorry for the man. "You have every reason to. But, there are better ways to deal with our differences than with more bloodshed."

Vallon wasn't ready to hear that. He let out another roar, a hazy eagle's mask materializing to cover his face as he prepared for battle. The crowd gathered around the perimeter of the circle shouted approval at the sure sign of gryphon violence.

"*P'don.*" Trystan muttered, heading towards the ring. "Knight, this is a bad idea. Come out of there and I..."

Vallon defiantly swung his mace straight at Galahad's head.
Calm and positive.

Galahad ducked under the arc of the swing, the timing of it second-nature to him. It was amazing how long practiced movements stayed with you. The speed of the ball and the angle of its path and the sound of it in the air... He could have avoided it blindfolded, just from muscle-memory.

Trystan's eyebrows shot up and he halted in his tracks.

The crowd of gryphons stopped cheering, confused by the lack of gore.

Galahad kept his eyes on Vallon. "A frank discussion of differences would get us a lot farther than fighting each other." He reiterated, as calmly and positively as he could. "Violence is rarely the answer to a problem."

Vallon disagreed. In a show of intimidation, he used his wings to propel himself ten feet above the ring and hovered there. Untouchable.

Except it would have been incredibly simple to pick up one of the red rocks encircling the ring and smash open his skull. Galahad refrained, of course, but Vallon's strategic positioning was all wrong. One well aimed throw would do it, and Galahad had been the star pitcher in Camelot's Charity Baseball League. No one had ever gotten a hit off him in over a thousand games. It had been kind of boring, really.

He felt like he should warn Vallon about his questionable tactics after the fight ended, so he wouldn't be so sloppy, again. ...In fact, he should probably just do it, now. If history was anything to go by, the other man would be in no condition to hear the warning later.

"You see that there are rocks all around us, right?" Galahad pointed them out. "You should make sure that I'm not able to access them. I could walk over and pick them up and use them against you. You want to *stop* me from doing that." He nodded, because it really was excellent advice.

Trystan blinked, like he was somehow mesmerized.

Vallon ignored the potentially life-saving tip and swept through the air, straight towards Galahad.

Why did things like this keep happening? Was it Galahad? Something he was doing that just set people off? He tried so hard to be friendly, but even a species born without emotions became furious around him. It was super discouraging.

Galahad pivoted out of the gryphon's path, still trying to get through to him. "We really could *talk*, instead of doing battle. It's the better way." He eyed Vallon, willing him to somehow feel the positivity and calmness. "Are you *sure* you want to do this?"

Vallon was sure.

He landed on the ground and swung the weapon again, even harder this time. That wasn't the best technique. It looked cool and took a lot of strength, but chain-maces were best for hitting men in armor. Maybe that was why Vallon used it now. Maybe he associated it with killing slow, armored knights.

Luckily, Galahad had been stripped of his armor when he'd been banished. It made him much more agile. He casually stepped to the side and watched Vallon stumble past him, as the flail knocked him off-balance.

Vallon fell to the ground, skidding in the dirt.

Trystan snorted. If he hadn't been a gryphon, it might even have been called a chuckle. He quickly tried to cover it with a scowl. "Knight, sooner or later, you will need to actually hit that dickhead."

"I'm not going to *hurt* the guy, Trys." He gestured towards Vallon, who really was a mass of pain and misplaced aggression. "It's not his fault he's like this. Without emotions, he can't even express how hurt he is inside. I think he's had a very hard life."

"Who cares about his goddamn life? I do not want to explain to Avi and Gwen that you died of stupidity and blunt force trauma while in my care."

Galahad shook his head. "I'm trying to defuse his hostility with positivity and calm."

"And he's trying to defuse your head with a mace. Stop fucking around and kill him."

"I asked you to *stop* me from hurting people, remember?"

"And I did not agree. It was a stupid request."

"You said 'fine.' That's an agreement, Trystan."

"No, it's not. I would have said 'yes' if we had an agreement. Why do you consistently struggle with your own language?"

The other gryphons looked fascinated with the argument.

Vallon got up, his eyes fierce. Clearly, he was used to clubbing people to death on a regular basis and he was pissed that Galahad wasn't cooperating.

"I don't want to fight you." Galahad tried for the last time, holding up his palms in a gesture of peace. "I don't want to fight anyone. We can end this and both walk away."

Instead, Vallon struck out with the chain-mace, again. In a

way, you had to admire his commitment to his goals. But, on the other hand, this was *exactly* the kind of scenario Galahad had warned kids about on his shows. Once you gave into the darkness, it clouded your mind.

Galahad knew that better than anyone.

Vallon wasn't going to listen to reason. In his travels, Galahad came across *a lot* of people who didn't listen to reason. In fact, he found himself in this precise situation with depressing regularity. Experience had taught him that a cooling-off period was often the best way to deescalate conflict.

...And that cooling-off usually happened best when the other party was unconscious.

Galahad bent backwards.

From the corner of his eye, he saw Trystan's head tilt, following the movement of his body. He seemed fascinated, his usually expressionless face reflecting open astonishment.

How could Trystan so clearly feel things, when the other gryphons couldn't? The metal sphere sailed over Galahad's head, before he could ask. As it came within inches of crushing his skull, he couldn't help but notice there were bits of blood and hair stuck to the spikes. God, he did *not* miss the gross parts of war.

Or really *any* part of war.

Still, the basics of combat were a part of him. Galahad knew more about fighting than he could ever forget, no matter how hard he tried. For instance, he knew that Camelot chain-maces really were terrible weapons for hand-to-hand fighting. They were nearly impossible to use effectively, unless you practiced for years.

And Galahad had practiced for years.

Keeping his balance, he moved towards Vallon and slightly to the right. It was a single, smooth movement that had him brushing passed the man's side and ending up behind him.

Caught off guard, Vallon tried to readjust his position. His face whirled to look over his shoulder, trying to see Galahad. It was what everyone instinctively did when they didn't know how to handle the weapon properly.

But in all physical movements, body followed head.

Vallon's arm automatically changed direction as he shifted his face around, altering the trajectory of the chain-mace mid-attack. His swing just... kept swinging. Kind of like a tetherball game. The metal ball circled around and slammed right into his own skull. There was a sickening clang as the helmet rang out in protest.

Trystan's lips parted in something like awe.

The rest of the assembled audience cringed in unison.

"Sorry." Galahad told Vallon with real sympathy, even though the other man was beyond hearing him. "But I didn't have to kill you. That's the important thing." He nodded, radiating positivity and calmness.

Vallon staggered back, his eyes glazing over. He wasn't going to die, thanks to the helmet, but his head would hurt like hell when he woke up.

Galahad grabbed the handle of the chain-mace out of Vallon's hand, right as the gryphon toppled backwards. Otherwise, the man would have brained himself with it again as he fell. Vallon landed with a reverberating thud, dust from the sandy ground wafting around him.

And then the fight was over.

In all it took about two minutes and it was still a colossal waste of time. Like most fights were, really. Why didn't anyone ever just listen when Galahad suggested that they try rational discussion instead?

There was a long beat of silence as the assembled gryphons tried to figure out what happened. Their eyes seemed to go from Vallon's fallen body, to Galahad, and then back again, like they were attempting to make the pieces fit.

Trystan's intense gaze stayed on Galahad, not saying a word for a long moment. "How did you ever convince Guinevere that you're boring and beige, knight?" He finally murmured.

"I *am* boring and beige." It was why people stopped coming to the charity baseball games.

"The bleeding victim on the ground disagrees." Trystan arched a brow. "Explain your desire to fight with calm positivity, again. The approach is surprisingly effective for knocking people unconscious."

Galahad made a face at him and dropped the chain-mace to the ground. "Well, Vallon's *calm*, isn't he?" He challenged, sensing judgement. "And I'm *positive* he'll be pleased when he wakes up alive."

If he hadn't known better he would've sworn Trystan's mouth curved. "Let me guess: you invented that weapon." He nodded towards the Camelot chain-mace.

"Of course not."

"You've won some sort of award in wielding it?"

"No. We haven't had that kind of contest in years, because people kept dying."

Trystan waited expectantly.

"Okay, I *did* design the Knights' Academy training course for the chain-mace." Galahad admitted, after a beat. Aside from his TV shows, it made him uncomfortable to discuss his various jobs and skills. People sometimes thought his resume was bragging or outright lies. It was better to just keep things to himself. He shrugged, feeling defensive. "It's only an elective in the spring."

Trystan's eyes glinted in something damn close to amusement. He glanced over at Ayren. "So... That went badly for you." It was a flat-out taunt. "Is there anyone *bigger* you can send against this wingless, bound, unarmed man? Or do you not wish to embarrass our race further today?"

"How was I supposed to know he could do that?" She defended. "No one should be able to do that." She waved a disgusted hand and there was something *familiar* about the gesture. "No other of their kind has ever stood in the ring. Next time we'll send in two men and..."

"I know you." Galahad blurted out suddenly. "You were in Camelot."

Every gryphon present switched their attention to him.

"I *know* you." He repeated, shocked to see her again. "You're the woman from the lab. I didn't recognize you, at first, because you don't have your eagle face on, but... It's you!" He was thrilled. "I'm so glad you're okay."

Ayren focused on him for the first time. Really looked at his features. ...And he saw comprehension dawn. "Oh, Lyrssa." She whispered in amazement.

Trystan glanced back-and-forth between them. "What the hell...?"

"I've met your knight before, Trystan." Ayren didn't take her eyes off Galahad. "When the wingless hoards came and I was captured, they locked me in a cell. Fed me poison to cloud my mind. Shaved my wings and tried to take my body." Her voice was far away. "I thought I would die there and never see the sky again."

"*This* man did that?" Trystan pointed at Galahad. "No." He shook his head sounding very sure. "You're mistaken."

Galahad was touched by that immediate show of faith.

"He didn't harm me." Ayren agreed. "Your knight *saved* me. He held his own man at bay. Pressed a sword to his throat and told me to flee."

Trystan hesitated. "He used a sword to attack another knight?"

Galahad winced a bit. The scene with Perceval had literally gotten Galahad banished from Camelot and labeled a traitor. Tales of treason weren't going to help him woo Trystan into bed. The gryphon was *very* clear about disloyal soldiers being on his shit-list, so that story was exactly the kind of thing he *didn't* need to hear.

"I gave up weapons not long after that." He interjected, trying to mitigate the damage.

That had been the first and last time he'd pulled a weapon in anger since the War. It had been a part of his uniform as Captain of the King's Men, forever affixed to his side. Later it had scared him how easily he could have used it that day. If Perceval hadn't let Ayren go, Galahad would have slayed his own soldier without a second thought.

Maybe that was the final push he'd needed to throw his sword away forever.

"After he pulled the other man away, your knight told me how to escape. He let me go and stayed behind to suffer the consequences alone." Ayren continued. "Then, he burned that lab to the ground."

Trystan's eyes flicked to Galahad. "This is why you were banished? Why you forsook everything you had? Because you sided with a gryphon over a fellow knight?"

"Perceval was an asshole, Trys. I swear, I didn't have a choice."

Trystan sighed like he'd reached the end of a very long road and was now stranded someplace he *really* didn't want to be. "*P'don*." He muttered tiredly and pinched the bridge of his nose.

That resigned curse didn't sound like someone dying to forge a meaningful relationship.

Ayren's head tilted, almost like a bird. "Your eyes are purple, knight." She said abruptly, reaching out and almost touching his face. "Like the twilight sky."

He wasn't sure what to say to that. "Ummm..."

"You were the one at Legion, weren't you?"

The question came out of nowhere, but now everyone was listening for an answer. All the other gryphons were focused on him, with various degrees of confusion and suspicion.

Trystan's head snapped up. "Legion was five years ago." He declared and it was a clear challenge to everyone who'd want Galahad's head. "There were many knights there. We will never know them all. We only know this knight is *mine*."

Ayren kept her attention on Galahad. "My younger sister was at Legion, hiding in the grass. Skylyn is a gifted storyteller. She told me of one knight, with blood dripping from his hands, who rode before the Rath."

Bedivere's face flickered through Galahad's mind. The young soldier's gaze blazing, as they stared at each other in the last moments of Legion.

Trystan's head tilted. "What's the Rath?"

"A weapon of their godless king." Ayren said when Galahad remained quiet. "It would have killed the last of the survivors, except for one man. A lavender-eyed knight." She kept her attention on Galahad. "This knight is you, yes?"

It wasn't really a question.

Galahad shook his head, not wanting to remember Legion. Not wanting Trystan to know what he did. Not wanting to revisit *anything* about that day. "I don't want to talk about the War."

"*I* want to talk about it." Trystan retorted. "Did you do something to stop this weapon? How? How could you have *possibly* convinced Uther to cease fire, given your abysmal 'reasoning' skills and his amorality?"

"I didn't convince him." Galahad said honestly. "He was already dead."

"Lyrssa flew off with Uther, while this Rath was still a threat to her people?" Trystan didn't seem convinced. "Why would she do this?"

Galahad shrugged.

"The knight is a lesser species, but he shows potential." Ayren shot Trystan a quick look. "Give him to me. I will mate with him and mold him into a true warrior."

"What?" Trystan's attention swung back to her. "No." The response was instant and absolute.

Galahad's eyebrows shot up, shocked by both of them.

Ayren frowned at Trystan, like she'd been insulted. "I will treat him well. Certainly, I will not tie him up and let large men attack him with maces, as you do." She waved a hand at Vallon's prone form. "You did not even give the knight a sword."

"That was *your* fault, not mine!" Trystan sounded outraged.

"And he has no hat. The wingless need hats to protect them from the sun. You should know how to care for his kind, if you plan to keep one."

"I know how to care for the knight." The words were a snarl. "I gave him a hat, but he lost it. Then I gave him *my* hat and he lost that, too. I will get another one, just as soon as I find one to steal."

"I do lose a lot of hats." Galahad admitted, backing Trystan up.

Ayren shrugged, her eyes still on Trystan. "Your wingless sister need not be concerned for the knight's safety. That is what I'm saying. I will claim him and..."

"*No.*" The denial was even more emphatic this time. "You will *not* claim him."

Her eyes narrowed. "You think to stop me, Airbourne?"

Several gryphons took menacing steps forward, their hands on their weapons.

"Try it." Trystan dared, glowering at them. "I've barely killed anyone today."

Galahad decided it was a great time to interrupt. "I like men." He blurted out.

Everyone turned to look at him again.

"What?" Ayren demanded distractedly.

"I'm very flattered. Truly. But, I can't be claimed by you, Ayren. It's a sweet offer, but... I like men."

Ayren glanced back to Trystan, as if asking for a translation.

"They tend to be a limited species, in many ways." Trystan explained, his gaze on Galahad. "Options confuse them. The knight has decided he will only consider offers to mate with males."

Ayren's eyebrows soared. "Can they do that? Consider only... *one*."

Trystan gave another elaborate shrug.

Galahad didn't appreciate being discussed like a science experiment gone wrong. Because he lived a life of truth, he also couldn't just end the conversation there. His claim wasn't entirely accurate. "Actually, at this point, it's not even that I only want to sleep with men. Like in general." He pointed at Trystan. "It's that I only want to sleep with *him*. In particular. That's the biggest issue."

Trystan did a double-take. "What?" He blurted out in un-gryphon-like astonishment.

"I'm working on seducing him." Galahad confided in Ayren, ignoring the oblivious jackass beside him and his almost comical surprise. "But mostly he just yells a lot and thinks I'm an idiot."

Trystan looked like he still couldn't catch up with what was happening. "Wait... *what?*"

"The Airbourne clan was widely known to be difficult." Ayren agreed, nodding at Galahad and also disregarding Trystan's shock. "Trystan is especially so. I blame his rearing."

"Yeah, you were saying about Trystan visiting zoos and stuff?" Galahad prompted Ayren, because it really was the most interesting part of the whole discussion, so far. "As a kid, his parents took him to a lot of places?" Surely, he hadn't gone to the zoo as an adult. The man carried two swords and an axe. No one would let him through the gate for fear of a safari.

Trystan shook his head, trying to refocus. "Wait, we do not need to discuss that. We need to return to the claim that...."

"Trystan was stolen from his village as a child, by the wingless hoards." Ayren interrupted, probably just to piss Trystan off. "They took him to your land and put him on display in a zoo. A 'primitive peoples exhibit,' I believe it was called. Their soulless eyes stared at gryphons through bars, reveling in their conquest."

Galahad blinked. "What?" He said blankly and had a feeling he sounded just like Trystan had.

Trystan looked up at the sky again, like he was beseeching the missing gryphon queen for patience. "Lyrssa, help me not to slay them all..."

"He lived in a cage with other prisoners, for... how long, Trystan? Four years?" Ayren nodded answering her own question. "Four years. Much of his childhood."

Galahad gazed up at Trystan, his horror shifting to fury. He didn't like to feel fury. Whenever he got angry, things tended to get out of control. He tried to pull back. Tried to see through the red haze. Maybe he was misunderstanding this somehow. "My people locked you in a *zoo?*" He repeated carefully, praying he was wrong.

"It was long ago. As she said, I was a child." Trystan muttered. He glowered over at Ayren, most of his attention on her. "Was that necessary? The knight was smiling and now he's not."

"Oh, their kind becomes emotional over everything." She waved another hand. "Who knows what sets them off?"

Galahad was finding it hard to breathe. He'd once fought for people who locked babies in zoos? How could he have been so blind to right and wrong? How could he have stood with evil against the innocent? The shame of it would never fade.

"I'm sorry. I'm so sorry." He didn't know what else to say. He wanted to cry. He wanted to rage and kill. "I didn't know. I swear. I didn't understand until it was too late."

Trystan's attention swung back to him. "I am *fine*." His eyes burned into Galahad's. "This is not your doing. You were a child yourself. And I was never harmed in that cage. The other gryphons cared for me. I was protected. They got me out."

"By the time he made his way back to our people, everyone else in his clan was dead." Ayren chimed in helpfully. "No doubt that's why he's so attached to this wingless clan he's claimed for himself." She paused, her tone echoing with distaste. "Well, that and his grandfather."

Galahad couldn't focus on her words. Imagining Trystan locked in a motherfucking *zoo* was pulling him under again. He could feel it happening. He needed to let it go, before it was too late. Had to stop himself from...

Son of a *bitch*.

He *couldn't* let it go. He couldn't. Fury was building, driving out the peaceful calm he'd been trying to master since the War. Blinding him, as it hadn't since Legion.

Darkness threatened.

It wasn't just the village, resurrecting old memories. This was the inevitable result of the savage and undeniable connection he felt with Trystan. The strength and ferocity and truth of the bond. You couldn't feel so much, so quickly, without it stirring up *everything* inside of you, Good and Bad.

And Galahad had *a lot* of Bad.

Deep down, he'd always known that he possessed both Good and Bad in nearly equal measure. It was one reason that he worked so hard to stay on the right side of things and never waver from righteousness. Because it would be simple for Galahad to fall into Badness and never climb back out. He felt it beckoning so often that he suspected it was a huge part of his character.

...And now some bastard zookeeper was about to prove his theory right.

Trystan might be Good enough to want to forget about being caged, but Galahad *wasn't*. He would see anyone who hurt the gryphon dead. There was no other option.

"My grandfather was a *great* man." Trystan told Ayren, sounding pissed, now. "He gave me my first sword and played catur with me often. Say *nothing* against him."

Galahad barely heard them. God, he *needed* to kill that zookeeper. It was like a compulsion. "Do you recall his name?" He got out in as normal a voice as he could.

"Of course I know my grandfather's..."

"No, the zookeeper's name. Do you remember where he lived?"

Trystan squinted suspiciously, reading his Bad intentions clear as a wishing well. Something like concern flickered across his face. "You live a life of peace, remember, knight?" He said softly. "Calm yourself."

Galahad's desire to live in peace did *not* extend to risking Trystan's safety. No way. That loophole was the size of a canyon. Avalon and Gwen and Trystan. He would risk the darkness for them, without a second's hesitation. The drive was so strong that he didn't even question it.

Galahad shook his head. "I just want to talk to this guy."

...And then stab him.

Trystan didn't look convinced. "He was ancient even then. He is probably dead, now. Leave it alone."

"He's going to wish he was dead." Galahad snapped, giving up on pretending to be calm. Darkness lived in him, always searching for an outlet, and it just found a *really fucking great* one. "I'm going to kill him, Trys. Get used to the idea."

"There is no need. That man was not the one who caught me and put me in that cage. He merely oversaw the zoo. He sometimes gave me apples, through the bars."

"Apples?" Galahad was losing his mind. It was the only explanation. "Fucking *apples?* Are you fucking kidding me? You think that somehow makes this okay?"

"I think I have far greater enemies than that old man." Trystan arched a brow. "And I think you are swearing, again. You try not to do that, remember?"

"I don't give a shit about my fucking language, Trystan! I can't have that zookeeper in the world. He contributes *nothing* to making it a better place."

"You do not need to fix the world." Trystan was trying to pacify him, like he knew that Galahad was about to lose control. "That is not how you make amends. You simply need to be a Good man. Which you *are*."

"I'm not that Good." In that second, he knew it was true. "Not all the way down. You have to sense it, too."

Trystan didn't deny that. "You are Good *enough*. You do not need to kill all those who wronged me. I am fine, now."

No, Galahad *did* need to kill them. He *would* kill them.

The more he considered his plan, the more it made perfect sense. How could he live a life of peace if that man was out there? No doubt he was still doing harm and should be stopped. Fucking *laughing* as children were dying in the grass and smoke spiraled into the...

One of the armed gryphons shifted in his peripheral vision, closer to Trystan.

And Galahad moved.

He didn't think about it, he just acted. Suddenly, the man was on the ground, with Galahad standing over him. The gryphon's weapon was somehow in Galahad's bound palms, the blade aimed at the man's chest. Other men were on the ground, too. Two seemed to be unconscious. Another was rolling around in pain. How had they fallen...?

Galahad froze, his mind catching up to the fact that he held a sword.

He must have done this. He must have hurt them. It had to have been him. There was no one else with a weapon in their hand. No one else standing over prone gryphons, as if they were burnt bodies under the August sun. Just Galahad. Only Galahad.

"Oh my God..." His stricken eyes went over to Trystan.

Trystan stared back at him, like he was seeing him for the first time. Like he was seeing straight into his soul.

"Look what he did!" Ayren was gaping around. "Trystan, are you *sure* you claim the knight? I really want to keep him."

"Do not even *think* about it." Trystan jabbed a finger in her direction, his attention still locked on Galahad. "You're safe, knight." His voice went soft, so much different from his usual surly tone. Almost a croon. "Put down the sword."

Galahad shook his head and backed up a step, afraid to get near him. Afraid he might hurt Trystan. "I'm not... I don't..."

"It's alright. Put the sword down. No one here threatens us."

"I'm sorry." Galahad dropped the blade into the sand, like it burned him. Visions of checkered grass vanished, leaving only the small town and his own shame. "I didn't mean to do that. I didn't mean to hurt anyone. I *told* you I could hurt them."

"They will all survive. It's alright."

"It's *not* alright! I wasn't even here."

"I know." Trystan caught him, as if he was afraid Galahad would run away. "I know what happened." He dragged Galahad closer to him. "But the battles you see in your head are long over. You're not there anymore."

"You *don't* know! You don't know what I *did!*" His voice broke on the word.

"It's alright." Huge wings moved forward to shelter Galahad. Wrapping around him, as he collapsed against Trystan's chest. "I have you." Trystan held him tight. "Goddamn it. I have you and I will not let you go." It sounded like a surrender.

Galahad let out a shaky breath, his head falling forward to

rest against Trystan's shoulder. A palm slipped up to rub the back of his neck, gentle words he didn't know murmured in his ear and Galahad found himself calming.

"That's it." Trystan's chin rested on his bent head. "It will be alright. You're with me and I will keep you safe."

It did feel safe in the cocoon of tattoos and feathers. The only times he'd ever felt safe in his whole life were when Trystan was holding him. The repeated assurances that everything was alright gradually broke through. Gryphons were wonderful with children and Trystan was clearly no exception. He was soothing Galahad just like he would with Avalon if she'd had a nightmare. And it was working. His heartrate returned to normal. The world seemed to slow down.

And the darkness receded, again.

"You see why I can't fight, anymore?" He asked when he was sure his voice would be steady. "You see, right?"

"I see Camelot shattered its greatest gift and then abandoned him to memories." One massive hand brushed over his hair, Trystan's voice soft in his ear. "But, there is too much light in you to stay broken and lost, Galahad. In time, you will heal."

"No." He wouldn't heal. He knew that. There was no more light in him, at all.

"You will fight through this." Trystan insisted. "You are a great warrior. What you just did here was... amazing. I have never seen the like of it." Genuine admiration shone in his tone. "To forsake such a talent is a mistake. You should use it to do Good. As you did when Ayren was threatened by Percival. It's why you were given the gift."

A knight protects those weaker than himself.

Galahad squeezed his eyes shut. That was the one thing he still believed in with his entire heart. The bedrock of his self. The oath he'd taken as a knight to guard the innocents of the world.

Why could he never live up to the vow?

He pulled away from Trystan, not deserving the comfort. "I'm sorry." He whispered, again. He was sorry for so many things.

Galahad looked over to Ayren, ready to apologize to her, too, and the poor guys he'd knocked on their asses. But all the gryphons were staring at him with understanding eyes. (The ones who were conscious, anyway) As if they knew all too well what images were burned into his head. As if they saw them, too.

"You *are* the same knight at Legion." Ayren murmured. "Aren't you?"

Trystan's gaze narrowed at her in warning.

Galahad squared his shoulders, swiping his wrist under his nose. "Yes. But, that's not who I am, anymore." He said with as much dignity as he could muster. "I'm *not* that man. I'm on a mission to make up for everything I did during the War."

Ayren gave him a strange smile that didn't reach her eyes. How could it? She had no emotions. "Aren't we all, knight? Aren't we all?"

Chapter Seven

I'm not about peddling conspiracy theories on this show. All my regular listeners know that.

But, just *think* about it...

Do you seriously believe that Sir Pelles just happened to be hunting with the king...? Just happened to get drunk...? Just happened to miss what he was aiming at...? Just happened have his arrow hit King Uther...? Which just *happened* to ensure that Camelot would have no more Pendragons from his loins?

For real, people, it's a conspiracy theory *not* to call bullshit on that bullshit. It's all a lie of the winged devils! They're all liars and we all know it!

A gryphon must have snuck into Camelot, hid in the forest, and shot Uther in the dick.

Plain and simple. It's the only theory that makes sense.

"Stopping the Savages" Podcast
Sir Dragonet of Camelot- Former Troubadour of King Uther and Host of the Program

Lyonesse Desert- Camcliard Flats

"I just do not see how you continuously lose to puppets." Trystan said, as he cooked the glatisant lizard on the fire. "A man who can defeat five gryphons can surely slay creatures made of felt. They do not even hold their weapons properly."

Galahad glanced up at him.

The knight had been abnormally reserved ever since they'd left Ayren's village the evening before. Trystan had spent much of their time together wishing Galahad would shut up for ten seconds, but now he found the silence far more irritating than the chatter had been.

Quiet didn't suit Galahad. Bizarrely, Trystan wished for the cheerful talking to return and speaking of the knight's abysmal TV program always seemed to inspire the man to conversation.

"You have to show children there is a struggle involved in any task worth doing." Galahad explained, his voice still flat. "In the end, Good always triumphs, though. That's the message of all my programs."

Trystan grunted and flipped the lizard, so it would be crispy on both sides. "This is a poor message. But then it is a very poor show."

The two of them were sitting across from each other, alone in the vast desert. Darkness had fallen, so Trystan had decided to stop traveling for the night. The knight had to eat and rest. He was Trystan's responsibility, so Trystan needed to ensure he was cared for.

He still wasn't untying him, though.

Galahad bit off of piece of his cactus root, more animated, now. For some reason, known only to illogical knights, he preferred to harvest vegetation, rather than eat the freshly killed meat. Trystan had been briefly concerned the man would poison himself on some unknown plant, but Galahad casually informed him that he "genome mapped cacti as a hobby" and so knew about them very well.

What the hell was Trystan supposed to say to that?

Nothing had sprung to mind, so he gave up trying to feed the man protein. Clearly, Galahad was stubbornly set on his "conscientious veganism." Watching Trystan catch and skin the lizard had seemed particularly distressing for him. It was very strange.

Glantisants lizards were oddly-shaped creatures, with long necks and cat-like bodies. They tended to bark fretfully when you caught them, which apparently pulled at the knight's heartstrings. They were also mean bastards, who fed on children, but Galahad did not want to hear that. If it were up to him, all of Lyonesse would be overrun with the carnivorous little fiends.

"I think you miss the message of my series." The knight decided, casting another disapproving frown at the cooking lizard. "You want it to be a fighting show and it's not. It's about making Good choices and showing kindness. It's about teaching children ways to *not* fight."

"So you wish to get children killed." Trystan summarized. "Why do you hate children, knight?"

"I don't hate children!"

"Then, why do you teach them to lose to puppets?"

Galahad was clearly aggravated by that inescapable logic. "Why do you even watch the show, if it bothers you so much?"

"*Avalon* watches it. I am merely in the room. Occasionally."

Every day.

He watched it every day, trying to make sense of the confusing stories and telling himself that the knight could not *possibly* be that attractive in reality. That he doubtlessly had a dark soul, given the things he'd done, so it was wrong to have such erotic thoughts about him. That the inexplicable pull he felt towards the man was his instincts misfiring, due to lack of more suitable companionship.

The mental lectures hadn't helped.

Trystan cleared his throat. "It's a very badly written program." He reiterated, because it was true. Trystan had always had an affinity for storytelling. He took the work of weaving a tale seriously. "With some help, though, you could improve the lessons you seek to impart to the young."

"Wait... *You're* going to rewrite my show, now?" Galahad's eyebrows soared. "Is that it? You think you can do better?"

"Of course I could." There was nothing Trystan didn't excel at. Even pointless things like television came easily to him. He was sure of it. "Much of your audience has grown up in the shadow of war. They must be taught about reality, so they can deal with what they have seen."

Galahad seemed agitated, now. It was a welcomed change from the silence. "Oh, the sponsors are going to be lining up for *this* program." He settled back with a grumpily expectant expression. "I'm all ears. Enlighten me on how you would script *Trystan's Musical Puppet Show Death Match*."

"To begin with I would remove the puppets."

The knight made a frustrated sound. "Jesus, why are you so against the poor puppets? What did they ever do to you?"

"They are talentless performers. Also, their dead eyes are unsettling."

"You want to stick *live* eyeballs on the dolls? Wouldn't that be even more unsettling?"

Trystan rose above the sarcasm and removed his cooked lizard from the fire. "I would teach the children *real* things." He stressed again. "You wish to say that Good will always win, but that is nonsense, knight. There is no point in deceiving children."

Trystan crunched down on the body of his lizard. It was cooked perfectly. He had lived on the creatures for much of his life, so he knew how to prepare them. Unlike the knight, he'd never had the luxury of agonizing over the morality of eating meat. Lizards and leprechauns had been the only food sources for the gryphons during the War. You ate them or you starved.

"What kind of 'real things' should I tell a five year old about battle?" Galahad demanded. "You think they want to hear about the bodies we pushed into mass graves? The wounded soldiers screaming over their missing limbs, as the fight raged around them?"

"I think you should tell children that sometimes evil will triumph, but they should stand against it, anyway. Life will be unfair, and unjust, and they will want to give up. They will often be alone and afraid. They may have to eat lizards to survive and so they should learn how to catch them. Because warriors do what they must in order to carry on with their missions."

Galahad's expression changed, becoming less annoyed.

"You tell them that life will be hard, at times. People will perish and kingdoms will fall. *No one* goes through life and never fails. It is the effort that counts, in the end. Many of their dreams will not come true, but they should continue to have them. Without dreams, people become ghosts."

Galahad seemed transfixed.

"Most of all, you tell children that their actions always matter and their stories will endure, long after they are gone. So, if they are on the right side, they should fight on, regardless of the consequences. They should *fight*, until they win or die. Because that is how the world changes for the children who follow them."

Galahad stared at Trystan for a long moment. "Yeah." He finally murmured. "That does sound like a good show."

Trystan grunted. "I know." He paused. "Also, you should show the young how to use an axe to defeat their enemies."

Now, Galahad looked almost entertained. "You want to train preschoolers to kill people with an axe? On Saturday morning TV?"

"Of course." Trystan really *should* write the show. Now that he was generating ideas, the program was coming together nicely in his head. "Axe-handling is a difficult skill to master. How will children learn to do it well, if they are not taught?"

Galahad's mouth twitched at one corner. "That's a fair point, Trys. If I ever work on another television show, I'll insist that we decapitate all the puppets, at least once a season."

"That would be a good start." Trystan was pleased to help the man see reason.

"So, what kind of dreams do you have?"

"What?"

"You said everyone has to have dreams or they die. So, what are your dreams?"

"To kill all my enemies." Trystan said without hesitation.

Galahad seemed puzzled. "That's it?"

"What else matters?"

"I don't know. It's *your* dream. It should be what you want most. What do you want most?"

Trystan frowned, uncomfortable with the question, because he wasn't sure of the answer. The man asked too many questions that had no answers. It was so... irritating. "I prefer discussing your TV show to discussing myself." He decided.

"You prefer *insulting* my TV show."

"Not entirely." Trystan wanted to be fair. "I did approve when you battled the fuzzy green whale on your program. That episode was *far* superior to the others."

Galahad's grin stretched wider. "I was shirtless and wet for most of that episode, wasn't I?"

Trystan shrugged, like he couldn't recall. "The plot was excellent. Very engrossing. I enjoy tales of the sea."

"Thanks." Galahad was happy, again, which was always a pleasure to witness. His gaze shone brilliantly, and his smile was magical, and Trystan experienced peace just from being in his company.

Trystan glanced away, irritated by the *rightness* of it all. "Fine."

Between them the fire crackled and popped in the dark night. Only bamboo, cactus, and wishing trees grew in this region of Lyonesse. Bamboo was the easiest to gather, but air pockets in the long stalks exploded when heated. Wishing trees were "too special" to cut down, according to the knight. That left dried up cacti as fuel, so that's what Trystan was burning. Thankfully, it hadn't spoiled the taste of his lizard.

"So," Galahad said out of the blue, "would you like to have sex?"

Trystan's head snapped up. "What?" The knight randomly said many strange things, but this *had* to be a translational problem. The common tongue was Trystan's third language, so...

"Sex." Galahad repeated and there was simply no mistaking the word. "I want to seduce you. Did you forget what I said to Ayren before?"

No. He hadn't forgotten. At all.

"I mean I've been giving you time to think about it," Galahad went on, "but I'm really, *really* attracted to you. When I look at you everything feels safe. And true. No one else has ever felt that way to me."

Trystan had no idea what that meant... but he didn't hate hearing it.

"So, I don't want you to think I come on to guys all the time." Galahad assured him. "It's really not like that. I've never been with a man, actually. I'm just thinking it's probably easier to ask you outright than use subtlety. I suck at subtlety." It was a trait he shared with Gwen. "You don't seem like someone who responds to subtlety, anyway."

"You've never been with a man?" How in the hell was that possible? *Why* was it possible? What did these puritanical people do to themselves? ...And why was it so appealing to know that no other male had ever touched the knight?

"No, I haven't." Galahad shook his head. "To be honest, I've never been with a woman, either. I considered that, when I was younger. I wanted to fit in. But it wouldn't have been right to sleep with someone who I wasn't genuinely attracted to. Someone I didn't have true feelings for."

Trystan stared at him.

"I'm living a life of truth." Galahad told him with earnest virtue. "I don't ever want to lie, again. And it would be a lie if I didn't tell you that I think you're beautiful, and interesting, and I want to have sex with you."

Trystan considered that. Considered everything.

"I'm not going to untie you." He finally said.

"Okay." Galahad agreed readily. "It's the part where we're *not* having sex that I'd like to be untied for, honestly. We can keep the ropes on for the sex part, if you like. I don't mind."

Looking at the knight's guileless face, Trystan saw how it would be between them. Shimmering blond hair caught in his fist, guiding Galahad's head... Lavender-blue eyes shining up at him as Trystan found release in his perfect mouth... The sense of connection he'd experience when he'd give Galahad pleasure in return... How exactly *right* it would all be. It wasn't just some fantasy or a product of his imagination. For just a second, he *saw* it.

That whisper of fate flickered in his head again.

Shit.

Trystan frowned and went back to eating his lizard.

Galahad grinned, somehow taking his silence as a positive sign. "You know you didn't actually say 'no,' right?"

"I didn't say 'yes,' either. Eat your fucking cactus."

"Okay great!" The knight lived in the sunlight, seeing only the brightest of sides. "Think it over and get back to me." He paused for approximately two seconds. "Are you thinking it over?"

Trystan rolled his eyes and bit off the lizard's tail. It was the best part. "Mostly I am thinking you're a twisting path. One I'm unsure I wish to walk."

"Jesus, you really just said that."

Trystan shrugged. "I do not know where you will lead me."

That wasn't entirely true. A part of Trystan already knew where the path was headed. He'd known it from the second Galahad bested Ayren's men and then fell apart in his arms. When the knight had held onto him like Trystan was the only solid thing in the world, *something* had moved inside of Trystan's chest. Something protective and tender and vast. Something that told him just where this path would go, if he continued down it.

Which is why he hesitated, now.

This wasn't a path he'd planned to take with a wingless knight who had been his enemy for years, and asked unanswerable questions, and possessed a reckless amount of optimism. It wasn't a path he planned to travel with *anyone*, in the foreseeable future. He needed to deliver Galahad to Gwen, then leave Camelot to kill all the men on his list. Then, eventually, he would choose a hero as his mate. *That* was his plan and he would see it through.

But his eyes kept returning to Galahad.

"You really *shouldn't* walk my path." Galahad admitted, his smile vanishing again. "I'm messed up in the head, and everybody keeps trying to kill me, and my name will always be tainted. You can do better."

"Probably." Trystan agreed.

"You saw what happened in Ayren's village. I can snap at any time." Galahad snorted. "I'm not even a knight, anymore. I was stripped of my title when I was banished. There was a ceremony and everything."

"You will always be a knight." Trystan ate some more lizard, still trying to figure the man out. The campfire smoke added a pleasant taste to the meat. "It seems to me that it is the deepest part of you, as all your terrible TV shows revolve around the glory of it."

"I don't glorify being a knight. I teach the importance of the Knights' Code."

A knight protects those weaker than himself.

Trystan knew that vow. But, none of the knights he'd ever met even attempted to live up to the simple rightness of the words. Galahad seemed to believe in it, though. Seemed to want to keep that promise, now. That was interesting. "If this code is important to you, why do you no longer fight?"

His eyes dimmed. "You know why."

"Legion?"

Galahad took a deep breath. "After Legion, nothing was ever the same." Apparently, he wasn't going to shut down all conversation about that day, as he had before. That was a promising sign.

"Ayren says you stopped the Rath, in the end. The weapon would have killed the last of the survivors. But you stopped it, yes?"

Galahad shrugged. "I stood on the wrong side of a massacre. That's the bottom line. Everything else is just details."

Trystan couldn't argue with that. Still, having met this man and spent time with him, he saw something... special. "No one goes through life and never fails." He reiterated. "Not even you. The only way to make up for the harm you've caused is to use your gifts to help others. Otherwise, you are squandering your abilities.

Galahad had defeated five trained men while his hands were bound. No one else could have done that. Trystan wasn't even sure *he* could've done it. He wasn't ready to agree that Galahad was the "best knight ever," but he was easily --*easily!*-- the greatest fighter Camelot had ever produced.

Only the man didn't want to hold a sword ever again, thanks to Uther and his fucking War.

Trystan believed Galahad's claim that the old king had kept him in the dark about most of the War's worst brutality. If you had to pull a cart through thick mud for miles on end, you didn't kill your best horse trying to accomplish the task. No. You sacrificed all the less significant, more malleable beasts in your stable on the grunt work. You kept your finicky thoroughbred safely tucked away from anything that might spook it or break its spirit, because you wanted to win races. Uther had needed Galahad committed to the cause and the man's soft heart would have gotten in the way of victory.

"Killing more people won't make up for Legion." Galahad sounded very sure. "It will just sink me deeper into darkness."

"Someone once told me that you should not judge a man on

his worst day. You should judge him on his best."

"Well, my worst day is pretty damn bleak."

"Yes."

"After the War, I was able to push it all down for a while. I had Gwen and Avi to anchor me. I did my TV shows. I tried to be normal, again. I thought, if I just kept busy, doing everything I could think of…" He trailed off. "But it never went away. And when I was banished, it just got worse. I can't even sleep most of the time."

Trystan had noticed that he stayed awake at night. It was not healthy. "Nightmares fade when you speak of them." He wasn't sure why he said that, but the words were just suddenly there. "Do you wish to speak of them with me?"

"No."

Trystan wasn't surprised by the answer. The knight preferred to do everything alone. For all his sociability, he kept the core of himself hidden. Galahad shared nothing he did not wish to share. And he did not wish to share much of importance. He had not mentioned his treasure lately or asked Trystan about the men he planned to kill in St Ives. He seemed to embrace the idea that their separate missions were *separate*. The longer they were together, the less inclined he seemed to try and recruit Trystan as an ally in his madness.

That was… fine

Obviously, Trystan wanted no part of whatever nonsense he'd dreamed up. He was pleased that the man seemed content to wait until they returned to Camelot to continue his quest for gold. Trystan's irritation was only because Galahad was in his care and the knight suffered with memories that could only heal if they were shared.

"You should tell these nightmares to someone, even if it is not me. You are the most popular man in your kingdom. There is *no one* you can talk to about the War?"

Big eyes met his. They were the exact shade of the sky just after sunset, when light still illuminated the clouds. No one else had eyes like that. No one else in the world.

From out of nowhere, Ban's voice sounded in his mind, giving him the advice that had helped Trystan find his way home, after the zoo: *"Do not move until you see the lavender hues of twilight. Purple.* That *is your path home."*

Shit… The thought was a sigh in his own head.

Purple is the path.

"The Galahad on TV is the most popular man in the

kingdom." Galahad told him, not noticing Trystan's distraction. "I'm just an unemployed, disgraced knight, convicted of treason."

"Camelot still has your face on every magazine at every supermarket." Trystan cleared his throat and refocused. "Last month, one theorized that you were working on a top secret project to reach the moon."

"I haven't been to the moon, yet." Galahad really, honestly, *literally* said "yet." "Magazines write all kinds of stuff and most of it is wrong." He arched a brow. "For instance, in any of the articles, did you read about my statement during the hearing on Legion?"

Trystan tilted his head, watching him closely through the smoke of the campfire. "No. I did not even know there *was* a hearing on Legion."

"Exactly." Galahad gave a humorless smile. "No one wanted to print my recollections. They wanted to weave fantasies about how they were in the right and build statues to their Martyr."

"You knew Bedivere?"

There was a beat of silence, like Galahad was weighing a careful response. "Yes."

"The hideous statue you refer to sits in the courtyard of the palace. It claims that he died a hero, saving children at Legion from a fire. Did you help him in this deed? Is *that* what Ayren was talking about?"

"No. I wasn't a part of anything Bedivere did. Truthfully, the only heroes I saw that day were all on the gryphons' side."

That might have been truthful, but it wasn't *all* of the truth. Trystan could tell that the knight wasn't sharing everything with him. The reports of Legion were wrong. He knew *that* much. This man could not butcher children.

"I have never lied about Legion." Galahad insisted, like he sensed Trystan's skepticism. "It's just nobody wants to hear what I have to say. After a while, I gave up trying to make them listen. What good would it do? The only true way to honor the dead is to keep the darkness down inside of me." He rubbed his eyes. "I'm Good. All the tests said so, when I was born. But I'm telling you... there is almost the same amount of Badness in me. I know it."

Trystan knew it, too.

Hidden beneath his golden hair, and his bright smiles, and his award-winning spoken-word poetry performances, Galahad possessed an edge. A mind that was shrewder than you'd suspect. A self-assurance that only came from knowing he could best everyone present if he needed to. A drive to get what he wanted, regardless of the consequences.

Every once in a while, some of the man's latent Badness would come out. Galahad would get some insane idea that no one else would even try and that small, fearless smirk of impending victory would flash. His mouth would curve at some magical angle and his eyes would sparkle like the stars and it was a revelation to witness. Divine and erotic and more beautiful than anything Trystan had ever imagined.

He cleared his throat. "Avalon is Bad, according to those same tests. So is my brother." He paused in his dinner to poke at the fire with a stick, building the flames back up. "None of the results mean anything to me. They have no bearing on a person's heart."

"In my case, it *should* mean something." Galahad looked tired. "I'm the most dangerous man you will ever meet, Trystan."

That was undoubtedly true, but it didn't matter. Trystan's instincts told him the knight was special and Trystan trusted his instincts. "I believe we all have Good *and* Bad within us."

"Scarlett Riding-Wolf's theory? That's what you're going with?"

"Yes, because it's right." Trystan didn't even question it. He finished off the lizard and tossed the carcass away, before Galahad suggested they hold funeral rites for the creature. "We all possess both qualities, in some quantity or another."

"The *quantities* are the key part, though. Even if her theory is right, I have *way* more Badness in me than you do."

"You don't know that..."

"Have you ever killed someone who posed no threat to you?" Galahad interrupted. "Did you ever lose *everything* you ever believed about yourself in one single moment of darkness?"

Trystan hesitated.

"Because I have." Galahad bit off a bite of cactus, with something like vindication. "I've been so out of control angry that nothing else mattered. I was almost back there again, yesterday. If that zookeeper was in front of me, he'd be dead. I promise you."

"Because he oversaw my captivity?" Trystan had a list of people to kill, but that old man wasn't on it. "I told you, there is no need for you to take that on yourself."

Galahad shrugged. "He'd be dead." He repeated with total surety.

Trystan believed him and for some reason it was warming. Few people had ever cared about him enough to plot the slaughter of his enemies. "If you were as Bad as you believe Ayren's men would be dead, too. Even in your anger yesterday, you did not kill them. You have more control over yourself than you believe. You would do well to let this Badness out more, so you can learn to channel it."

"What if you're wrong? What if I have a sword and someone dies?"

"You still ascribe all the power to the weapon." Trystan arched a brow. "But the power is not *in* the weapon. The power is in the *warrior*. Only you can find a way to balance the forces inside of you."

"I won't risk being armed." Galahad repeated stubbornly. "Especially around you. I could hurt you, if I lose control."

Trystan tilted his head. "You truly think you would win, if we fought?"

"I think that I usually *know* I'm going to win. With you," he paused, considering it, "I'm not sure."

Trystan was intrigued by that answer. The knight was the only one who could ever pose a credible threat to him. The two of them were the best at what they did. Nobody else even came close. Galahad's skills should be a cause for concern, but instead Trystan found the idea of fighting an equal... stimulating.

Galahad polished off his cactus with a sigh. "We don't have anything for dessert, right?"

"I could catch you a lizard."

"I'll pass." He sighed again. "It's times like this that I really miss Gala-Chips. Of everything I've ever invented, they're my favorite." He paused for a beat. "My popcorn and chocolate chip idea has a lot of potential to be popular, right? I'm thinking of calling it 'Pop-Chocolate.' Or do you like 'Gala-Corn?'"

Gods, it really was like talking to someone who existed in two worlds at once.

Trystan shook his head, trying to return him to the matter at hand. "If you do not like weapons, why do you collect guns?"

"I don't collect them. I don't really collect anything. I've really getting into minimalism, lately. Not just because I'm broke, but because --like-- how many," Galahad made a vague gesture, as if trying to think of an object to complain about, "*pairs of shoes* do we all really need?"

"An interesting mindset for a man with his own athletic sneaker."

"Do I have a sneaker brand?" Galahad frowned, like he couldn't recall. "Maybe."

"Definitely. 'Gala-Soles' are red and hideously festooned."

And had sold eighteen million pairs.

"Whatever." Galahad lifted an unconcerned shoulder. "Consumerism is still a problem. Plus, minimalism is the most moral choice environmentally. So much pollution goes into our oceans from manufacturing." He paused for a beat. "Speaking of oceans, do you think fish ever get thirsty?"

"No. Fish absorb water through their gills."

"You think so?" Galahad pondered that. "How can you be sure?"

"I think that you *used* to collect guns, before Arthur outlawed all firearms in Camelot." Trystan answered, vainly trying to keep the man's limitless mind on track. "You gave Gwen a gun to protect herself from him, in fact, even *after* they were banned, yes?"

"Yes." Galahad allowed, finally focusing again.

"It was a Good choice." Trystan grunted, respecting the man's actions. "Gwen also said you are an expert in antique weapons. This is why you have been dragging around that rusted hunk of metal from the ogre girl?"

"I know a little about guns." Galahad hedged, without really answering. "But it was never about collecting them. I mostly like repairing them."

"Why?"

"Guns remind me of me. We were both made to kill and now we can be... better. We get a second chance to be something beautiful and treasured." He shrugged. "I like to give them a new life."

Trystan slowly nodded. "Alright. Fix the broken revolver, then." There was certainly no harm in it. "But, you need a functioning weapon, as well."

"No."

Lyrssa, the knight was stubborn. "It is stupid for you to remain vulnerable in a land where so many beings hate you. You seem to have even more enemies than I do and I would have said that was impossible of anyone."

"I think you're not as big of a badass as you pretend to be." Galahad told him, sounding very sure. "I think underneath the sarcasm and grisly threats, you're kind of a pushover, in fact."

Trystan snorted. "The four hundred and eighty men I've killed would disagree with you."

"Four eighty?" Galahad waved a hand to dispel the smoke when the wind changed direction, keeping his attention on Trystan. "What about the attack of the Mynyw Garrison?"

"What about it?"

"Well, there *is* no more Mynyw Garrison, for starters. You leveled it, along with the five hundred and twenty-six men who were sleeping there."

"I knocked down an enemy stronghold in an effort to stop Camelot from setting up a base there. They would have used Mynyw as a staging point for raids along the western frontier. Uther's goons were not specific targets. They were just in the building." Trystan shook his head. "No, they do not count as men I slayed."

When Trystan actually killed someone, they *knew* he'd fucking killed them, because he was standing over them with an axe. To Trystan's mind, those lives at Mynyw were all on Uther's head, because he was the one who'd hired mercenaries as the auxiliary forces for the War. He'd paid every scumbag with a sword to come to Lyonesse and then set them loose on the far reaches of his territory, weakening local resistance before the King's Men even arrived.

Before Galahad was there to see their cruelty.

Trystan suddenly understood the strategy in the king's plan. Would Galahad have stopped the mercenaries, if he'd witnessed their heinous actions? Trystan doubted it, but maybe Uther had thought it too big a risk.

The knight was unpredictable.

Galahad sighed, like he still disagreed with Trystan's tally. "I fought against you in the War, Trys. I'm just saying that four hundred and eighty kills seems really low."

"I've kept count."

"Creative math aside," Galahad went on, "if you killed *everyone* who crossed you, I'd be dead by now, too. All I do is cause you trouble. You said it yourself."

"There are only four people in the world I know I will never kill. You are one of them." Trystan said honestly. "The trouble you cause me is outweighed by the fact that you are...." he shrugged, "special."

Galahad smiled at him, the shadows lifting from his eyes.

Trystan glanced away. Shit. The path was looming before him treacherous and incredibly goddamn tempting. It was hard to recall why he was even avoiding it. It was hard to recall anything but how much he desired the man.

"Can I touch your wings?"

Chapter Eight

Uther became determined to restore his body to what it had once been, regardless of the cost.

His goal was impossible. All told him that no amount of magic or medicine could regrow flesh. Still, he would not accept the truth. He began ransacking other lands for their treasures, hoping to find some powerful amulet or mystical potion to do the impossible.

Then he heard of the graal. Heard of its magic and what it might be able to do.

And he set his sights on finding it.

How the Wingless War Happened
Skylyn Welkyn- Gryphon Storyteller

Lyonesse Desert- Cameliard Flats

Trystan stared at the knight over the fire, trying to keep up with the way his mind worked.

"Can I touch your wings?" Galahad repeated, because of *course* he would ask something like that.

Trystan exhaled a shuddering breath, knowing this was stupid and suddenly wanting it too much to stop. "Fine." He muttered. If he was going to become a complete moron, he might as well enjoy it.

The knight beamed.

Trystan was unused to making anyone smile. It affected him in some way, deep in his chest. Galahad's smile was always perfect and knowing he was the one who'd caused it made it even better.

There simply wasn't a more attractive man of any species.

Galahad immediately headed over to stand in front of him, like he was afraid Trystan would change his mind. Trystan really should change his mind. He knew that even as he rose to his feet and unfurled his wings.

The knight's interest in them seemed strange and exotic. To Trystan, wings were ordinary. He'd never viewed them as particularly sexual. But Galahad seemed enthralled by the span of them and it had Trystan's blood pounding. The knight reached out, his wrists still bound together, and gently smoothed his hand over the white feathers.

They both groaned.

Shit.

Trystan closed his eyes, his head automatically dipping down closer to Galahad's. The knight was large for his species, but still smaller than Trystan. And his lack of wings made him seem almost vulnerable, despite his fighting skills. It stirred... *something* within Trystan. Something protective and predatory, at the same time.

"So soft." Galahad seemed mesmerized by Trystan's wings. His palm brushed over the downy feathers beneath the larger ones and Trystan jolted. Galahad drew back. "Did I hurt you?"

"No." It was hard to get oxygen. "Do it again."

The knight smiled in understanding, his hands growing bolder. His fingers slid deeper into the thick feathers, grazing the delicate skin beneath and Trystan forgot how to breathe. He'd never known that someone caressing his wings could be so erotic. How had he not known that? It was a revelation.

"How did you get these scars?" Galahad's fingers traced along the crisscross of bare ridges marring Trystan's wings.

"Escaping the Wicked, Ugly and Bad Mental Health Treatment Center and Maximum Security Prison."

"Only Bad folk are supposed to be locked up in there." Galahad frowned, his thumb touched one of the scars like he wanted to erase the pain that caused it. "It was against the law for Uther to put you in that place."

"Laws mean very little to your people. Especially, when they seek information from their enemies." Trystan shifted closer to him, unable to help himself. Everything in him was pushing for more. He wanted this man pinned under him, his body naked and his purple eyes filled with desire that only Trystan could satisfy. And he wanted it *now*. The intensity and speed of the craving was shocking.

Concerning.

"Uther put you in there because you knew something?"

"He suspected I had knowledge about the Looking Glass Pool, so I was sent to prison as an incentive to talk. I still did not wish to talk. And so I was there for three years." Nearly twenty percent of his life had been behind some kind of bars or another. It gave him a deep appreciation for freedom.

"I'm sorry." Galahad said sincerely. "I'm so sorry, Trys. I swear to you, I had nothing to do with you being arrested."

"I know. You were not there that day." The knight was not someone Trystan would forget seeing. Ever. His face and hair and body were all very… memorable. His palms ran down the wingless surface of Galahad's back, intrigued by how smooth it was compared to a gryphon's.

"I was temporarily demoted, at the time." Galahad went on. "Uther was pissed at me."

"You must have done something right, then."

"I thought so. No one else agreed." Galahad sighed dejectedly, a frown tugging at his perfect mouth, and it was adorable. "I didn't win a battle."

Trystan arched a brow. "You deemed it *right* to lose a battle? I thought you had never failed at anything, knight."

"I didn't *lose* the battle. I just didn't win it."

"A failure to win is called 'losing.' Are you sure this is your native tongue?"

"You're such a wiseass." Galahad smiled and leaned up as if to kiss him.

Trystan shifted back slightly, unsure. He'd never kissed anyone before. That wasn't a gryphon custom. Since it was new, he wasn't going to be great at it and Trystan didn't often do things he wasn't great at. Especially, when it directly related to having sex with the knight. He intended to be great at that. Kissing was not a smart idea, at all.

Galahad's bound hands fisted in the fabric of Trystan's shirt, tugging him closer. "It's okay." He said quietly, sensing Trystan's hesitation. "I won't hurt you. I won't do anything you're not alright with."

Their lips were only millimeters apart now, but Galahad wasn't trying to close the small distance. Instead his mouth shifted, gliding down Trystan's jawline. His teeth nipped his neck and Trystan's body jerked. The unexpected dominance of the move was oddly arousing. Being dragged towards the knight and then marked during passion made is blood pound. No one had ever been that aggressive with him before. Maybe because he scared them. He always scared people.

Except the knight.

Galahad said he felt safe with him. Galahad was telling *Trystan* that he wouldn't hurt *him*, for Lyrssa's sake. Galahad was smiling at him like he was excited and happy and full of ideas. This whole experience was pleasing. Trystan wanted it to continue.

Kissing the man probably wouldn't be *that* bad, now that he considered it.

Galahad looked smug, sensing that Trystan was no longer resisting his pull. "This is the part where I seduce you into saying 'yes.' I've been thinking about how to do it, for a while. Let me know if it's working."

His hands returned to caressing Trystan's wings in every way imaginable. It was torturous and beautiful and could only lead to disaster… and Trystan didn't do a damn thing to stop it. Instead, he stood still and nuzzled the man's temple, soaking up the attention. Needing it. Nothing in his life had prepared him for the avalanche of lust that cascaded through him. It blew common sense to bits and who the hell missed it?

Galahad's palms memorized the placement of every feather on his wings. "They're just so big." He whispered, measuring their wide span with his hands. "I love how big they are. How strong they are."

Trystan's wings shifted without conscious thought, wrapping around the man and dragging him forward. He couldn't help it. Instincts were beginning to take over.

Galahad automatically moved closer, herded against Trystan's body. Plastered tight against him, the knight suddenly felt the iron length of his arousal. Galahad's surprised expression was so genuine and so unexpectedly innocent that Trystan made a sound of helpless lust. It dimly occurred to him that the knight had truly never been with another. It seemed like a small thing, but it kicked Trystan's desire into an even higher gear.

Galahad's eyes went back up to Trystan's face and he slowly smiled, smug over the reaction he'd caused. "*Sooo* big." He teased. He leaned back into the cocoon of white down, content to be surrounded by the wings and also pressed against Trystan's growing erection. His hand continued to touch the feathers, his fingers gentle and curious, and Trystan was fast losing the ability to think.

Gods, he was going to come just from this man stroking his wings.

Trystan swallowed thickly, trying to concentrate and failing miserably. "If you become unsure about this path, just pull back at any time." It was hard to know what went on inside any of the wingless race's heads and Galahad was especially confusing. But the knight was new at this and in his care. Trystan needed to protect him. "I will be fine. I will not stop you."

Galahad flashed a smirk at him, cocky and unafraid. "Oh, I'll bet you a lost treasure that I can *make* you stop me from stopping."

A growl left Trystan's throat at the sight of that wicked smile, imagining it wrapped around his throbbing shaft. He was harder than he'd ever been and Galahad hadn't even touched his body, yet. The knight really *was* seducing him. Trystan knew it was happening, but he was powerless to resist. It was as if he was under a thrall. Hypnotized by the magic of the man.

He was so lost, he wasn't sure he'd ever be able to find his way back, again.

Galahad seemed pleased with his spellbound reaction. "Seems like my seduction is working." He said, as if reading Trystan's mind. His attention drifted back down to Trystan's erection. "...Or is adrenaline causing it again, you think?"

If Trystan knew how to laugh, he would have laughed at that. "You have really never done this before?" He asked, even though he knew it was true. It just didn't seem possible. "How the hell are you doing this to me, if you've never done this before?"

"I'm usually good at everything I try." His fingers danced along the edge of Trystan's wings in a way that made Trystan believe in all the gods in the heavens. "Give me some time to practice and I'll be the best."

Trystan caught Galahad's chin in his hand, meeting his eyes. "You will practice with me and no one else. Yes?" It was a demand, not a question.

"Just you. Just so it's just *me*."

"Fine." Trystan couldn't focus on anything but him. "Yes. Just you. Continue practicing."

As a boy, Trystan had thought those gryphons in the stories were foolish for wasting their lives chasing figures made of moonbeams. Suddenly, he understood their hopeless quests, though. You could not unsee extraordinary things, even when they doomed you. Once you had gazed at those otherworldly creatures, nothing else would ever seem beautiful enough.

Nothing else could ever shine with the same light.

"Trys?"

"Yes?"

"I'm going to practice something new." Galahad's hand shifted away from his wings and towards Trystan's chest, edging under his shirt and trailing across his skin. Tracing the muscles of his abdomen. It was like being bathed in light. "Okay?"

Trystan sighed in surrender, his forehead coming to rest in the knight's shimmery hair. "Whatever you want." He agreed without even a moment's hesitation. Wherever Galahad wanted to touch him was *fine*, just so he kept touching him.

All the reasons for denying himself the man had vanished from his mind like mist. Galahad was unclaimed. Why shouldn't he take him? Shit, even if he *had* been claimed, Trystan would have taken him. He would fight whoever he needed to, in order to keep Galahad looking up at him like this. No one would stop him from...

"I told you we'd catch up with you, knight." A new voice declared smugly and a Crooked Man stepped into view. "I warned you this day would come."

Trystan's head snapped around, breaking the spell that had fallen over him.

The stranger's body was all jagged angles, his features bent into sharp folds that didn't quite line up correctly. He held a sword in his twisted hand, all his attention on Galahad. Two other crooked figures circled in the darkness, casting misshapen shadows in the firelight.

"Oh thank Lyrssa..." Trystan had rarely been so pleased to be ambushed by cutthroats. The crooked strangers had shown up before he did something epically stupid. He still planned to kill them all, but their timing was impeccable.

Galahad wasn't nearly so relieved with the interruption. Frustration was etched all over his face as he stepped away from Trystan. "You fucking *assholes*." He scraped a hand through his hair, pissed off and gorgeous. "*Fuck!*"

Trystan's body might never recover from its thwarted release, but at least he got to hear the sunny, cheerful knight's florid cursing. For some reason, he enjoyed it when Galahad got angry enough to begin swearing. It felt like Trystan was seeing *more* of him. The knight should let his temper explode for real. Trystan saw now that course would be best. Not just because it would reassure him that he wouldn't lose control and kill everyone, but because Trystan wanted to see *all* of him. Especially the parts Galahad had hidden away in his mysterious core.

"You ruined our lives!" The Crooked Man shrieked

dramatically. "Now it's time for us to return the favor."

"You three followed me, *all this way*, because of that damn rug?" Galahad sounded incredulous. "*Really?*"

"What did you think we'd do?" The Crooked Man shot back. "We have nothing left, since you wrecked our business, you bastard."

"You wrecked it yourself." Galahad retorted, his stymied sexual energy making him sharper than usual. That bit of latent Badness truly was delightful. "You and the Cat and the Mouse have been screwing people over for years. Suddenly *I'm* a villain, because I didn't fall for it?"

None of the others agreed with that assessment. The Crooked Cat and Crooked Mouse stomped into view, both oddly formed and both of them screeching out their own versions of what happened at some village fair. The Crooked Man was listing all the reasons why Galahad was completely wrong about gods-only-knew-what. Galahad was shouting about the inferior quality of their wares.

It was all extremely loud.

Trystan sat down, his body aching with unfulfilled desire. "This is five times you've been attacked, since I found you, knight. You know this, yes?"

"Five?" Galahad flashed him a frown. "How do you figure?"

"Pigs, snake god, ogre girl, gryphons, these dickheads." Trystan held up a finger for each one and ended up with an open palm, in case Galahad wanted to count for himself. "Five."

"No. No way. We're not counting the ogre girl. She wasn't an actual threat."

"You refuse to fight, so even she would have been able to defeat you, if she wished. The number is five." Trystan wasn't budging on that. His math was always sound. "It's unbelievable. No one is attacked five times in such a short span. You are a magnet for lunacy."

Galahad shot him a put upon look. "Well, no matter how you add it up, it's not my fault it's happening *this* time."

"Who else's fault could it possibly be?"

"*Their* fault obviously. I don't start this shit. I'm a normal, boringly beige person. Ask anyone." He paused. "Except them," he swung an arm at the newest group of morons plotting his death, "because they're liars."

"*You* started this, not us!" The Crooked Man cried. "And now you'll die for it!"

Trystan ignored the jackass and shook his head at Galahad, somewhere between charmed and exasperated. "Are these the men who used to be under your command? The ones you were traveling with, until they tried to murder you?"

Galahad pouted a bit. Under other circumstances, it would have been adorable. Actually, no. It was *still* adorable. "No, that's a different group of guys." He grumbled.

"A different group? An *entirely different* group of villains wishes you dead, now? How do you even keep track?"

"Well, I told you I was lousy at making friends. Did you think I was joking?"

"No, people wanting to kill you is totally understandable. I was just not expecting their numbers to reach so massive a scale. If they ever join forces, your enemies will be able to surround Camelot."

"Most of the time it's all just a big misunderstanding."

Trystan rolled his eyes. The knight was a walking disaster area. Trystan wanted to rip out his own hair, dealing with all the messes he caused. He also wanted to sink into his warm, welcoming body, murmuring soft promises of how he would fix all the man's problems.

Yes. This was definitely concerning.

"We have no quarrel with you, gryphon." The Crooked Cat told him. "If you flee now, we'll spare your life and only kill the knight."

Trystan snorted. "Do not tempt me."

"Look, if anyone has a right to be angry it's me." Galahad went on passionately. "I don't like to get angry, though, so I'm going to stay calm and positive."

"Yes, that worked so well in the Welkyn village." Trystan deadpanned.

"I know." Galahad agreed, taking him seriously. "But, even through my calm positivity, it's crystal clear that *I'm* the only one here who has a real grievance."

"You ruined our lives!" The Crooked Man objected, again. "How are you the victim?"

"Because *I* was the one nearly swindled in Bisnagar and just now you morons interrupted a very nice moment I was having with him." Galahad gestured to Trystan. "I think he was about to say 'yes' to sleeping with me and you screwed it all up." He looked at Trystan. "Were you about to say 'yes,' Trys?"

"I was considering it." He'd been about thirty seconds away from having the man naked and spread out before him like a banquet. That counted as "considering" in their rather limited dialect.

"See?" Galahad turned back to the Crooked Man. "Happy now?"

"We weren't swindling you, dumbass. The rug was real. *All* my rugs are real. It's not my fault you were too dim to work it."

Trystan tilted his head. Clearly, he was going to have to save Galahad from dying horribly. (Again.) But he might as well know *why* he was about to kill the three crooked beings first. "This is about carpeting?"

"Look, I was in Bisnagar, minding my own business." Galahad explained, like he could somehow make this madness sensible. "And these three crooked crooks came up, trying to sell me a magical carpet. I asked them to prove it could fly, because otherwise it's just a rug with an ugly pattern, right?"

"It's not ugly!" The Crooked Mouse hissed through its buck teeth. "It's stripes. Stripes aren't ugly."

"That's a matter of opinion and yours is wrong." Galahad retorted and then looked back at Trystan. "Anyway, they *couldn't* show me the rug flying. They couldn't show me anything but it lying on the ground being a rug with an ugly pattern. Obviously, I'm not going to pay for that."

"Obviously." Trystan concurred. "Also, you have no money."

"You couldn't even *pay* us?" The Crooked Cat cried, like that was somehow the final insult.

"At the time, I had *some* money," Galahad's voice went mumble-y, like he was hoping no one would hear the next part, "but then I used it all to buy a unicorn."

"You bought a unicorn." Trystan rubbed his temple, not even surprised. "Yes. That is *exactly* what I would've predicted you'd spend the last of your gold on."

"The unicorn was being abused." Galahad assured him, eyes wide with Good intentions. "Trapped in a horrible sideshow and forced to do tricks that it hated. See, I was investigating my mission, looking for clues. And I was kind of working at the circus, temporarily..."

"You were working at the *circus?*" Trystan interrupted incredulously.

"It was a weekend job." Galahad defended. "I had to eat while I was in exile, didn't I? I know how to do some trapeze tricks, so it was an easy way to make a little money."

"Why the hell do you know trapeze tricks?"

"Everyone knows trapeze tricks. It was getting shot out of the cannon with the grizzlies that took practice." Galahad waved it all aside. "Anyway, I explained that the unicorn was unhappy, but the circus owner wouldn't listen. So, I bought the poor thing and set it free. It was a good use of gold, Trys. Way better than giving it to jerkoffs who sell fake magic carpets."

Was this all an elaborate joke being played on him? Sometimes Trystan wasn't sure.

"Carpets don't just fly on command!" The Crooked Man glowered over at Trystan like he was the judge of the matter. "Tell him! You need to focus your mind for them to levitate properly."

"That is true." Trystan told Galahad, because it was true.

Galahad didn't look convinced. "The carpet was fake." He insisted. "They run a crooked business. We argued about it. Pretty soon a crowd had gathered around, and then the authorities were there. Turns out these three were wanted for about a thousand crimes and so these crooked crooks got arrested." He waved a hand at the jagged-y beings. "I'm not to blame."

"You *are* to blame!" The Crooked Man shouted. "Do you have any idea what bail cost us? When we skipped town, they took everything. We lost our little crooked house because of you."

"You were *cheating people!*" Galahad repeated like he was the last sane man in the world. "*That's* why you lost your house."

"And *that's* why we're going to kill you!" The Crooked Cat bellowed, its crooked hair puffing up in all kinds of twisting directions. "We're going to chop you into pieces, wrap you up in a magic carpet, and send you flying over the moon, knight."

"That threat might mean something if your rugs actually flew. But they don't, so…" Galahad trailed off with a taunting shrug that was absolutely adorable. The knight might've been determined to stay "calm and positive," but it was clearly a struggle for him.

"Oh, it'll fly, but you'll be too dead to see it." The Crooked Mouse unfurled a blue and yellow floral carpet, heading for Galahad. "You've lived your last day, dickhead."

"If you make me kill you, I'm going to be pissed." Galahad warned. "I mean it. I don't like to get pissed and I don't like killing people, but you're *seriously* pushing me."

The Crooked Man, the Crooked Cat, and the Crooked Mouse didn't seem impressed with the threat. They advanced on him with weapons (and rug) drawn.

Trystan really should let them slay Galahad and be done with it. It would save him no end of trouble. Unfortunately, only one path appealed to him and it was a complicated, beautiful, unicorn-saving mess.

He sighed at his own stupidity. "I told you something like this would happen, knight."

"No, you didn't. You always say 'told you so' even when you didn't tell me anything."

"Well, I'm telling you *now*, aren't I?" He flicked a hand at the crooked trio. "These beings look very serious about your murder."

Galahad made a face. "People look like that a lot around me."

"I've noticed." Trystan's future would be spent listening to rambling accounts of why random assholes were attacking and then digging graves for the random assholes. It was inevitable given Galahad's popularity. "As you refuse to pick up a sword, like a normal person, would you like me to handle this for you?"

Galahad frowned over at him. "I can deal with it myself."

Did knights have mottos? If so, that should be the one Galahad engraved on his new silver shield. "You are going to deal with it alone? How?"

"I'm going to diffuse the situation with reason."

"Oh Lyrssa save us…"

"Reason is going to *work*." A pause. "One of these times."

Gryphons didn't laugh, but Trystan came damn close. "Fine." He leaned back, ready to watch the catastrophe unfold. At least he would be able to steal another hat for the knight off of the Crooked Man's corpse. He really did lose them with ridiculous regularity. "We'll hope for the law of averages to kick in, then. Always a sound strategy. I give it a minute, before you fail."

The knight cast another affronted scowl in his direction. "I told you, I don't fail at things."

"Yes, I heard you make that claim. It was just before the swarm of killer snakes attacked you, wasn't it?" Trystan crossed his arms over his chest, enjoying the knight's insanity despite himself.

Those extraordinary eyes narrowed. "You really don't think I can stop these guys without bloodshed?"

"No." Trystan fully anticipated stepping in to fix this mess in forty-five seconds or so. "I think I will have to kill them all."

Galahad's jaw tightened at the challenge and Trystan felt his blood thickening in desire. Gods, the man was gorgeous when he got defiant. He wasn't sure why that surprised him. Every crazy thing Galahad did increased Trystan's desire. That shadow of fate flickered through his mind, again. The sensation that something had guided him to this one man above all others.

The idea that the knight was the only one who could offer him… everything.

The Crooked Cat stepped closer to Galahad, ready to stab

him. The Crooked Mouse held up the rug, ready to wrap the knight's bleeding carcass in it. Trystan's muscles tightened, about to intercede.

And that's when Galahad pulled a gun from the back of his waistband and aimed it right at the Crooked Man's head.

Everyone froze. Even Trystan.

What the hell...?

It took him a second to realize it was the ancient firearm the ogre girl had used in her robbery. The one that Galahad was repairing. Trystan remained unconvinced that it would ever fire, again. And even *more* unconvinced that Galahad would be the one who fired it. The knight didn't hold the same aversion to guns as he did to swords, but he was stubbornly set against killing anyone. Even the people who so clearly deserved it.

The crooked beings didn't know any of that, though. All of them seemed to believe that the knight was about to fire right into the Crooked Man's skull.

"How much do you want for *that* rug?" Galahad asked in the sudden silence that fell over the group. "Maybe we can make a deal."

"Oh for Lyrssa's sake..." Trystan sat up straighter, unable to believe this new foolishness. "Are you out of your mind?"

Everyone ignored him.

"You say that magic carpet is real, right?" Galahad gestured to the hideous piece of woven fabric the Mouse held, the gun steady on the Crooked Man's crooked face. "Well, I'm still in the market for a magic carpet, so I'm willing to buy it from you." He paused for dramatic effect. "...Or I could just shoot you all and take it."

The Man, the Cat, and the Mouse stared at Galahad, weighing his resolve.

"Bear in mind, I *really* don't want to kill you. That would mean he wins." Galahad nodded over to Trystan. "As much as I want to sleep with the guy, he can be kind of arrogant. Have you noticed that? You must've noticed that. How could you miss it?" The knight flashed him another aggrieved look.

Trystan arched a brow in reply.

Galahad turned back to his would-be assassins. "Anyway, I don't feel like listening to 'I told you so's for the next hundred miles, if you all wind up dead." He went on. "So, I'm open to reasonable offers, here."

The crooked trio must have found the "Trystan's an arrogant prick, so let's prove him wrong" argument compelling, because they conferred for a beat about the price of the rug.

Galahad waited patiently.

"Sixty gold pieces." The Crooked Cat finally decided. "We'll call it even for sixty gold pieces." The other two nodded in agreement.

"Forty." Galahad offered.

"Fifty," said the Cat.

Galahad grinned victoriously and lowered the useless gun. "Deal."

Trystan shook his head. "That is still twice what the carpet is worth, knight."

"Yeah, but they lost their crooked house." He apparently felt sorry about their self-imposed misfortune, despite his annoyance at them. "We really should help them out."

Trystan had never before met such a soft-hearted lunatic. "How do you plan to *pay* for the rug?" He asked, even though there was only one answer.

"I plan to rob you." Galahad told him blithely. "I have the gun of the most famous highwaywoman in Lyonesse, after all." His eyes were now bright with humor.

Trystan's insides gave a strange and pleasant twist. Few people ever wanted to share a joke with him. Gryphons were generally born without emotions, after all.

"If you want my gold, you'll have to steal it yourself." Trystan decided, going along with this stupidity for no real reason. "I told you before, I don't like giving my belongings away at gunpoint. Especially the point of *that* gun."

Galahad tilted his head, considering his options. "You could just toss it to me."

"No." Trystan crooked a finger at him. "Come and take it."

Galahad moved over to him, wary but enjoying this game that had sprung up. "I'll pay you back, you know." Trystan wasn't standing up, so he crouched down in front of him and Trystan's whole body tightened in response. "I swear." His hand went down to the money pouch at Trystan's waist.

"I thought you squandered all your funds on unicorns."

"Well, I happen to have a treasure map. That should help."

"Knowing you, finding piles of gold would end up *costing* us money."

Galahad leaned closer, lowering his voice. "Well, let's negotiate, then. You can have whatever you want, Trys." He very slowly drew the sack of gold from Trystan's belt, dragging it free so the weight of it pressed against some very interesting spots. "You know that."

Trystan's jaw tightened, desire burning through him.

"Teasing me is a bad idea, knight."

"I told you, I have some Badness in me." Galahad grinned. "Sometimes I feel it."

"Right now, I 'feel' it, too." All over his body.

"I'm not teasing you, though." The knight's palm brushed against Trystan's thigh and Trystan's eyes flickered shut in throbbing desire. "I'll let you do *anything* to me. Just say 'yes' to us having sex and it's yours."

The man was simply the most alluring headache ever born. "Not yet." Trystan decided, somehow holding onto his sanity. He might be stuck on this path, but he wasn't quite ready to run headlong down its stupid, unpredictable, hazardous surface.

Yet.

Galahad smiled, hearing the inevitability implied in the word and knowing he'd already won. How did he always seem to win? "Alright." He tossed the stolen bag of money up and caught it with a flourish, even with his hands bound. No one should be able to do that and make it look so graceful. "I told you, I can wait."

Trystan wasn't sure he could. His whole body was on fire. "Go pay those morons, before I forget I'm not killing them... and you."

Galahad flashed him another beaming grin and went back to the crooked thieves.

Trystan blew out a long breath. Gods, he really was becoming a pushover for the man. "Knight?"

"Yeah?"

"Why do you want a flying carpet?"

"I promised it to Avalon, as a gift."

Trystan had been afraid he was going to say that. The man had remembered his promise to Avi. There was little else Galahad could've done that would have impressed Trystan more.

Shit.

There really was no escape from this path, was there?

Chapter Nine

Battle of Legion
End of the Third Looking Glass Campaign

Like lightning on the edge of clouds, there were warnings before the final storm broke. Rumbles of danger. Flashes of violence. The Looking Glass Campaigns had flared up, again and again, for decades. An unsustainable cycle of fighting and death and hatred. It came as no surprise there would eventually be a final reckoning.

Except everyone was surprised.

Especially Galahad.

In the end, of course, most people in Camelot shrugged and sighed and justified the carnage. But most people weren't there to witness the massacre. Galahad had been there, though, so that horrible day became a part of him. A pivotal moment seared into his memories for the rest of his life. It never really faded. The screaming and the smoke and the gryphons fearlessly lining up to face them...

And the tall August grass.

The gryphons lived in mountain villages, hidden away from the world. Their unofficial capitol was Legion, which resided in a valley between two of the tallest peaks. It was a place of peace, where the young were kept safe and the old could rest.

Surrounding Legion, inexplicably, grew the Checkered Plains. The grasses there were thick and lush and nearly endless. And checkered. No one knew why. Trained gryphons could navigate the optical illusion of symmetrical squares, finding their way when others would be hopelessly lost. They used the squares to confuse their enemies and hide their most vulnerable. Those who could not fly.

Galahad didn't know that most of the residents were civilians. Not then. Legion was supposed to be an enemy stronghold. A city of warriors. That's what the Yellow Boots had told Uther and he'd believed them.

Galahad had believed so much that he should have doubted.

The King's Men arrived at Legion on horses. They were Wonderland's elite guard, King Uther's strongest and most loyal men. Over six hundred of the soldiers, armed with the latest weapons and a sense of righteousness. They surrounded the town and the vulnerable people within.

Galahad had been the one to find the path to Legion. Later, he'd hate himself for that. Hate that it was his hard work that had led them to the abyss. His choices that doomed them all. His blindness to reality that allowed the slaughter to happen.

When they arrived at Legion, he'd felt satisfied that he'd cornered his enemies at last. That the interminable War was nearly over. If the wooden village was not how he'd pictured a supposedly fortified city, he didn't yet allow doubts to enter his mind. He'd still believed he was in the right.

Until that day, he'd believed in so much.

Galahad climbed down from his horse, standing in the waist-high grass and took a second to admire the beautiful vegetation. When the strands waved in the breeze, mixing the blocks of black and white, everything became the perfect gray of a stormy sky.

Within moments, blood and fire would turn it all red.

Later, most people in Camelot would shake their heads and say it was all the gryphons' fault. Really, they'd brought the final destruction on themselves with their backwards ways and stubborn natures. Why hadn't they just relented in the face of overwhelming force? Why hadn't they surrendered to the inexorable pull of civilization? Why did they fight so hard?

But most people weren't there to see the grisly results of Camelot's victory. Galahad had been there, though. So, he knew where the blame lay.

King Uther issued his ultimatum. He had taken the gryphon queen, Lyrssa Highstorm, prisoner several days before. Drugging her with angelycall, a mineral that incapacitated gryphons. It was the second and last time he would hold her prisoner. She watched her capitol surrounded from inside a caged wagon, her one-eyed gaze intent. Uther demanded that everyone in the town surrender. Bow before him, right in front of their queen, pledging loyalty.

The gryphon were not about to do that. Perhaps they knew Uther better than Galahad did. Maybe they knew that surrender meant death. Instead, the few warriors in Legion decided to fight. The very young and very old could not fly away. The warriors said they would hold off the King's Men while the children and the elderly fled on foot.

      None of them had ever heard of the Rath, so they had no idea what was about to be unleashed. Even if they had known of its existence, they would have chosen the same fate. The warriors would never have abandoned the weak to save themselves. It was not their way. Perhaps that was why they lost, in the end. But it was also why their honor remained, even in death. Anyone would be proud to have that action as their final story.

      Without even knowing it, they upheld the Knights' Code to their dying breaths.

      A knight protects those weaker than himself.

      Galahad stood on one side of the battle lines, watching the gryphons line up, shoulder-to-shoulder, on the other. He didn't know the discussions being held within the city. The decision to protect the children and the old above all else. He just knew he'd never seen braver fighters. That he never would again. Selfless and courageous, they stood against overwhelming odds, ready to die for their cause. It was exactly the kind of action that every knight aspired to. The ideal of chivalry.

      It was... beautiful.

      And that was when doubt first tickled Galahad's mind.

      At the Knights' Academy, they'd taught recruits that doubt on the battlefield meant treason. That it was the mark of cowards and idiots. Later, Galahad would wonder if that indoctrination was why he ignored the sudden feeling of apprehension that gripped him. Ignored his own instincts. His instructors had all seemed so *sure*.

      But, those smug bastards had never stood over the bodies of dead children, knowing it was your fault their lives had been extinguished forever. Galahad had, though. So, he knew that doubt was sometimes the only thing that stood between right and wrong.

      Life and death.

      Despite the years of training, on that horrible day, *doubt* filtered through the decades of anti-gryphon propaganda he'd endured all his life. For the first time, he questioned his orders. If Legion was an enemy stronghold, why were the defenses so minimal? Why were there so few gryphons preparing to fight?

      The young knight next to him was jittery, his finger moved closer to the trigger of his gun, frightened by the show of strength in their opposition. Bedivere. He was a low-ranking soldier, but Galahad knew the names of all the men under his command. The boy's movement distracted Galahad from his momentary confusion and the moment of doubt was lost.

Galahad shoved the muzzle of Bedivere's rifle towards the ground, preventing him from firing. "Don't you dare." He warned. "We're not monsters."

He'd believed that, then. But he'd been wrong.

The next day, in taverns throughout Camelot, everyone was drinking a bit more than usual as they watched the news come in that the gryphons' resistance was finally annihilated. Whatever had happened up there on the Checkered Plains *had* to happen. Most were sure of that. It was inevitable. The gryphons' time had come and gone. And Uther had been killed in battle, too. Surely that showed that the gryphons had been vicious to the end.

Surely the knight's fighting had been formidable, but fair.

Perhaps the gryphons thought the same thing before the Rath began firing. Perhaps, for all their fierceness, they were a bit too trusting. Put a bit too much faith in their enemies' honor. Like Galahad, perhaps they'd believed when they should have doubted. It was a mistake, though few of them lived to realize it.

In Camelot's official report, issued months later, it was decided that the gryphons rushed the knights' lines. *That* was why the King's Men started shooting and the Rath was unleashed. In Galahad's mind, the knights' had shot first. Nervous recruits like Bedivere pulling their triggers without orders. Or maybe they'd *had* orders, from Perceval or one of the other lieutenants.

Or, most likely, Uther himself had issued the command.

He could never be sure, though. He hadn't seen it happen. He definitely remembered the gryphons refused the knights ultimatum. He definitely remembered Uther's voice screaming for the Rath. He definitely remembered the feeling of doubt that filled him and how he ignored it.

His memory of all that was crystal clear and always would be.

And mostly he remembered that one shining moment of admiring the gryphons. That was an image that didn't fade. It stood out so clearly to him that, even as an old man, he'd be able to recall the way their feathers blew in the wind and the resolute looks in their eyes. He'd remember each and every one of them. They had been so... beautiful.

And then that moment was gone forever.
And all at once, death was upon them all.
And Galahad was lost in darkness.

Chapter Ten

Why was Galahad *really* banished? Do you ever think about that?

Now I'm not in the business of speculating. We're only about facts around here, people. But *maybe* Galahad knew too much. Maybe he was exiled because the Powers That Be are trying to keep something secret from Good, honest folk.

Maybe Galahad was banished for trying to tell us all the truth.

Why was his testimony about Legion sealed? What are they hiding from us? I have my suspicions, that's for sure. I think --and the evidence is there to support me-- that the King's Men were infiltrated by radical gryphon sympathizers that day.

Again, not a conspiracy theory. This is *real*. I read it on the internet.

"Stopping the Savages" Podcast
Sir Dragonet of Camelot- Former Troubadour of King Uther and Host of the Program

Lyonesse Desert- Brocéliande Oasis

"Your people's concept of virginity interests me."
"Well, *there's* a conversation starter you don't hear every

day."

Trystan ignored Galahad's dry comment, leaning against a palm tree. "Gryphons are not as repressed as the wingless. We enjoy sex. We don't attach judgement to engaging in it. None of my kind would abstain from it entirely, as you have chosen to do."

"I like men and liking men was against the rules of the Knights' Academy. Abstaining was kind of the only choice."

"In a school full of boys and then countless military encampments, not a single male approached you?" Trystan sounded skeptical. "No *other* men were pleasuring each other in these places?" He snorted. "This seems unlikely."

Galahad sat down by the water, enjoying the shade and the sound of the river rushing past. After days in the desert heat, it was a joy to be surrounded by so much green.

He'd insisted on stopping at the oasis, which was one of Lyonesse's most beautiful and mysterious spots. Trystan had been against the idea. Huge surprise. Travelers tended to avoid the oasis, because of its reputation for unstable magic.

Which was a shame, because it could have been a real tourist destination. A thick forest of bamboo and palm trees sheltered a fast-moving river. The largest waterfall in Lyonesse tumbled from the red cliffs above, tall and thin. A ribbon of turquoise in the barren desert. Sure it was ominously called "The Vale of No Return," but it was still lovely.

Instead of enjoying the stunning landscape, though, Trystan wanted to discuss Galahad's virginity. Why? It wasn't that stimulating a topic.

"You have been banished from Camelot for over a year." Stimulating or not, Trystan didn't seem willing to let the subject drop. "If nothing else, that surely opened up some opportunities for you to select a partner, yes?"

"It's not easy to find someone." Galahad muttered, unenthusiastic about this whole conversation.

"It's always been easy for me to find someone. I have found many someones."

Gee, that was *just* what Galahad wanted to hear. "Congratulations."

Trystan seemed to miss the sarcasm. "Yes, I excel at everything." He shrugged dismissively. "But it would be even easier for you, looking as you do. I would wager it might take you all of," he mentally calculated, "five minutes --perhaps?-- to find a willing man in any bar. Three minutes, if you smiled."

Galahad shook his head, because that wasn't true. "I told you, people don't get close to me. At first, they're usually happy to talk to me, yeah. But then I say something strange or they start to get bored. I think my personality annoys them."

"Your personality is *fine*." Trystan defended fiercely and then paused. "Once someone becomes accustomed to it. No, you *choose* to keep people at a distance."

Galahad slanted him a glare. "I've let people in. Not sexually, but in ways that matter."

"I count three: Gwen, Avi, and King Uther. Have I missed any?"

Galahad ignored that question, because those three names were indeed the entire list. "Look, maybe I could've had sex with someone by now, but..."

"*Maybe?*" Trystan interjected. "No. It is biological fact."

"...But I didn't want some random guy at a bar." Galahad finished emphatically. "It might seem like a foreign concept to gryphons, but my kind attaches feelings to sex. At least I do."

"You wanted emotions." Trystan summarized in an unreadable voice. "Without them, no man is good enough." He shifted his position against the tree and crossed his arms over his chest, like he was troubled by the answer. "In any case, you have remained in an untouched state, until now. In your culture, when I touch you, I will therefore be defiling you in some way."

"Defiling?" Galahad made a face. "Really?"

"You prefer deflowering?"

"You're not going to be 'deflowering' me, when we have sex." Galahad tossed his boots onto higher ground. "Even if the term wasn't antiquated and a little creepy, it wouldn't fit me. Men don't get 'deflowered' the first time they have sex."

"The word is not gender specific. It is *your* language, knight. You really should know it better."

"'Deflowered' *is* about gender, though. Maybe not in the dictionary definition, but in what it really *means*."

"The dictionary *says* what it really means. That's why the book was written. To say what words really mean."

"No, see, you're missing the chauvinistic subtext... Oh forget it." Trystan just wasn't going to accept that he was wrong. God, it was like talking to a brick wall, covered in tattoos. "Look, I don't live in a box. I lack some firsthand experience, but I understand sex. This isn't as big a deal as you're trying to make it. So, can we please analyze something else that interests you about my culture? Like *anything* else?"

"Nothing else about your people has captured my attention." Trystan watched Galahad roll up his pant legs with an idle sort of indulgence. "As I understand it, there is a belief among the wingless that once a virgin is deflowered..."

"Jesus Christ." Galahad stood up and shook his head. "Be glad I don't carry a sword anymore, because I would be stabbing you, right now."

Trystan kept going, not looking particularly threatened. "...that the virgin's purity is blemished in some way. A lasting mark now invisibly mars their body." He paused to consider that for a beat. "This is a stupid concept, obviously. Purity is not a physical trait. It is within a person and cannot be tainted by another's actions."

"Agreed. And yet we're *still* discussing it."

"But, as ridiculous as the idea is," Trystan lifted a shoulder, "I am intrigued by this notion of... despoiling you. Of tarnishing something pristine, as I take you for the first time."

Galahad glanced at him sharply. Okay, *now* they were getting somewhere. "Yeah?"

"The irrevocability and carnality of it is appealing. The possession." He looked Galahad up and down, like he was imagining his fingerprints all over his skin. "This is perhaps why your backwards people invented the concept. It is stealing something valuable for their own and they always enjoy stealing valuable things."

"You won't be 'stealing' anything. I'm the one seducing you, remember?" He'd been working on it for days now. "To be honest, my current 'untouched state' is kind of *your* fault. Are you ready to fix it and say 'yes' to sleeping with me?"

"Not yet."

Galahad lost interest in the conversation, again. "Right." He unbuttoned his shirt and wrestled it off, which was no small feat with his hands still bound. "Seems like since your kind is so enlightened and uninhibited, you shouldn't be dragging your feet about having sex with one simple guy." He wadded up his shirt and tossed it over with his boots.

"You are far from simple." Trystan's hooded gaze lingered over his bare chest. "With you, I am still considering many options."

The appreciative survey of his half-nude body did nothing to make Galahad feel better about being turned down. Again. "What kind of options are you considering? Like *where* we can do this or *when* it might happen...?"

Trystan cut him off. "Is that the key you found in that

tomb?" His attention had been caught by the ruby encrusted key Galahad still had around his neck. The chain reached the middle of his torso, so it was usually hidden under his clothes.

"Yeah."

"And you still wear that?" He didn't sound pleased. "I thought you had agreed to abandon your mission, until we returned to Camelot?"

Galahad had no idea why he'd think that, but the misunderstanding worked to his advantage. He wasn't going to lie to Trystan about anything. He lived a life of truth. He just wasn't in a hurry to clarify things that didn't need to be clarified.

"Well, this key was kinda hard to get, Trys." He shrugged like maybe it was just a fun souvenir to hang onto and let Trystan draw his own conclusions.

Trystan still seemed suspicious. "You nearly died at that snake tomb, knight. Anything that comes from it is dangerous. Whatever that key opens can only lead to disaster." He paused. "Do you know what it opens?"

"Not exactly."

Trystan frowned at that non-answer. "You know… if you had an overriding compulsion to discuss your treasure hunt with me, I would not fault you. I know that you have no one else to talk to." He cleared his throat. "I could listen to you briefly explain what that key might do. There is little else to focus on here. It would be no bother."

That was nice, in a Trystan-y kind of way. "Thanks, but I'm fine."

Trystan's forehead creased into an even deeper frown. "You must have many ideas on this topic. You *always* have many ideas. There are none you wish to share?"

No, there were absolutely *none* Galahad wished to share. "I've got it all under control. I appreciate the offer, though."

Trystan brooded for a beat. "Fine."

"If you want to talk about your mission to kill that guy in St. Ives, I'll listen to you, too." Galahad said, unsure what that terse "fine" meant in Trystan-ese.

Trystan snorted. "I do not wish to talk, either." He decided firmly. "No matter. When we get back to Camelot, I will assist you in selecting professionals to search for this treasure you want so badly, yes? In the meantime, you should get rid of that relic." He gestured towards the key. "Whatever it does."

"Yeah, I think I'll get rid of it today." Galahad said honestly and unbuckled his belt, making a production of tugging it free.

Trystan blinked, his attention drifting... downward.

Galahad smirked, thrilled on multiple levels with how easy it was to distract Trystan. "I don't want to pressure you, but maybe you could *really* focus on the pros and cons of having sex with me." He suggested conversationally. "That might help you make up your mind faster. Like, for instance, you could start with even *naming* a con to the idea, because I can't think of any."

Galahad wasn't surprised by Trystan's hesitance to sleep with him, of course. Trystan could do better. Anyone in Lyonesse would be happy to tell him so. But that was just too bad, because Galahad wanted this man and no other.

And, judging by the spellbound look on Trystan's face, Galahad was well on his way to getting him.

"You listening, Trys?" He prompted, when Trystan just stood there watching him undress. The weight of his stare was like being physically touched.

"What?" The word was vague.

"Are you listening?"

He clearly wasn't. Galahad's pants sat low on his hips and Trystan's full attention fixed on the strip of skin just above the waistband. His jaw was tight, and his eyes were hot, and it was *awesome*.

"Trys?"

Trystan shook his head, like he was trying to clear it. "What are you doing, knight?" He asked, his voice thicker than usual.

"I'm taking my clothes off."

"I fucking see *that*." Trystan dragged his eyes back up to his face. "Why? Whatever you are plotting, it will not work."

"You sure about that? I'm pretty convincing."

Galahad had always been good at distractions, dedicated to his goals, and very, very patient. It was how he'd won most of his battles against this man. Trystan might be a military genius, but Galahad was way more unpredictable and he could wear down an opponent like water on rock.

"At the moment, though, I'm not 'plotting' anything nefarious. I'm just going in the river." He added the belt to his pile of discarded clothing, like nothing unusual was happening. "Do gryphons swim?"

"Generally, no."

"Too bad. You stay here and keep considering, then. I'll be right back."

Trystan's brows came together. "Last time you said those

words to me, you were nearly killed with a chain-mace."

"I'm just going upstream. I'll be fine."

That assurance didn't reassure Trystan. "I can think of six ways for you to die merely by walking a foot in any direction. Knowing you, there are a dozen more possibilities that no one could even predict. You could be sucked into a magic lamp or eaten by a tiger, at any moment."

"I thought you liked tigers?"

"I *respect* tigers. There is a difference."

"I don't even think there *are* tigers in Lyonesse."

"I do not put it past you to find them, anyway. This entire idea is..."

Galahad fixed him with a flat look, cutting off the complaint, before this debate went any farther. "I'm going to take a bath, because I'm tired of being covered in dust and smelling like a horse." He said, breaking things down very plainly. "It's possible I'll be naked when I do this. I often am when I bathe."

Trystan's lips flattened, like he suddenly saw the problem.

"If I'm naked around you right now, I feel like we're going to have sex." Galahad continued, spelling it all out. "Am I wrong?"

Silence.

Galahad nodded in triumph. Damn, he was good. "Exactly. You just told me you weren't ready to sleep together and I am respecting your decision. Ergo: You should wait here, while I go towards that waterfall alone." He started down the shoreline. "Give me twenty minutes, okay? And don't leave without me." He wasn't sure why he added that last part, but it was suddenly there on his tongue and in his mind.

Trystan squinted at him. "Do you honestly regard that as a possibility? At all?"

Yeah. He did.

Galahad had always had a gift for knowing when a fight was winnable and when it wasn't. It was why he'd never been defeated. Because he picked every battle, and saw every move, and knew the probable outcome before the first shot was fired.

With Trystan, though, he was going into the fight with no idea how it would end. There was a very real possibility that Trystan would vanish one day. Especially, if he learned more about Legion. But still Galahad found himself getting deeper and deeper with the guy. It was a huge risk. One that he'd never taken before and one that he wasn't sure would pay off.

"Well, I doubt you'll leave until you 'deflower' me." He

replied, so he wouldn't have to give a real answer. He'd already shared more then he would have liked.

Trystan's eyes gleamed. "It is good that my plots to assassinate you during the War always failed. The world would be dimmer without you in it, knight."

Galahad smiled at that very Trystan-y compliment.

"Do not run off, because I don't want to waste time chasing you." Trystan ordered. "And do not get directly beneath the waterfall and drown. And do not talk to anyone, as they are most likely villains. Just do nothing dangerous or stupid. I will sit right here and keep watch for possible murderers."

"I feel safer already."

Galahad continued on his rocky path towards The Vale of No Return. He eventually found a spot where the water was calm and he dove into it. Instantly, he felt better. He'd told Trystan what he planned to do and that's just what he'd done. He'd absolutely, unequivocally taken a bath. No doubt about it. Why he felt cleaner already. Galahad surfaced wiping the water from his face.

Now that his bath was over, if he happened to find a magical doorway just sitting around... Well, anyone could see that wouldn't be breaking his word. Even Trystan. Humming an unknown tune that had been playing in his head, Galahad climbed up onto the rocks. They grew bigger as he reached the base of the waterfall.

On the map, there was a lopsided picture and the words "sapphire door" at this spot. He wasn't sure what that meant exactly. Whoever had drawn the map wasn't much of an artist, so the whole thing was difficult to decipher. But, he was currently in possession of a ruby key, so, odds were, it fit into the sapphire door. The falls were called the "Vale of No Return" and a "vale" was kind of a door, wasn't it? ...Or was that "veil?"

Shit. What was the difference between "vale" and "veil?"

Trystan would know. The man loved to obsess over the nuances of language.

Either way, Galahad was pretty sure he was in the right spot. His eyes traced along the stone wall in front of him, looking for clues as to his next step. Nothing seemed particularly sapphire-ish. All the rocks just looked gray and wet. The illustration on the map showed a lopsided blue archway, so he was kind of expecting to see something like that. Also, it should glow. In his imagination, magical doors always glowed.

Sadly, nothing was glowing.

Maybe this door was at the top of the waterfall? The map

was two dimensional, after all. It couldn't really show verticality. So maybe the doorway was above him somewhere. Galahad's eyes traveled allll the way up the length of the cliff, not enthused about climbing up hundreds of feet on slippery rocks.

He was debating how to start the assent when whispers sounded in his mind. Words in the gryphons' language that he didn't understand. He knew they were telling him he was on the right track, though. They were trying to help him. Just then the sun caught the cascading water at the perfect angle... and the entire waterfall seemed to glow.

Galahad's head tilted.

Hang on...

What if he was considering this all wrong? What if the door way wasn't *at* the waterfall? What if the doorway *was* the waterfall? What if that damn, wobbly, lopsided doorway on the map was actually meant to be a drawing of the waterfall itself?

"Got it." He told the voices, although possibly he was just crazy and they weren't real.

Unfastening the chain from his neck, Galahad wrapped it around his palm, so he wouldn't drop it. There was a big rock right next to the base of The Vale of No Return. Getting out there would be next to impossible. White water churned and raged. It would be like swimming through a washing machine.

Luckily, he'd won two medals at the All Kingdom Olympics in pole vaulting.

It took ten minutes for him to find a fallen bamboo trunk that was long enough, but then it was fairly easy. He just ran forward, slamming the pole down into a semi-sedate spot in the river, and levered himself out to the rock. His form wouldn't have impressed any judges, but Galahad easily made it to the rock at the center of the waterfall. Heavy spray drenched his skin as he surveyed the falls up close. He didn't exactly see a keyhole anywhere in the torrent, but magic didn't really play by the traditional rules.

He inserted the key into The Vale of No Return and turned it sharply.

A click sounded, the key vanished, and a small window opened in the curtain of water. It *actually* glowed, which he approved of. A magical, golden light lit the edges of a perfectly square cubbyhole, about the size of a shoebox.

Inside was a chunk of painted rock.

It looked like someone had chiseled it off a wall. It was a little bigger than an index card, featuring pieces of various lines and a green X.

    Was it part of another map? It looked like it, but why would the treasure map lead him to *another* map? He tilted the thin piece of stone sideways, trying to figure it out. The next stop he was supposed to make was at a mural in a cave. Maybe this was a piece of that...?

    A horse neighed.

    Galahad's head whipped around, thinking it must be one of the stallions he and Trystan were riding. But that didn't make any sense, because they were way downstream. It would've been impossible to hear them over the cacophony from the waterfall. This horse was closer. Horses, since it sounded like many of them, now. Their hooves drew closer, almost like they were riding over the water.

    So, yeah... That seemed wrong.

    He was still trying to figure it out, when the golden outline of the cubbyhole seemed to enlarge. As he watched, it grew bigger and bigger, expanding from the size of a shoebox, to the dimensions of a barn door, and then to the entire scope of the falls. The whole waterfall glowed with magic and --honestly-- the effect didn't seem so cool anymore.

    The Vale of No Return *was* a doorway and there was something waiting on the other side, trying to get out.

    "Knight!" Trystan bellowed from someplace to his left

    That was *more* great news. Trystan was definitely going to blame Galahad for this. (Whatever *this* was.) Galahad could already envision the ranting. He needed to get the hell out of there before things got worse and Trystan never let him hear the end of it.

    Galahad stuffed the painted rock into the zippered pocket of his pants, bracing for a disaster to strike. Even he was surprised, though, when he was caught in a stampede.

    "Shit!" Galahad and Trystan shouted in unison, as fifty hippocamps came tearing out of the waterfall.

    With heads like horses, tails like sea serpents, and huge wings that looked like iridescent fins, they were impossible to mistake for any other creature. Hippocamps were usually frolicking around oceans and lakes, not corralled in waterfalls. Someone must have magically trapped the whole herd there to guard the painted piece of stone.

    Thrilled to be free, the hippocamps ran hell bent for leather down the river, knocking Galahad off the rock, just like the stone shard's protector had probably intended. He was thrown into the river, miraculously missing any submerged rocks that would have cracked his skull like an egg. Christ. This was *exactly* the kind of thing that Trystan would hold over his head all night as evidence that he made lousy choices.

He got his face above water, briefly sucking in oxygen.
"*Galahad!*"

He heard Trystan on the riverbank and realized that he'd jump into the torrent after him. Trystan would die himself, before he let Galahad drown. In that second, Galahad knew it as he'd never known anything. Anyone sensible would leave him, but Trystan would fly and/or dive right into the water stampede, heedless of danger. Heroism was in his heart and in his nature.

And the son of a bitch couldn't swim.
Goddamn it.

His lungs burning, his body thrown and crashed in the current, Galahad tried to orient himself in the water. There wasn't time to figure this problem out in a logical way, since Trystan was about to kill himself. Galahad was just going to have to wing it, as usual. Fortunately, he was a good swimmer. He had four All Kingdom Olympic medals in that sport. Even with his hands bound, he could figure it out.

Galahad's feet found the stony bottom and he propelled himself upward, grabbing for a handhold. It took a couple tries and then he hit a hippocamp. His fingers seized onto the creatures long pastel mane, using its momentum to his advantage. Through sheer effort of will, he managed to hold on as the animal lifted him from the water. He only had one equestrian medal, but it was a gold.

He loved horses and this was just a big, flying horse. He could handle a horse.

Galahad got his leg around the hippocamp's wings, used all his strength to heave upward. And then he was sitting on its back.

The creature's soft hide glistened like fish scales beneath him. Its front feet were like a horse's and they ran along the surface of the water, while the gossamer wings somehow kept its back suspended in the air. Its body shimmered like a rainbow, all around him.

Had anyone ever ridden a hippocamp before? Galahad wasn't sure, but he always kinda wondered what it would be like. Turned out it was smoother than he'd imagined, because the hippocamp wasn't actually touching the ground and it wasn't exactly flying. More like it was swimming without water. It glided forward at an incredible rate, not even noticing Galahad's extra weight.

Galahad's head turned back towards shore, making sure Trystan was still alive. The other man was standing in the shallow water. Apparently, he'd been wading into the river when he spotted Galahad. Now he was staring after him, perfectly still, a stunned expression on his face.

"You okay?" Galahad shouted at him.

Trystan seemed to rally himself. "What the *hell* are you doing?! Get off of that thing before it kills you!"

"It's not going to kill me!" Galahad decided, based on a lot of hope and very little evidence. "I think it likes me!"

Trystan threw his hands up like he was too pissed to even yell about that idea.

Galahad waited until he was well away from the waterfall and the river was calmer. Then he jumped back into the river, diving deep. He looked up at the surface as the hippocamp herd raced by, seeing their hooves graze the surface above him and it was just... beautiful.

There were so many beautiful things in the world that he'd never seen before. So many small, magical moments that he wanted to experience for himself. Some days that alone kept him going forward.

Galahad surfaced again, using his legs to keep him afloat. Okay. Well, that hadn't been *too* terrible. It could've gone better, obviously, but he'd done fairly well. Maybe Trystan would give him some points for improvising.

Probably not, though.

He made a face and started for shore.

"I knew something like this would happen, if I left you alone." Trystan was waiting for him, still standing in knee-deep water and seething. "I told you so."

"I knew you were going to say that." Galahad complained good-naturedly, as he waded towards land.

"What else would I say, in the face of your staggering recklessness?" Trystan bellowed, not appreciating his casual tone. "I scouted this area and no hippocamps were here thirty minutes ago. Suddenly they appear out of thin air, the moment you leave my sight?"

"They came out of The Vale of No Return, actually." The name was wrong, because things could *clearly* return. Somebody should explore what else was back there. It was probably awesome.

"If they came from the waterfall, then you did something to release them or create them! Those are the only explanations."

Galahad frowned, guilt striking him. Poor Trystan. He was really getting worked up and it kinda *was* Galahad's fault. "No matter how it all happened, it's fine now."

"No matter how it all happened, *you* are somehow responsible." Trystan snarled back, following him onto the rocky beach. "So much for your 'life of truth.' You said you wished to bathe and instead you incited a herd of…"

"I did take a bath! Look how wet I am."

Trystan automatically looked down at Galahad's wet chest and then jerked his gaze back up with a scowl. "Do not distract me. You are *not* naked. You said I could not come with you, because you would be naked."

"I said I *might* be naked. I didn't say definitely. Not a lie."

Trystan's eyes narrowed. "I *might* let you live through the night. Am I lying?"

Galahad laughed at that, because it was a funny comeback, and he was happy to have survived yet another brush with death and, because Trystan was… Trystan.

Trystan wasn't nearly so amused. "You may be suicidal, but you are still in my care." He leaned in closer, so their noses nearly touched. "My life is tethered to yours, whether you like it or not."

Galahad rolled his eyes. "I was the highest ranking knight in Camelot for most of my career. I don't need a bodyguard, as I've mentioned repeatedly."

"I promised Gwen that I would care for you." Trystan shot back. Giving up on intimidating Galahad, he stalked over to sit on a rock, so he could pull off his boot and dump the water out of it. "I will guard your fucking body or die trying. If you have no regard about your own safety, attempt to give a shit about mine."

Galahad swiped an arm over his wet face. "Your safety is the *most* important thing to me. That's why I try to keep you away from all the trouble that follows me around."

Trystan blinked like he'd been flying and just run smack into a window. "Wait… You think to protect *me?*"

"I've been protecting you this whole time." Wasn't it obvious? "Aside from the tomb, when you ignored me and stayed in the tunnel, you have never been in any danger with me. I had the gryphons and those crooked assholes, and the hippocamps under control." He paused. "The pigs were getting a little out of hand, granted, but I think I could've…"

"You're out of your mind!" Trystan interrupted at a shout, vaulting to his feet, again. "You are in *my* care, not the other way around."

Galahad didn't think so. "I might no longer be a knight, but I still live by the code. I took an oath to protect innocent people. It's my responsibility to keep you alive."

And that meant keeping him away from most of the shit Galahad did. The longer he was with Trystan, the more Galahad wanted to keep his mission quiet. It seemed so much safer to keep him far away from it. Nothing was worth Trystan's life.

Not even finding Atlantis.

Trystan squinted. "You see *me* as innocent?"

"I see you as Good, straight down to your soul. Way, way better than I will *ever* be." Galahad said sincerely. "Even if I'd never given my word to protect the innocent, though, I would still always risk myself before you. *Always*."

Trystan stared down at him, breathing hard. For once, he didn't seem to know what to say. He almost looked lost. "Why?" He finally asked in a serious voice.

Galahad moved closer to him. "Because I'm crazy about you." He leaned up to press his lips against Trystan's in a quick, chaste kiss. "Your fun-loving personality has just totally won me over."

Trystan jolted at the feel of Galahad's mouth against his. It didn't take a genius to know that nobody had ever kissed him before, even in a G-rated way. He seemed puzzled and a little hesitant about the whole idea. ...He wasn't pushing Galahad away, though. His lips softened almost imperceptibly as Galahad's mouth brushed across his.

Galahad took that as a great sign.

The kiss was over in less than a second, but his own heartbeat sped up with desire. "Kissing isn't a gryphon custom?" He guessed, reluctantly shifting away, so he didn't scare Trystan by pushing for more than he was ready to give.

"No. But, I am not opposed to learning how, if you need it." He sounded defensive. "I will no doubt excel at the skill, once I grasp the mechanics."

"No doubt." Galahad smiled and flipped the wet hair out of his eyes. "Just so you learn the mechanics with me, I am all for that plan. Later." He could wait for Trystan to be completely ready to kiss him back. He'd always been patient. "Right now, I need to dry off."

Trystan's gaze watched the beads of water trailing from Galahad's hair and down his body. "Yes. You should dry off." He agreed vaguely. "It will be easier to focus on yelling at you, if you're not so bare and… wet." One of his fingers ran down Galahad's chest, like he just couldn't help himself. Creating a warm path on his cool skin. Gathering up water droplets on his finger and then sucking it dry in his mouth.

Galahad stared up at him, momentarily hypnotized.

Trystan gave his head a clearing shake. "*P'don.*" He quickly stepped back, his voice returning to normal. "You're seducing me, again, aren't you? How do you keep doing this? It won't work."

"Of course it will work. All my plans work, once I figure out what they are." Feeling more confident than ever, Galahad headed towards his clothes. "You know, if hippocamps weren't wild, I could open an aquatic dude ranch with them for underprivileged families." He said randomly. "Like that *just* popped into my head and it would be amazing, wouldn't it?"

Trystan's jaw locked, watching him walk away.

Galahad sighed for what might have been. "Can't do it though, because hippocamps are wild animals that deserve to run free. Still, what a fun place that would be for kids. We could have a waterslide."

"I know that your mind does not work as mine does." Trystan ground out, following Galahad. Clearly, yelling at him while wet wasn't *that* hard. "I know that you like to distract and misdirect with your ideas. I know that you prefer to live alone in some other world, filled with art and light and mist. But your new plot to 'protect me' is *not* acceptable, in any reality."

"How do you figure?"

"Because it's fucking nonsense! I was more ruthless than you in every battle we ever fought. Your people called me a goddamn demon!"

"They're wrong. You're Good straight to your soul, Trystan. A hero."

Trystan blinked.

Galahad made his way along the rocks. "I'm not like that." He continued. "I wish I was. But, I've got too much darkness inside of me. When I *have* to win --when it's all on the line-- I will *always* out ruthless you. I will go places and do things that you *never* would."

Trystan let out a long, controlled breath. "You have a pumpkin-curd flavored chewing gum named after you. I am a wanted criminal in several kingdoms." His tone was filled with pained composure, as he enunciated each word. "I am *clearly* the more ruthless of us. We are not even arguing about something so obvious."

"I'm not arguing, at all." Galahad had been stating an incontrovertible fact. "And it's a *caramel-and-whey* chewing gum." He made a face at the repulsive combination. "Super trendy, but disgusting. Still, all the proceeds go to a dedicated veterinary hospital for tarantula surgeries. They need *really* specialized care, because of all their legs." Galahad was happy to lend his name to such an underfunded cause, even though he would've preferred 'Gala-Gum' to have a different flavor-profile.

Trystan rested his head in his palms, like he was developing a migraine. "You will give me your word that you won't ever risk your life for mine." He decided, refocusing on that dumb idea. "*Now*, Galahad. Before I lose my temper and frighten you."

"Oh, I won't be frightened if you lose your temper." Galahad reached for his shirt, not worried about the threat and not promising a damn thing. "I think you're really handsome when you're angry. Has anyone ever told you that?"

The pupils of Trystan's eyes dilated as if he was so astonished and frustrated and a dozen other things that his brain just couldn't process it all. Like smashing every letter on a keyboard down at once, his face reflected a bottleneck of incoherence and rage.

Bull*shit* this man was emotionless.

Possibly due to the fact that he wasn't supposed to feel feelings, Trystan's sometimes had a hard time expressing the feelings he wasn't supposed to feel, but he sure as hell felt them.

"Fucking fucking *fuck*." Trystan's façade of patience collapsed and he went stomping off, swearing in three languages. He was losing his temper alright, but it wouldn't have frightened a butterfly.

Such a pushover. Galahad's mouth curved, more encouraged than ever.

If Trystan had emotions... Well, then there was no reason he couldn't fall in love, was there?

Chapter Eleven

The Looking Glass Pool is a gateway.

It is said that if you look into its reflective surface, the gods see who you truly are. If you are the *ya'lah*, you will be allowed to pass through.

If not... you are drowned in the dark waters of unknowing, forever beyond the reach of light. Such was its power that our ancestors erected Listeneise around the Looking Glass Pool. A building to protect it and the sacred object that it shields. No one has seen the graal since the time before my grandmother's grandmother, but I believe it's still down there, locked under the silver surface of the pool.

Waiting for a hero.

How the Wingless War Happened
Skylyn Welkyn- Gryphon Storyteller

The Town- Edge of the Wilds

Trystan directed his horse down the dusty street. The town they'd finally arrived at had no official name. Situated on the edge of the Wilds, it was the last place to get water before the final trek towards the Pellinore Mountains. "Civilization" ended beyond this place. As a result, ramshackle buildings had sprung up around a muddy pond, as well as a shop to resupply and some bars to sit awhile and reconsider all the choices that brought you to such a shithole.

Travelers heading to the Moaning Sea or St. Ives stopped, because they had no choice. A few desperate people lived there because they had nowhere else to go. No one else visited, at all.

Last Trystan heard, a group of mercenaries had overtaken the town, so maybe they'd named it. It didn't much matter to anyone, either way. Everybody in the town, no matter its name, was wingless, though. *That* mattered to Trystan, because it meant his presence would set off tensions. He therefore planned to spend as little time as possible in the dreary place.

But, at least the wingless were Galahad's own kind. Perhaps no one would try to murder the knight for an hour or so. That would be a pleasant change from the past week.

"What a sad town." Galahad said in a sad voice.

"It's a wasteland of despair and hate." Trystan agreed. "We're only staying for an hour. We need to be far from here, before nightfall. Mysterious creatures roam the desert in this area."

"Tigers?" Galahad guessed good-naturedly.

"Worse. Sandmen."

"Sandmen aren't really the savages they're made out to be, you know."

Trystan rolled his eyes at that predictably naïve response. "Have you ever *met* a sandman?"

"No. But the Knights' Academy told the cadets horrible stories about them. The same kind of horrible stories they'd teach us about the gryphons. They lied about your people, so odds are they lied about the sandmen, too."

Trystan glanced at him, saying nothing.

Galahad was quiet for a long beat, seeing something in his own head. "They lied about *everything*. They wanted me to be a killer and it's easy to kill someone you hate and fear. It's easier if you don't see people as people. I realize that now. I wish I had when I was younger."

Trystan could identify with that lament. Had he known Galahad before, he would have made different choices. He'd once sent a pissed off rock ogre to assassinate this man. He would not do that, again.

…Even though the knight had survived and the rock ogre had somehow gone on to get a master's degree in comparative literature. According to the stony creature's valedictorian speech, he'd been inspired by the pep-talk Galahad gave him, after the knight won their fight.

Galahad perked up, like something new had just occurred to him. "Well, there *was* a bright side to the Knights' Academy showing me so much propaganda about your kind." He sighed reminiscently. "That's how I saw *Corrupted by the Winged Devil.* A masterpiece of filmmaking about a poor, innocent knight taken captive by an evil gryphon. Unspeakable things are done to his poor, innocent body."

Trystan glanced his way, intrigued. "*How* unspeakable?"

"The knight is tied up in a cave, a slave to the gryphon's unholy desires. Soon the deluded fool is tricked into craving that barbarian's touch. Submitting to the constant, shameful demands of his captor's insatiable appetite." Galahad shrugged. "It's a fate worse than death. The narrator told me so."

"That does sound like a fascinating tale." Trystan allowed. "Far better than most your people tell." Storytelling was a vital part of any culture, so it was noteworthy that the wingless had come up with at least one worthwhile piece of fiction.

"I know *I* really enjoyed it." He hesitated. "...Well, up until the part where the gryphon devoured the guy's lungs. The ending always seemed tacked on."

"Gryphons are not cannibals." Trystan scoffed. "And even if we *were*, lungs are unwise to eat from any animal. They require specialized preparation. If you ate meat, like a normal person, you would know this."

"I learn so much about 'normal' from you. It's a lot different than I thought it would be."

"And I know of no knights who were held as sex slaves by my people." Trystan went on, disregarding that dry remark. "Any wingless who stayed in our villages were there willingly."

"You're ruining the magic for me, Trys."

Trystan nearly chuckled at the lament. "I assume this film was supposed to teach you that gryphons are a carnal menace of some kind? Or unnatural in our desires? Or a threat to your masculinity, perhaps? Because I do not think any of those messages took hold with you, knight."

"Yeah, I was never great at picking up on subtext." A dashing, jaunty, pleased-with-himself smirk curved the edges of his mouth. "I just know that watching that movie is how I figured out I like guys."

Trystan's desire rose like a tidal wave, dumbstruck by the beauty of the man. Lust was never at a low-ebb around the knight, but anytime he smiled with that hint of Badness things got serious. Fast. Galahad's grin held all sorts of wicked ideas, and Trystan knew he truly was in the presence of something beyond this world. Some creature made of moonlight straight out of Elaine's stories.

Galahad must have sensed how far gone Trystan was because his smirk took on a delightfully smart-ass quality. "I think the moral of the film was: Even when I'd been brainwashed into not liking your kind... I thought gryphons were *incredibly* hot."

Trystan was listening intently, because how could he not?

"I memorized the whole script." Galahad went on persuasively, seeing that he was winning over his audience. "No pressure, but if you wanted to act it out..." He gestured to his bound wrists. "We're already halfway there. We could do this, Trys. Right now."

Trystan shook his head to clear the images away. Galahad was the real carnal menace. "One hour." He repeated, getting back on track. "Focus. We will leave this town, on schedule."

Galahad made a face at him. "We have a schedule? Did you pencil in 'sex' anyplace on it? Because, I feel like we keep skipping that page."

"*One hour.* I mean it." Not even the knight could cause too much damage in sixty minutes, right? Speaking of which... "Do you see those men who tried to kill you, by any chance? The ones you were looking for the treasure with?" He added the second part to differentiate them from the scores of *other* people who were plotting to assassinate the knight.

Galahad sighed and abandoned his seduction plans. For the moment. "No. I told you, I left those guys farther east. They have no reason to follow me."

"No reason, at all... Except you told them that you know the secret pathway to a hoard of unimaginable wealth." Trystan sighed. "Never mind. I'll just kill them when they get here."

"I don't think you should kill so many people. I've felt much better since I stopped."

"I'd be much deader if I ever did. ...You would be deader, too." Trystan muttered. "Your refusal to see reason on this is frustrating. How can you be the best knight ever, if you do not kill your enemies?"

"I never said I was the best knight ever. Who said I was the best knight ever?"

"Avi said it and Avi is always right. *Usually* always, anyway." Trystan paused. "Interesting that she would grant you the title and not

Bedivere, yes? As he was the one who died saving children at Legion."

Galahad shrugged, saying nothing.

Whenever the knight was silent, you knew there was much more to that story. But, Trystan let it drop. Pushing Galahad would not gain him what he wanted. "Avi also asked me to remind you to bring her a magic carpet, which I did not need to do." He was still completely won over by the knight remembering Avalon's gift.

"Yeah." Galahad patted the magic carpet behind him. "Hopefully, this one isn't fake."

"It's real."

"I'll have to take your word for it, since I still can't get it to fly." His struggles with operating the magic carpet annoyed the knight, because he typically excelled at everything without effort. His brooding over the delay in his inevitable success was very endearing.

"I told you, you have to clear your mind and concentrate on what you want it to do. Otherwise, it is no more than a regular rug. The problem is, you're unable to focus on anything for more than two sustained seconds."

The knight would have argued, except something new had already caught his attention.

Trystan's mouth nearly curved. He might grouse at Galahad, but half of the man's success came from having no limits on his mind. It was forever buzzing with strange questions. Trystan was slightly in awe of how quickly Galahad picked up on new concepts and how freely his thoughts flowed together.

This man was an artist.

His creativity was always working. Always driving him off in unexpected directions. He was not firmly affixed to the world, instead flitting into other realms and bringing back ideas. Trystan had never cared much for art, but now he saw the appeal of those who made it. They possessed a magic that lit up the bland landscape of reality.

"Hey Trys, what are those elves over there doing?"

Trystan glanced in that direction and saw some scrawny creatures fruitlessly tilling the dry soil. "Farming."

"They're farming? In sand?" Even the knight seemed to know that was a bad idea and, captivating as he was, the man was the most illogical being on the planet. "Will that work?"

"No. But they are a very stupid people."

Galahad frowned like he wanted to open a soup kitchen for the misbegotten bastards. "We should help them." He decided. "I know a little about growing food. I set up this whole urban garden project in Camelot and we fed all the orphaned children in the kingdom nutritious lunches for a year. I bet if we build an irrigation ditch from that pond, we could get..."

"No." Trystan interrupted firmly. "Leave the people of this town to rot. Believe me, they are not worth the effort it would take you to care about them."

"But..."

"*No*. You already cost me half a day's riding with that leprechaun, this morning." He wasn't forgetting that moronic side-quest any time soon. Or any of the *other* moronic side-quests that the knight constantly instigated. "Then, you wouldn't even let me eat it."

"It was going to die, if we didn't help it. It was caught under a rock. You wouldn't eat a helpless creature, caught under a rock."

"Of course I would. Leprechauns are delicious, so long as you avoid the lungs."

Galahad sighed, still looking around the town for some Good deed to do. "The irrigation ditch would be easy to dig." He tried persuasively. "All we'd need are some shovels. Someone around here must have some. It could be a community project."

Trystan inhaled a deep breath and decided to break it down for him slowly. "Those people are growing poisoned herbs... probably on the orders of an evil overlord... to sell to wicked witches... to make magical potions... that will facilitate horrible spells." He explained very carefully. "Are you *sure* you want to help them succeed at that plan?"

Galahad blinked over at the withered plants. "Those are poisoned herbs?"

"Yes."

"Oh." He subsided with a frown. "I didn't know that."

Of course he didn't. Galahad wouldn't know poisoned herbs if they arrived in his salad. For a man who claimed to possess Badness, he seemed incapable of seeing it around him. Trystan would count himself lucky if he only had to kill a half-dozen people protecting the knight from his Good-doings today.

He softened his tone, trying to be gentler. "This part of the world is a cesspit of spells. They are always developing newer and stronger magic. It's very dangerous and it will get even *more* dangerous as we move towards St. Ives. Understand?"

Galahad nodded. "Sure." Guileless eyes scanned around, again. "Is there a school here? People wouldn't have to turn to crime and magic, if there was a quality education system in place. Maybe we could talk to someone."

"NO!" Trystan gave up on being gentle. He sucked at it. "Do not *speak* to anyone. Do not *help* anyone. Do not *look* at anyone. Do not *proposition* anyone. Alright?"

Galahad had the gall to grow insulted. "I'm not going to proposition anyone. I don't do things like that."

"You proposition me thirty seconds ago."

"That's because you're *you*, though. I've never propositioned anyone *else*."

That was a fair point. Since he'd met the knight, Trystan hadn't seen him even look at anyone else. Other men had looked at *him*. Trystan had sure as hell seen *that*, but all of Galahad's propositioning was reserved for Trystan and that was what mattered.

Trystan wasn't unreasonable. The knight couldn't help his alluring appearance, or the wonder of his ideas, or the fact that his smile was like a spotlight shining upon only you. It wasn't *his* fault that other males desired him.

It was quite obviously the fault of the other males.

Two days before they'd come across a wingless man who'd been revoltingly eager to win Galahad's favor. The knight didn't seem to notice the man's slavish attention, but it had set Trystan's teeth on edge. Trystan had been forced to talk to the asshole, when the knight was distracted. Unlike Galahad, Trystan knew how to *actually* apply reason. Hard, flat, simple reason. Just a few hard, flat, simple words and the other male had taken off through the desert, running as fast as he could. He was probably dead of heat exhaustion, by now.

It was a satisfactory result.

Trystan grunted, appeased by the knight's defense. "Fine."

Galahad still seemed affronted by the accusation that he'd proposition others. Trystan had very clearly admitted he was wrong when he said "fine," but it apparently wasn't enough.

"I live a life of truth now and when I look at you it feels true." Injured lavender eyes frowned at him. "*That's* why I want to sleep with you, Trys."

Trystan still wasn't sure what that meant. "You have never even been with a male." He muttered, wanting the knight to say something that would make it clearer for him. Something to make his hold on Galahad seem less precarious. "It would probably 'feel true' with any man you're attracted to."

"I don't think so." Galahad assured him sincerely. "I've been a lot of places and met a lot of people. I can never get close to any of them. It doesn't feel like this with anyone except you."

Yes. That was *exactly* what Trystan wanted to hear. "Fine." He reigned in his horse, pacified again.

Galahad kept talking, ruining the semi-peaceful moment.

"...At least, it hasn't yet."

Trystan's head snapped up, his gaze narrowing. "*Yet?*"

His mind whirled with new, highly agitated thoughts. For all his outgoing smiles, the knight was elusive and mysterious on some level that Trystan sensed, but had not touched. The man still did not share his deepest thoughts or rely on Trystan's care.

Maybe because he was waiting to give himself to another.

Something swelled within Trystan like a gale at the idea of Galahad smiling up at another male, leaning against another male, causing endless headaches for another male, trusting another male with his secrets...

"No." The word was a flat command.

"No?" Galahad repeated like he had no clue what it meant.

"*No.* You will touch no other men. Get the thought from your mind, knight. *Now*."

"I don't *have* that thought in my head!" Galahad protested like Trystan was being irrational. "*You're* the one saying I should start sleeping around, not me."

"I did *not* say you should sleep with anyone else. Are you out of your mind?" It was the last thing in the world he wanted. "Why would I say that?"

"You insinuated that I should have meaningless sex, just to reach some magical number of partners that finally qualifies me to be sure of who I really want. But, I don't care if you like that idea or not, I'm not going to..."

"*No.*" Trystan leveled a finger at him, cutting the whole confusing discussion off before he ended up killing some random asshole from sheer irritation. "No one else, Galahad. If it ever 'feels true' with anybody but me, you fucking suppress it, unless you want the son of a bitch dead in the street."

Galahad beamed at him, unperturbed by his threats. "Are you ready to say 'yes' to sex with me, then? Because there's probably a hotel around here."

"No." Trystan jumped off his horse, pissed off at the world. "Come inside, before you start a tornado."

"How could I possibly start a tornado?"

"I have no idea, but I have total faith that you'll eventually stumble upon a way." Trystan headed towards the listing storefront. "There is no disaster you can't cause. Let's go. I have no more time to save your life today."

The knight made a face and looked up at the sign above the mercantile shop promising "cold drinks, hot ammo, and snacks." "Hey, if they have Gala-Chips, can you get me some?"

"No." Trystan repeated and kept walking. "They have the same nutritional value as glass shards. Your eating habits are abysmal and I will not contribute to them. No meat, but plenty of sugar. You will be dead within a year on that diet."

"I want peanut butter flavor." Galahad called, disregarding Trystan's lecture. "Really, anything but caramel-and-whey, is fine." He made a face. "Don't get caramel-and-whey."

"I am not getting *any* of them. I will not feed you poison. Now, let's *go*."

"I'm tied to the saddle with enspelled ropes. How am I supposed to get off the horse without help?"

"Figure it out." Trystan had no intention of putting his hands on him. He was already too far gone in his need for the man. Galahad was allegedly the "best knight ever." He could problem solve.

Inside the store was an impressive selection of dirt and items no one wanted. Trystan ignored the cobweb covered shelves, heading for the back wall of the shop. He'd been there once, before the War. He'd been *everywhere* before, which is how he knew the whole world was a cesspit. The only place he wanted to be was home with his clan.

"We don't allow gryphon in here." The old man behind the counter snapped as Trystan stalked by. "No monsters of any sort. Grundys' orders."

"Shut the hell up." Trystan kept walking, right past the Gala-Chip display. They only had caramel-and-whey flavor. The knight would not be pleased.

There wasn't any cellphone service in Lyonesse, thanks to the mountains. However, there were still a few landlines sprinkled about and this hellish store had one of them.

It was impossible to fit in the glass box of the phone booth with his wings and height, so Trystan had to stretch the dingy cord out and crane his neck to talk on the receiver. "I don't care how much it costs." He snapped at the operator. "Charge Midas and put me through."

The old man went stomping out of the store.

Trystan didn't care. His brother was on the line within moments. "Trystan?" Midas' voice was deep and echoed with the rough accent of his birthplace. "Are you okay? We've been worried. You were supposed to call."

"I *am* calling." How was that not obvious? "Is the child safe?"

"Avalon is fine. She drew you a new picture."

Trystan relaxed a bit. "Has Gwen started another war, while I was gone?"

"Not yet. But it's only Wednesday."

He grunted. "Tell her I have the knight. He is so far unharmed, but I make no promises. The man is irritating the shit out of me."

"You found Galahad?" Midas sounded impressed. "Already? How?"

"Gwen and Avi wished him retrieved, so I've retrieved him." Trystan did everything his clan wanted to the best of his abilities and his abilities were second-to-none. There should be no surprise over any of his stellar achievements. "I am bringing the knight back to Camelot soon."

"Are you bringing any more ogres home with you, too? Because I have the royal guards picking up some girl, who called and said you promised her a new life in Camelot. She also says she's the greatest highwaywoman in Lyonesse, so *that'll* be interesting."

"Saving that felonious child was mostly the knight's doing. His heart is pitifully soft. And he gives away money even faster than you do. I will soon be penniless."

"Uh-huh." Midas didn't sound convinced. "And you're such a hardass with kids."

Trystan looked towards the door, making sure Galahad wasn't there. "Can I ask you something, *j'ha*?" He switched to the gryphon dialect.

"Anything. You know that." Midas obligingly adopted the language, too. He was the only person in Trystan's life who could speak in his native tongue fluently, which was always a blessing when you needed to not be overheard by irritating blond knights.

"When you first met Gwen, you knew instantly it was *ha'na*. You just... knew."

"Yes. I knew she was the one. I met her eyes and saw everything."

Trystan kept his gaze on the door of the store. Where was Galahad? Why could the man not do the simplest thing without complications? "Did she also irritate the shit out of you?"

Midas instantly understood the meaning behind the question. "I'm Bad, Trystan. I knew Gwen was my True Love, just by looking at her, and it *still* drove me crazy. You're Good, so it will probably be even harder for you to adjust to finding your mate. That's just how it works." He paused. "Are we talking about Galahad?"

Trystan winced. "No." He muttered.

Midas ignored the lie. "Galahad's attracted to men, huh?" He made a considering sound. "That makes me like him more. I used to worry he was in love with Gwen."

"He says he is attempting to seduce me. I think it might be working."

"Well, great! Do that, then. Gryphons don't care about genders. Jesus, why are we even having this discussion? If he's the one you want..."

Trystan cut him off. "Galahad will want a True Love, yes? As all your kind do."

There was a pause, like Midas saw the problem. "Yes." He said quietly. "He will."

"And I cannot give him that." Trystan rubbed at his temple, his insides roiling. "Gryphons are born without feelings. We do not have True Loves. I do not possess what he needs and he will soon see that."

"Your people are generally born without feelings." Midas allowed and then his tone became more pointed. "*Generally*."

Trystan froze.

"Some of you have them, though, even if you don't admit it. Some of you can feel everything, if you try hard enough." Midas paused. "...Can't you?"

Trystan stared at the wall of the phone booth, saying nothing to his brother's question.

Midas continued undaunted on the other end of the line. "I've seen a gryphon *almost* smile when he's bickering with my wife, and allow my daughter to put sparkly bows in his hair, and protect my life before his own, simply because his devotion to us is a part of him."

"You are my clan." Trystan whispered, his heart pounding.

"You are mine, as well. You would be my clan, even if you had no emotions. But Trystan, you *do* have them. I've seen it more and more since Avi and Gwen came to us. I've seen you with them and your feelings are crystal clear to me. I don't know how you got them, but the emotions are there."

Trystan's lips pressed together. "My grandfather was your kind." He muttered at length.

Midas made a sound of frustrated surprise. "And you're *just* mentioning this."

"Yes." It was not something he often thought about. His grandfather had simply been his grandfather. "I am not sure what land he came from, exactly. He wandered into gryphon territory and my grandmother decided to keep him."

Her preference for wingless men might explain why Trystan was so drawn to Galahad. Maybe this warped attraction to their baffling species was in his DNA.

"My grandfather was a great man, who taught me much." He went on, his memories filled with special moments between them. Like most of the adults in Trystan's childhood, his grandfather had been protective and doting. "I believe I am the only gryphon who ever learned to swim and it was because of him."

Generally, gryphons couldn't swim. Trystan hadn't been lying when he told Galahad that fact. But Trystan's grandfather had insisted that he acquire the skill. The old man had cared deeply about keeping Trystan safe, so he'd imparted all the lessons he could. Trystan now did the same thing with Avi.

"Your grandfather sounds like a wonderful person."

"He was a skilled warrior. As am I. He had brown eyes and I also have brown eyes." Trystan hesitated. "He had emotions."

"And you have emotions, too." It wasn't a question.

"I don't know." Trystan ran a hand through his hair. "Perhaps. I have never really considered it."

Something was inside of him and it was growing bigger. It had always been there in the background, but he'd really started noticing it when he'd met Midas. It had gotten worse with Avi and Gwen around. The pull to be with them and see them safe and content. At first, he'd been able to explain it away as simply --*finally*-- having a clan of his own to care for. With Galahad, though, the *somethings* inside of him were worse. Stronger than he'd ever experienced.

"How do I know how many feelings I should have? Or what they *mean*, if I do have them?" Trystan demanded, not liking how irrational these *somethings* inside of his mind and heart seemed. He liked to be in control, but *they* were driving his actions, now.

"Your grandfather didn't explain any of this to you?"

"No. Perhaps he planned to, but Yellow Boots killed him and I was sent to the zoo. So I ask you: How can I know what I feel and what I don't?" It irritated Trystan how... intangible it all seemed. He wanted to deal with things he could identify. Things that made sense. "There are not even words in this language to describe different feelings. How can I even know what something *is*, if I have no term to describe it?"

"Use the common tongue. You speak that, too. Try and place your feelings into *those* words." Midas switched back to his own language. "Joy, sadness, love..."

"Love?" He scrubbed at his eyes, knowing it was hopeless. Whatever paltry emotions Trystan had, they couldn't sustain something that big. They weren't good enough. It was obvious. "Shit. I cannot do this. You *know* I can't."

"If you try to deal with these feelings, you'll succeed. You are the *best*, Trystan. The best at everything you do."

Trystan grunted, conceding that point. "This is true."

"Don't fuck this up." Midas continued. "If you've found *ha'na*, then it's a gift. You need to calm down and…"

"The knight is the problem here, not me." Trystan interrupted, not wanting to hear more of what he didn't want to hear. "If it's fucked up, it's *his* fault, not mine. I have been the soul of conciliation, while he does nothing but irritate."

"By all accounts, the man is naturally, inexplicably, singularly exceptional at everything he does. *Obviously* he irritates you. He irritates me and I've never even met him."

Trystan frowned, not appreciating that remark. "Galahad is not *that* irritating." He muttered defensively. "He cannot help his many talents."

Midas started laughing.

"It's not funny, asshole." Trystan pinched the bridge of his nose in frustration. "The knight asked me what I dreamed of and I said I wished to kill my enemies. But I am not sure that's really the answer. Why am I not sure of something that should be so clear?"

"If Galahad's turning you off your stupid revenge mission, then I'm on his side."

"Nothing will turn me from my mission." Trystan snapped, meaning it. "And Gwen is the one who sent me into this confusing mess. It is all a deliberate plot on your woman's part to drive me mad. You know that, yes?"

"Oh, I'm sure matchmaking was her stretch-goal. But Gwen could've given Galahad to anyone and she gave him to *you*. She just handed you the World's Most Eligible Bachelor on a silver platter, so you really can't complain."

"Have you not been listening? I have *many* complaints about this man she chose for me."

There was a display of coats, next to the phone booth. The sign above them read: "Sale! Down-Filled and Enspelled with Protective Magic." Trystan began flipping through the rack, looking for a garment large enough to fit the knight. He would need a coat as they neared St. Ives.

"Seems like you're the one choosing him." Midas hesitated

again. "You know that Galahad led the Battle of Legion, right?"

Trystan's jaw tightened, anticipating what his brother was going to say. "Yes."

"As perfect as Galahad seems, the King's Men were monsters and he was a part of it."

"I do not understand all that happened that day, but Galahad is *not* a monster. I know that, Midas. He has the same crazed idealism that Gwen possesses." Trystan paused. "Speaking of Guinevere, I warn you now, the two of them will be impossible to reign in when they are together. We will need to establish rules or Camelot will quickly become a recycling plant. Galahad spent four hours yesterday lamenting the horrors of 'micro-plastics.'"

"It's hilarious you think we can lay down rules. Is that working out for you with Galahad? Like at all? Because Gwen would just laugh at me, if I tried."

Trystan made a face, admitting the truth. "No. It does not work. I am keeping the knight tied to a horse and he still won't listen to reason."

"You've *tied him to a horse?*" Midas echoed. "Fucking hell, Trystan... *That's* how you romance your *ha'yan?*"

"I am trying to keep him alive! He would wander off into the desert, if I did not have him safely tethered. I've watched him become distracted by a pretty flower and ride in a complete circle." Trystan picked out a coat and held it up to check the size. "That *literally* happened. The man is alive only by the grace of the gods."

Midas sighed. "Galahad is an *actor*."

"Debatable. Have you seen his show?"

"An actor could trick you into seeing a *lightness* inside of him that's not really there."

Trystan snorted, even though he'd considered the same thing when he'd first met Galahad. "The man once refused to kill a poisonous sand-eel, because 'it might have a family.' Trust me. He's dismally Good."

"He's still a knight." Midas persisted. "Are you really okay with that? You fought his kind for years, Trystan."

In his mind, Trystan again saw Galahad falling into pieces after defeating Ayren's men. Saw his horror and shame. Saw a warrior, like himself, who had witnessed far too much, in battles not of his choosing, and now wished for a brighter life.

"Different men fought in the War." He accepted Galahad's words on the matter, as he had no better ones. "I would not want you to know all that I did in combat, Midas. I would not want Gwen and

Avi to ever hear the tales. You would look at me with changed eyes."

"Nothing you ever did, or could ever do, would change the love we feel for you, Trystan. You are our clan. You never need to feel a moment's concern about that."

Trystan shut his eyes and leaned his forehead against the side of the phone booth. Inside of him, the morass of unidentified *somethings* warmed at Midas' words. He wanted to say something warm back to him, but he didn't know how.

"I like Galahad." Midas went on. "In theory. He guarded my wife from her asshole first husband, so that's a big plus in his column. If he is your mate, then I will help you win him. You know that. I'm just saying, you've claimed a complicated *ha'yan* for yourself."

Trystan looked back towards the door. Still no Galahad. Perhaps he was avoiding Trystan, now. Was irritation an emotion? If so, he could definitely feel it.

"I have yet to claim the knight." He grumbled. "I have not fully committed to this path."

If Trystan claimed the man, Galahad would own a piece of him that could never be taken back. Trystan had already lost two clans. He knew what it was like to be left all alone. Losing his mate would cripple him and the knight was so... ephemeral. Galahad could slip between his fingers and back into mist, at any time. Then Trystan would be forsaken in a world without his magic, forever searching for what he couldn't hold.

Midas sighed in a commiserating way. "The path is already beneath your feet, brother. All you can do now is follow it. That's how *ha'na* works. Trust me, I've been there."

Trystan frowned, refusing to accept the truth of Midas' words. His contradictory thoughts wished to both grasp Galahad tight and also resist claiming him. It made no sense. He knew it and still he continued on. "I am considering many options." He reiterated firmly.

"What options?" Midas sounded exasperated. "You get *one* mate. You're confusing yourself with something that's very simple. When you look at Galahad do you see everything?"

Trystan's jaw ticked, that shadow of fate flickering in his mind.

"Because, if you *do*," Midas continued smugly, "then the only 'options' are mating with the handsome movie-star who says he has 'true' feelings for you or spending the rest if your life alone and miserable. I just don't understand how that's a hard choice."

Trystan snorted. "Because you have yet to meet the knight."

"Was that a joke? Are you telling jokes, now?"

"I wish to speak to Avalon." Trystan decided, rather than answering. He hung the coat up on the door of the phone booth, so he could buy it if and when the shopkeeper returned. "I am tired of listening to you. I would hear her voice before I hang up."

"I genuinely have no clue what Galahad sees in you."

"Would you shut up and put the child on the phone?"

Midas saw that simple request as a learning opportunity, because he was a jackass. "*Why* do you want to talk to Avi? Try to think of the word for your feelings."

"Oh for Lyrssa's sake..."

"Just try it, Trystan. What could it hurt?"

Trystan took a deep breath, scrounging the recesses of his mind and heart for a clue. Humoring Midas, for no logical reason. Nothing would happen. It was all a waste of time.

Even as he thought that, though, Trystan also knew that Galahad would not want someone who didn't feel enough *somethings* for him. The wingless prioritized emotions in their mates. If he didn't figure this shit out, Galahad would choose another male to irritate.

Trystan closed his eyes, forcing himself to concentrate.

"Trystan?" Midas prompted, after a while. "You still there?"

"I... have not seen the child in weeks." The *somethings* were connected to his thoughts about Avalon. Telling him information. If he listened, they began to form into words. "I do not like being parted from her, for so long. She will do many cute things and I will not see them. She will need me and I won't be there. She will forget me."

"Avi won't forget you." Midas assured him distractedly, sounding excited by Trystan's dismal attempt at feeling feelings. "Now, what emotion do you think all that is?"

"I... um..." Trystan floundered for a beat. *P'don*, this was hard. He squinted, focusing with all his strength on deciphering the *somethings*. "I... miss her?" It came out as a guess, but he suddenly knew it was true. "Yes. I miss Avi. I miss you and Gwen. I am not content to be separated from you." He searched for the right word to describe his restlessness. "I am *unhappy* when I am away from home. Yes. *Unhappy* without my clan to care for."

A long pause. "My God..." Midas finally breathed in amazement.

"Is that wrong?" It was probably wrong. He knew it would be.

"No! No, it's not wrong." Midas sounded ecstatic. "You actually did it! Trystan, you just felt an emotion and identified it! No other gryphon has *ever* done what you just did. Do you know how incredible it is?"

Trystan rubbed the back of his neck, uncomfortably. That had been difficult and strange. He didn't want to talk about it anymore. "I wish to speak to the child." He reiterated.

"Alright." Midas agreed, still dazed. "Hold on, I'll get her." He must have tilted the phone away from his mouth, because his voice became muffled. "Princess? Come here. Trystan is on the phone for you. He says he misses you."

Avalon was apparently in the room with him. No great surprise. Midas was Avi's *first* best friend. She spent most of her time playing with dolls under her father's desk, drawing all over his possessions, and otherwise wrapping him around her little finger.

"Hi, Trystan!" Her perfect little voice came on the phone and Trystan's tension melted away. "Yous far away, in a sandy place!"

"I know." He agreed, his tone growing softer. "It's a desert."

Hearing the child calmed him. Knowing that she was safe and that she remembered him. He didn't care what Midas said, he wanted to be sure.

"Yous in a mean town, too." He could picture Avalon's blonde ringlets bouncing as she bobbed her head. "Mean people is running it. Gal won't like them."

"I have no doubt. We're leaving here very soon, though."

"To go find the treasure?"

"No. That madness was the knight's initial plan, but I talked him out of it."

"You did?" Avi sounded surprised. And honestly, now that Trystan considered it, it *was* strange that Galahad had given up his mission so easily. The man was not usually so reasonable.

He frowned. "Galahad has not spoken of his treasure hunt in days. He accepted my decision not to help him die in some mad scheme and the matter has been laid to rest."

"You sure?"

"Of course." Trystan *had* been sure, anyway. Now he weighed the chances that Galahad was still plotting something stupid. "I will talk to him, again. Do not concern yourself. I will keep Galahad safe." No small feat given the man attracted trouble like porridge attracted bears.

"And he'll keep you safe." Avi chirped. "Then yous can both find the big glass bubble!"

Trystan's mouth curved ever so slightly. "Yes. I will find your gift soon. I promise." How hard could it be to locate a glass ball of some kind? They were surely sold in many shops. Trystan had already set his mind to the task and what he set his mind to he readily accomplished.

"'Kay. I love you!"

The *somethings* didn't feel messy or confusing. Not with her. "Watch over our clan for me." He ordered softly and knew he should hang up. Instead, he took a deep breath. "Avi?"

"Yeah?"

"Is Galahad truly the best knight ever? You saw this?"

"Oh yeah, Trystan. He's going to help break the curse."

A feeling of... *relief* flooded Trystan. Fisher had said that no one was the *ya'lah,* but Trystan would put his faith in Avi and Galahad. The child was always right and Galahad was special beyond understanding. Maybe there was still a chance for some kind of future for the gryphons, if the knight fought for them. Maybe if he picked up a sword...

Avi's voice interrupted his thoughts. "Gal's not good at making friends, though."

"I noticed that." Half of the man was always in some other realm, so it was little wonder. "I believe it is because he does not try to connect with people. I have told him so."

"Well, he is *really* not trying, right now."

Trystan froze, his gaze once again scanning for the knight and not spotting him. "Now?" He repeated, hoping he was misunderstanding her. "He's not making friends, *right now*?"

"Oh yeah. A lot."

P'don.

Trystan dropped the phone, racing for the front of the store.

"Bye-bye, Trystan!" He heard Avi call over the dangling receiver, her voice still cheerful. "Be careful of the other Galahad."

Chapter Twelve

I am soooo glad to be out of Camelot, now. So glad I can live free, out here in Prendergast, remembering all the Good men who fought in the War.

Bedivere… Martyr of Legion, tragically taken from us while saving gryphons from the very fires they set.

Percival… Who understood that the winged devils can *never* be assimilated into any civilized society.

Galahad… The knight Uther loved as a son, expelled from our kingdom for some damn reason, probably dead now, in a foreign land at the hands of a foreign savage.

What would those brave knights think about us now?

What would they think about the false stories being told about our glorious king? I think, like me, they'd be *glad* to be far from Camelot and its lies.

Glad to be in a better place, among true heroes.

"Stopping the Savages" Podcast
Sir Dragonet of Camelot- Former Troubadour of King

Uther and Host of the Program

The Town- Edge of the Wilds

A sandman was being dissolved in a water tank.

The creature was made entirely of grit and dust, so water turned him to sludge. He'd been locked in a large, vertical container filled with liquid, ensuring that he couldn't take his humanoid form. Every time the sandman tried, he dissipated into nothing but gooey mud on the bottom of the tank and particles swirling in the water.

That would happen again and again. Forever. Unless someone saved him.

Galahad looked around, hoping to see someone rushing forward to save him.

Trystan wasn't going to like it if he got involved. It was hardly Galahad's fault that people kept falling into peril all around him, but Trystan would still blame him. It was inevitable. Trystan had been super clear about wanting to stay away from trouble while they were in town. And he'd been super, *super* clear about not helping anyone else today.

Unfortunately, nobody else on the dusty street seemed concerned about the grisly torture of a fellow being. They were too busy enduring their dejected lives, dully tilling the dry soil, and plodding from place-to-place with their heads down. It truly was the saddest town he'd ever seen. Maybe the citizens were so inured to its dirt and cruelty that they didn't even notice the suffering of others. They weren't going to help the sandman

Shit. That meant *he* was going to have to do it.

Galahad sighed and started towards the glass cage. Hopefully, everyone would be reasonable about the sandman and this whole thing would get resolved before Trystan heard about it. Since Galahad was trying hard to seduce the guy, he would've liked to get through at least twenty minutes without pissing Trystan off.

He bent down to pick up a rock, which was no easy feat, considering he was holding the saddle. It was balanced over his bound hands, because he couldn't get completely free of it. He'd had to remove the saddle from the horse while he was still sitting on it in order to bypass the enchanted ropes tying him to the pommel. It was the quickest escape he could come up with, but it inhibited his mobility. The damn thing was bulky with leather trim, thickly padded, and weighed a ton. Also, there was a flying carpet tied to it.

Galahad's eyes flicked around the glass cage, counting four scruffy looking men lounging on the wooden sidewalk. Weirdly, they all looked identical. They were all so dirty and unshaven that it was hard to make out their individual features. Smart money was on them being directly responsible for the sandman's suffering.

One guy was manicuring his too-long nails with a switch blade. Another was napping in a chair, his wide-brimmed hat pulled down over his eyes. The last two were playing cards on a barrel top. All of them looked like professional scumbags and none of them looked reasonable.

Galahad took a deep breath, pressing forward with determined optimism. "Hey, fellas." He said easily, stopping in front of them. "Nice afternoon, isn't it?"

The men fixed him with identical glares. It was a hundred and ten in the shade.

Galahad pretended not to notice. At this distance he could see a hand-printed sign was taped to the front of the huge water container. It read: DIDN'T PAY HIS MONSTER TAX!

"That's not really a thing, you know." He pointed to the piece of paper.

"Sure it is." The guy picking his nails with the knife declared in the exact same tone the upperclassmen at the Knights' Academy used when stealing all the younger kids' food. "It's the tax monsters gotta pay if they wanna live in our town."

Galahad made a "huh" sound. "That seems a bit unfair. Is there a sheriff around here? Because I'd love to talk to him about it."

"This town doesn't need a sheriff." The man spread his hands like a cheap carnival wizard who'd just made a rabbit disappear. "It's got us."

The card playing guy hooted in agreement. The one who'd been napping tipped his hat back and sat up a bit straighter. There was a small gun in his lap and his hand was resting on it. None of them said any actual words, though. It was... odd.

Galahad kept his attention on the switchblade guy. He seemed to be the one in command. "Okay. So who are you gentlemen, then?"

"I'm Solomon Grundy. These are my brothers. Thursday, Monday, and Wednesday. We run this town."

Oh. *That* explained the oddness.

Galahad squinted, looking for the former soldiers through the grime and finally recognizing them. It was surprising he hadn't before. After all, how many men had magical duplicates of themselves? Solomon called them his "brothers," but they were more like multiples. Mute clones, who acted independently, but who he also somehow controlled.

Maybe?

Honestly, Galahad had never fully understood the phenomena. The King's Men had treated the eight Grundys as separate beings, just as Solomon claimed. (Coincidentally, that allowed him to cash their eight separate paychecks.) Galahad had never been so sure they were really individual people, though. It always seemed to him that Solomon was the center cog of a hive mind.

A very sadistic, homicidal, screwed-up hive mind.

"You were elected by these people?" He asked doubtfully.

Solomon snorted. "Hell, no. We did what *all* kings do: We took control. Expanded our empire. Demanded obedience. Executed traitors." He seemed pleased with the analogy. "Back home we might have been nobodies, but, around here, we're royalty."

That was exactly why Galahad had had seven of the Grundys court-martialed. He'd seen the way they treated everyone weaker than themselves. The eighth "brother" he'd had tried, convicted, and shot by a firing squad. Which was no small feat in the King's Men. The rape and murder of gryphons hadn't exactly been high on Uther's list of worries.

"Hardly seems just that you takeover a town and enslave everybody." Galahad pointed out mildly, his gaze moving between the replicas/siblings. No doubt the other three Grundys were lurking nearby, too. Probably on the rooftops.

"Seems just to me. Might makes right around my kingdom and *I've* got the might. That means our kind does what we say or they suffer the consequences. And their kind?" He pointed to the elves, who were fruitlessly farming poisoned herbs in the sand. "They work or they die."

Jesus, it seemed like every dishonorable soldier in Uther's army had decided to stick around the land they'd helped conquer, eager to take whatever they could get. The exploitation of Lyonesse would drag on forever, at this rate. Something really needed to be done.

Galahad glanced towards the dying vegetation. "Not to change the subject, but wouldn't it be smarter to build an irrigation ditch for that garden? It would be so simple to run it from that pond, straight onto the plants." Was he the only one who saw the sense in that plan?

The three lesser-Grundys frowned at the pond, then the

garden, then back again. Like setting up an irrigation system had never occurred to them before.

Solomon's jaw clenched. "Don't recall asking for your opinion," he spat in the dirt, "Captain."

Great. Solomon remembered him, too. That sure wasn't going to calm this situation down.

Galahad's hand tightened on the rock in his hand. "I'd appreciate it if you let the sandman go." He tried, getting back to the point.

"Now, why the hell would I do that?"

"Because what you're doing is torture. I never did abide torture."

"So I recall." Solomon scoffed. "You always were a pussy." He hopped off the wooden sidewalk. "I should have dealt with you back when you killed Sunday, for no goddamn reason."

"No reason? He forced himself on a little girl and then hacked her wings off with a hatchet. He left her to bleed to death in the mess tent."

"She was a *gryphon!*" Solomon advanced on him. "My brother died because of *you*. Because you're soft on monsters. You always have been."

"We're all monsters. It just depends on who's looking at us."

Staring across an abyss of hate and fear, your enemies always looked like something evil. Something *other*. If they didn't, wars wouldn't work. It was the same on every side and it was all lies. Galahad had learned the truth when it was all too late, but now he saw it so clearly.

"Bullshit!" Solomon stabbed a finger at him. "You've always been a dirty monster lover."

Galahad shifted his stance, his eyes flicking to the sandman's glass cage, gauging the distance. "I follow the law." He said calmly. "Gryphon or wingless, everyone should be treated the same. That's what I did with your brother. Sunday was fairly tried by a military tribunal."

Everyone else on the street was watching them, now. The elves had stopped farming, their small eyes darting around. The other three Grundys were on their feet, supporting Solomon like off-kilter mirror images. Several people ducked into the nearest building, sensing a brewing fight.

"Where does the law say gryphons should be treated the same as us?" Solomon demanded. "You're making that up. It was *never* a law."

"It should have been."

"This is just like the Battle of Flags," Solomon raged at Galahad, not accepting that legal theory, "when you didn't even let us fire on the gryphon. When you made up some goddamn excuse not to kill them all. Uther was *right* to demote you, after that. He should have kept you locked up for the rest of the War."

Remembering his two months in the stocks had Galahad's temper crackling. During that time, Trystan had been captured. If he'd been there, Galahad would have been able to get him free. He hadn't known Trystan then, but one look at that man would have changed everything that came afterwards. Galahad knew himself too well to think otherwise.

There wasn't a chance in hell Galahad would ever meet Trystan and then allow him to be harmed. Not under any circumstances. His bond with Trystan was inexplicable, but it had been *true* right from the first moment they met. Galahad trusted it in a way that would always trump everything else. He would have *never* allowed Trystan to be illegally shipped off to the Wicked, Ugly, and Bad prison. Not even if freeing him meant his own life.

He gave his head a shake, pushing down the darkness that threatened to rise. Thinking about Badness happening to Trystan was *not* going to help him stay in control.

"Well, now the War's over, Captain. Now, *I'm* in command, so I suggest you get your ass outta here, before I put your monster-ass-licking corpse in the ground."

Galahad gave reason one last shot. "Let the sandman go," he reiterated quietly, "or I'll free him myself."

Solomon slowly smiled. "I was kinda hoping you'd want to do this the hard way."

His "brothers" moved in on Galahad from different angles, preparing to surround him. Solomon stalked closer from the front. No one on the street seemed willing to lend a hand and it didn't seem like this was the day that reason would win out against morons.

Shit. It was times like this when Galahad almost missed carrying a sword. Too bad all he had in his hands were a rock and a saddle.

...And a magic carpet.

Galahad glanced down at it, an idea suddenly dawning.

"You know, I'm glad you showed up in my town." Solomon sneered out, already anticipating victory. "This thing between us goes beyond what you did to Sunday."

"There's a thing between us?" Galahad asked,

surreptitiously untying the hopefully-not-fake flying rug from the saddle.

"You bet your dick there is. Seeing your picture everywhere, and reading about your movie deals, and listening to your stupid album over and over and over…" Solomon made an aggravated sound. "Let's just say, I've been wanting to kick your ass for a *looooong* time."

Galahad winced a bit at that complaint. It had never been his intention to be a pop star. He'd only recorded that album as a joke for Gwen's birthday, so it was a little embarrassing that it somehow went triple-platinum.

"The goddamn songs played on every radio station." Solomon went on like he'd been personally targeted by the music. "It got so I was *dreaming* them. I almost went crazy."

"Yeah, to be honest, I really don't think I deserved to win so many awards for that album." Galahad tried not to shy away from valid criticism, even when it came from assholes. It was the only way to grow. "I only played three of the instruments on the tracks." He paused, recounting in his head. "No. *Five.* There was a harp and…"

"Shut up!" Solomon roared, cutting him off. "*This* is why no one could ever stand you!"

"My music?" Galahad pretended not to notice as the magic carpet fell to the ground. "Well, I've always seen myself as more of an actor, so…"

Solomon interrupted him again. "No. That everything you have is some kind of dumb luck." He jabbed a finger at Galahad. "It's all just handed to you, when you do jack-shit to deserve it." His face was red with rage. "And --just so you know-- you're not a great actor either, dickhead. Your TV show sucked!"

Galahad frowned. "Which one?"

"*All* of them."

Okay. *Now* he was getting annoyed.

Trystan said the key to using a magic carpet was concentration and Trystan was the most capable person ever born. Galahad was sure as hell willing to go with his advice. He closed his eyes and focused his thoughts on the carpet, instead of them men drawing nearer. Focused on lifting it off the ground. Focused on sending it through the air. Focused on the trajectory.

After a beat, something happened. A buzzing energy crackled in his head and he knew it was connecting to the rug. He could feel the carpet levitating a bit, which was a good start. But how did he make it really *go?*

"Take his head off." Solomon ordered his brothers. "We'll

stick it in a box and charge people for a peek." He chortled, already envisioning the advertising. "'Come and see Galahad's head in a box.' That's *gotta* be worth some tourist coins. I can't be the only one who'd pay to see this bastard dead."

Galahad tuned him out, all his focus on the flying carpet.

"The old fella at the general store came runnin' up before, telling me there's a gryphon in the shop." Solomon moved closer. "That winged devil wouldn't be with *you*, now would he, Captain? One of your monster friends?" He snorted. "Not that it matters. We gotta keep this town's riffraff under control. He's a gryphon so, either way, he's gonna die."

Galahad's eyes snapped open... and the magic carpet took off flying.

"What the *hell!*" Solomon screeched in panic. The heavy fabric slammed into his knees, knocking him right off his feet. He hit the dust face first, bloodying his nose. "Stop!"

Galahad didn't stop. The carpet ricocheted between the other Grundys. Spinning them around like tops. Covering their eyes, so they couldn't see. Knocking weapons from their hands, as it zipped past them. Keeping them off balance and thoroughly occupied.

Galahad might have known nothing about magic carpets, but he'd been the eighth grade laser-pinball champ. (Also, he'd invented the game.) The key was to keep the ball moving. The magic carpet never let up on its assault, even as the brothers tried to swat it away. It wasn't going to stop them for long, but all he needed was five seconds.

Galahad launched himself sideways. Throwing a rock with his hands tied and the saddle weighing him down was hard as hell. But, Galahad really had been the star pitcher of Camelot's Charity League. The baseball-sized stone slammed into the large tank holding the sandman, cracking the glass into a spider web. There was an ominous creak. A second later the weight of the water burst through, emptying the whole container in a wave. Liquid whooshed out, washing through the cracks on the wooden sidewalk and into the dirt below.

Galahad lay on the ground and flashed Solomon a triumphant smirk. He wasn't sure what the next step of his plan would be, but, he wasn't worried. Situations like this seemed to come up all the time and he always figured them out. For the moment, he was winning.

"You *prick*." Solomon raged, holding his bleeding nose. "I've hated you since you fucked us over at Flags and now I'm going to finally...!"

A dead body hit the sand, interrupting his threat.

It landed two feet from Galahad, with a morbid crunch of bones and its limbs all akimbo. It slammed into the dirt so hard, you'd almost think it was thrown straight down. Its head exploded like a watermelon, so blood and goo leaked all over the sand.

What the hell?

For a heartbeat of time, no one moved. They just stared down at the crumpled, sticky remains, trying to understand where it came from. It was like the man had dropped from the sky.

"Saturday?" Solomon said in a blank tone, gaping down at the dead guy. "Is that you? Jesus, what *happened?*"

The dead guy didn't answer.

The mystery didn't last long, though, because another dead guy quickly joined the first. There was a muffled shout of panic and then a shadow passing overhead. Everybody looked up as a figure went pin-wheeling through the air. He sailed above their heads, almost gracefully. Then, inevitably, he fell towards the ground and... *splat*. Galahad rolled sideways to avoid getting crushed by the impact.

And nearly got hit by a third guy.

This one silently screamed all the way down. It was kind of eerie. And his rolling crash into the sand twisted his head the wrong way around, which was even eerier.

Solomon gave a choked gasp of shock, trying to process what was happening.

Galahad was beginning to understand, though. The final dead guy's wrong-way face survived the collision, so it was easy to recognize Tuesday Grundy. (He was the only one missing a nose.) The three dead brothers had indeed been keeping watch from on top of the buildings lining the street, no doubt acting as sentries to keep the elves in line.

Solomon dragged his eyes away from his dead brothers and onto Galahad. "*You* did this." He seethed.

Galahad got to his feet. "Technically, no."

He could take an educated guess as to who *was* responsible, though. God, Trystan really did belong on television. The man had a true flair for drama.

The Grundys began scanning rooftops. They didn't have to look hard, since Trystan now stood on the edge of the nearest building, unconcerned about all the angry people below. His face wore the misty veil of battle, giving his features the look of an eagle. A hot desert breeze plastered his clothes to the strong, hard lines of his body.

No one else had ever been so beautiful.

For one timeless moment, everything went still and there was only Trystan. Invincible and Good and extraordinary in every way. Voices whispered in his head and Galahad understood *exactly* what they said. He couldn't translate the gryphon dialect they were speaking, but he knew the truth they told him.

Because he saw it too.

"Holy shit..." Solomon's eyes went wide, horrific memories from the War flashing over his face. "It's *him*. I seen him once. It's that goddamn demon!"

Galahad didn't even hear him, transfixed by Trystan. His wings were impossibly huge behind him, perfect and white as an angel's. A warrior sent to protect the innocent. A gift from God. In that second, gazing up at Trystan, Galahad saw the future. He saw *everything* right there in front of him, silhouetted against the cloudless sky.

And it was beautiful.

"That's Trystan Airbourne!" Solomon screamed at him, like maybe Galahad didn't comprehend what was happening. "It's really him!"

"I know." Galahad felt his mouth curve, seeing his path so clearly that it dazzled him. "That's the man I'm going to marry."

Chapter Thirteen

Uther was determined to have the graal. This is what started the first Looking Glass Campaign.

He rallied all of his gold, and all of his knights, and all of his weapons. Then he marched into Lyonesse, cutting a swath of destruction and pain. He demanded that the gryphons show him the location of the Looking Glass Pool and vowed not to stop the slaughter until he had claimed it for his own.

Even if we had known the location of the lost temple, we would not have told it to him.

How the Wingless War Happened
Skylyn Welkyn- Gryphon Storyteller

The Town- Edge of the Wilds

Seeing an opening to overthrow their oppressors, the toiling elves began to rush forward. Hoes and rakes held high they charged the lesser Grundys. Thursday, Monday, and Wednesday were swarmed with angry serfs trying to win back their freedom. The men began beating them away, but the small creatures were coming in waves.

The rest of the town began joining in the fight, although it was hard to determine whose side they were on. Mostly they were just panicked. Guns began firing out windows, aiming at anything that moved. Solomon and Galahad had to rip their eyes away from Trystan and duck behind water barrels on opposite sides of the street to avoid being hit.

This whole plan could've been going better. Why did no one ever act reasonably?

"Flags was the battle you were punished for losing, knight?" Trystan called from the rooftop, calm in the midst of pandemonium. He must have been listening to Galahad's argument with Solomon.

Galahad winced a bit. He didn't like Trystan knowing about his part in the War. Nothing Good could come from it. "I didn't lose the battle. I just didn't win it."

"Fucking *pussy*." Solomon reiterated, glaring at Galahad. Blood dripped from his injured nose onto his chin.

Trystan ignored him, his attention fixed on Galahad like he was fascinated. "Uther demoted you, because you ordered your men to stop firing on the gryphons?"

"Technically, I was demoted for 'showing mercy to the enemy in wartime.'"

That rule was ridiculously vague and not at all in keeping with the Knights' Code. Galahad had stated as much at his disciplinary hearing, not that anyone cared. He'd received his rank back after a couple months, though, when the king needed him to kill more people.

Trystan considered that for a beat. "Well, not to agree with Uther, but stopping the assault at Flags *was* a terrible strategy. Why would you do something so stupid?"

"Because the gryphons were *retreating*." Galahad yelled back. That was the same question Uther had bellowed at him after the skirmish. Right before he locked him in the stocks. "You don't shoot people who are retreating. Not if there's another way."

Trystan's scoff was audible even at a distance. "You do, if you want to win."

"In war, there *are* no rules." Solomon insisted loudly. "Even the gryphon knows that and he's a goddamn demon!"

"If you're killing unarmed people, then it's murder." Galahad knew *that*. "It's a rule, no matter if it's wartime or peace."

"You pious little prick! The gryphons would have picked us off, if the situations were reversed." Solomon looked up at Trystan like the two of them were suddenly on the same side. He must not have heard the part about Galahad intending to marry the man. "Wouldn't you have picked us all off, Airbourne?"

"When men come to kill me, I kill them first. It's why I yet survive."

That was true. Under Trystan's take-no-prisoners command, ten knights died for every gryphon and most of them had never seen it coming. The man was a genius at guerrilla-style combat. Galahad wasn't. He was willing to admit that. He'd tried to strictly follow the rules of engagement.

But Trystan had been fighting armed knights, who knew what they were getting into. Galahad had been trying to wage a war in towns and villages, surrounded by civilians. When he'd encountered non-combatants, he stopped his troops and let the people peaceably disperse. Even if warriors slipped away with them, the alternative had always seemed far worse. Galahad didn't apologize for erring on the side of caution, when it came to sparing innocent lives.

Not when the alternative was children dead in the grass.

"Damn right, you kill them first." Solomon nodded at Trystan's words. Somehow he was blaming Galahad for all this, even though Trystan was the one who'd tossed his brothers to their deaths. "If Trystan Airbourne was in charge, we'd have *won* the goddamn War."

Galahad was getting pissed, now. "We *did* win the War!" Unfortunately. "I did what I had to do at Flags and I'd do it again. There were women and children in the crowd."

"So the hell what?"

"So I'd *never* fire on women and children! No true knight would."

Trystan froze.

Galahad was beyond noticing, the argument with Solomon bringing back memories he'd rather forget. "Innocent people are *not* my enemies. It's my job to protect them. It's right there in the Knights' Code."

"You're the only one who ever gave a shit about that code!" Solomon screamed. Blood from his nose had gotten into his mouth and coated his teeth, giving him a demonic look. "*You're* why Bedivere died saving those little bastards at Legion. You *had* to be. I knew him and he wouldn't have done something so stupid on his own."

Trystan's head tilted.

"I never made Bedivere do anything." Galahad didn't like to get angry, but this entire conversation was pissing him off. "He made his own choices and he lived with them."

"Bullshit!" This time it was a screech. "It's your fault he's dead. I wasn't even there and I know it was all your doing." Solomon turned his attention to Trystan. "Hey, Airbourne! You and me don't have a problem here."

"I disagree." Trystan intoned. "You have upset my knight. This is a problem for you."

"This ass-clown was Captain of the King's Men. He's your sworn enemy. Now, you might be a monster, who just murdered my brothers, but I'm thinking it's really *his* fault." Solomon jabbed a finger at Galahad. "Everything is always *his* fault."

"I have noticed this, as well. The man's very aura creates disruption."

Galahad sighed, praying for patience.

"Both of us have reason to hate Galahad, gryphon." Solomon was warming to his own logic. "He's fucked us *both* over, just by being such a do-Gooding bastard. Go ahead and kill *him* and we'll call it even."

"That's a remarkably tempting offer." Trystan allowed. "The knight is no end of trouble to me. He cannot even enter a store without igniting a shootout in the street."

Galahad rolled his eyes, no longer on the verge of losing his temper. Trystan's calm voice soothed the edges of his anger, even when his future husband was being a jackass.

"Yet, I have a deep and confusing interest in keeping the knight alive." Trystan continued and nonchalantly jumped off the roof, his huge wings keeping him aloft. "So he will stay alive."

Jesus, the man truly did look like an angel. Galahad gazed upward, in total and complete wonderment. Everything Trystan did was just *so* beautiful.

"Abandon your plan to harm my knight and I will cease killing you and your multiples." Trystan told Solomon. "Don't and I will rid this town of all of you for good."

"Screw that!" Solomon screamed back. "You side with him, you *both* die!"

Galahad's eyebrows soared. Hang on... Was Trystan calling him "*my* knight?" That was awesome. Did Trystan *try* to be awesome or did it just come naturally to him? God, it didn't even matter. No one else in the world could *ever* compete with this man.

Around them, the firefight continued to rage. It seemed like the whole town had been a powder keg, just waiting to go off and Galahad had lit the fuse. Most people were aiming at the Grundys, though, so that was a positive sign. Galahad always tried to look on the bright side. Solomon and his brothers had apparently pissed off everybody with their tactics, because now they were the targets of a lot of pent up frustration and hate.

A couple of the lesser Grundys managed to escape the elves. The other one was ominously still, with a shovel planted in his chest. The two remaining men made their way toward Solomon, crouched down to avoid all the flying bullets targeted at their heads.

Trystan didn't seem to notice the chaos. He landed on the ground, smoothly transitioning from flying to walking. He didn't miss a single step. Didn't even hesitate. He just strolled through the battle, with total confidence.

It was *awesome*.

One of the Grundys raced towards Trystan and Galahad slammed the flying carpet right over his head. Trystan didn't really need his help, but Galahad couldn't help his instincts. He protected Trystan, first and always. The dense weave enveloped the Grundy's skull like shrink wrap, winding round and round. The man hit the ground, gasping for air and trying to pry it off his face before he suffocated.

Trystan glanced at the struggling moron and then arched a brow at Galahad. "*Now* you wish to fight?"

"A rug isn't a sword, Trys. I'm well within my rules of nonviolence."

The Grundy continued to thrash around like a beached fish.

Galahad ignored him, his eyes on Trystan. "Hey, did you get me any Gala-Chips?"

"They only had the caramel-and-whey ones."

"Ew. I hate caramel-and-whey. Why does *anyone* like it? Why is that always the best-selling flavor?"

"I am shocked any of your gods-awful concoctions sell." Trystan stomped a boot into the man's stomach reaching down to pry the carpet free. "But, at least you are focusing better and managing to make this thing fly." Galahad eased back on the pressure he was exerting to keep the fabric in place and Trystan removed it from the guy's face. "I told you so. The rug is authentic, yes?" He tossed it back to Galahad. "Do not damage Avalon's gift. She will have words for us both."

"Kill Galahad, brothers!" Solomon ordered. "We'll see him dead and then get the rest of these monsters under control. They're all about to learn who they're dealing with!"

Trystan's attention flicked to him, again. He looked like a gunfighter, all set for a shootout. Galahad had *always* had a thing for cowboys and he had an even bigger thing for Trystan.

Jesus, Galahad was just completely sold on the man. Planning-their-dream-wedding, adopting-an-adorable-dog-together

SOLD. For real. Galahad was already up to the step where they bought and restored their dream home. Which he could totally do, because he had a contracting license and a real interest in historic architecture.

All that stood in the way of a future filled with fuzzy puppies and claw foot tubs was convincing the way hotter, way cooler, way more awesome half of their partnership that they *had* a future together.

Trystan headed up the center of the dirt road like he owned the whole damn town. "Are these the former King's Men who want you dead because of the map, knight?"

Galahad cleared his throat. "No, this is a *different* group of ex-soldiers who hate me."

"For Lyrssa's sake... I think the wingless soldiers despise you more than the gryphons."

"I explained that I had a problem making friends, didn't I?"

"This is not a problem. This is an epidemic. Everyone we meet wants you dead."

Solomon nodded, like Trystan was once again making a lot of sense. "Preachy do-Gooder deserves it, too." He stood up, ready to make his last stand, and looked at his brothers. "*Kill Galahad.*" He repeated in a commanding tone. "No matter what, he dies today!"

Trystan's head tilted at some predatory angle. ...And then Solomon was in the air. Trystan launched himself into flight, blasting down the street and hitting Solomon like a torpedo. Solomon shrieked in fury and terror as he was lifted into the sky. Ten seconds later, he hit the ground again, only now he was in two separate pieces.

Galahad cringed a bit at the mess.

The last two Grundys raced at Galahad, eager to carry out their brother's final order. They only made it a few steps when the sidewalk behind them exploded. Wooden boards were propelled twenty feet in every direction, along with about a ton of dirt and rocks. A new being stood in the center of the crater that was left behind.

The sandman had re-formed himself.

Galahad had never actually seen one before. His body was shaped like a man, but it was made of swirling dust and grit, creating the sensation of motion even when he was standing still. It was remarkable. Like a cyclone had been given life.

Everyone in the town ran for their lives.

The sandman's glowing topaz eyes fixed on the last two Grundys and the ground beneath them began to churn. The men screamed as the dirt rose up, spinning and reeling around them at incredible speeds. The whirlwind was concentrated on the Grundys, but its colossal strength fogged the entire street with debris. Galahad had to shield his eyes from the power of it. Then, just as quickly as it began, the grinding wind stopped and the air stilled, again.

And all that was left of the Grundys were sandblasted bones.

"Holy shit." Galahad whispered getting to his feet.

The sandman's attention switched to him, an unreadable expression on the ever-changing features of his grainy face.

"Uh... Hi." Galahad raised a hand at him, wondering what to do next. "Listen, what do you say we have a reasonable discussion about this?"

The sandman started towards him, but he didn't get far.

Trystan landed right between them.

He slammed down with massive force, hitting the ground in an animalistic crouch. Holy *shit*, the man was awesome. Slowly straightening up to his full height, Trystan braced his legs apart, ready for the next fight. His back was towards Galahad, his face towards the sandman, and it really was like an angel intervening. No one could have defeated Trystan. Galahad believed it without reservation.

The man was the greatest warrior in the world.

The sandman hesitated. "I am not a threat to your knight."

"*Nothing* is a threat to my knight." Trystan's eyes stayed trained on the sandman's swirling form. "Not for long, anyway. I make sure of it."

Yeah, he had *definitely* said "my knight" that time. Galahad's mood soared. That was a really optimistic sign for his seduction plans.

The sandman and Trystan continued to watch each other. They both seemed to be waiting to see what the other would do next.

The sandman relented first. "I doubt a fight would end well for either of us, gryphon." His voice was like listening to sandpaper scrape across wood. "And there is no need for one. I simply want to speak with the knight. I owe him a debt. I was locked in that water cage for over a week. I do not understand why he helped me, but I thank him."

"You're welcome." Galahad said with a friendly smile. See? *Now* things were going smoothly. You just needed to stay positive. "I'm glad you're okay."

The sandman stared at him, like he was waiting for the other shoe to drop.

"Uh... You don't *literally* owe me anything, you know." Galahad assured him, in case that's what he thought. "Really. I was happy to help."

The sandman squinted a bit. "You freed me with no thought of reward? That's... ridiculous." He glanced back at Trystan, as if he needed to make sure he wasn't imagining this whole thing. "You see that is ridiculous, don't you?"

"Yep." The word was infused with all the frustration in the world.

"Does the knight do these ridiculous things often?"

Trystan arched a brow, apparently deciding the sandman wasn't a danger now that he was agreeing with Trystan's point of view. "Yep."

"Well, you should stop him."

"I've tried." Trystan gestured around the decimated town. "Witness my success." He was pissed. Galahad had been totally right about that prediction. Now that he'd decided the threat was over, Trystan was ready to start shouting. The man was the most emotional man ever born without emotions. Ever.

Sure enough, brown eyes narrowed in Galahad's direction. "When I said you were capable of starting tornados, knight, I didn't expect you to prove me right quite so quickly."

Galahad made a face. "It was a sandstorm, not a tornado. And why are you blaming me for it?"

"Who else would I blame?" Trystan roared. "It's *your* fault. That man I ripped in half was correct on that score. It's *always* your fault. You throw yourself headlong into danger --Unarmed and with no plan in your empty blond head-- and bedlam ensues."

"He does not even have a sword?" The sandman lamented with a sad "tsk." "Gryphon, your man will not survive if you allow this kind of ridiculous behavior."

Trystan made a "finally someone understands my pain" sort of sound. "You see, knight? Why do you not comprehend what is obvious to all others?"

"I used to kill people professionally." Galahad scoffed. "I've undoubtedly had more training than anybody else in Lyonesse. I've won every battle I've ever fought. You can relax, because *I know what I'm doing*."

Trystan wasn't convinced. "You have *not* won every battle, knight."

"Sure, I have. Ask anyone."

"What about the pigs who nearly barbequed you? Shall I ask *them?* They had you tied to a pole, when I arrived. You somehow count that as a victory?"

"Oh, that wasn't a battle." Galahad snorted dismissively.

"And I probably would have pulled through it okay. I was getting my second wind."

"You were forty seconds from death when I arrived. Which was still better than this mess." He waved a hand at all the various pieces of Grundys.

The sandman wasn't done complaining about Galahad, either. "The sun here is too harsh for his kind, as well, gryphon. The knight is going to be baked in no time."

"I won't get sunburned." Galahad said, but no one was listening.

The sandman reached down and took the hat off a dead Grundy for him. "Put this on."

Trystan snatched it from him, before Galahad could take it. His eyes fixed on the sandman, like he was back to thinking up ways to kill him. "*I* care for this man." It was a warning coated in icy death. "Not you. Only me."

The sandman held up his palms in conciliation and took a step back. "I was just trying to help keep your knight alive."

Trystan relented. Slightly. "Well, the lunatic needs all the help he can get, that is obvious." He unceremoniously dropped the hat over Galahad's hair. "Here."

It smelled. The fact that he kept the ratty thing on his head was proof of Galahad's devotion to this man. "I don't like hats. I always lose them."

Trystan ignored that, too, adjusting the brim. "It begins to make sense now, why I could never predict your battle strategies in the War. You *had* none. It's no wonder I was forever confused by your actions."

"I had plenty of great strategies!" Galahad defended. "Remember when I led your guys in a big clockwise circle and got them all stuck in that briar patch...?" He stopped, a sudden thought popping into his head. "Hey, why do you think clocks go clockwise? Who decided that?"

Trystan covered his eyes with a palm and sighed.

The sandman smiled, amused by Trystan's frustration. "I envy you, gryphon. You possess a true gift."

"I possess a true pain in the ass. ...At least until I kill him and free myself." Trystan went back to glowering at Galahad. "*That* plan makes sense. You are determined to die anyway, so I might as well have the fun of finishing you off, yes? Afterwards, I can go looking for Mount Feather and live with the old clans, forgetting that wingless knights even exist. I have no idea why I don't."

"Because you're not a fool." The sandman intoned. "And only a fool would let such a mate slip through his fingers."

Trystan glanced at him sharply.

Galahad's eyebrows climbed, suddenly liking the sandman a lot.

"I had a woman with a heart like his, before the War." The sandman held Trystan's gaze. "She drove me crazy with her desire to save the world. When I was with her, I had everything. Without her..." He trailed off and his sigh was filled with sorrow. "I have *nothing*."

Trystan remained silent, but his eyes were intent.

"You do not want to be where I am, gryphon." The sandman pointed at Galahad. "For your own sake, do what you must to guard this man. Hold him. *Tight*. Believe me, the world is dark without beings like him to brighten it for us."

"We're sorry for your loss." Galahad told the sandman. The creature's grief was real and vast, so it seemed appropriate to offer condolences. "Aren't we, Trys?"

"Yes." He said softly and it sounded like he actually meant it.

The sandman moved his hand and a pouch somehow appeared in his palm. "Here." He tossed it to Galahad. "I fulfill my debts, whether or not repayment is required. Use this to protect yourself, the next time you're in trouble and save the gryphon from my fate."

Galahad caught the small pouch, clumsily, because he was still tied to the saddle. He examined the parcel and realized the sandman had given him sleeping sand. Jesus, that was super rare and super valuable. The finely milled dust was infused with the sandman's powers and it worked on everyone. It was natural magic, so even Galahad would feel the effects. A few grains would send someone into a deep sleep for hours. *More* than a few grains and they'd never wake up, at all.

Galahad had no clue what he was going to do with it, but it was still a thoughtful gift.

He looked up, wanting to say thanks, but the sandman was already gone. He deteriorated into a mist of dirt, floating away into the desert. It was actually very pretty to witness. Galahad turned to watch the trail of dust drift away, the sun glinting off the particles.

...And that's when he noticed the Grundy with the gun.

The brother who'd been napping when he'd first walked up, the one who'd been impaled by a shovel when the elves attacked, was still slightly alive. He'd rolled onto his side. Using his last ounce of strength, he pointed a revolver at Trystan's back. Before he died, he wanted to take out the man who'd killed Solomon.

His finger squeezed the trigger and Galahad stepped forward, into the line of fire. His hands came up, blocking as much of Trystan as possible, and then the bullet hit. The force of it had Galahad staggering backwards into Trystan.

Trystan's head snapped around, taking everything in with one sweeping glance. "*P'don*." He dragged Galahad closer, scanning him up and down. "Are you alright? Are you hurt?"

For a second, he wasn't sure.

"*Galahad, are you hurt?*"

"I'm fine." Galahad gave his head a clearing shake and held up the saddle. "It was a small caliber. The leather stopped the bullet. I'm okay."

Trystan stared down at the hole in the side of the thickly padded saddle, like he was trying to wrap his brain around a complex puzzle. "You knew that would happen? When you stepped in front of me, you *knew* the saddle would shield you?"

"...Sure." Galahad tried to sound confident, but he could tell from Trystan's answering growl that he wasn't successful.

"Son of a bitch." Trystan made a wrathful sound and his gaze whipped over to the last Grundy, but the man had already slumped over dead. "Son of a *bitch*." He looked back at Galahad, his chest rising and falling too fast. "Do not ever --*ever*-- do that again. I would *never* choose my life over yours. What the hell were you thinking?!"

"I was thinking that without you," Galahad shrugged and told the truth, "I'd have nothing."

Trystan looked up at the sky and squeezed his eyes shut. Trying to calm down. A long moment past.

"Trys? You okay?"

"I was *at* the Battle of Flags." Trystan opened his eyes to look at him, picking up the earlier conversation like nothing else had happened. "We weren't expecting Uther's men to cut us off like that. Not so close to the village. I thought your side would kill us all and that would be the end of me. It was a clever maneuver, knight."

Galahad brightened. "Thanks." *Finally* some positive feedback on his tactics.

Trystan wasn't done. "Afterwards, I questioned whether I had been overestimating you as an opponent. I thought you must be the biggest imbecile in creation for letting us escape, after you trapped us so effectively."

"Thanks." This time the word was sardonic.

"No one else, on *any* side of the War, would have stopped

their advance. And all others of your kind would have ridden their enemies down, slaughtering men, women and children. Only *you* would have let us get away."

Now, Galahad was getting annoyed. "I just didn't want to shoot retreating gryphons for no damn reason, when we could possibly reach a peace agreement or…"

Trystan cut him off. "You misunderstand me." His hand came out to grip the back of Galahad's neck and Galahad's insides tightened in pleasure. "Only *you* would care about having an honorable victory, instead of an easy one. Only *you* would choose a path without personal glory, out of kindness and hope. Only *you* would willingly accept demotion for showing mercy to an enemy. Only you, knight."

Galahad's jaw dropped, shocked that Trystan had just said such a beautiful thing to him.

"So this?" Trystan gestured around the town again, still not letting Galahad go. "All this must *stop*." He gave him a small shake. "You must stop risking yourself. The War took the rest of your breed. You are the last and you *must* survive." His eyes met Galahad, his gaze intent. "At least one hero should be left in the world."

Chapter Fourteen

Battle of Pen Rhionydd
Start of the Second Looking Glass Campaign

Inside the zoo, Trystan had no idea what was happening in the rest of Pen Rhionydd.

He had no idea that Lyrssa Highstorm's forces had overrun the city and were burning the wingless supply depots. He had no idea that Uther's forces were retaliating with bombs and guns. He had no idea which side was winning or losing or if it even mattered. Even later, he didn't know all that happened outside the cage that held him.

But he recalled *exactly* what the other gryphons in the zoo did in their last moments.

He carried it all with him, using the memories to help guide him for the rest of his life. Bits and pieces of it would return to him at odd moments, letting him know he was on the right track. The gryphons who raised him were *always* with him. They were his clan.

Even Fisher.

"Do you know why Uther locked us up in here, boy?" Fisher got to his feet and hobbled closer to Trystan. "It wasn't to preserve our species, or whatever that plaque out there says." He waved a disparaging hand to the sign on the front of the cage, which described the "Primitive Peoples Exhibit" to visitors. "No. It's because he wants our secrets."

"We don't know where the Looking Glass Pool is." Trystan argued. "Why would he...?"

"It's in Atlantis." Fisher hissed, cutting him off. "That is where our people built Listeneise. Inside of that building is our oldest holy site. The first temple. Uther knows some of that, which is why he's burning *all* of our temples. He's looking for the secrets hidden in the first one. He won't find them, though." His eyes were sly. "I made sure of that."

Trystan tilted his head, not knowing what to believe. Fisher wasn't an entirely reliable source of information. Sometimes he talked to the grass. "You've been to this place?

"I've been everywhere. I've seen fire that lives and horses that swim. I've seen statues older than time, in fields of the stony dead. I've peered into the Looking Glass Pool." He leaned down, crouching next to Trystan, his bones creaking. "And it looked back at me."

Trystan blinked.

"I couldn't go into the pool to get the graal, though. Oh no. It would have killed me, for sure." He shook his head. "It wasn't my mission. I'm not the *ya'lah*. No one is."

Trystan's heart sank. "No one?"

"No one is enough." The old man's head tilted at a slightly-wrong angle. "Count higher."

"Huh?"

"All of Atlantis is below the sea, you know." Fisher was getting spacey again, losing his grip on the real world. That happened a lot. "It was an accident that I found Listeneise. The voices of dead gryphons spoke to me that day. Showed me a path. Told me to *leave* a path, so he can follow it to the graal."

Trystan was reluctantly fascinated now. Fisher said many strange things, but this tale was actually pretty good. "What kind of path?"

"I drew it all out on a few maps and hid them in foreign libraries, far from Uther's reach. Maps go in libraries. Smart people go in libraries and look at them, even with wizards around. And a shield, just as the voices told me..." He stopped. "Or '*her*.' Not just '*him*.' I said 'him,' but it could be 'her.' Any gender can be a *ya'lah*." He nodded, like that all made sense. "'Them.' I left a path for *them* to follow." His head tilted, at a strange angle. "Yes. In the end, it will be them."

"You just said there was no *ya'lah*." Trystan argued. "Were you wrong?"

"I'm never wrong." Fisher sounded insulted. "My mate was a *ya'lah*. She died defending our children and our clan. Then, they died, too. That was seventy-two years ago, before the Wingless War.

She was the one who spoke to me the clearest, that day over the water. It's why I knew to listen. I remembered her voice, even after such a long time..." He trailed off and stared at nothing for a moment.

"I remember my mother's voice." Trystan said quietly. "She used to sing to me."

Fisher jolted himself out of his memories. "When my *ha'yan* died, I started traveling everywhere, looking for gems and magic. People say I was obsessed, but that wasn't it. I just had nothing else to do. No bright hopes or true path." His eyes went wide. "A ghost!"

Trystan glanced around. "A ghost?" Fisher was always talking about ghosts, but Trystan never saw them. "Where?"

"Right before you. *I'm* a ghost. Without dreams, people become ghosts, boy. They're dead in a living world." His milky eyes met Trystan's. "Don't be like me."

Trystan was slightly disappointed by the lack of a poltergeist haunting them. "Okay." He agreed distractedly. "So, if there's no *ya'lah*, what's the point of anyone searching for the graal with your maps? It won't do them any good, even if they find it. Only the *ya'lah* can break the curse."

Fisher ignored that logic, stuck on his tangent about ghosts. "Find a dream and follow it, boy. And when you're lost and your dream follows you...? Tell it not to look at the horizon. Look straight *down*." He slowly pointed at the ground and Trystan's eyes followed the gesture, half-expecting to see an island appear beneath them.

The whole exchange made very little sense, even when Trystan reflected on it later, but it would see him locked in prison for three years.

Once Uther and Marcus realized that Trystan was the last one alive from the zoo, everything would change. They would inadvertently kill Fisher before he could lead them to Atlantis, evidence of his travels uncovered long after the Battle of Pen Rhionydd. They would reason that Trystan might harbor Fisher's secrets. They were right. Rather than kill Trystan outright when they captured him, they would be determined to learn everything that the old man had said. But, even when they tossed him in prison, Trystan would never tell them any of this conversation. He gave Uther *nothing* of his clan, even when he'd seen no value in Fisher's words.

He would one day tell Galahad, though.

"Trystan," Elaine landed beside them, resolve lighting her face, "we must speak, child."

"Fisher says no one is the *ya'lah*." Trystan reported, not wanting to believe it. "Do you think that's so, Elaine?"

She flashed the old man a frown. "You told him that?"

"It's true!"

She shook her head. "We do not have time for this nonsense."

"This is the only time we have left." Fisher scoffed. He got to his feet and limped back over to the tree. "The last time for any of us." He settled down against the trunk, not perturbed by their fate. "It's a good day to die, yes?"

"Not for Trystan, it isn't. He has other days ahead." Elaine petted the top of Trystan's head, as she spoke. "We are going to get him free of this place."

"But, I want to be with you." Trystan protested. "I don't want to go out there." The world beyond the walls of the enclosure was foreign to him, now.

"This is not your path, Trystan." Elaine's hand cupped his cheek. "Your path is long and important and far from here. You have stories left to tell. Lives left to touch."

The *booming* sounds outside were getting progressively louder.

The other gryphons landed on the floor of the cage, like there was nothing else to observe outside the glass of the dome. As Trystan watched, they began hacking off their warrior braids with the rock-edged tools they'd created, just in case they ever needed weapons. Warriors never cut their braids, so all their hair was thick and over a foot long.

What was happening?

"I don't want to leave." Trystan repeated, a little wildly. "Don't make me leave."

Elaine began weaving the braids together. "Ban, speak with him." She urged. Her blonde hair was short, now. It looked wrong.

This was *wrong*.

Ban came over and scooped Trystan up. "You have to be strong, child." His thumb traced down the center of Trystan's face from his forehead to his nose. "You are likely the last of your clan. You must survive."

Trystan's arms wrapped around his neck, holding tight. "*You* are all my clan."

"If the curse did not stand in between us, I would have adopted you, Trystan." Gryphons were generally born without emotions, but *something* shook Ban's voice. "I promise you, you would be my son. All of us would do the same. All of us claim you as our clan. And, in doing that, we vow to always keep you safe, no matter the cost. You must live now and be the last of *this* clan, too."

"That is too much for any child." Cador shook his head. "I lost one clan and it nearly broke me. Now *two* are taken from the boy? We send him out there with *no one*. We should consider alternatives."

Cador liked alternatives. It had been his job to find flaws in battle plans and he'd been excellent at it. Naysaying other's ideas fit perfectly with his pessimistic nature.

"What alternatives?" Lunette shouted back. She was of the Redcrosse Clan and they were not a people for strategizing. They preferred action. "Do you wish him to perish or to fight on?"

"I would rather die than leave you." Trystan interjected frantically.

Cador glanced at him, his eyes tracing over Trystan's face. "No." He said quietly. "That is *not* an alternative. Not ever."

Ban nodded. "You cannot stay here, Trystan. But, you will soon have two clans guiding you from the next world. Listen for us, yes? When you need us, we will be there."

"I need you *now*." Tears began escaping down Trystan's cheeks. He couldn't help it. "Elaine?" He looked over at her. "Don't make me do this without you. Don't make me be alone."

"I will be with you in memory. As your mother is. This is what she would ask me to do, were she here." The warriors' braids were braided again, Elaine's fingers flying over the tight knots, securing them into strong ropes. "Who has the sticks?"

Lunette came forward, carrying thick limbs from the tree. "They're getting closer."

Just as she said it, something exploded outside, shaking the very foundation of the zoo. Above them, the "unbreakable" dome cracked.

"*P'don!*" Cador bellowed, staring up at the ominous shards in disgust. "The wingless cannot even build a prison right. Fucking morons."

"I am happy to see this place fall to ruin." Lunette shot back. "I just wish we didn't have to be standing beneath it, when it happened."

"The glass will fall." Ywain intoned. He rarely spoke, so when he did all listened. "Ten minutes, at most."

"We have to get him out." Elaine tossed the ropes she'd made to Ywain and Olwen. "*Now*."

No one mentioned the tears in Trystan's eyes. Gryphons didn't cry. As he grew, Trystan would realize that they must have all suspected that he had wingless blood. They just didn't care. "I can't do this." He whispered.

"You can do *anything*." Lunette stabbed a finger at him. "Let no one tell you otherwise, not even yourself. We have raised you to be a great warrior and so you are."

Trystan nodded, the certainty of her words breaking through his panic.

Gryphons always raised children to believe in themselves, but Trystan *really* believed in himself. How could he not? His mother and father had showered their only child with endless attention. Any dream he had, they supported. His four doting grandparents all had high expectations that he would one day lead the Airbourne Clan. In their eyes, he'd been born for glory. At the zoo, the other gryphons protected him and patiently passed on what they knew. Different people came and went, but they all treated the youngest prisoner with care.

In a very real way, he was the only child of a dozen selfless parents.

Every day of his life, he'd been told that he was valued, and smart, and special. As a result, Trystan would always have a lot of faith in himself and his own abilities. Right then, he decided he could do something to save his clan. He could find a way. He knew it.

He just needed to think of a plan.

Ban ran a hand over his back. "Trystan, listen very carefully, alright? When you get outside, fly away, as fast and as far as you can go. Head west, towards the mountains. Stay off the roads. Look for leprechaun tracks to find food and water. Travel only at night. Take cover during the day and do not move until you see the lavender hues of twilight. Purple. *That* is your path home. Can you remember all that?"

Trystan nodded. "Yes."

And he did. Far in the future, Trystan would meet Galahad's violet eyes across the campfire and he'd remember Ban's words. He'd remember that purple was his path home.

"Do not talk to the wingless." Ban continued. "Do not approach them. Find a gryphon…"

"Not a Yellow Boot." Lunette interjected.

"…A gryphon who is *not* a Yellow Boot." Ban agreed. "Look at their shoes before you get close. When you find someone safe, tell them who you are and where you come from. They will protect you, until you are older. The innocent belong to all who would care for them. You will be safe with our kind."

"Not with the Yellow Boots." Lunette said again. "They are traitors, who deserve to die on pyres of their own bones."

"Not with the Yellow Boots." Ban repeated dutifully. He and Lunette were mates, so he tended to humor her bloodthirsty ideas.

Trystan swiped a hand over his cheek, still trying to think of a way out of this. "Maybe we can all get out through the dome." He pointed up at the spider-webbed glass. "We can break it and fly away together."

Except there was a heavy iron grate above the dome and it was still locked in place.

"We will attempt to escape, after you are gone." Elaine promised distractedly, but she didn't think it would work. Trystan could tell. She helped the men thread the braids around two of the bars that were right next to each other. "Okay, try it now." She fitted the large sticks into the loops, so the men could twist the branches and tighten the ropes. "It should act like a vice."

"Or a garrote." Olwen muttered. In his old life, he had done things he did not speak of, but he woke each night shouting from nightmares. "Ready more sticks, in case these break. Sometimes a garrote breaks." He turned his piece of wood in fast circles, twisting the rope, again and again.

Ywain did the same.

By the tree, Fisher began reciting the gryphon death prayer. You only said it during your final battle and the words were terrifying for Trystan to hear. He'd heard his grandmother saying them, just before she killed three of the wingless and the Yellow Boots had slaughtered her. More bombs were going off, so loud that they hurt Trystan's ears. He could smell a fire close by. Something burning its way towards them.

It was too much. All of it. He was trying to be brave, but he wasn't sure what to do.

He covered his ears and hummed the song his mother had often sung to him, trying to block it all out, so he could think of a plan. Trystan hoped that the other gryphons' efforts would fail and he could just stay where he was. That would be the *best* plan. Only here, in the care of his clan, seemed safe.

"All will be well." Ban's chin rested on Trystan's hair, his voice comforting. He had been a holy man, once. A *fennix*. One who accepted that you sometimes had to rise from the ashes of unfair events and press forward on a new path. "You will have a new clan to care for, one day. You will find a *ha'yan* and live a life filled with light."

"When you choose a mate, select a heroic one." Lunette told

Trystan, but her eyes were on Ban. "They are a rare breed, but well worth the hunt."

"Yes." Ban agreed quietly, staring back at her. "Even at the end, you will stand beside them with pride and know you hold... *everything*."

Even through his desperation, Trystan took that advice to heart. He would never settle for less than Ban and Lunette's quiet pledges of devotion. He would wait until he looked at someone and believed the man was a hero.

The rope braids were strong and the gryphons' resolve was stronger. Using their jury-rigged winch, they were able to pry two of the cage's iron bars apart. The iron bent, slowly but surely, until a hole was forged. A few precious inches with nothing blocking the path.

"Can he fit through that?" Olwen demanded, panting from exertion. His strange eyes measured the distance. They were the yellow of an eagle's and saw just as much. "I think he'll fit."

"He'll fit or I'll rip the goddamn bars off with my bare hands." Elaine would do anything to shield the child she cared for. When he met Gwen, decades later, Trystan would recall this moment and he'd see Elaine in his sister's determination to protect Avalon. "Trystan is getting out of here. He *will* fly free." She looked over at Ban. "It's time."

Trystan clung tighter to the man, dreading what was about to happen.

"You will find a new place to belong." Ban promised again, carrying Trystan towards the small opening. "But, remember us, yes? Remember both your clans and the lessons we taught you. Take what you know and learn more. Your new clan will need you, as we have. You will have to protect them, with your strength and your knowledge."

Trystan didn't doubt that, but he knew he had to protect *this* clan first.

Trystan swallowed and steeled his will. Staying here wouldn't work. He had to come up with a better plan. Something to get them all out. To *stop* this. The other gryphons were touching his face. Saying good-bye. He didn't want to say good-bye. Everything was a daze to him. His first clan had been ripped from him and now he was losing another.

He had to fix this.

Ban handed him to Elaine, who held him against her, for a long moment. "Go, Trystan." She murmured into his hair. "When you are older, tell my tales to a child that you care for, yes? You must carry them for me, now."

No. He would rewrite this tale. He would save them.

Trystan began squeezing through the narrow opening between the bars. The others were helping him. Pushing him and yanking on the bars, maneuvering his small wings so they fit. Forcing him out of the cage through sheer willpower.

And then he was on the ground, outside the Primitive People's Exhibit, staring back at them.

Trystan gaped around, shocked to be standing there. He had not been outside of the cage in so long that he'd forgotten what anything else even looked like. Seeing the world from this new, wingless perspective seemed... wrong. Looking at the others, while he stood apart was *wrong*. A huge part of him just wanted to sit down and wait for the zookeeper to let him back into the enclosure.

Except, he couldn't do that. It was all up to him to save his clan, now. He couldn't let them down.

"*Go*, Trystan." Elaine repeated firmly, gripping the bars that still caged her. "Don't hesitate. *Run*."

Trystan took a step backwards, away from her. "I'll be back for you all." He promised.

And then he ran.

Chapter Fifteen

All gryphons are liars. How many times do I have to say it?

They don't have emotions. Without emotions, you don't know Good from Bad, right from wrong, truth from lies. That's why, when people come crying to me saying, "Oh, noes, you guys treated the gryphons worse than animals," I answer, "Damn right we did!"

Why?

Because animals are *better* than gryphons! Animals have emotions. Gryphons are unfeeling demons.

"Stopping the Savages" Podcast
Sir Dragonet of Camelot- Former Troubadour of King Uther and Host of the Program

The Town's Hotel- Edge of the Wilds

"This is the stupidest thing I've ever done." Trystan decided, gesturing around the hideous hotel room. "And, since I met you, most everything I've done has been stupid."

Galahad disregarded his grumbling. He had the map spread out on the faded bedsheet, next to the silver shield he'd taken from the tomb. The strange writing on each of them was similar. Not quite gryphon, but also not quite *not* gryphon. He was guessing it was an old dialect of their people.

There were a few words from the common language on the map, acting as translations for some of the foreign writing. Using those, he was attempting to make out what the engravings on the shield said. He didn't have a particular reason for wanting to decipher it, except the whispers of the dead gryphons seemed to think it was a good idea.

Luckily, Galahad liked playing with codes. For fun, he'd developed one for marine biologists, based on soundwaves. Everyone hoped it would soon lead to direct communication with dolphins. That would be nice. Galahad was interested in what they had to say.

Also, translating the shield distracted him from lustfully staring at the man beside him. Trystan was lying on the floor, restlessly switching through channels on the static-y TV. He'd taken his shirt off and it was hard for Galahad to focus on anything else. The man was so beautiful.

"This town is still filled with terrible people." Trystan announced, not noticing the furtive, longing looks Galahad was sending his way. "We may have gotten rid of the Grundys, but many more remain. They will no doubt attack us during the night. When they inevitably arrive, you *will not* complain at me as I slay them, understand? I do not wish to hear it."

"We're not going to slay the townsfolk, Trys, because they're not going to attack. We just freed their town from Solomon. They're very grateful."

The town did indeed seem pleased that the Grundys were gone. They had been celebrating all day, the elves frolicking in the streets and the bars passing out free drinks. It was heartening to have such a positive impact on a community.

"I think we should help this town --like-- build a factory or something." Galahad decided. "In the future, that would give them an independent livelihood and help keep them free of tyrants."

Trystan fixed him with a flat look.

"Just a small factory." Galahad promised.

Trystan's eyes rolled towards the ceiling and he went back to watching the TV.

Galahad decided to take that as a "maybe."

"It was a very stupid day." Trystan opined again. "The only useful accomplishment was buying you a coat."

"That was very thoughtful of you." Galahad agreed. "But I don't need a coat..."

"You do need a coat."

Galahad kept talking. "...And this *particular* coat is filled with down. I'd really rather a vegan alternative. I only want to wear clothing that's ethically sourced."

"I *have* feathers. They are warm. Letting you freeze to death would not be ethical, so you will wear a warm coat. The end."

Galahad hesitated at that firm summation. Shit. Trystan *did* have feathers. That kind of gave him the moral authority in the debate. "I promise you, I won't freeze." He tried. "Really."

Trystan didn't even bother to answer that assertion. "And now we must stay here, at this god-awful establishment, where you will undoubtedly contract a horrible disease from the filth. Then Gwen will blame me for not properly caring for you."

The hotel *was* pretty horrible. It smelled like decay and rodents. The rooms all opened onto a dirt courtyard, filled with trash and scorpions. As far as Galahad could tell it didn't even have a name. Whatever industry the town developed, it was not going to be in hospitality.

"It does not help matters that you requested *one* room with *one* bed." Trystan continued. "I told you not to do that, even as you did it. You do not listen."

"I like rooms with one bed." Galahad said, straight-faced. "Two beds crowd the space."

"You think this is a joke?"

"No. I think you're funny, a lot of the time, though." Galahad said honestly. He leaned against the headboard, at ease with the world. "Speaking of us sharing this room... Are you ready to say 'yes' to having sex, yet? Because this *does* seem like a great opportunity."

He could hear Trystan's teeth grinding together. "Once you start down some paths, you cannot return, knight. I will not *let* you return. So, you should take time to think it through, before you continue asking me to say 'yes.' Be very sure."

"I *have* thought it through."

In the single second it took Galahad to look at Trystan in the pig village, he'd thought it all through carefully. ...And come to the simple conclusion that he was head-over-heels in love with the man.

Nothing was going to change that. Not even Trystan's grumpiness. The two of them were a perfect fit, as far as Galahad was concerned. Trystan needed some more time to realize their connection, but he was already starting to crack. He'd called Galahad a "hero" after the fight with the Grundys. Galahad *wasn't* a hero, of course. Trystan was the only hero left and everyone with eyes could see it. But if Trystan was blind enough to think Galahad might be heroic, too, even for a second... Well, that was a really optimistic sign for Galahad's seduction of the man.

"Some things are just fate, Trys. Accept it."

Trystan went back to glowering at the TV. "I do not know why I even talk to you. It is impossible to use logic with someone who has none."

Galahad smiled at the gryphon-y pouting. If Trystan had *really* wanted a different room, he just would've gotten one. His protestations were just Trystan being Trystan. Completely at ease, Galahad absently whistled a little tune as he worked on translating the map.

Trystan's head snapped around to stare at him. "My mother used to sing that song."

Galahad's eyebrows went up in surprise and pleasure. Trystan had never spoken to him about his mother before, so this was more progress in their relationship. "Yeah?"

"It is a gryphon hymn." Trystan watched him closely. "A song of our gods. Very few people would know it, now. Where did you hear it?"

Galahad's enthusiasm for the topic vanished. The voices of the dead gryphons had been humming the song. *That's* how he heard it. "I didn't know the song was sacred. It's just been playing in my head."

Trystan kept staring at him, like he was trying to read his mind.

Galahad cleared his throat, eager to change the subject. He hunted for something else to say. "Do you think trees sleep?" He asked randomly. "They're alive, right? So, do they need to rest and dream, sometimes?"

Trystan arched a brow.

Galahad winced, because that question had been weird even for him. "Sorry."

"Hearing about the workings of your mind does not bother me. Even when you use your ideas to distract and confuse and not answer my questions. It is when you *don't* speak of your thoughts that I brace for trouble."

"I tell you everything." He paused. "...Mostly."

Trystan gave a derisive snort. "No, you don't. You show the world what they want to see, even if it is not entirely truthful. This includes me."

Galahad was hurt by that claim. "I don't lie to you, Trystan."

"No. But you share nothing that you don't choose to share. And you do not choose to share most of the core of you. Trying to catch hold of you is like grasping mist."

It was hard for Galahad to connect to people. It always had been. He tried to give them what they wanted, but they always seemed to slip away. This one time, it was vital that Galahad keep someone with him, though. Without Trystan, he would be lost.

He thought for a beat, figuring out what to do next. "What do you want me to share?"

"Do you still intend to have dinner with your 'fan' in St. Ives?" Trystan asked from out of nowhere.

"Yes." Galahad frowned, surprised by the question. What was going on in his head, now?

Trystan's finger jabbed down on the remote key with unnecessary force. "Fine."

Galahad's eyebrows shot up, interpreting what that surly "fine" really meant. Trystan was jealous. That was so cute! "Trys, *I have no interest in Mordy*." He made the words very clear. "I've never met the guy and he already *has* a husband. He's mentioned that before."

"This Mordy person wants to have sex with you. I guarantee it."

"No, he doesn't." Galahad scoffed. "Even if he did, I'd just politely decline. Mordy seems like a nice guy, but I'm only meeting him so we can get into St. Ives. He can open the gate." He arched a brow. "That's why you're even here with me, in the first place, isn't it? Because your goal is to go kill some guy who lives there and I'm your ticket into the town."

"Of *course* you try to make this lunacy seem like a favor for me."

"It's not a *favor*. We had a deal."

Trystan shook his head like Galahad was being ridiculous and clicked to another channel without even stopping to see what was on the last one. "Fine." It didn't sound fine.

"You're worried over nothing." Galahad persisted, wanting to reassure him.

"Gryphons do not worry. We simply foresee likely disasters." Trystan muttered. "Do not discuss your treasure map with Mordy, either. You remember I told you it isn't safe, yes?"

"Mordy's already rich. I doubt he's going to steal it."

"If you think any of your kind is ever rich enough, you do not understand them."

"*I'm* rich enough."

"You have no money, at all. What wasn't confiscated, you spent on unicorns or gave away so hellhounds in pet shelters could have new rubber balls."

"Oh, that's because hellhounds love playing catch. They're very playful animals, but their six rows of fangs are hard on toys. If I don't get them replacements every day, it will break their little hearts. I had to set up a trust for it, before I was banished."

No one could sigh like Trystan. It was deep, and extended, and theatrically long-suffering. The man really should be an actor. "Anyway, since you bring up this mission of yours..."

"Wait what? *I* brought it up? Jesus, are we back to that?"

He ignored the interruption. "Why have you not spoken of your map recently?"

Galahad hesitated, wary now. "You said you didn't want to talk about it."

"I *don't* want to talk about it. But I also don't want you silently plotting about it."

"I'm not 'plotting.' You always say I'm plotting."

"And I am always right. It is a burden, at times."

"I've just been keeping the planning to myself. That's not plotting. It's what I'm *supposed* to do, according to our agreement." Galahad wasn't sure where this was coming from, but now he felt attacked for following the rules. "We agreed that we wouldn't interfere with each other's missions, remember?"

Trystan didn't seem to like the indisputable facts of that argument. His jaw ticked, his eyes on the television. "Fine." This time the "fine" was brooding and unconvinced.

"Look, I get you into a lot of crazy shit." Galahad assured him, still trying to fix whatever was bothering the man. "If I were you, I wouldn't want to help me, either."

And that was probably for the best. At first, Galahad had liked the idea of becoming allies. Honestly, he *still* wanted that. Trystan was smart and capable and a gryphon. All of that would be a big help. But, now that he knew Trystan better, Galahad also worried what Trystan might uncover if he joined the quest. He asked Galahad questions with only terrible answers, his brown eyes seeing far too much. Galahad couldn't lie to him, but there were things that he preferred Trystan never, ever know.

"I did not say that I wouldn't help you." Trystan muttered.

Galahad arched a brow at that revisionist history. "You didn't?"

"No. I will *always* offer you assistance. It is my duty." Trystan nodded righteously, as if he'd been begging to be included this whole time and Galahad was cruelly excluding him.

"You *specifically said* you didn't want to help! Multiple times, Trystan."

"Well, I have changed my mind." Trystan shot back. "If you require assistance, *I* will do it. Not Mordy." He sounded legitimately angry, now. "It is *my* duty to care for you, Galahad. No one else's. *Mine*. Gwen gave you into my keeping, until we return to Camelot. I told you this."

Galahad ran all that through the Trystan-translator he was developing in his head. Trystan defined himself through caring for others. He didn't use the word "duty" like most people did. For him, it was more like a calling. Trystan had apparently decided that "caring" for Galahad was some right that he'd earned. He saw it as a rejection when Galahad didn't accept his gryphon-y, overbearing-ish, usually begrudging help.

It hurt all the feelings that Trystan wasn't supposed to have.

That was the last thing Galahad wanted. He would sooner refight the War than make this man unhappy. He sighed and gave up being annoyed at Trystan's stubbornness. "You've *already* caught hold of me, Trys." It was the stark truth. "I know that, even if you don't."

Trystan's gaze flicked over to him and stayed there.

"I would like for us to *trust* each other." Galahad pressed. "For each of us to trust in the other's abilities and choices. Do you think that's possible?"

Trystan considered that idea for a long moment. "Fine."

"Good." Galahad marked that cautious "fine" as agreement. "Now, there's a mural I have to see. My map says it's in the Pellinore Mountains. I'm going up there to find it."

Trystan sat up straighter. "And you just mention this intention *now?*" He demanded, ready to get angry all over again. "How did you plan to hide the fact we were diverting north for three days, into the depths of the Wilds?"

"I planned to ride off and do it alone, obviously. I would've been back, though."

"I *knew* you were plotting."

"Do you want to argue about this some more?" Galahad challenged. "Or do you just want to skip to the part where you come see the mural *with* me?"

Trystan forestalled his brewing rant, looking surprised. "You are inviting me on this futile side-trip?"

"Yes. So long as you promise to let me handle the important part, where we get into the cave and see the mural, you and I can do this together."

Trystan considered that idea for an even *longer* moment. Galahad waited.

"Fine." This time the "fine" was mollified, like Trystan's non-worries had been soothed. "I suppose we can spare a few days."

Trystan's tension relaxed, now that he was being included. Galahad was satisfied. This trip was going to be complicated, but what else could he do? Making Trystan feel better was worth the headache. The man was worth everything.

Trystan stretched out in a more territorial way. Taking up space, like everything in the room --from the carpet, to the lamps, to Galahad-- belonged to him. "This map of yours is probably a fake. You know this, yes? I would not like to see you disappointed when you reach the end of your mission and find nothing."

"It's real. I'm sure of it."

"And your surety is based on what, exactly?"

"Somebody told me. Somebody I believe."

"You would believe a witch offering you a poisoned apple." Trystan switched to a new station. The television only got so many channels, so it wasn't going to do him much good. "When this treasure is revealed to be the fantasy of some depraved liar, I will not say I told you so. But," he shrugged again, "I told you so."

"I appreciate your restraint." Galahad told him straight-faced.

Trystan nodded, like he was being the soul of consideration. "And I think trees know more of the world than we do." He decided, like he'd been mulling Galahad's strange question over and had finally settled on an answer. "They sleep, and dream, and see all paths, which is why they are so patient in their growing."

Galahad's mood lightened. God, he was just insanely attracted to every single part of Trystan. Even his eyelashes were perfect. "You really can lie on the bed, you know. If you're not ready for us to have sex, I can wait. Honestly. I promise not to touch you."

"It's not *you* touching *me* that I'm worried about." Trystan grumbled.

"Yeah?" Galahad grinned at the admission. "Well, you have *incredible* self-control around me, so I'm sure that won't be a problem, either. I bet you can last at least ten minutes, before I talk you out of your pants."

Trystan's eyes stayed fixed on the TV. "You would lose that

bet."

Galahad blinked at the dry remark and then laughed in delight. Trystan's mouth absolutely, one hundred percent, no-mistake-about-it curved into a tiny smile at the happy sound. It was impossible and beautiful and *real*. Trystan could smile. Trystan could do anything.

"I am crazy about you." Galahad said sincerely, dazzled by the man.

Brown eyes glowed warm, even as Trystan shook his head in frustration. "None of this is helping me to stay down here and..." He trailed off suddenly, his attention fixed on the screen. "Is that man supposed to be you?"

Galahad glanced at the television and felt his heart drop. That goddamn unauthorized, completely fictitious, made-for-TV account of the Battle of Legion was on. The one he would have sued every goddamn person involved for making, had he not worried that it would draw more attention to the goddamn thing. It was a goddamn lie from the opening title screen to the end credit crawl.

"Turn it off." He said, his amusement gone.

Trystan ignored that, watching the horror show play out in badly-scripted detail.

"We must save our men!" The jackass who played King Uther cried to the troops. He was thinner and younger than King Uther had been, with a cheap-looking crown on his head. "Don't let the savages win! Push them back for Camelot!"

A screaming mass of gryphons descended on the knights. Hundreds of extras, all with fake wings attached to their backs and raging with out-of-control hatred. The smaller force of King's Men was eviscerated, the ruthless gryphons hacking them apart in grisly close-ups.

Trystan's head tilted, taking it all in.

"Sire!" The son of a bitch portraying Galahad bellowed. "They are overtaking our lines!" Real-Galahad tried to be a positive person, but there was simply nothing Good to say about the dyed-blond asshole playing him. Nothing at all. "Bedivere has already perished, bravely trying to save young ones from this hoard!"

"Bedivere!" Fake Uther screamed into the sky. "*Nooooooo!* He was the best of us all!"

The music swelled and misty flashbacks of fake-Bedivere glistened across the screen. The fake-warfare paused for some reaction shots of fake-knights weeping over the fake-hero. They weren't alone. Back in reality, all of Camelot had mourned the Martyr of Legion.

Galahad's lips flattened together.

"The barbarians will destroy us all, if we don't do something drastic." Phony-Galahad continued, dramatically resting a hand on his forehead. He was a terrible actor. Utterly talentless. Galahad detested him.

"Turn it off, Trys." He said again, unable to look away from the abysmal spectacle.

Trystan didn't seem to hear him, just as mesmerized by the dishonesty and bad production values.

"You'll never defeat us, knight!" The scenery-chewing, scantily-clad villainess meant to be Lyrssa Highstorm shrieked with maniacal glee. The actress shook the bars of her rickety prop cage and was lucky when the cardboard sides held together. "It's too late for your wingless kind! We will destroy Camelot and all of you with it!"

"Never!" Fake-Galahad roared. "We knights shall triumph, for we follow a code of true justice!" He raised his plastic sword over his head and the shaky camera captured the heroic set of his jaw. The grandeur of his cause. The *rightness* of his mission. "Fire the Rath!"

"Turn it off!" Galahad reached down to grab the remote from Trystan's hand. "Turn the fucking thing *off!*" He slammed his finger down on the power button and the TV went blessedly silent. He closed his eyes, breathing hard.

For a long moment they sat in silence.

"That shit is even worse than your singing puppet show." Trystan said thoughtfully.

Galahad's eyes popped open, looking down at him in surprise.

"Did you not wish to be in this program, knight? Is that why they hired such an ill-favored man to portray you?"

"I would *never* be in that movie." It was a snarl. "My shows were all focused on teaching children about compassion and truth. That," he pointed to the screen, "is a goddamn travesty."

"Lyrssa was there, though. That part was truthful. Did you *truly* see her?"

Galahad blew out a long breath, trying to calm down. He wanted to be a peaceful man, but some days it was hard to remember why he bothered. "Yes."

"I never met the Queen. I have not even met anyone who met her. All she fought beside are gone."

"That's because we killed them all."

Trystan didn't respond to that bleak comment. He seemed

fascinated by the idea of Galahad interacting with the gryphon queen. "You are one of the few who would recall her, now. What was she like? Was she as fearsome a warrior as they say?"

Galahad looked back at the blank TV screen, remembering everything as it had truly been and wishing he didn't. "You followed the right leader, Trystan. You were on the right side, with the right leader, and the right warriors. The gryphons were so brave. The better fighters, by far."

"I do not think anyone is a better fighter than you, knight."

Galahad slowly shook his head. "The warriors could have escaped, but they stayed and faced us, because of the children and the elderly. They were protecting the innocent." Galahad's sense of justice had never recovered from Legion and the unfairness of it all. The fact that Good didn't triumph. "*I* should have lost. *I* was the one on the wrong side."

"Yes." Trystan agreed quietly. "Perhaps, though, for some men, it's easier to lose on the right side, than win on the wrong one."

Galahad rubbed his eyes, refocusing on the original question. "Lyrssa was at Legion, but that damned movie was right about her being in a cage, for most of it. Perceval had captured her days before, while I was on reconnaissance." Yellow Boots had helped him, under direct orders from Uther. Galahad had not been involved in that, which had no doubt been the king's intention. "She didn't participate in the fighting. Nearly everyone was dead within minutes, so I doubt she could have done much. In the end, she got free and flew off with Uther and..." He trailed off with a shrug. "I never saw her, again."

No one had.

"Oh." Trystan seemed disappointed not to hear stories of his lost queen, but he nodded. "This makes sense."

The conversation could've ended right there.

Galahad knew it was smarter to let the topic drop. Legion was a poison, threatening to infect everything he was trying to build with Trystan. There was no need to tell Trystan anything he didn't need to know. The man had plans of his own in St. Ives, that didn't include Galahad. Since no one in the history of creation had ever changed their plans for Galahad, it was a really lousy sign for their future. He knew that and he was a typically optimistic guy. It would be better to work on *that* problem, rather than creating new ones.

But he also wanted to make Trystan happy and tell him about his queen. Wanted to give him more than just that surface answer, because Trystan had had a point before: Galahad kept a lot of his deepest thoughts to himself. That wasn't how a true relationship worked. If he ever wanted Trystan to open up with him, he needed to open up to Trystan. At least a little.

He had to give Trystan some trust.

"I spoke to Lyrssa." Galahad said before he could talk himself out of it.

Trystan looked at him in astonishment, shocked by that news and the fact that Galahad had offered it. "You did? When?"

Galahad shifted, still wary of this whole topic. "During the massacre. I spoke to her, through the bars of her cage."

Trystan sat up straighter, again. "What did she say?" He was engrossed, now.

"She screamed at us that there were children in the village. She begged the knights to stop firing." Galahad handed the remote back to him, not meeting his eyes. "They didn't listen."

"Anything else?"

"She tried to decide if I was a lunatic."

"A debate I regularly engage in, as well."

Galahad paused. "And she told me that darkness wasn't the path."

Trystan's eyebrows soared. "She talked of your *path?*" He echoed incredulously. "That is a very important thing to speak of, knight. I told you, it is vital to our beliefs. What did she say *exactly?*"

"'Only light protects the innocent.'" Galahad quoted without hesitation. "'Only light can save us. Choose Light.'" The words would stay with him forever.

Trystan blinked, seemingly struck speechless.

"She said she saw my path as clearly as her own." Galahad stared off at nothing, reliving it all in his head. "She said I should fight for something better."

Trystan studied Galahad, like he was trying to see into his memories. "Why did she tell all this to you?" He asked, sounding mesmerized.

"I don't know."

"There must've been a reason for her to say such a thing, at such a moment."

Galahad was uncomfortable with this whole tangent. "She didn't give me a reason."

Trystan wasn't giving up. "Knight, her words were a *seywa*. A...uh..." he hunted for the right translation, "a hopeful teaching. A *blessing* for you. Why would Lyrssa give *seywa* to an enemy soldier? What did she see in you that day?"

Galahad took a deep breath and gave in. "Darkness."

"Darkness?"

"Yes." He could never lie to this man, even when he wanted to. "There's darkness in me. There always has been. During the fighting, it came out. I *let* it out. Mindless rage and killing. She saw it." Maybe the dead gryphons did too. Maybe that was why they spoke to him. They were trying to keep him from becoming a monster. ...Or maybe he was crazy.

Trystan instantly shook his head. "No."

"*Yes*. *That's* what Lyrssa saw. She was trying to stop me from being lost forever, I think. But I was already damned."

Trystan was still shaking his head. Refusing to see the truth. "No. You think I don't feel the pull of darkness waiting to swallow me, as well? *All* warriors sense that abyss, regardless of which side they fight on. You got closer to the edge than the rest of us and what you saw there frightened you, but it's *not* inside of you. You fight it back each time it threatens. I am alive today, because you held it at bay at the Battle of Flags." Trystan nodded with total confidence. "You will continue to do so."

That was one of the longest speeches Galahad had ever heard him make. He frowned at Trystan, a little annoyed that he was so self-assured. "You seem pretty confident in my sanity. Too bad I'm not."

"It is very clear to me. You are a *ya'lah*."

"What's a *ya'lah*?" Trystan had said the word before.

"A *ya'lah* is a champion of legend." Fathomless brown eyes met his. "Someone who gives all they have in the service of others. Someone who does glorious and courageous things, for glorious and courageous reasons. Someone who stands against wrong, no matter the consequences. Someone who protects the innocent. Always."

Galahad blinked.

"*Ya'lahs* are born different." Trystan continued. "They think and act in exceptional ways. They are the guardians of their people and the world. The heroes that all gryphons aspire to be."

Galahad sighed, wishing he didn't have to tell the truth. Wishing he could pretend to be the hero that Trystan wanted. "Trys, I'm so sorry. You're wrong about me. I'm not special, at all. Can't you see that?"

Trystan arched a brow. "I take you home to my clan, knight. If I did not see you clearly... you would not go."

There was nothing else Trystan could have said that would have reassured Galahad so fast. Trystan was *fanatically* protective of his family. He would never, *ever* endanger them by exposing them to someone drowning in darkness. Someone who couldn't be redeemed. If Trystan looked at him and saw something special, maybe there was hope for Galahad's recovery. Hope that he could regain his honor one day and be a fully-functioning partner for the man he loved. Maybe, with Trystan beside him, he wasn't damned, after all.

Galahad gave him a dazzling smile. "Thank you, Trys. You're completely wrong about me being the *ya'lah*, but I feel better." Opening up a bit hadn't resulted in disaster. In trying to get Trystan to connect with him, Galahad now felt more connected to Trystan.

It was awesome!

Trystan's gaze traced over Galahad's face in something like resignation. "Let's turn the light off." He muttered. "It will be easier to stay down here, if I don't have to look at you."

"Well, you don't *have* to stay on the floor. Seriously, you're going to throw your back out. What if we agree to just innocently practice kissing on the bed and see where it...?"

Someone pounded on the door, cutting off Galahad's persuasive words. Both their heads swung towards it. Townspeople were outside, demanding entry.

"Crap." Galahad muttered, knowing what was coming next. "Don't say it."

Trystan arched a brow, perversely pleased to be proven right. "I told you so."

Chapter Sixteen

The first Looking Glass Campaign dragged on for years. Frustrated that he could not win by force, Uther called a meeting with Queen Lyrssa, claiming he wanted to forge a treaty.

Pledging that he wished to stop his war on the gryphon, if only Lyrssa would have words with him.

Promising peace.

It was a lie. All wingless are liars. I say this often, because it is true.

King Uther trapped Lyrssa in his castle and told her that she must reveal the location of the Looking Glass Pool or face his wrath.

But he had greatly miscalculated. The queen told him that the gryphons would never surrender the graal.

Even if we'd been able to reach it, we would never hand such a treasure over to evil.

How the Wingless War Happened
Skylyn Welkyn- Gryphon Storyteller

The Town's Hotel- Edge of the Wilds

"Gryphon!" An angry voice shouted from outside the hotel room. "We want to see the knight? We know you're holding him prisoner! Hand him over or we'll come in there and get him!"

Trystan grunted. "Shall I slay these men now or do you want to drag out their suffering with your 'reasoning' first?" He asked conversationally.

"Don't start." Galahad climbed off the bed. "I will deal with this." He stepped over Trystan, who was still lying on the floor, between the bed and door. "It'll be fine. Just try not to kill anyone, unless you have to."

"Life teaches that I *always* have to."

Galahad shook his head in exasperation. "And let me do the talking, okay? When you do the talking, things get depressing and violent." He headed over to the door and yanked it open. "Hello, gentlemen." He smiled determinedly at the assembled men. "Is there a problem?"

Eight of them were standing in the dilapidated courtyard, several carrying torches. Jesus, did people still make torches? Why? Where did they even find the time? Sometimes Galahad wondered if he was the only one with an actual plan for his life. Everybody else just seemed to be wasting their energy on shit that didn't matter.

"Sir Galahad, we're here to set you free." The largest of the men declared, he had a bushy red beard and a torch in his hand. "You saved our town from the Grundys and now we'll save you."

"That's thoughtful, but not necessary." Galahad blocked the entire doorway, positioning himself between the men and Trystan, in case the makeshift posse didn't want to listen to reason. "I'm actually..."

The bearded man cut him off. "We know that the gryphon is holding you here, forcing you to do God-only-knows what."

Galahad made a rueful face. "Mainly we're just watching TV, but I'm working on it."

The man ignored that attempt at humor, caught up in his dramatic spiel. Maybe he'd been practicing in his head. "Come with us now and we'll keep you safe from him. Our town will no longer be party to injustice."

"I fully support your new focus on social issues, but..."

"No one is taking my knight." Trystan interrupted flatly. He remained sitting on the ugly carpet, like he was too bored to bother standing up, but his eyes were watching everything. He leaned forward to glare at the men around Galahad's body. "*Leave.* While you can still walk." His voice was the stuff of nightmares and legends.

Four men took off running.

Galahad had to bite the inside of his cheek to keep from laughing. Only Trystan could half the number of enemy forces facing him without even getting to his feet.

"Cowards!" The bearded leader screamed after them.

Galahad cleared his throat and kept a firm smile on his face. "See the thing is, guys... I'm really happy here with Trystan. I don't need to be rescued. Thanks, though."

The leader of the posse glowered at Trystan. "You're making him say that, aren't you?"

Trystan was silent in a not-particularly-friendly way.

The bearded guy turned to Galahad. "He's making you say that, isn't he?"

"Trystan's never made me do anything. I'm usually the one forcing him into situations, actually. He's kind of a pushover."

Trystan gave a contemptuous scoff.

The bearded man didn't believe that honest assessment of their relationship, either. "Come with us, Sir Galahad. We'll save you from this demon!"

Galahad felt sorry for him. "This is *exactly* the kind of thinking that's kept our people apart for so long. Truly, I've been where you are, brainwashed by the propaganda, but it's all bullshit. The gryphons aren't all devils and the wingless aren't all heartless. And Trystan is *certainly* not a demon. The man is Good straight down to his soul."

Trystan stood up, which put a slight damper on Galahad's earnest praise. Huge feet thudded on the floor, his massive body rising up in one smooth, ominous movement. It was like watching a mountain come to life and start towards you, carrying an axe.

Galahad quickly started to ease the door closed, before he had to spend all night cleaning up a grisly crime scene. "So, I'm fine! See? I appreciate your concern, though. Really."

Beard-Guy put his foot down in the jam, stopping the door from closing. He was either brave, drunk, or stupid. Possibly all three. "If you're not being held against your will, why are you tied up?" He demanded, still not convinced.

Galahad glanced down at his bound wrists. "Oh... this?"

To be honest, he'd forgotten about the ropes. He was pretty

sure he could figure out a way out of them, if he needed to. He had a hundred-and-seventy-eight Knights' Academy Junior Survival Badges and one of them was for untying magical knots. But pointlessly securing him was such a quirky, harmless, Trystan-y thing to do that Galahad hated to disappoint him by escaping.

"Um…" His mind raced for a reasonable reason as to why Trystan tying him up and abducting him didn't really count as being tied up and abducted.

Nothing sprang to mind.

"No one. Is taking. My knight." Trystan repeated, spacing out each word. He dropped his axe so its handle was resting against the wall, right by his side.

His hands slammed onto the doorframe on either side of Galahad's head, his body positioned directly behind Galahad's and it was… awesome. Somehow protective and territorial, at the same time. His eyes stayed on the leader of the small group over Galahad's shoulder and, if Galahad hadn't already been crazy in love with Trystan, the total bad-ass-ness of the man would've won his heart.

Every single person in the rescue-mob took a step back.

Trystan watched them in the animalistic way of an eagle sighting prey. "My knight will be upset if I kill you all." He paused for a beat. "Don't make me upset my knight."

Another posse member stumbled away in terror.

Galahad never would've guessed that possessiveness would be a turn on, but Trystan's dominant stance behind him and the way he said "my knight" in that deep tone *really* worked for him. Tattooed arms were arranged so Galahad was surrounded without being touched. So there was no mistaking who he belonged to and where he was staying.

Galahad found himself leaning backwards, wanting to be even closer to Trystan's bare chest. His body brushed against Trystan, instinctively needing… more.

Trystan's fingers went white around the doorframe. He gave a low growl and moved forward slightly. Apparently, he wasn't worried about Galahad being upset by his erection, because the hardness was unmistakable and Trystan didn't seem to care if he felt it.

Wow. That was *awesome*.

Galahad's gaze went up to Trystan's chiseled profile, intrigued. "Adrenaline, again?" He whispered, wanting to soothe the man's temper, at least a little. Trystan always seemed to like that joke, although it made no sense for a gryphon to like *any* joke.

Trystan's chin very subtly rubbed against Galahad's hair in a caress. "No." The word was almost soundless. "This is all you."

Galahad suppressed another smile. "Just remember we're letting me deal with the guys reasonably." He whispered back.

Trystan's mouth shifted closer to Galahad's temple. "I say many stupid things around you, knight." His lips grazed against Galahad's skin. "But I don't ever recall saying anything *that* stupid."

Galahad swallowed. Trystan was pressed against his back, his perfect voice was in his ear, and the heat of his body was enveloping him, uniting them. It was the most erotic moment Galahad ever experienced.

Inspiration struck.

"I'm tied up for sex!" Galahad looked back to the leader of the gang and beamed. "Trys and I play bondage games."

Trystan's face snapped down to stare at him. The other three men blinked, like that was the last thing in the world they'd expected to hear. ...But no one was threatening bloodshed, anymore.

Galahad triumphantly nodded, pleased with himself. "Trystan and I are dating." He decided. "Exclusively. Right, Trys?"

Trystan's eyebrows compressed. "Think about what you're doing, Galahad." Whenever he used Galahad's actual name, you knew he was serious. "You are coming very close to claiming me and you cannot take that back."

"Claiming's that thing where you're made a part of my family, right?"

"A part of your clan. Yes." His voice was pitched low. "It is *very* important, in my culture. If you continue on this path, you are irrevocably pledging a part of yourself to me."

Galahad snorted. "Well, that happened --like-- four days ago."

Trystan regarded him with open mystification. As if he had no idea what to say.

"It's already done." Galahad translated with a shrug. "Sorry." He wasn't sorry. "I already claimed you. I didn't know you didn't know." It seemed obvious, so he wasn't sure why Trystan was surprised.

Trystan's lips parted. "You're really going to do this?" He sounded different. Almost vulnerable. "In front of these men, you're really going to claim me? Do you not understand what it means?"

"For the purposes of this conversation, I'm thinking it means you're mine."

Trystan's head tilted.

Galahad mimicked the gesture, pleased that he had the

upper hand. He liked winning. He felt his mouth curve into a triumphant smirk. "Or did you want us to date *other* guys?"

Trystan's eyes narrowed slightly at the challenge.

Galahad grinned at him. For once, having a little bit of Badness inside of him was kinda fun. "Yeah... Didn't think so." He taunted, cheerily.

"Be careful, knight." Trystan's eyes were intent. "I am a pushover with you, but I can also push *back*. And I have much more experience on this battlefield."

Trystan's hips shifted so his erection was in a *really* interesting spot and Galahad gave a choked gasp, caught off guard. Trystan had never done that before. *No one* had ever done that before and Trystan knew it. His gaze flew up to Trystan's, astonished that the other man was being so open about their connection, especially around other people.

Maybe it was *because* of the other people.

Maybe Trystan liked being publically claimed.

"Try to 'date' another male and see what happens." Trystan eased forward with the tiniest bit of pressure and Galahad forgot how to breathe. "See what happens to the Mordys of this world, if they touch you. See what I do to anyone else you look at with that shiny, taunting smile on your face. The man will survive only to linger on in never-ending pain. I promise you."

Holy *shit*. The possessiveness was seriously, *seriously* working for him. Galahad swallowed. Hard. "I don't want anyone else, Trys. I told you. There's only you."

"Good." Trystan arched a brow, calming at the instant agreement. "Continue telling them that you belong to me, then. For once, you're 'reasoning' makes sense."

"Um..." Galahad gave his head a shake and tried to concentrate. "Right." He turned back to the gaping men, hoping his voice was steady. "Like I said: It's Trystan and me against the world."

"Which might be fair odds, if you ever picked up a sword." Trystan muttered. One hand ran over Galahad's hair, like he just couldn't help himself. He let out a long sigh, his fingers tangling in the loose curls. "Fuck."

"You're dating a guy? A *gryphon* guy?" The bearded man blurted out at Galahad, finally seeming to catch up with what was happening. He tried to rearrange his thinking and it looked almost painful. "But you're a knight!"

"I was. Luckily, Trys is willing to overlook that."

Trystan made a sound that could only be called a snort of

amusement.

Galahad glanced at him with an arch look. "Emotionless" his ass.

Trystan quickly tried to cover the betraying sound. "Enough. The knight stays with me." Aggravated, sexually frustrated, and absolutely gorgeous, he dropped his hand from Galahad's hair and shot the gathered men a glare. "Do you plan to fight or leave? Decide. *Now*. Before I decide for you."

Two more men retreated into the night, leaving their bearded leader alone.

Galahad pretended not to notice. "Don't mind Trys. He's always moody." He told the man, who was looking a little confused and *more* than a little worried. Like he had no idea what his next step should be. Luckily, Galahad had a great idea. "Actually, I'm glad you're here. You seem like a very reasonable person. Are you the mayor of this town?"

The guy was visibly flustered. "The town doesn't have a mayor, anymore. The Grundys killed him."

"Well, as the former Captain of the King's Men, I'm going to appoint you the new mayor, then. Until we can set up a fair election." Galahad wasn't sure he could legally do that, but who was going to stop him?

"Can you do that?" Trystan demanded doubtfully. "I do not think you can do that."

"Well, we can check the rules and call the lawyers..." Galahad shrugged at the bearded guy, indicating what a long and drawn out process that would be. "But, my way would be so much more efficient. We have to get things moving, right? The town needs leadership."

"Sure." The guy bobbed his head. "We gotta move. Absolutely." He paused. "Where are we going?"

Trystan rolled his eyes.

Galahad tapped the bearded man on the chest with his index finger, like a recruiting officer offering a young cadet some grand new adventure. "We're going *forward*. And you're the only logical choice to take us there."

"I am?"

"He is?" Trystan asked at the same time.

"Of course! It's important that a community have someone responsible at the helm and I can tell you're a man who gets things done. I admire that."

The thwarted-savior looked fascinated, now. "Really?" He

tossed his torch away, like he thought it wouldn't be a good look for his new political career. Scorpions scattered. "You think I'm a leader?"

"You bet I do. Look how you rallied your men to rescue me. It was inspiring."

"His men fled." Trystan intoned sourly.

Galahad rose above that negativity. "What's your name?" He asked the bearded man.

"Uh, Ted."

"What do you know about sand, Ted?"

"Sand?" He seemed to wrack his brain for a moment. "Well, there's a lot of it on the ground around here."

"Exactly!" Galahad praised. "It's so perceptive of you to notice that potential."

Ted beamed. "I notice it all the time." He boasted. "It gets in my boots."

Trystan pinched the bridge of his nose and sighed dramatically.

"Now, Ted, the other day Trystan was telling me that there's a lot of strong magic, in this part of the world."

"I told you that, because it's true." Trystan put in, seeing a golden opportunity to list off potential dangers, again. "The spells out here are more primal and unpredictable. It will get worse as we move west and leave even this much 'civilization' behind." He waved a disparaging hand around the hotel. "You need to be careful and use your head. *That* was my point, knight. Although you seemed to have missed it, entirely."

Galahad ignored that last remark. "So you see, Ted, the sand in this desert is filled with magic. It's why the sandmen like it so much." Galahad was surprised that he was the only one who'd put that together. He'd been thinking about it since his experience in Medusa's tomb. "Now, we don't have their powers, so we can't make genuine sleeping sand. But, I was thinking maybe we could make lower-dose sleeping *potions* to help insomniacs."

"Lyrssa save me." Trystan groaned, seeing where this was headed.

Ted seemed baffled. "You wanna put people to sleep?"

"No. Well, *yes,* but only medicinally. We can refine the sand and sell it to pharmacies, all over the world. Lots of people would buy it. It can relax them. It's a whole industry, just waiting for the right man to develop it."

Trystan had heard enough. "*No*, knight." He shoved away from the doorframe. "I'm not paying for a factory. I don't care how shimmery your hair is." He flopped down onto the ancient carpet by the bed, again, slanting Galahad a frown. "And how the hell does your hair stay so shimmery, when you are forever without a hat to protect it?"

"With industry comes jobs and prosperity." Galahad told Ted, disregarding Trystan's complaints.

"There's not going to *be* an industry." Trystan insisted. "Why are you still talking about this?"

Galahad kept talking. He'd been the Knights' Academy's entire debate team and they'd never lost a championship. Even the year he'd had to argue against himself in the finals. "With prosperity comes less crime and more education. You see that, right, Ted?

"I guess. We could... buy books, maybe?" It sounded like a question.

"Books!" Galahad clapped his hands together like that was a genius idea. "I should have thought of that myself. We'll use profits from the factory to buy books. Great thinking."

Ted seemed pleased with himself. "I got --like-- four books at home."

"I'm *not* building this shithole town a factory or buying them books." Trystan repeated a little desperately. "You're wasting your time with this little play you're preforming, knight. I am unmoved."

That sounded like a dare.

"It's amazing how you're willing to confront the cycle of poverty head on." Galahad told Ted persuasively, even though Trystan was his only real audience. "As the standard of living goes up, bigotry and scapegoating will go down. Children will be raised and protected in happy homes. Children who had no say in where they were born. Blameless little beings, who just need some help to survive."

Trystan flashed Galahad a withering glare. "I am not expending resources on these hopeless people. You are not a skilled enough actor to sway me."

"I'm not acting. I truly think there's always hope in children and we should nurture it. I think it's our duty to help them, no matter their race or their parents."

"You think I will do whatever you wish, because I *always* do whatever you wish. But, I am *not* doing this. Not even for you."

"I'm not trying to make you do anything that you don't want to do." Galahad glanced at him over his shoulder and went in for the kill. "But, I think the innocent belong to all who would care for them. And I think you think so, too."

Trystan's jaw tightened.

Galahad arched a brow.

The bedrock philosophy of gryphon culture lay between them for a moment.

...And then the fight was over.

"God*damn* it." Trystan seethed, folding because he was too Good a man not to. "I should have just let them abscond with you, knight." He clicked on the TV again, stunningly beautiful and pissed at the world. "It would have saved me no end of trouble."

Galahad suppressed a grin. Trystan really was a pushover. It was adorable. He looked back at Ted. "Soon, this place will be a haven for all types of people and every one of them will admire you, Mayor. I can see it all in my head. Can't you?"

Ted slowly nodded. "Yeah." He breathed, drawing out the word. "Maybe they'll even name the town after me. How 'bout that?"

"Sounds great!"

"Sounds fucking wonderful. I'm going to own a sand factory in Ted-ville." Trystan shook his head in resignation. "Of *course* I am. How did I not see it coming?" He brooded for a beat. "And I am *not* claiming you back, knight. I do *not* say I am yours. Not yet."

Yet.

That was fine. Galahad could be patient. Half of his military successes came about because he was willing to just straight-up outlast the other guy.

"I mean it." Trystan continued. "I'm not claiming you tonight. I'm not sleeping with you, either. I have many other options I am considering, when it comes to dealing with you."

No, he didn't. Trystan was his and there was nothing the gryphon could do about it. The battle was over. Now, he just had to wait for Trystan to realize it, too.

Galahad kept right on smiling at Mayor Ted, disregarding all the pessimistic muttering from the love of his life. "So, let's talk about infrastructure..."

Chapter Seventeen

I was with King Uther on two of the campaigns and you know who answered directly to him, every single day?

The fucking Yellow Boots! Remember them? Even *gryphons* knew gryphons were assholes. Yellow Boots wanted to work for *us*. They were thrilled to be cleaning our tents and telling us the savages' secrets.

Because they *knew* that was their rightful place. Serving their betters, as we swept the world clean of the gryphons' filth.

"Stopping the Savages" Podcast
Sir Dragonet of Camelot- Former Troubadour of King Uther and Host of the Program

Pellinore Foothills- West of Ted-ville

Three nights later, Galahad woke up, covered in sweat, his heart pounding and a shout caught in his throat. In his head, he could still smell the smoke and hear the cries of the dying. Legion never left him. It never would. He didn't deserve to sleep without dreaming of it.

Goddamn it.

Breathing hard, he tried to wipe the images from his mind. It was impossible. They were seared there like acid burns. Nothing could make them fade short of death. At his lowest point, Galahad

had considered that option, but it was a path without redemption. More than anything he wanted to be a Good man. Wanted to live up to the Knights' Code and protect the innocent.

And so he always kept trying for another day.

He laid his head back down, knowing he wouldn't get back to sleep. Trystan had fastened the ropes to a rock so Galahad's arms were stretched above his head. He'd also arranged the saddle blankets under him, so he'd have a mattress and pillow. He'd grunted when Galahad thanked him and went off to sleep on his own side of the fire.

Alone.

Who could blame him for that part, really? Optimism was easier to find in the light. Galahad could feel assured of winning Trystan over all day, but at night the doubts rose. Why the hell would someone like Trystan want someone like him? Galahad let out a shaky breath and squeezed his eyes shut, wishing he was somebody else. Anyone else. Someone beautiful.

"All warriors have nightmares, knight."

Galahad's eyes popped open to find Trystan standing over him. Just seeing him made the panic recede a bit. "Memories come back at night." He admitted, still trying to calm his heartrate.

"They do." Trystan agreed. "And they will until you let the past go. You are beyond them now. You are a different man than the one in those recollections, yes?"

"What if I'm not?" It was a whisper. "What if I'm still the Butcher of Legion?"

"You are incapable of butchering anyone." Trystan crouched down next to him. "Whatever happened that day..."

"I killed an unarmed man." The words were stark.

Trystan regarded him in surprise.

"I ran him through with my sword, because I was... gone. In that second, I was *gone*, Trys, and someone else was inside of me." Galahad stared at something far away. "...And that person in my body? He could have killed everyone in the world."

Trystan sighed. "Yes. I have been to that place, too."

Galahad glanced at him, pulled from the terrible recollections. "You have?"

"In war, darkness calls to us all. I told you this. But it fades, after we are away from the battle and reconnected to our clan. All soldiers have done things that haunt them. Terrible things. Do not let these memories consume you."

"Have you ever killed an unarmed man?" Galahad seriously

doubted it. "Ever in your life?"

"I threw Sir Perceval through a window, once. He may or may not have been armed, when he died on the ground below. I honestly didn't notice."

Galahad blinked. "You killed Perceval?"

"Technically, the fall killed him. I do not count him among those who died by my hand. I've only slain four hundred and eighty-four men. The rest all died of natural causes. I told you this, yes?"

By Galahad's count, Trystan had killed *nine* people, since the last time he gave the tally, but somehow he was only crediting himself with four. Which four and why was anyone's guess.

"Tossing someone out a window isn't a 'natural cause,' Trys. Neither is a sword through the liver, during a battle. Even if some of those guys in the War died in a hospital tent, *you* killed them."

Trystan didn't agree. "The men still breathed when I was through with them. I cannot be blamed that your army employed substandard medics and did not retrieve the wounded fast enough. Just as it is not my fault that Percival cannot fly." He paused. "You are upset at what I did to him?"

"No. Percival was a terrible person, who I'm *sure* did something to start that fight. He hated gryphons. It was zealotry. At Legion, he and Bedivere were laughing..." He broke off, not wanting to remember.

"The Martyr of Legion was laughing during the battle?"

"It wasn't a battle." Galahad said quietly.

"But he was *laughing* as children died?"

"I think half of the knights were laughing. In my memories, it's as loud as the screams."

Trystan rubbed his eyes, like he was exhausted right down to his soul.

A long moment passed. Too ashamed to look at Trystan, Galahad stared up at the sky. They were traveling into the mountains, now. The higher they went, the brighter the night sky became. Sometimes he dreamed of visiting the moon, where absolutely no one knew him. "How many stars do you think there are?"

"Two thousand and four."

Galahad glanced at him, surprised by that very precise answer.

"I used to count them often, during the War. Trying to sleep. Two thousand and four was as high as I ever got."

"I do the same thing. I counted to thirty-eight hundred once. By then it was morning."

"You would sleep easier if you spoke of your nightmares." Trystan's palm ran over his hair. "Do you wish to tell me of them? I will listen without judgement. I give you my word."

Galahad didn't say anything.

Trystan nodded, accepting the silence. "Rest, then. I will watch over you."

Galahad could have let it go at that. Trystan clearly expected him to. But not sharing his memories suddenly seemed harder than remaining quiet. "I was the one who found the path to Legion." He announced without preamble.

Trystan's head tilted, but he stayed quiet, like he was afraid anything he said would cause Galahad to stop talking.

"It was my fault." Galahad continued. Trystan would probably hate him and he deserved it. "Uther never would have gone there, if not for me."

"Did you know it was a town filled with civilians?"

"No. Of course not. It was the capitol of your people, so I thought it was a military stronghold. That's what the Yellow Boots told Uther. At least, that's what *he* said that they said. Who can know if it's true? Maybe he misunderstood them. Maybe he just lied to me." He swallowed. "Christ, there's so much I believed that turned out to be lies."

"That's how you found Legion? The Yellow Boots told you the way?"

"No. You have to be taught to navigate the Checkered Plains and none of them had ever been given the instructions. I don't know why."

"Many Yellow Boots came from the Sunchase Clan. They lived like feral beasts, even before the War. They were *never* to be trusted, so it would make sense that the information would be kept from them."

"I don't know." Galahad repeated. "I didn't know any Yellow Boots. They answered directly to Uther. In the end, I paid a drunk gryphon in a bar for the instructions. He'd been born in Legion, so he knew the path. He was pissed at the town. I think he said they'd demoted him from sentry or something."

Trystan's calm façade faltered. "Some random gryphon *sold* you directions to Legion? For spite and drinking money?"

"Yes."

Trystan made an aggravated sound. "Then the bastard would have sold it to another knight, had you not been there. Uther would have gone there, anyway. There is no need for you to take that weight upon yourself. That *gryphon* was the one who betrayed his people." His voice spat out the last part.

Trystan hated traitors more than anything. Even knights.

Galahad sighed. "But the guy *didn't* sell it to someone else. He sold it to *me* and everyone died. There were so many children lying in that grass afterwards, Trys. So many. Not all of them were gryphons, because your people took in orphans from other races." Gryphons treasured children. How could Trystan even look at him, knowing what he'd done? "My people slaughtered them. It wasn't war. It was murder."

"I do not believe that the same knight who let my men escape at the Battle of Flags, rather than shoot us in the back, executed children at Legion." Trystan murmured. "You told Solomon that you do not open fire on women and children. That it violates your code."

"It *does* violate the code."

"Then explain to me what happened that day."

"Uther was there and that took me out of direct command. Usually, he was far from the frontline, but we all knew this could be the last battle. I think he wanted to be there, for the history books. So they could write about him facing down the enemy. He was there, giving orders…" Galahad could still hear his voice screaming for the Rath. "*Everything* knights are supposed to stand for was broken."

"I have never seen you go against what you stand for. Not even once." Trystan shook his head, like he still didn't accept the story. "This is why Uther did not have you burning temples, yes? Because even he knew you would not violate the oath you took as a knight."

"It was the end of the War, so he didn't care what I saw. And it was all happening so *fast* and I was so *stupid*. So brainwashed into hating your kind. So sure I was on the right side. I didn't stop, even when I had doubts. I didn't understand until it was too late. I should've questioned…"

Trystan cut him off, deciding to go with more direct questioning. "How many children did you slay, Galahad?"

"All of them." The answer was immediate and true.

"*All* the young died by your sword?" Trystan sounded skeptical. "I doubt that. Your memory of that day plays tricks on you."

"I didn't kill them directly, but it was my fault."

"How many children did you kill with your own hand?"

Galahad hesitated. "Technically, I guess… none."

"None." Trystan's eyes glinted in satisfaction, like he'd just proven himself right. "How many of the old and sick did you kill? You *yourself?*"

He wasn't getting it. "None. But, Trystan, I was..."

"How many women?"

"*None.* Alright? That's not the point, though."

"How many men did you kill that day?"

"Why are you so focused on numbers? What do they prove? Even one was too many."

Trystan grunted, like that was debatable. "Sometimes you must do what is necessary. I killed a man this morning. I do not dwell on it."

"You killed *two* men this morning." He arched a brow at Trystan's blank stare. "The guy by that big rock."

"Oh. *Him?* He does not count." Trystan waved the dead guy aside in a typical show of Trystan logic. "I am saying that warriors often kill each other. You were on the wrong side of the battle, but your guilt over this is..."

Galahad interrupted him. "It wasn't a battle. It was murder. And it was my *fault*." His voice rose. "That entire town burned before my eyes, and the children died in the grass, and it *was all my fucking fault*." His words echoed through the night.

Fingers brushed through his hair, comforting him when he didn't deserve it. Galahad leaned into Trystan's palm and felt his defenses crumbling at the gentle touch. He hadn't spoken of Legion since the official inquest. As much as he didn't want Trystan to know about that day, the words began to pour out of him.

"The slaughter of it was... unbelievable, Trys." He closed his eyes. "People ran, and my men just kept firing, and the flames kept spreading. And it was like I was frozen, just watching it all happen. I can see it all again, every time I close my eyes. Every knight there was to blame, but especially me."

Trystan's head tilted. "So, *no* knights acted honorably?"

"No."

"Not even Bedivere?"

"No."

Trystan made a frustrated sound. "They built a statue to Bedivere's bravery. You know this, yes? Now you tell me it is all a lie." He paused. "That bronze monstrosity will come down, as soon as I return to Camelot."

"What good will that do? People will still believe what they want."

"It will improve the look of the courtyard, for starters."

Galahad shook his head. "I don't care what anyone else thinks. I just have to try and make amends, for that day. That's all that matters, now. I have to live a life of truth and peace. You see that, right?"

Trystan's hand continued to caress Galahad's hair. "I see that Legion was *not* your doing. It was perhaps not even Perceval and Bedivere's, as terrible as they were. It was *Uther* who sent you all there and Uther who gave the commands. Leave him behind you. That is how you will heal."

His voice was like a balm. The timbre of it and the accent soothed Galahad somehow. Just listening to it pushed some of the darkness away.

"I'd followed Uther since I was a boy. I loved him like a father. I truly did." Galahad blinked hard against the stinging in his eyes. "…And now I hate him. I hate what he did to me and to the world. What kind of son hates his father?"

"A son whose father is a monster."

"Can you ever stop loving your parent, though? Even when you discover they're twisted and wrong? Can you just turn that off? Ordinary people can't, right? I think it's the Badness in me."

"You are far beyond ordinary. And whatever Badness is in you, it is a drop in the ocean of your Goodness. And Uther was *not* your father."

"In my heart, he was. *That's* my point. Uther… shaped me." Once Galahad began talking, it was like uncorking a bottle. "Lyrssa carried him away, but his ideas and teachings are still somewhere inside of me. Recruits for the Knights' Academy are taken from their real parents when we're young. I barely remember mine. In all the ways that matter, Uther *is* my father." He paused. "Maybe I do still love him, down deep. Would that be worse or better?"

Trystan's comforting hand hesitated in Galahad's hair, ignoring the question. "Your parents did not come back to that school to visit you?"

"No. They sometimes promised to, but they always had other plans. More important places to go. I'm not someone who people changed their plans for."

In Camelot, there were few things that would help you climb the social ladder faster than having an offspring selected for training into knighthood. In his shadowy recollections, Galahad saw his parents as proud strangers, waving him off as he left home. Honored that their son had been chosen for greatness, because it would help their own status. More interested in the glory he'd bring to the family name than in the actual child, crying to stay at home with them.

Maybe he hated them, too.

Trystan drew in a deep breath, like he was trying to calm himself. "The Knights' Academy is an abysmal system for training warriors." He decided. "The entire school will be immediately changed. Children must be raised with care or they become damaged."

No shit.

"When I was very small, I had this fantasy where my parents would come to the Knights' Academy and demand to have me back." He looked at Trystan. "Would your parents have come to save you from the zoo, if they'd been alive?"

"Yes." The word was certain.

"I'm glad." Galahad said honestly. "I'm so glad you had that, Trys. I wish my parents had been like yours. For years, I thought maybe they'd miss me so much, that they'd take me back home. But they didn't. They died before I graduated and I never..." He trailed off with a sigh. "Anyway, by that time I'd replaced them with Uther and Camelot and being a King's Man. I followed *everything* they taught me. Did *everything* he asked. Why did I do that?"

"Because if you were successful enough, and Good enough, and won enough, you hoped you would be wanted. If you never fail, perhaps you will not be forgotten by those who should care for you."

Galahad looked at him sharply.

Trystan arched a brow.

Shit.

Galahad sighed. "In my head, it seems more complicated and less pathetic."

"It is not pathetic to desire a clan. You said yourself that Uther was your surrogate father. You wished to make him proud of you. To win his praise and affection, so he would value you as a son. He used that desire against you."

"That's all the more reason I can't ever be a man who would follow Uther, again. I can't *ever* be like him."

"Your concern over this is pointless. You are not like the dead king. His teachings did not warp you."

"You're so sure, huh?" Galahad certainly wasn't.

"Yes. If you were like Uther, you would not dream of the past with pain and regret. You would remember it with thirst."

Galahad snorted. There was very little in his past worth remembering, at all. He spent most days trying to forget his life even happened.

"You wouldn't care about buying a magic carpet for Avalon, either." Trystan continued. "Keeping your word to her would mean nothing."

Galahad shrugged. He would give up both his lungs for his goddaughter, so buying her a gift seemed like a very small thing.

Trystan paused for a beat. "And you *certainly* wouldn't wait for a gryphon's consent, if you desired his body. You would scheme to take what you want by force and my wishes would be meaningless."

That possibility had never occurred to Galahad. Not even once. "I would never hurt you, Trystan." He would die first, without even a moment's hesitation. "It's my job to protect you."

"I know you believe this. Would Uther ever seek to protect another?"

Galahad blinked. No. The old king hadn't cared about anyone. Not Galahad or Arthur or Avi or the people of Camelot. Just himself.

Trystan rubbed a lock of Galahad's hair between his thumb and forefinger. "Uther was a monster." He repeated. "You are not. I would not lie to you about such a thing, knight. I also try to live a life of truth."

Whether it was because of the bluntness of his words or his reasonable tone, Galahad felt strangely comforted by that promise. Maybe it was just Trystan himself, being so close to him, that brought peace. Jesus, the man was flawless inside and out. Galahad didn't want to recall the nightmare, anymore. He wanted something else. Something beautiful and clean.

He wanted Trystan.

Galahad looked up at him, his body super-charged with sudden need. "Speaking of desiring you, are you ready to say 'yes,' yet?" He asked abruptly. "I've been seducing you for days."

"No."

"Why not?"

"You are not ready."

"Yes, I am. *You're* the one who wants to wait. Sex was my idea, for Christ's sake."

"No, you are wounded and need comfort. It is not the same thing as desiring a mating. I would be taking advantage of you and you are in my care."

"I don't mind."

"I mind."

"Shit." Galahad banged his head back, frustrated but unsurprised. Trystan really was an angel. Gray areas didn't exist for him. There was just honor. "Well, could you go back over there in the dark, then? Looking at you is making some things worse for me."

Trystan's eyes went down to the huge bulge in the front of Galahad's pants.

Galahad arched a brow at him. "See?"

"I do not want to be in the dark, either." Trystan said quietly. "I would prefer to stay in the light with you."

Christ, he was really hard. It was painful. Trystan got that this was painful, right? "What if you just untied one of my hands?" He tried. "Then I can fix my problem and…"

"I could fix it for you."

Chapter Eighteen

When Lyrssa refused to give Uther the graal, he brought in Igraine to curse her. The sorceress was born Good, but used very wicked spells. She cursed Lyrssa to known Uther's pain.

To never be able to have more children.

But she went farther than Uther's condition and ensured that the gryphon would have no young to raise. No births. No adoptions. No surrogates.

No one to carry our stories.

Like a disease, this curse slowly spread outwards. At first, a few were effected, then a few more. Eventually, it was all gryphons who bore the weight of the spell. We tried many ways to get around the terrible words of it, but nothing worked. Our adoption rituals did not seal. Our women did not become pregnant. Our male's seed was dead as soon as it was spilled.

There was nothing we could do except hand over the graal. And we could never hand over the graal.

How the Wingless War Happened
Skylyn Welkyn- Gryphon Storyteller

Pellinore Foothills- West of Ted-ville

Galahad stopped short at Trystan's calm offer. "Huh?"

"I will not mate with you tonight, but I also do not wish to witness your suffering." Trystan declared, like he was the soul of consideration. "I will get no sleep, knowing I am not caring for you properly. Besides, you've claimed me, yes?" He asked that a lot, like he wasn't sure Galahad really meant it.

"Yes. I claim you." Trystan was everything to him. It was that simple and that complicated.

"I do not claim you, yet."

Yet.

Galahad suppressed a victorious smirk at the word. Trystan was still planning on claiming him, despite everything. That was enough. "I can wait." He assured him.

Trystan's eyes lingered on Galahad's triumphant grin and he sighed in something like surrender. "When you get that wicked smile on your face, I see your mind working in all kinds of Bad ways and I am... lost."

"I noticed that. It's working out great, for me." Galahad nodded, enthusiasm for this plan rising. "Can you start 'easing' me now? I promise, I will smile at you *a lot*, both during and afterwards."

Trystan's mouth almost seemed to curve. "I have no idea how you've stayed a virgin. It certainly wasn't by playing hard-to-get."

"It was simple, actually. Things just have to feel true for me to seduce a guy and they only feel true with you. Cuts way down on who I let 'deflower' me."

Trystan's gaze met his. "I am not complaining that you refuse all others, but it seems remarkable that casualties have not resulted. If you chose to seduce another like this, I would wage war on the man. And I'm good at war. I would win and he would die." It was a warning. "You understand this path goes only one way?"

"You're the only direction I'm heading, Trys. Don't worry about that."

"Gryphons do not worry." His hand went to the front of Galahad's pants, finding the pulsating erection under the fabric. Rubbing in some magical way that made Galahad think of beautiful things, again. "We don't *have* to worry."

"Oh my *God*..." Galahad breathed in awe.

Trystan made a pleased sound. "So, you need me to care for

this, yes?"

Galahad lived a life of truth, so he didn't even hesitate. "Absolutely fucking *yes*."

Trystan's eyes gleamed, as the size of the bulge increased. "Never with another man." His tone was arrogant. "But look how ready you are for me. Perhaps I am seducing *you*."

"Perhaps I just like you more than everyone else." It was a massive understatement.

"I think you like that I have you captured like this. The uniqueness of being at someone's mercy often interests warriors. We like to take and, sometimes, we also like to be taken."

Crazily, he *did* like that. All his life, Galahad had had to be the strongest and the most aggressive in order to rise. He liked that Trystan was so dominant. So completely sure of himself and so totally Good. Galahad might fall into darkness again, but Trystan *never* would. He liked the feeling of safety that gave him.

Plus, he just kind of liked being tied up.

Galahad lay there helplessly, as Trystan's free hand began removing his shirt. The buttons gave way under his nimble fingers and the whole experience was glorious. Trystan exposed the bare skin of Galahad's chest, his palm spreading wide over the surface. Rubbing against the thick muscles, like he was claiming Galahad's body as his own. Galahad was sure as hell not fighting that idea.

He instinctively tried to move his arms, wanting to pull Trystan even closer, but his hands were still bound above his head. He made a frustrated sound, even as the restraints enflamed him further. Trystan's fingers skimmed over his nipple and Galahad's whole body jerked. He'd had no idea that would be so sensitive.

"Trys..." His voice was thick and needy.

Trystan made a soothing sound, dipping his head. "It's alright." His lips encircled the tight bud. "You will come quickly the first time. Just let it happen. It's what we both want."

Galahad could barely think. His body yielded to Trystan's touch, pressing against his hands. Needing more.

"That's it." Trystan's teeth scraped against the opposite nipple. "Give yourself to me. I will take such good care of you."

"I know you will." Galahad didn't want to miss any of this. He craned his neck to watch Trystan's tongue lap at his skin, shivering at the sensation and the erotic sight. "Did I ever tell you that you look like an angel?" He got out. "Because you really, really do."

Trystan began slowly popping open the buttons of Galahad's pants with his other hand. "An angel?"

"Yeah." Galahad tried to focus on his words, so he didn't come right then and there. "You know, technically, I still own a production company and a bunch of shows. Not just my shows. Other ones."

"I know." Trystan lifted his head. "You also own several art galleries, a string of bookstores that only seem to sell coffee drinks, a robotics manufacture which creates artificial limbs for amputees, the most successful thoroughbred horse farm in the world, and an eco-conscious bicycle shop. All of them, *somehow*, turn a profit. You are talented at starting businesses." He rolled his eyes. "And yet you still have no money."

Galahad smiled, slightly distracted by that rundown. "You memorized my whole resume?"

"I learned all I could about you before my search. No one could memorize the *whole* of your resume, though. It would be like memorizing a phonebook full of impossible lunacy, shiny awards, and TV ratings."

"Hey, my ratings are always awesome. That's easy to memorize. And if you ever want a job on a television series, I could get you one in like two minutes. For real. Take your pick. It's not nepotism. Casting agents will *adore* you. I..." He trailed off with a gasp, as Trystan undid the last button and tugged his pants down. "Oh God, *I* adore you."

Galahad's aching staff broke free of the confining fabric. The tip was already weeping. Trystan looked smug, as he took in the size of the erection he'd caused. Galahad was too far gone to feel embarrassed by his need.

"Hurry." He begged.

Trystan didn't seem to be in much of a hurry. "I do not wish to be on TV." He murmured, like they were having a normal conversation. He studied the hard flesh he'd uncovered with devouring eyes, but he didn't end Galahad's torment by touching him. "Honestly, I would prefer writing the show to acting in it. I enjoy stories. I have many ideas to improve your strange programs and help children learn valuable skills."

"Like how to behead all the puppets." Galahad swallowed. "I remember."

"Not *all* of the puppets. Only the weak and pathetic ones, who cannot fight back."

Despite his current situation, Galahad laughed at that. There was no way to stop it. The man was just so... Trystan.

Trystan's mouth twitched upward, as if he was pleased that

he'd made Galahad happy. It was a *smile*. The emotion was right there on his face. It wasn't just in Galahad's imagination.

It was *real*.

"You feel things, don't you?" Galahad blurted out, unable to stop himself.

Trystan hesitated, the flash of humor fading. "...Some." He allowed cautiously. "My grandfather was one of your kind."

"I knew you had emotions. Every time you look at me, there's *something* in your eyes."

Trystan met his gaze. "Yes." He said again and the word was vast. "For you, I feel many somethings. I do not have words for them all."

Jesus, Galahad was so completely in love with the man. "Well, tell me what you *do* know then. Tell me something that you like about me."

Trystan tilted his head. "Something that I like about you?"

"Can you think of anything? Anything at all?"

"I like that you want me." Trystan said softly and his hand hovered just over Galahad's straining flesh. "That should be obvious, knight. I like that you claimed me, right in front of your own kind. I like the artistic ways your mind works. I like the wonder you see in the world and the questions you ask."

Galahad arched upward, needing contact. "Please, Trys."

"I like when you shorten my name." One finger trailed down the full length of him and Galahad saw stars. "I like when you share things with me that you do not tell anyone else. I like that you are a hero. I have always wanted one of those."

Galahad frowned slightly, trying to think. "I told you, I'm not this *ya'lah* guy, right?"

"Yes, you say many ridiculous things. I like that, too. I find it endearing." Trystan made a low sound in his throat, rubbing the very tip of Galahad with his thumb, spreading the moisture around. "I like that you never hide your desire for me."

"Touch me." Galahad offered desperately, twisting beneath him. "Now." Being tied up really was making this even better for him. Intensifying the sensations. "Touch me *now*, Trys." He commanded, unable to wait anymore.

Trystan arched a brow. "I like that you are patient in all things..." His massive hand wrapped around Galahad's erection without the slightest bit of self-consciousness. "...Except in your need for me."

Galahad let out a choked groan as Trystan began stroking

him. Over and over. Hard and long. Sooo hard and sooo long. It was incredible. Like his black-and-white existence was suddenly infused with color. His head went back, his sightless eyes staring up at the moon, knowing that nothing else would ever compare to this. To this man and this feeling he had whenever he looked at him. Whenever Trystan touched him, he was cleansed.

"I like that you fret over being a Good man, when your heart is so pure." Trystan watched his hand work with an engrossed expression on his face. "I like that you ask what I dream of. I like that you defeated five gryphons, barely even trying."

Galahad's hips moved in his tight grasp. "Oh, Trystan. Oh *yes*..."

"I like that you win all arguments with me, even the ones where I'm right. Which is most of them." Trystan continued, enjoying how responsive Galahad was to his touch. "And I like the lavender hue of your eyes. When I look into them, I think of the sky and the setting sun. I think of home." He gave a small, perfect smile and it was world-changing.

Right then, at that very moment, Galahad realized the truth: He wasn't a Good man, at all. He never would be. Not entirely.

Because, he knew Trystan was his True Love.

From the second he'd seen Trystan, he'd known it. He could admit that, now. He'd felt the *truth* of their connection from the first. Bad folk always knew when they met the other half of themselves. The bond was instantaneous. Galahad had long suspected there was as much Bad as Good in him. Now he had proof there was more wickedness than he'd even imagined.

It should have traumatized him, but instead he found himself grinning up at the sky, wanting to shout in triumph.

He had his True Love. *Finally.* It was beyond anything he could have hoped. Beyond anything he deserved. He truly wasn't damned. He saw it now. How could he be? He'd just been given an angel.

"Kiss me." He ordered, joy filling him.

Trystan glanced at him in surprise.

"Kiss me." Galahad repeated, the tendons in his neck standing out from the strain of holding back his release. "Please. Give me what I need, Trystan. You're the only one who can."

"Always." The word was immediate. The grip on his shaft changed, as well. Becoming more territorial. Ownership and want and dominion went into each stroke. Galahad's whole body shuddered. "*I* protect you. *I* comfort you. *I* touch you." His wings spread out, like he was instinctively shielding Galahad. "*Only me*."

Galahad made a helpless sound of lust, seeing the incredible feathers above him.

"No one else, knight." Trystan seemed to be dwelling on this topic, for some reason. "Anything you need, *I* will provide. Understand?" It wasn't a question, but he seemed to want an answer. He knew how attracted Galahad was to his wings and he used it to his advantage. His feathers very deliberately brushed against Galahad's throbbing arousal, seeking the agreement he desired, and it was fucking *awesome*.

Galahad lurched upward, craving the softness of the downy feathers. "Oh Jesus. *Again*. Please. More."

"Mine." Trystan murmured, doing as he asked. The tip of Galahad's staff was dusted with those magical wings again and the whole world was beautiful. "All mine. Say it."

"You're going to be *really* possessive, aren't you?" Galahad guessed with a smile, loving all of this and resisting Trystan's demand just to play.

A pause. "Yes." Trystan sounded startled. "Yes, that is the word for what happens inside me when I picture you depending on another, or desiring another, or accepting emotions from another." He nodded, as if he'd just solved a puzzle. "I feel very... *possessive* of you."

"I noticed."

"It is overwhelming. It fills my head with noise and many *other* emotions. All tell me to kill any other man who would try and claim you."

Galahad totally understood that. "I know. I feel it, too."

The thought of Trystan loving someone else made the darkness rise within him. He would kill that other bastard, before he even realized it happened. And when Galahad came out of his haze of grief and jealousy and anger and saw what he'd done... he'd only feel satisfaction and glee. He knew that. No one would take Trystan away from him and survive.

Poor Trystan. His True Love was such a lunatic.

"You feel possessive?" Trystan seemed surprised and pleased. "Towards me?"

"Of course. Probably even worse than you do, because I'm not half as stable." Galahad felt like he should apologize for ruining his chances at a normal life. "I need you, even when I know I'm not Good enough for you, Trys. Even when I know you could find a better man. Like someone who can fly and who's not so fucked-up, for instance.

I'm so sorry you're stuck with me, but I can't let you go."

"You concern yourself with very odd things." Trystan lamented, with a shake of his head. "All who have seen us together know that I have no intention of choosing another. It's absurdly clear." His hand tugged a little bit harder and Galahad's hips arched in ecstasy. "*You* do not seem as certain, though."

"I don't?" Galahad managed a snort. "You haven't been paying attention, then. You're the only one I want. You can tell by how I keep telling you that *you're the only one I want*."

"Yet?" Trystan's voice was silky.

"Huh?" It was hard to focus.

"In that accursed Ted-ville, you told me you were not planning to be with another man... *yet*." The implications of that word had clearly pissed him off. "I do not like that. At all. It is only me. *Always*."

"*That's* what this is about?" Galahad would have rolled his eyes, if he wasn't so busy reminding himself how to breathe. "Jesus Christ, tell me you've been brooding all this time over semantics."

"I understand the subtleties of your language, even if you don't. Your words indicated that you may soon desire another. Of course I think of it often."

"I never said I desired another! Why would I desire another? Shit, we were arguing over some crazy thing *you* said and I was... *God!*" His hands fisted around the bindings, his body taut and shaking. "Again. Oh God. Whatever you just did, do it *again*."

He did it again and Galahad had never loved him more. "You chose this path, knight. When you claimed me, you made me a part of your clan. A part of yourself."

Sure. That sounded right. "Okay."

"You've pledged yourself to *me*." His teeth nipped the side of Galahad's neck, marking him and it was every goddamn fantasy of Galahad's life come true. "And I keep what's mine."

Galahad had to grind his own teeth together to keep himself from coming. His glazed eyes went back to Trystan's massive wings looming above him. The beautiful, exotic sight did nothing to help him regain control. "Oh God..." He would die if he didn't find relief. "I can't hold on much longer. Please."

"Not yet. Tell me who you belong to first."

"You." It was a low moan.

"Who?" The hand continued its glorious work. "Say my name, Galahad. You know I like to hear it."

"*Trystan*." He met his gaze, feeling both victorious and

conquered. "I'm yours, Trys. Always."

"I like it when you're sensible. It happens so rarely." Trystan's free hand came up to brush the golden locks from Galahad's face and he gave a captivated sigh. "And I like your hair. I like the way it shimmers."

"You like it… when I give into your caveman tactics…" Galahad's voice was coming in pants now.

"That, too." Trystan lowered his mouth to Galahad's. "Kissing is your people's custom, not mine. Show me what you need and I will provide it."

His lips touched Galahad's in the lightest brush imaginable… and Galahad came.

"*Trystan.*"

His body stiffened, his mouth falling open as the biggest orgasm of his life rocked him. It was so much better than he'd ever imagined it could be. So much deeper and truer. Because he was so totally in love with the man who'd given it to him. It went on for so long, Galahad thought he would die from the pleasure of it.

Trystan milked him dry, obviously pleased with himself. "I'm good at kissing." He decided. "As I am good at all things. I knew I would be. I told you so."

Galahad went slack, barely able to suck oxygen into his lungs.

Trystan glanced at his palm, like he wanted to see Galahad's release on his skin. Then, he gave a satisfied sound. "I *like* that. Fuck. I didn't expect to like that, so much." He leaned down to nuzzle the side of Galahad's head and sighed contentedly, like he was the one who'd found release. "I like *everything* about you, knight." He murmured, his voice warm and tender.

Galahad turned his face to rest his forehead against Trystan's, feeling closer to this man than he'd ever felt to anyone. "I like everything about you, too, Trys." He whispered, closing his eyes in bliss. "God… You can deflower me anytime you want."

Trystan's mouth curved. "Oh, I plan to." His hand went back to work. "I will have you again, now. Give me what I want, like a Good knight."

Damn if Galahad's staff didn't rise to the occasion at that order. His dazed eyes met Trystan's in surprise. He had no idea he could recover that quickly.

Trystan arched a brow. "It's not fair to keep something so big contained for so long. It will take several rounds to satiate it. You really should have let me take care of this sooner."

"I've been begging for over a week." Galahad scoffed,

exhausted and exhilarated at the same time. "If I'm not playing hard-to-get hard enough, you're playing it *too* hard."

"I'm not playing, at all. I *am* hard-to-get."

Galahad gave him a crooked grin. "*I* got you."

"At the moment, I would say it is the other way around." Trystan's palm squeezed in some absolutely perfect spot and Galahad was suddenly more aroused than ever. "That's it. That's what I want." Trystan looked proud at how easy it was for him to accomplish his goal. "It all belongs to me, yes?"

"Yes." Galahad nodded and his body certainly agreed. It responded to Trystan like it was starving for him. He *was* starved for him. "I'm all yours."

Trystan's feathers brushed Galahad's skin and he gave a contented rumble, feeling Galahad swell beneath him. "At least twice more before you can rest, knight. Then, several times tomorrow. Depravation isn't healthy. You will need me to do this very often, I think."

"I will never get enough of you, Trystan." Galahad breathed enraptured by the man.

Trystan seemed satisfied with Galahad's total capitulation. Not that it had been much of a fight. "Tell me again of your school film. *Corrupted by the Winged Devil*, yes? I wish to hear *exactly* which barbarous acts the gryphon used to desecrate the knight's untouched body. I intend to invent even more depraved things to do with *my* innocent prisoner. It will not be difficult. I am excellent at telling stories and the wingless have dismal imaginations."

Galahad felt drugged. "Jesus..." He melted into Trystan's touch, soaking it all in. Trystan was a genius at knowing how to extract every single reaction, from every single nerve-ending. "You're right. You really are *incredible* at writing scripts."

If the Knight's Academy had gone with Trystan's ideas for their propaganda film, there would have been a line of cadets wanting to be the eager sexual hostages of the gryphons.

"I have not even started on the scene." A second hand joined the first and Galahad literally whimpered in elation. Trystan made that low sound that was nearly a chuckle, liking that reaction. "You are becoming a fan, yes? Now, I will show you how that gryphon *really* would have defiled his helpless virgin."

"Defile me in every way you can dream up." Galahad said, while he still had the air to talk. "But untie me first. I want to show *you* something."

Trystan glanced at him with an undecided frown. "Untie

you? But then you could leave."

Galahad shot him an incredulous look. "Are you deranged? Look where your hands are, Trystan. It took hard work for me to get them there. I'm not about to *leave*, now that I finally have you right where I want you."

Trystan wasn't convinced. "I am…" he seemed to flounder for a word to describe his feelings, "*vexed* by the idea of releasing you. I like you tied. I know where you are and that you are not wandering off into trouble. You are safer this way."

"Untie me or I'll untie myself. You know I can figure it out if I have to." Galahad struggled into a sitting position, adopting the tone he used to command troops. "*Now,* Trystan."

Trystan grudgingly reached over and unfastened the ropes. "This is ridiculous. I don't know why I listen to you. This is what I'm talking about. Even when I'm right, you somehow managed to…

Galahad cut him off. The second his hands were free, he was dragging Trystan's head down to his.

Trystan jolted, startled by the fierceness of the kiss. Whenever Galahad was aggressive, it seemed to catch Trystan off guard. It dimly occurred to Galahad that nobody else had ever taken the lead with the man. Trystan was simply too intimidating for most people to even consider it.

Or maybe he just allowed Galahad to do things he'd never tolerate with anyone else.

Galahad's tongue surged into Trystan's mouth, showing him what he wanted. A heartbeat passed and then Trystan hesitantly responded. His tongue touched Galahad's like he wasn't sure he would like it. Then a hungry groan escaped him and he was all in. Within seconds, he was a full participant in the kiss. In less than a minute, he was the aggressor. His lips devouring and demanding more. You might be able to startle Trystan into submission for a moment, but the gryphon would always take charge, in the end. It was his nature.

Galahad loved it. Loved him.

He finally pulled away to look at Trystan, wanting him to understand. "*That* is kissing." He told him, breathlessly.

Trystan's mouth curved. "I like it."

Chapter Nineteen

Let me ask you this, gryphon shills out there:

If the War was so hard on them and the curse was so terrible...

Why didn't they just hand over the graal and be done with it?

"Stopping the Savages" Podcast
Sir Dragonet of Camelot- Former Troubadour of King Uther and Host of the Program

Pellinore Mountains- Below Corbenic Cave

Trystan stared at the cave for a long moment. ...Then his eyes slid over to Galahad.

Galahad smiled back at him, like everything was normal and under control.

Trystan arched a brow, saying nothing.

Galahad's expression dimmed a bit. "It's going to be *way* easier to get in there than it looks." He assured Trystan earnestly.

Trystan snorted and glanced back up at the cavern. It sat high on a black monolith, surrounded by jagged rocks. Inextinguishable flames burned in an impenetrable wall around it, blocking the entrance. Below, everything within half a mile was singed black or still aflame. Yet, the interior of the cave somehow shone brilliant white through the smoke. It looked enticingly cool and pristine inside the mysterious space. That was possibly why so many people had died trying to reach it.

"This is the Fire Cave of Corbenic." He said unnecessarily. "A place of legend and horror."

Galahad blinked with contrived innocence. The man truly was a terrible actor, as his TV shows so amply proved. "Is it?"

"You *know* that it is."

"Well, I mean it doesn't have a sign out front, so..."

Trystan cut off that nonsense. "We are not entering the Fire Cave of Corbenic, Galahad. I mean it."

It wasn't often that *exactly* what you desired was delivered into your grasp. The night before, though, it had happened to Trystan. Galahad had shared his thoughts and his body, in ways that he'd never done with anyone else. The last thing Trystan wanted to do was backtrack on the progress he was making with the man. Disappointing Galahad was not desirable, at all.

...But neither was watching him burn to death.

"I need to see a mural up there." Galahad pointed to the cave. "You agreed that we could go look at it, remember?"

"You did not tell me where the mural was located!"

"To be fair, you didn't ask."

"Why would I *ask* if you planned to venture into a cavern of certain death?" Trystan paused and gave a scoff. "Although with your track record for lunacy, I suppose I should probably be asking that twice a day."

"This is going to be *so* easy." Galahad assured him, again. "I was a volunteer firefighter in Camelot. I rescued eighty-nine people and sixteen cats from fires." He brightened. "Oh and I delivered a baby for this super-nice fairy who was stuck in an elevator. She named the little girl after me, too. Galahada. It was an amazing moment. ...Then, I had to go stop a volcano from erupting."

"You make these stories up, don't you? There is no other explanation."

Galahad pretended not to hear that. "Anyway, I can handle this cave, no problem. I'm figuring out a whole strategy."

"My blood runs cold at that sentence. I have heard it as a portent of disaster at least a dozen times, with you." Trystan scanned the area, continuing to run various scenarios in his head. None seemed promising. "How important is this mural to you?"

"On a scale of one to ten? I'll give my life for it, but not yours. So like a nine?"

Trystan didn't like that number. "Do not give your life for *anything*. Not even me." It was an order. "Nothing is worth the cost of you in this world."

"I'm crazy about you, too, Trys."

Trystan grunted.

"I *need* to do this." Galahad went on. "But I have it all under control. You wait here. I'm going to just go in there and find the mural..."

Trystan cut him off, his head whipping around. "I will wait here, while you go in the cave alone? This is your strategy?"

"Right." Galahad nodded. "It will be safer to just let me handle the important parts. You agreed to that, remember?"

"No, I do not remember that, because I did not say it."

"Yes, you did. And I have more experience in dealing with evil caves than you do. I stumble across them *a lot*, weirdly enough. I should go in there alone, so you don't get hurt."

Trystan squinted in bafflement. The knight was trying to protect him, again? Why did this keep happening? And why was it not insulting? Instead, it felt... *pleasant* that the man cared for his safety. Stupid, but pleasant.

"I will not sit here, while you go off to die, knight. Are you crazy?"

"I'll be right back. I'm just going to go up there and take a look around." Galahad climbed off his horse, pulling a pack from the saddle and looping it over his shoulders, cheerful and confident. "You worry too much."

"Gryphons do not worry. We just know a shit plan when we hear one." Trystan sighed in exasperation. "You have called me a hero, yes?" He liked that claim, although it was not true. The knight was the only true hero left. "Would it not be wise to have my help, then?"

"You *are* a hero, Trys. That's one reason I need to keep you safe. You're too special to risk on anything."

Trystan snorted at that logic and surrendered to the madness. "I can get you to that cave. This is a better plan, yes? I could fly us over the fire and land right at the mouth of it."

Galahad's head tilted, like he was thinking over the proposal and seeing nothing but flaws. "I don't know if it's such a good idea to be allies on this." He hedged.

Trystan searched for a way to win him over. Emotions seemed like the quickest answer. Galahad responded well to emotions. "I would feel... *lonely* if you did this on your own." He tried, hunting around in the *somethings* for the right word.

Galahad blinked. "You'd feel lonely?"

"I think that is the emotion. Yes. On the other hand, I would feel... *happy* to be allies with you in this mission. Can you consider making me happy?"

Yep. *That* did it.

Galahad's hesitance vanished with an endearing swiftness. "If it makes you happy, we can be allies, Trystan. My God, of *course.*"

Trystan felt a surge of triumph at his easy victory. Possessing such a kindhearted knight was so satisfying, at times. "Fine." He got off his horse, pleased with himself and at his new status within Galahad's pointless quest. "This is still a shit plan, but we will do it together."

"You really need to let me take the lead on this one, though. Remember how we talked about trusting each other to know what the other one's doing? I meant *you* need to trust *me.*"

Trystan grunted again, heading towards him. "We will see."

"You *promised* me I could handle the important parts of this, back in the hotel room."

"We have different memories of that event." Trystan waved a dismissive hand. "You and I are the best at what we do, so we will be able to find a balance in our alliance. It will just take some compromises." He paused. "Mostly, they will be on your part."

Trystan had no idea how it happened, but he knew his path was no longer his own. He now shared it with Galahad and so Galahad was going to have to adjust. It only seemed fair.

Galahad brightened. "You think I'm the best at what I do?"

"I think you are special in every conceivable way. This is why the dead gryphons speak to you. Why you hear our ancient songs, yes?"

Galahad's head snapped around to stare at him.

Trystan arched a brow.

Galahad winced and began climbing the rocks, towards the cave. "Hey, do you think a pumpkin is a gourd or a squash?" He asked randomly. The knight always said odd things, but never more so than when he wished to confuse, mislead, or otherwise change the subject.

"A pumpkin is a gourd *and* a squash. And also a fruit." Trystan said, refusing to be distracted. "How long have you heard the dead gryphons?"

Galahad stayed quiet for a beat. "I started hearing that song in my head when I was banished." He finally muttered, which was more of an answer than Trystan had expected.

Trystan was pleased that the knight was giving him some of his secrets.

He also noted that Galahad looked fucking adorable in his coat. The weather was colder here, because of the altitude. Trystan had insisted that Galahad put on the jacket he'd bought him in Tedville, ignoring the man's complaints that he "didn't need a coat." He was not going to let the knight freeze. Besides, the coat was "Enspelled with Protective Magic." Trystan wasn't sure what that meant, but he liked the sound of it. And he liked how the blue fabric showcased Galahad's eyes.

This area was warmer than the rest of the region, though, thanks to the heat from the fire cave. No snow stood on the ground. Instead, it was covered in thick, black powder. Trystan's boots crunched against it. Mixed in with the dark soot, he could see small bits of white glinting.

Teeth.

Wonderful. They were standing in the middle of a crematorium of previous travelers. He glanced around, gauging the size of the wide swatch of black stretching out for hundreds of yards in every direction. *A lot* of previous travelers. Given the lack of tourism in this area, this creature must've been killing for a very long time to accumulate so many victims.

"Communicating with my ancestors is a mark of honor." He told Galahad absently, his eyes on the landscape. "They did not choose you lightly."

"The dead gryphons don't *exactly* speak to me." Galahad told him, like he was trying to make sense of it. "I can't even understand your language. Sometimes I just... hear things."

"You hear the old gryphon speaking to you." Trystan agreed, still studying the dusty mountains of dead. Not even a dragon could have done this much damage. Whatever had killed these beings, it was not a beast he'd fought before and he'd fought just about everything.

The Pellinore Mountains were filled with many rare creatures, though. The magic was so strong that most explorers stayed away. This left all sorts of beasts to spawn and thrive in the cold isolation. Whatever this creature was, it was sure to be unknown and horrible. Hopefully, Galahad would let him kill the damn thing without extended chiding about how "monsters have souls, too." Trystan could recite that particular lecture by heart, at this point.

Galahad stopped on a large rock and turned to glance back at him. "Something wrong?" He asked, noticing Trystan's distraction.

"Not yet. I'm sure it will be, though." Trystan looked around for some sign of the creature who'd slaughtered thousands, but he didn't see any footprints. "Are you *sure* exploring this cave is of nine level importance, knight?"

"Maybe even nine-and-a-half."

Trystan sighed. "Fine." He'd deal with whatever this disaster was, once it actually befell them. He shook his head and returned to the topic at hand. "My ancestors only talk to those with great destinies. Do you understand this? It is not a Bad thing you hear them. It does not mean you are crazy or wrong. It means you are *chosen*."

Galahad didn't answer.

Tired of walking upon charred corpses, Trystan used his wings and flew upward, landing beside Galahad on the rocks. "They see something special in you. As I do."

"I'm *not* the *ya'lah*, if that's what you mean. I'm *not* some 'champion' guy. I'm certain of that." Galahad hesitated. "The word does sound sort of familiar, though. I keep trying to remember where I heard it."

"The dead gryphons probably called you by the title."

"No, they didn't! Jesus. You just make up your mind about something and refuse to listen to anything else."

Trystan disregarded that nonsense. "Why are you scaling these rocks?" He asked instead, because it was a legitimate and pressing question. "I can fly you up the entire way."

Galahad snorted. "I'm too heavy for you to carry for long. Relax. I have this under control." He jumped up to seize a handhold, using upper body strength to catch himself before he tumbled to his death.

Trystan's stomach jolted in terror at the casualness of the stunt. Terrified, he flew upward, keeping pace with Galahad, so he'd be able to catch the knight if he fell. "What about the magic carpet? We have one of those. You could use that to scale this cliff, yes?"

The wingless were fragile in many ways. Without the power of flight, they could not protect themselves properly. If the knight lost his balance, he would be smashed beyond repair.

Galahad glanced back at Trystan's arms ready to steady him and his mouth curved. It looked like he wanted to say something, but then he changed his mind.

Trystan didn't like that. "I would hear whatever you wish to tell me, even if I will not be pleased to hear it." He said and it was true.

When Galahad shared his thoughts, it became less likely that he would slip back into his own mysterious world. Also, his words were often... interesting. Trystan could never predict what new idea the knight would come up with.

"Well, I was just thinking about the gryphons..." He trailed off.

"The dead ones or the living ones?"

"Living ones." Galahad got that speculative expression he always got just before he asked something that was so insane it just might be genius. "Did you ever wonder why gryphons don't have emotions?"

Trystan's eyebrows shot up. "No." He said honestly.

"Who decided that they couldn't feel things? Did *they* decide it?"

Trystan floundered for a beat. "I don't..."

Galahad cut him off. "I doubt it, right? Because how would gryphons know what they didn't feel unless someone came along and told them they didn't feel it? It would be like someone telling me I couldn't smell the number six. The idea that it even *had* a smell never even entered my mind, so it wasn't like I knew that I was missing it, right? There's no test to quantify emotions. Maybe gryphons *do* feel things, you just feel them *differently* and that's okay."

"Except we don't feel things."

"Are you sure about that? *You* feel them."

"Because, my grandfather was wingless. You know this."

"But, what if it's bigger than that? I mean, I'm sure you feel more emotions and feel them deeper, because you inherited them from your grandfather. But what if a lot of gryphons feel... *something*?" Galahad tilted his head. "I keep remembering how Vallon got so pissed at me, back in Ayren's village. I think he was feeling things that he had no framework to express."

Trystan blinked, trying to wrap his head around the idea. "Vallon tried to kill you. Yet, in your mind, he is now a tragic victim, filled with sensitive emotions?"

"I didn't say he was a victim. --Although, I think he kind of is.-- I said that he has a lot of emotions, which he has no idea how to channel, because he has no idea he even *has* them."

"Or he's just an asshole."

Galahad flicked him off, somehow not losing his grip on the rock. "*You*, on the other hand, deal with your emotions by making snide remarks, yelling at me, and hovering a lot."

"It is *your* fault, I must yell and hover. You leap around on cliff sides and deliberately drive me crazy."

Galahad opened his mouth and then closed it, again.

"Say what you are dying to say. It cannot be any stranger

than gryphons with feelings."

"I just don't want you to think I'm arrogant."

Trystan shrugged. "You should boast of your abilities *more*, not less." He might scoff about the man's lengthy list of accomplishments, but he saw no purpose in Galahad trying to hide any of his talents. It was a doomed effort. You might as well try to box up the sun and mail it from the sky. "Besides, we are past the point where we shield parts of ourselves, yes? Be fully Galahad with me. Always. This is what allies do."

Galahad smiled at him, his expression lightening. "Alright." His hand lodged in a crevasse that Trystan hadn't even noticed. "Well, it's cute you're worried about me, but I've got this. I've set records for free-climbing every mountain in Camelot. Twice. The second time, I wore a blindfold, as part of a charity event." He swung sideways, his body twisting at an impossible angle. At the last instant, he released his hold, so he sailed through the air.

Trystan had literally been tortured without flinching, but now he cringed in horror.

The knight landed on a near vertical surface, his feet digging into the stone to stop himself from sliding into oblivion. "I vloged my fastest ascent and it broke the internet." He went on with a shrug. "Seriously, it was out for three days."

"Millions of people were no doubt wagering on how quickly you would flatten yourself on the rocks below. That would take much bandwidth."

Galahad rolled his eyes. "I *promise* you, I'm not going to fall, okay?" Not even noticing the dizzying drop, he easily grabbed onto an outcropping to the left of his original position and kept going up. "You have to trust that your ally knows what he's doing."

"Fine." Trystan's pulse was thundering in panic. Everything within him wanted to grab the man to safety. Galahad might be the best at all he tried, but it was still a nightmare to witness his death-defying feats firsthand. To distract himself, Trystan tried to refocus on the dead gryphons. "Uhh..." He swallowed hard. "Even if you refuse to see you are the *ya'lah*..."

"I'm not the *ya'lah*."

Trystan kept talking, his eyes riveted on each millimeter of Galahad's climb. "You must see that my ancestors would not be speaking to you at all, if they did not believe you have a great destiny. What are you planning to do that has them convinced you are on such a path?"

"*If* they were talking to me, I guess it would be because of the art school I'm going to build, once I find the gold."

Trystan's heart was in his throat, as the knight sprang to a new rock. Did gravity not work on him? "Gryphons don't value gold. Whatever they see in you, it isn't that."

Galahad looked back at Trystan, hanging by one arm for no possible reason except he wanted to cause Trystan distress. "Shit." He whispered. "You're right. They wouldn't consider gold worth very much, would they?"

"Can you grasp that rock with *both* hands?" Trystan demanded, unable to fully concentrate on anything except Galahad's precarious grip. "I trust that you know what you're doing, but you are still in my care."

Galahad twisted his body so he was holding the rock more securely, but his eyes never left Trystan's. "What *would* they consider a treasure?" He asked, with a strange expression.

"A future for our people." Nothing else mattered, now. "The gryphon cannot have children, even through surrogates or adoption. Without young, who will tell our stories?"

The knight would want young to raise. That thought flickered through Trystan's head, causing him to frown. Galahad loved children. He would wish for a mate who could provide them and Trystan couldn't.

P'don.

"Midas' mother adopted him." Galahad argued. "You told me that. And she was a gryphon."

"That was early in the curse's power. It has been spreading and getting stronger. At first, *some* children would be born. *Some* could be adopted. But those rarities have been over for many years." Most of the last of that group had died at Legion. "Not Igraine's death, nor Uther's, has lifted the spell. The gryphons will be gone soon."

Galahad considered that with a concerned expression. "I don't think I can do anything to fix that curse, Trys." He heaved himself up onto a small flat area beneath the cavern. "I would if I could, but I've got zero insight into magic and curses."

"I know." He landed on the knight's new perch. "But there is *some* reason the dead gryphons have chosen you. You have no idea what it might be?"

Galahad shrugged in a stubbornly silent way.

Trystan sighed and gave up on his fleeting hope for any kind of rational behavior from the man. "I should have kept you tied up." He muttered. "You were easier to deal with."

"I was?"

"Not really. You're always a pain in the ass." Trystan frowned down at him, irritated and intrigued that the exertion of the climb had added an appealing glow to his skin. "If we both survive this lunacy, you will owe me a boon, by the way."

"Rock climbing lessons?"

Trystan leaned closer to him. "No. But you will be using your hands."

Galahad gave a slow smirk, filled with gleaming Badness and delightfully carnal ideas. "Well, that sounds promising."

Gods, Trystan would follow that beautiful, wicked grin right off a cliff.

He grabbed the fabric of the knight's shirt, dragging him forward. "Hold onto me." His arms went around Galahad's waist, gripping him close. Trystan was unwilling to go through another moment of watching the man's acrobatic skills. His heart couldn't take the strain.

Galahad gave a start of surprise, automatically clutching Trystan's shoulders as huge wings lifted them into the air. "Holy shit!" He gave a laugh of elation, enjoying the sensation of flight. "Holy *shit!* I can't believe you can do this and we're not *always* doing this."

Trystan's mouth curved. "Perhaps, I did not want you to think I am arrogant."

"You *are* arrogant." Galahad leaned up to kiss him. "And it *really* works for me."

That was fortunate, since Trystan *really* liked kissing. He liked the way it tightened his insides with desire and the feel of Galahad's lips softening beneath his own. As with all things he liked, he was now devoting himself to the mastery of it. The wingless culture had contributed little of value to the world, but kissing was truly a great achievement for their people. Trystan intended to perfect their invention.

The knight seemed delighted with his enthusiastic response. His mouth parted, accepting Trystan's possession. He leaned into Trystan's body, putting himself into Trystan's care. And all the *somethings* inside Trystan agreed that was exactly how it was supposed to be. A hungry sound escaped him, as he deepened the kiss. Oh yes... This was all *exactly* right.

Trystan carried them over the wall of fire and landed on the smooth white entrance to Corbenic Cave, his mouth still drinking in Galahad's moonlit taste. Everything about this man was perfect. The light of his smile, and the million artistic ideas in his head, and the way he flew without looking down.

Everything about him was... *everything.*

"Trys?" Galahad finally pulled back. "Hang on, okay? I gotta do something real quick."

Trystan gave a growl of displeasure at his retreat. "How quick? I want my boon. *Now.*"

This area seemed secure, for the moment. The fire was safely behind them and that was always good news when exploring a fire cavern. No creatures were attacking, yet. Also, a positive sign. Trystan saw no reason to release Galahad, when he didn't have to. For weeks, he'd been in a state of near constant need. He didn't want to stop touching the one person who could give him some relief.

Easing someone with your hands was seen as more meaningful among the gryphons than it was with the wingless. Trystan had never given or received pleasure that way before, because the idea of it was too intimate for his liking. But in the knight's culture, it was regarded as a smaller step on the path to further mating, so Trystan had given it a try for Galahad's comfort. Oddly, Trystan had liked the experience.

A lot.

He liked that the knight faced him when they engaged in the act, his dazed eyes on Trystan's. He liked the feel of the man's release on his skin. He *liked* the intimacy of it all. With Galahad, it was not so uncomfortable to be close to someone. It felt *right*. Trystan now wished to try the experience again, with the knight's palm stroking him this time. He already suspected it was going to be revelatory.

"Give me ten minutes." Galahad's teeth nipped the edge of his jaw and Trystan's whole body jolted. "I'm in the lead up here, remember?"

"I do not remember agreeing to that or anything else you've been claiming."

"It was implied."

The knight slipped away and Trystan reluctantly let him go. The night before, Trystan had made the choice to delay his own pleasure. It was hard to remember why that had ever seemed like a sound strategy. His gaze lingered on the width of the knight's shoulders and then drifted downward. Very, very hard.

Galahad unlooped the satchel from around his body. "You wait here and... wait." His eyes flicked down to the bulge of Trystan's arousal and he looked anything but sympathetic. "Not for nothing, but you wouldn't be this *impatient* if you'd let me handle that last night."

"Oh, you will be handling it very soon. I promise you."

Galahad arched a brow, amused and interested. "Give me

five minutes." He revised and pulled his shirt off over his head, without bothering to unbutton it. He stripped off his pants and shoes next. Then, he dumped all his clothes in a pile. "Can you watch these for me?"

What the hell?

As much as he appreciated the sight of the man's naked body, Trystan was baffled by that action. Even by the knight's standards, it seemed odd. Still, if Galahad wanted to undress, Trystan certainly wasn't going to complain. His tongue ran along the edge of his teeth, tilting his head to get a better view. This was turning into one of the better misadventures that the knight had dragged him on.

Galahad glanced at him, noticing the increasing hunger of his gaze. "Five minutes." He repeated and dug around in the satchel. He pulled out the silver shield he'd found in Medusa's tomb, spinning it around with a practiced toss. "Maybe less."

Trystan frowned, coming out of his trance. Wait... Why did he need that shield? "Knight? Do you know something about this cavern that you have yet to mention?"

"Well, I don't *know* it. It's just a theory." Galahad headed straight for the mouth of the cave. It loomed like a white abyss around him. "I've been really interested in encryptions, ever since I started decoding the secret language of dolphins." (Of *course*, he was talking to dolphins.) "And lately I've been using the map to decipher the engraving on Evalach's shield. It says some stuff about the cave, actually."

A feeling of foreboding gripped Trystan.

Evalach had been a gryphon warrior of great renown. His weapons had all been forged with magic and purpose. Why would he have led Galahad to the weapon? Why would any of the ceremonial writing on the shield match up with Galahad's cheap treasure map?

Unless it *wasn't* a cheap treasure map. Unless Trystan had been a total idiot to dismiss it so easily. Unless Galahad had *let* him dismiss it, because it was easier than revealing things he didn't want to share. Unless the unpredictable Captain of the King's Men had outflanked Trystan all over again and was actually questing after something *real*.

Son of a bitch.

For the first time, all of Trystan's focus locked onto the knight's mysterious "mission." "Galahad, where did that map come from?" He demanded, his mind sharpening.

Galahad glanced at him, hearing the new intensity in his tone and looking wary. "I told you, in a library on Sarras." He stopped right at the entrance to the cavern, his feet braced apart.

"You found it on Sarras, but who *made* the map? Why would someone match the writing on it to the *seywas* on a gryphon's shield?"

Galahad said nothing.

Son of a bitch...

"It's a gryphon map." Trystan whispered, answering his own question, because it was obvious, now. "You are on this mission to find a *gryphon* treasure."

Galahad muttered a curse, frustrated that Trystan was onto him now. "I'm not going to steal the gold." He assured him, like that would be Trystan's first concern. "I'm going to build an art school with it."

Trystan stared at him in total shock, his mind whirling.

"I was going to try and split the gold up among all the gryphons I could find, but I was worried they wouldn't take it. They hate me. ...With good reason. But, you guys love kids, so a school seemed like a perfect way to honor your people. The gryphons who left it behind would want it helping children, way more than just staying buried someplace, right?" He sighed. "Except, now I'm sure there *isn't* any gold. I'm looking for 'a treasure beyond price,' but I'm not sure what that actually means."

Trystan was pretty fucking sure what it meant.

He took a deep breath. "So, we are here to see a *gryphon* mural?" Oddly enough, that idea struck him as the most unlikely part of all. "Gryphons do not make art. They don't make maps, either."

...Except memories flickered through Trystan's mind. Fisher talking to him about hiding maps in libraries, as the city of Pen Rhionydd burned around them.

Holy. Shit.

"I don't know who made the mural." Galahad assured him, not noticing Trystan's stupefied stare. "But, I'm sure the map came from a gryphon. I've been following the clues on it and they led me here."

Trystan gave his head a clearing shake. Okay. One step at a time. "Why are you taking off your clothes to see a mural made by *anyone?*"

"Honestly, I'm afraid they'll get burned, when..." He stopped short, his gaze suddenly going to the ceiling. "Hang on."

Trystan looked up, too, his attention shifting. Inside Corbenic Cave, nothing moved. Nothing even seemed to live. Trystan saw nothing but white walls and a curved ceiling that stretched back to a far off vanishing point. ...But Galahad was braced for a battle.

Son of a *bitch*.

He drew his sword and stalked forward, ready to fight whatever was about to attack them. "Knight, move away. I will…"

A hand made of fire dropped out of the ceiling. Twice the size of a tabletop, with flaming fingers, it slammed down like it was swatting a bug.

Right onto Galahad.

Trystan's world stopped. "*No!*" The conflagration completely engulfed the knight's body, swirling like a vortex as the fiery fist clenched around him. No one could survive that attack. It was impossible. Trystan knew that even as he moved. He ran for the hand-creature, ready to reach right into the flames and somehow pull Galahad out. …But he never got the chance.

The fire-hand let out a sudden shriek of otherworldly pain and reared back, away from Galahad. Rather than a flattened pile of ash, the knight was still standing there. Completely unharmed, the silver shield held above his head and not a mark on his muscular body.

Trystan's mouth dropped open in relief, and astonishment and… wonder.

He gaped at Galahad. In that second, he saw the hero who wouldn't open fire on his retreating enemies. The warrior who'd defeated five gryphons with shackles on his hands. The idealist who withstood banishment to free a gryphon hostage from torture. The artist whose ideas brightened the world. The kindhearted man who'd remembered to buy his goddaughter's flying carpet. The only being alive who could possibly, *maybe,* rival Trystan in battle.

He saw his mate.

Unable to kill the knight, the fire-hand began crawling towards Trystan, its fingers propelling it along like a spider. Trystan dragged his attention away from Galahad and scanned the creature's intangible form for a place to stab.

"*Stop!*" Galahad shifted position, keeping himself between the fire-monster and Trystan. "It'll kill you! It won't kill me!" He turned his head, frantic blue eyes meeting Trystan's. "If you are ever going to trust me at any moment in your life, *this* is the moment."

Trystan's gaze held Galahad's for a heartbeat of time and he did the stupidest thing a warrior could do: He stopped fighting.

Trystan stepped back, his heart pounding. "Do not die." He got out hoarsely.

The knight's eyes widened, like he was surprised that Trystan agreed.

He wasn't the only one. "You have twenty goddamn

seconds." Trystan couldn't believe he was agreeing to even that long. "Then, we are both *leaving.*"

"We agreed on five minutes!"

"I never agreed to that!"

Galahad's mouth curved, a confident smile glinting. "We'll compromise on three." He spun the shield around and slammed it into the huge fiery hand.

Fisher had been wrong, when he said no one was the *ya'lah*. He'd never met Galahad of Camelot. The knight was glorious. Every move was perfect. No one else in all of creation could fight as he did. That ridiculous match against Vallon had been beautiful, but this was… art. Gods, if they survived this, Trystan was going to *insist* that they try sparring. It would be an absolute revelation to cross swords with an equal.

The massive hand hit against the shield, crazed by Galahad's continued evasion. The light of its fiery fingers seemed to intensify, reflecting off the mirrored surface. Rather than killing the creature, the shield seemed to be feeding it.

There was no way Galahad could keep holding it back forever. No matter how skilled he was, the creature was monstrous, now. It grew brighter and brighter, bigger and bigger, its color changing from yellow, to orange, to brilliant red. Smoke rose off the shield, as the hand tried to reach Galahad. The fire-monster was getting stronger.

Trystan shook his head, unwilling to continue this madness. "Knight…"

"Trystan, do not move!" He bellowed, as if he could feel Trystan's struggle to stay still. "I've got this." He kept the shield up, pushing back against the force of the hand. It was soon white hot and swollen to a monstrous size.

Trystan wasn't sure how Galahad had survived so far, but he wasn't about to push his luck. "Twenty seconds are *up!* That thing is about to explode. Let's go!"

"We agreed on three minutes!"

"I never agreed to…"

The hand exploded.

For one timeless instant, Trystan was sure Galahad had detonated with it, his body blown apart and his light gone from the world. The shield somehow absorbed the fire and energy, sucking it into its supercharged surface. A blast of power went out, so bright that Trystan squinted against the glare. Then, the blinding glow faded. A small shower of flames and sparks rained down, but with nothing to burn, they quickly fizzled out, leaving everything quiet.

And the knight still stood there, not a scratch on his perfect body.

Trystan collapsed forward, bending at the waist, so his hands rested on his knees. Every prayer of thanks, to every god of his childhood, ran through his mind on a loop. He was fairly sure he would never recover from witnessing that.

Galahad made a "huh" sound, not even winded. "The writing on the shield was right. That *did* work." He gave the silver surface a knock with his knuckles, like he was trying to figure out where the fire had gone. "Is it like a battery or something? Maybe a portal? The engravings didn't say."

Trystan very slowly turned his head to look at him.

"You were amazing, by the way." Galahad enthused. "I can't believe you trusted me to handle that. This is a huge step forward in our relationship." He paused the way he always did when some new, bizarre thought entered his head. "Hey, do you think that hand-thing was an animal or just an enchantment? I'd hate to have killed an endangered species."

Trystan straightened up to his full height. "Knight," he said in a very calm tone, "why are you still alive?"

"Oh, right." Galahad made a self-conscious face. "I'm impervious to fire."

"You're impervious to fire." Trystan could barely hear his own voice over the pounding in his ears. "This seems... unusual."

"Yeah, it's kind of a new thing." Galahad agreed. "It's just my skin and hair that's fireproof, not the clothes I'm wearing. I learned that the hard way. But the spell is still a lot more useful than I thought it would be." He hesitated. "It's a protection spell. Did I mention that? See, when I was traveling around, looking for the map, I met the Princess of the Salamanders. Really sweet girl."

Trystan's head tilted, almost hypnotized.

"She'd lost her golden ball down a well, right?" Galahad went on. "Her dad had given it to her, before he ran off with this local frog-woman. That affair was a *huge* scandal. So, the princess was crying because the ball was gone forever and I wanted to help. Luckily, I'm pretty good at free-diving." He shrugged. "And the well wasn't *that* haunted and bottomless."

Trystan stifled a wince.

"So, I got the ball out and she was like, 'I have to reward you.' I tried to refuse, but I think it's a cultural thing with salamanders to repay favors. So she says, 'Let me make you impervious to fire.'"

Galahad nodded like all of that made perfect sense. "Turns out, all salamanders are fireproof. I'm not sure why. Anyway, I didn't want to be rude, so I said okay."

"Good choice." Trystan said vaguely.

"Right? For some reason, I've always been slightly immune to *consumer* magic. Like those weird potions people sell. But, the salamanders' magic comes from nature, just like the sandman's sleeping dust. That's *way* more powerful and it seems to work great!" He spread his arms, casually pleased. "And it *is* pretty cool to be fireproof. I never have to wear a hat, because I don't get sunburned, either." He paused. "I thought I'd be okay when I was tied to that pig pyre, too, but it turns out I'm *not* impervious to smoke. The princess didn't mention that part."

Lyrssa save him...

Trystan reached up to pinch the bridge of his nose, still trying to calm down. Caring for a *ya'lah* was stressful. He felt stress. Was that an emotion?

"You okay, Trys?" Galahad headed over to collect his clothing, his brow furrowed. "You weren't hurt were you?"

"No. I am fine." Trystan cleared his throat. "I am just considering many, many things."

Galahad still looked troubled as he pulled on his pants. "Considering whether you want to stay allies?" He guessed in a more serious tone. "Because I keep getting you attacked?"

"No." The knight was the only path he would ever take, even if it turned Trystan's wings prematurely gray. The undeniable feeling that he'd found his mate had taken root and would not fade, no matter how he tried to ignore it. "Our alliance is irrevocable."

"Alliances are irrevocable?" Galahad didn't seem upset by the revelation, just surprised. "Is that a gryphon rule?"

"Yes." Trystan had just created the rule and he was a gryphon.

Galahad smiled and it was like the sun shining in a cloudless sky.

Trystan jabbed a finger at him, refusing to be distracted. "But this was the *only time* I will let you fight alone, understand? At least, against dangerous enemies. I will happily watch if you wish to slay *weaker* ones. That would be enjoyable. But I cannot repeat this trauma."

"I know how difficult it is for you to not kill things." Galahad commiserated.

"Exactly!" Trystan flattened a hand over his own chest,

trying to express the hardship he'd just endured. "As I stood there, I felt... *worry*."

"Gryphons don't worry about anything, Trys." He pulled on his shirt. "You've told me that forty-thousand times."

"I know! And yet *you* made it happen within me, knight. I was *worried*." That sounded like an accusation, because it was. "It was the least enjoyable emotion I have ever experienced. Do not ever make me feel it, again. Promise me."

"I live a life of truth. So, I can't promise you that." Fully dressed again, Galahad crossed over to him. "But I promise to try, okay?"

"Try *hard*." He gripped the back of the knight's neck. "I mean it."

Galahad gave him a quick kiss. "You're worrying, again."

Trystan sighed, lost in the man. "Gryphons do not worry... often." His fingers brushed through his shimmery hair. Touching him calmed much of Trystan's panic, refocusing him on the next step of the mission. "Now, where is this mural?"

Chapter Twenty

Battle of Legion
End of the Third Looking Glass Campaign

The Rath was like no other cannon ever built, so it was no surprised that the gryphons didn't understand what they were dealing with. It fired weaponized magic. Abnormal, burning hot magic, cooked up in a lab. It had never been fired before the Battle of Legion.

It would never be fired again.

Galahad would later ensure the cannon was lost in the deepest hole he could find, never to be resurrected. But that was in the future. Far too late for the gryphons at Legion. On that day, it scorched the world.

Vivid green lightning streaked from the Rath's huge barrel with an unearthly roar and ignited the air itself. The horrific sound and sizzling brightness had most onlookers cringing away

But Galahad hadn't shielded his eyes. He couldn't. He was frozen.

The phony magic looked like withered, grasping fingers as it enveloped the village. Wooden houses exploded like they'd never been there at all. Galahad hadn't known that any weapon could do so much damage. Hadn't even imagined it was possible. He hadn't questioned what the Rath even was, when Uther arrived with it from Camelot.

He *should* have.

God, he should have done so much. But he didn't and then it was too late.

The Rath fired and, instantly, Galahad knew he stood on the wrong side of the battle. It seemed impossible that he hadn't seen it long before. Was it egotism or stupidity or naivety that made him so blind? Did it even matter? In that second, everything became tragically, unforgivably clear. And it was too late.

He stood there --The general of an army of villains-- trying to make sense of it all.

For one precious moment too long, the gryphons just stared, as well, as their minds tried to take in the horrible spectacle. None of them could comprehend the scale and speed of the devastation.

"*Stop!*" Lyrssa shouted from her cage. "*There are children!*"

Galahad had heard her. Surely the others did, too. Why didn't anyone else react? Why didn't they stop? He would never understand it.

Her cry was certainly enough to jolt him from his horrified stupor. His head whipped around to meet her one-eyed gaze, dread filling him. "What?" He bellowed, hoping he'd misunderstood and knowing he hadn't.

"The town is filled with the young and the very old!" She looked right at him, her words desperate. "Your king won't listen to me. I've told him, but he does not care. He'll kill them all!"

Galahad's entire world changed, leaving nothing as it was before.

"*Stop!*" He bellowed to his men, believing her claims.

In fact, he believed the woman --his enemy in countless battles-- so quickly that, later, he would realize that he must not have trusted King Uther, at all. Which was worse somehow. He hadn't trusted the man and still he'd followed his orders for years? Still saw him as a father? Still loved him? What did that say of Galahad's character?

His honor?

Instead of stopping at his orders, the knights opened fire with their rifles. In Camelot, guns would later be outlawed, because Arthur far preferred the sweep and majesty of swords. Even Galahad's collection of antique firearms would be deemed illegal. But on that day, a hail of bullets rained down unchecked. The gryphons did not possess a single firearm. There were three hundred and seventy men, women, and children in the village at the beginning of the siege. Within seconds, one hundred and sixty-three of them were dead in the August grass.

And that was just the beginning.

"Cease fire! Goddamn it, *stop!*" Galahad roared, but it was no use. The bloodlust of battle was upon the knights, now.

"Kill them all!" Uther bellowed. "Kill all the heathens and cleanse the land, boys!"

The warrior gryphons tried to fight back against the King's Men. Grabbing their swords, they flew at the knights. All of them fell, shot out of the sky. Automatic rifles cut them down like broken dolls, their limbs spasming in grotesque dances as they tumbled to the ground.

The elderly gryphons who remained fled into the Checkered Plains with the children.

Galahad ran for Uther's horse. "Your majesty, make them stop!" He shouted, frantic now. "They're killing old women and babies!"

For a heartbeat, he'd thought he could get through to Uther. That the king would be the man Galahad had imagined him to be. That Uther would see what was happening and order the men to cease fire. That everything would somehow be... fixed. Somehow. Galahad had been so stupidly gullible, right up until the end.

Instead of commanding a stop to the carnage, Uther laughed.

Fucking *laughed*.

"Why do your people always bother about protecting children?" He shouted at Lyrssa, sneering out the words. His face was alight with malicious pleasure. "It makes it so easy to pick you off in battle. Stupid and pointless, like all things you heathens do. Most of the little bastards aren't even of your race."

Lyrssa eyed him with palpable contempt. "The innocent belong to all who would care for them. True warriors know this."

Uther would never understand that philosophy. Not even at the end.

"This is our chance to wipe the winged devils out for good, men!" He shouted at the soldiers and Sir Percival led a cheer at the words, *laughing* as he fired on the gryphon. "Leave none of them alive! We're cleansing the world of these savages, once and for all!"

The knights stepped on the piles of dead and dying, picking off any survivors they found.

Later, nobody but Galahad would swear under oath that King Uther had personally issued the command to kill the wounded, so the official inquest would gloss over his account as unsubstantiated. The tragic death of Uther had so affected Galahad's recollections that nothing he said about the day could be relied on. That was what the bureaucrats in charge ruled, when they sealed and discounted his testimony. Grief had muddled his mind.

But Uther *had* bellowed at the troops to take no prisoners

and the soldiers *had* followed those instructions to the letter. Thanks to years of Knights' Academy propaganda, most of the King's Men saw the gryphons as little more than animals, so their murders were not really murders at all. More like a righteous defeat of evil. If you were entirely right, then your enemies must be entirely wrong. They must be less than you. Different than you. A threat to you.

Even Galahad had believed all the lies he'd been told about the gryphons being dangerous monsters... Until that moment, when the world started to burn. At that moment, he no longer believed in anything.

Some of the gryphons crouched down into the tall grass, desperate to hide. It didn't work. The knights set the Checkered Plains ablaze to drive them out. Whether through accident or design, the flames spread quickly in the summer wind, surrounding the village. Trapping many of the gryphons who were left inside a wall of fire.

"No!" Galahad bellowed, instinctively starting forward. "Stop!"

"*Don't stop!*" Uther contradicted at a roar, kicking Galahad back. He reeled on his horse to block Galahad's way. "What the hell's the matter with you, boy?! You want to confuse the men? We're in the middle of a battle here! *Fight!*"

Galahad barely heard him, frantic to stop the knights before all the gryphons were slaughtered. In a haze, he recognized Bedivere, the boy on the line who'd been so scared, helping to ignite the grass. Heard the little bastard laughing as children screamed.

The anguished wails of people being burned alive mixed with the ceaseless gunshots and roar of the fire and all the goddamn laughter, creating an unholy cacophony. Soot and ash rose, choking the air. It was all chaos.

No one could process it all.

So it was little surprise that no one knew exactly what happened next. That no one could give a fully accepted account at the inquests, or to the newspapers, or even make sense of each individual moment in their own minds.

That, in the end, no one knew exactly how the Queen of the Gryphons escaped.

Chapter Twenty-One

Some would ask why not just give Uther the graal? Yes, he was an evil man, but is it not also evil to allow his war to ravage Lyonesse, if you have the means to stop it? Shouldn't have Lyrssa have given into him, for the Good of all?

The answer is no.

Even if we could have acquired it for him, does anyone think that Uther would have been content to heal himself and then leave the graal's power alone?
Of course not.

He would use it to enrich himself. To gain power and enslave all who stood against him. Giving him the graal would not have stopped the War.

It would have allowed Uther the means to destroy the entire world.

How the Wingless War Happened
Skylyn Welkyn- Gryphon Storyteller

Pellinore Mountains- Corbenic Cave

The mural took up the entire back wall of the cavern.

It had been painted on the smooth white stone, the colors running together in some places and the perspective all wrong. Whoever had created it hadn't been much of an artist. To Galahad, it looked like a castle map from an old video game. A badly-rendered view of many interconnected rooms, with no writing to explain what it all meant. Over the years, Galahad had had fourteen video games based on his adventures, so he knew what their maps looked like.

Trystan seem transfixed by it. "Your map led us here?" He whispered.

"Yep. If I'm translating it right, I'm supposed to be looking for an emerald trail." He frowned. "But I don't see an emerald trail. Do you see an emerald trail?"

"The mural is incomplete." Trystan didn't tear his gaze from the wall, but he pointed to a jagged hole at one corner. "It could be there. Do you know what is missing?"

"Oh! Yeah, good point." Galahad reached into his pocket and came up with the jagged hunk of painted stone he'd found inside the waterfall. "I got this just before the hippocamps stampeded."

"I *knew* you were not just taking a bath."

Galahad ignored that muttered comment. When he slid the piece of stone into place, it completed the map. Instantly, a magical spell was triggered and a dotted line appeared on the mural. An emerald-green trail guiding a path through them maze of rooms and then straight upward to a spot marked with an X.

Treasure maps should always have Xs. It just made everything so much cooler.

"My gods." Trystan breathed.

"You recognize this place?" Galahad asked him softly.

"Who gave you this mission, knight?" Trystan's eyes traced over the labyrinth of misshapen rooms. Memorizing them.

Galahad hesitated at the direct question. He didn't want to lie and he didn't want to tell the truth, so he said nothing.

"Was it a gryphon?" Trystan persisted, glancing his way. "Did a gryphon tell you to find this?" He pointed at the mural. "They must have. The knowledge is lost to everyone else, except perhaps Avi. The child knows everything."

"I don't want to tell you about who sent me on this mission."

"Why the hell not?"

"Because, then you'll ask me about thirty other things that I don't want to tell you. You won't believe me, anyway."

"That is ridiculous. Tell me everything. *Now*."

Galahad shook his head, his heart pounding. "No."

"Knight..."

"I don't want to tell you!" Even Galahad was surprised when he shouted the words. He stood there, breathing hard and staring up at Trystan's face. "I don't want you to know anything more about my mission, okay?"

Trystan's head tilted and he edged closer to him. "Why?"

"Because, when I got it, I was covered in the blood of the man I'd just slaughtered *and I don't want you to know about it!*"

Trystan caught hold of him when Galahad would have turned away. "It's alright." He tugged him against his chest, big arms and even bigger wings enveloping him. "What you did *then* makes no difference to how I see you *now*. I have told you this."

Yeah, Trystan had told him that. But, Galahad didn't believe it. At all.

"There is no one alive who can better understand the horrors that you've seen and done." Trystan's palm rubbed the back of his neck. "I was in the War, too."

Galahad rested his forehead on Trystan's shoulder and let out a shaky sigh. This mission was so much harder than he'd thought it would be. It brought up everything he wanted to forget. "What you did is not the same as what I did."

"Of course it is. Truthfully, you and I were waging war upon *each other*, for most of the last campaign. You would move, and then I would move, and then you would move. We were two sides of a coin. Even then we were connected." His mouth curved. "Only I hated you."

Galahad gave a snort of reluctant amusement. "I mainly just admired your abilities. I thought you were a military genius. I still do."

"Many times I plotted to capture you and torture you to death."

"I know. I remember the rock ogre who tried to eat me, on your orders. It took me three days to talk him out of it. It's shocking I'm still alive."

"I am not shocked, at all. This is the only possible path for either of us." Trystan's lips brushed his hair. "Now, tell me why you are searching for Atlantis."

Galahad pulled back to look at him. "This mural is of Atlantis?" He looked back at the maze of rooms. "I guess it *has* to be, but..."

"This mural shows Listeneise." Trystan explained when Galahad trailed off. "The first temple of my people was in Atlantis." He shook his head. "Perhaps it is the last temple, now. Uther and his men burned the rest."

"You're sure *this* is that temple?" Galahad pointed at the map. To him, it looked like a hundred buildings in a hundred lands.

"I am sure that this symbol signifies Listeneise." Trystan nodded towards a circle-y shape at the top of the painting. "And that symbol?" He gestured to another one at the bottom. "That is a signature. A man named Fisher drew this." He made a face at all the squiggly lines and poor color choices. "We are not an artistic people."

"Fisher was that old gryphon you were in the zoo with, right?"

"Yes. The only one who knew the location of the Looking Glass Pool."

Galahad's eyes widened. "Oh hell..." His head whipped back around to Trystan. "*That's* what I'm looking for? The graal?" Galahad tried to process that idea, but it was kind of impossible. "Seriously?"

His incredulous response had Trystan's smiling. "Only you would go on a treasure hunt with no clue of the treasure, knight."

"I thought it was gold! She just told me to find Atlantis. She didn't tell me why."

"*Who* told you? Avalon?"

Galahad hesitated. "No, it wasn't Avi." He admitted after a beat. "Lyrssa told me to find Atlantis."

Trystan squinted. "Lyrssa? Queen of my people?"

"Yes."

"Lyrssa Highstorm sent a knight of Camelot on a mission to find *the one thing* that Uther most wanted to claim? The one thing that could save or destroy the gryphons?"

"I told you you wouldn't believe me."

"I believe you, I just do not understand it." Trystan paused, like he was thinking it all over. "Unless she knew you were the *ya'lah*."

"For the last time, I'm *not* the ya'lah. In fact, Lyrssa said..."

And that's when Galahad remembered where he'd heard the word before. His mouth snapped shut, staring at Trystan as comprehension dawned.

Holy *shit*.

"What did she say?" Trystan prompted when Galahad went quiet.

"Um..." He cleared his throat, trying to think. "Explain what the *ya'lah* does, again."

"The *ya'lah* is a champion of the gryphon people. He or she is chosen to perform a great task. In this case, the *ya'lah* is fated to be the one who will remove Uther's curse and allow the gryphon to have children, again. When Igraine cast the spell, she attempted to make it unbreakable by stipulating that the *ya'lah* must come from wingless blood. This is why it is important that *you* are the one on this mission."

"Right." Galahad's head tilted. "Your grandfather was wingless, wasn't he?"

"Yes. He died many years ago, though. He is not the *ya'lah*."

"But he's *biologically* your grandfather?"

"Of course. I have his eyes."

Galahad felt his mouth curve, pieces fitting together for him. "You have his blood."

It took Trystan a moment to catch up with that logic. "What?" He did a double-take. "Wait... what the hell are you talking about?"

"I remember where I heard the word before. Lyrssa said it to me." He'd all but forgotten about it in the haze of everything else that happened that day. But now he saw the workings of some higher power guiding him to this very spot. "She said she saw the *ya'lah* on my path. I didn't know what it meant."

Now he did, though. It meant his True Love was the greatest hero in the world. That was awesome!

Trystan was shaking his head, seeing where this was going and already denying the awesomeness. Why did he always want to be a downer? "She meant that you would *become* the *ya'lah,* as you continued on your journey, knight."

"No, she meant I'd meet *you* on my journey. Your grandfather was wingless and you have his blood. You are also a gryphon, and a Good person, and presently on a quest for the graal. This is *your* destiny, Trystan. It all fits!"

Trystan's eyebrows compressed like he was having difficulty keeping up. "No, it doesn't. *You* are the *ya'lah*. I have known since nearly the day we met. Why are we debating what is obvious?"

"You're the *ya'lah*, Trystan." Galahad repeated. He held up a hand when Trystan began to protest. "Stop and think about it."

Trystan didn't stop and think about it. "This is not..."

Galahad cut him off. "*Stop and think about it.*" He repeated. "Don't entrench and argue with me. Just take a breath and process what I'm saying."

"What you're saying is crazy. Why should I process something crazy? You think I would not know if I was the *ya'lah*?"

"Do you think I wouldn't know if *I* was the *ya'lah*?" Galahad retorted.

"*I* know you are!"

"I know *you* are!"

The two of them stood there, staring at each other for a long beat.

"We will *both* process this." Trystan finally decided. "Then you will admit that I am right. You are not thinking clearly and need time to adjust to your great calling."

Galahad rolled his eyes. "You need time to not be such a dumbass."

Trystan disregarded that and pointed a finger at the mural of the temple. "This is what's important, right now. How do we get *here?* This is the place where your map leads, yes? Where is it?"

"To the west, beyond St. Ives. On an island in the Moaning Sea."

"There are no islands in the Moaning Sea. There is *nothing* in the Moaning Sea. That ocean is enspelled with icy magic that freezes all who touch it. Few beings alive could withstand the frigid waves."

Galahad opened his mouth and then closed it, again. He cleared his throat.

Trystan stared at him for a long moment. "You're impervious to freezing, aren't you?"

"It's not as weird as it sounds." Galahad defended, raising his palms. "See there was this really nice yeti, who I helped out, right? And he gave me this..."

"No." Trystan waved a hand, cutting him off. "I do not wish to know the details. I am still recovering from your last insane tale. We will just accept the fact that this is yet *another* ludicrous skill that you possess, but have not told me about."

"Well, I told you I don't need a coat." Galahad defended.

Trystan shook his head in exasperation. "The point is, Atlantis is long gone. Even Fisher agreed with this. I remember him speaking of the land's submergence."

"Well, the map says there's an island." Galahad dug it out of his pocket and handed it to Trystan. "See for yourself."

Trystan made a face at the lopsided sketch. "Fisher no doubt drew this, as well. He was not an entirely stable man. Most likely it's a fabrication of his broken mind. ...And a poorly rendered one at that." Trystan just couldn't stand to be optimistic. It was like an allergy or something. "The old man spoke of hearing his dead mate." Trystan gave a vague shrug. "Of finding the Looking Glass Pool by accident and then leaving a trail for others to follow. I did not understand it all."

"Did he say anything specific that might help us find the graal?"

Trystan rubbed his forehead. "It was over twenty years ago. I was a child. I do not remember all the words precisely. But on the last night he lived he told me to follow a dream and then..." He floundered for a beat, like he was trying to accurately translate something that didn't quite make sense into Galahad's language. "'When your dream follows you, it should look down.'"

"Look down?"

"Not at the horizon." Trystan pointed at the floor as if unconsciously mimicking a gesture that Fisher had made. A slow, deliberate sweep of his index finger. "*Down.*"

Uh-oh.

"So... this gryphon temple is underwater?" Galahad surmised with a concerned frown.

"This would be my guess."

"Then how did Fisher see the Looking Glass Pool?"

"I do not know. As I said, his words never made much sense. But, if Listeneise still stood above the waves, someone would have surely seen it by now. We may be too late."

"No." Galahad didn't accept that. "I hear the dead gryphons whispering to me..."

"You are finally ready to admit this?" Trystan interjected smugly. "I *knew* that was happening, all the way back at the snake tomb. I told you so."

Galahad kept talking. "...and I don't think they'd bother if this was all bullshit. I think they're trying to help me on my mission. And I don't think Lyrssa would send me on this path without a purpose. She told me to find Atlantis."

"Fine." Trystan said, which meant he agreed and was on board with the plan. Galahad was getting much better at translating Trystan-ese. "I suppose the only way to be sure of the map's veracity is to check for ourselves, then."

"Yeah?" Galahad grinned.

"Yeah." Trystan sighed and handed the map back to him. "Shit. Now I am hunting for a mythic treasure. You really do cause me no end of problems, knight."

Galahad folded it up again. "Well, it's your duty to fix problems for me, isn't it?" He asked casually. All in all, he was pleased with how well this was going. At this rate, they could find the graal, lift the curse, and be back in Camelot in time for Avi's birthday.

"Did I agree to fix your problems?" Trystan went back to memorizing the mural. "I might as well agree to move the desert, one grain of sand at a time. I must have been out of my mind with desire for you, if I said such a thing. It does not count."

"*I* agreed to it when *I* was out of my mind with desire, actually. You very specifically told me that you're the only one who's supposed to be caring for me. I said 'yes' to that idea, along with everything else."

Trystan's head snapped around. "You choose to be in my care?" From his tone, it sounded like that was another one of those important, gryphon-y rituals that Galahad didn't fully understand.

"Aren't I already in your care? You sure say it enough... *hey!*" He broke off in surprise as Trystan seized hold of him. "What the hell, man?" Galahad didn't struggle as he was dragged backwards and pinned against the mural, but he did frown in exasperation. "Why can we never have a normal conversation?"

Trystan stared down at him intently. He looked even more focused on this discussion than he'd been on the hunt for the graal. "Gwen claims you as her brother."

"Uh-huh..." Galahad's eyebrows went up. "I claim her as my sister, so it works out fine."

Trystan gave his head a shake. "Gwen *put* you in my care. That is my point. I protect you as her proxy. You did not choose me. You have said you wished to be free of my custody. Many times."

"Well, you can be a little overprotective." Galahad defended. "How many ugly hats have you made me wear since we met?"

Trystan didn't seem to hear that. "Without your consent, I will have to withdraw my care of you, once I return you to Gwen." He shifted closer and one hand slammed out, impacting the wall beside Galahad's head. "I will have no more duty to watch over you, unless you grant it to me."

Galahad's eyes went to the massive tattooed arm and then back up to Trystan's taut face. Holy shit. The man typically was a perfect gentleman, asking permission before they even touched. Now, he was aggressively boxing Galahad in, his hard body radiating heat and dominance. This was unexpected and kind of awesome. Galahad ran the conversation through his Trystan-translator and began to make sense of things.

"You will have no more *right* to watch over me." He rephrased quietly.

Trystan's jaw ticked. "Technically, this is correct."

"And that worries you?"

"Gryphons do not worry. Often. It is merely an irritating fact that occurs to me several times an hour. You will be dead within days, without proper care."

"And only you can give that care to me, I'm guessing."

"Yes." His head dipped down to Galahad's ear, his voice a dark rumble. "Gwen put you in my care… But, now you must *choose* to remain there. That would give me the rights I desire. Rights that should belong to no other. Rights that are *mine*."

"Okay." Galahad breathed.

"Okay?"

"Okay, I'll choose to remain in your care." He met Trystan's gaze. "It seems to make sense. Who else could care for me like you do?"

Trystan's eyes burned hot. "No one." It was a quiet vow. "No one else in the world could care for you as I do."

Galahad shined a smile at him. "I believe you."

"You give yourself to me too easily." Trystan warned in a dazed voice, like he was shocked at how simple it was. "I am not as kindhearted as you, knight. I will take everything that you offer and perhaps more."

"If I'm in your care, you'll just have to watch out for me, then."

"All I do is watch you."

Galahad shifted his hips forward, so they brushed against Trystan's. "Have you noticed that you have me trapped against this wall, then?" He asked conversationally.

"I like you there." Trystan seemed right on the edge of control, his body rock hard and demanding.

"So you're not going to let me go?"

"Not yet." Trystan caught hold of his wrist, dragging it down. "First I will have *more*."

Galahad's breathing grew harsher as Trystan's hand held his palm over his manhood, pressing his fingers to show him what he wanted. Galahad could feel the heat of him right through the fabric. "Soooo… caring for me means I'm your sexual hostage, then? Hopefully." Because, he kinda loved that idea.

"Caring for you means I see that you are safe and protected." Teeth grazed Galahad's neck hard enough to leave a scratch. Galahad's body shuddered in response, tilting his head to accept the mark. "Holding you captive until your hand eases me is a separate issue, knight."

Galahad certainly wasn't going to argue. His hand rubbed over Trystan's arousal, giving a low sound of appreciation at the size. "You really are… big." Gleaming blue eyes met Trystan's, curious and hot. "Are you sure you're going to fit, when we finally have sex?"

The question seemed to kick Trystan's desire into an even higher gear. "Very soon, you will take *all* of me." It was somewhere between an order and a reassurance, his stance becoming more forceful. "I will hold you beneath me… And I will touch your untouched body in places no one else ever has… And when you are ready, I will push deep inside of you, again and again, until neither of us knows where we end and the other begins… And then I will finish deep within you, marking you as mine and mine alone… And you will like it *all*. Understand?"

"Yes." Galahad bobbed his head, dazed. "I'll give you more than just touching, right now. If you're ready to say 'yes' I'll sleep with you, *right now*."

Trystan hesitated, his breath sawing in and out, like that was *exactly* what he wanted. "No." He decided anyway. "Not yet."

"Not yet" was another one of his favorite things to say. "Why?"

"I am… *uncertain* what would happen afterwards."

Galahad wasn't sure what that meant. What could possibly happen after sex that would change Trystan's mind about him? That Galahad wouldn't be good at it, maybe? That didn't seem like a Trystan concern.

But if his True Love wasn't ready to sleep with him, then Galahad could wait.

"Okay." He agreed. "Have I mentioned *Corrupted by the Winged Devil* takes place in a cave? I'm not as good at scripting scenes as you are, but I'm confident I can draw on it as inspiration for all kinds of fun, third-base activities."

"Actually, in my culture…" Trystan stopped short and Galahad glanced up at him.

"Yeah?"

"Um…" Trystan cleared his throat, hunting for words, again. "In my culture, using hands on each other has more significance that it does to the wingless. It is sometimes not even done between mates. It is very… intimate."

Galahad blinked at that news. "You already did it to me."

"Oh, I remember. Trust me."

"And you didn't *tell* me it was some super-special thing to do in your culture?"

Trystan's head tilted, like the question confused him. "*Everything* I do with you is special. Because you are special."

Galahad smiled at the simple explanation. "Well, I still owe you that boon, right?" His hand massaged the front of Trystan's pants. "You want to try this very intimate, very special, *very* satisfying thing with me, right now?"

"Gods, yes." Trystan's knuckles tipped Galahad's chin up, so he could languidly kiss him. "Only with you."

Trystan really liked kissing. And Trystan was really good at being really good at things he really liked. His kiss was deep and slow and possessive. Galahad's mouth opened to give him access and Trystan drank his fill. Being the sexual hostage of this man was a dream job.

Trystan gave a low moan as Galahad kissed him back without reservation. "This will be over too quickly, knight. Having your hand on me is erotic enough, but your game has also put thoughts of the War into my head. I envision having you back then, as I have you now, and it is *very* appealing."

"Didn't you say you wanted to torture me to death during the War?"

"Obviously. You were a vexing opponent." His palm slipped to the zipper of Galahad's coat, tugging it down. "But first I would have captured you, intent on extracting information and prolonging your suffering."

Galahad snorted. "Sounds very romantic." He deadpanned.

"And once I had you in my grasp and began speaking with you... Once I saw your eyes and your smile and the brightness of your ideas... I would not have been able to hurt you." Trystan stripped Galahad's coat off, his hands slipping under his shirt and running over the thick muscles of his chest in appreciation.

Galahad struggled to breathe. "You sure about that?"

"I have never been more sure of anything. I would have kept you for my own, even if I had to shackle you to my bed." His head dipped to lick Galahad's ear, his mouth curving when Galahad jolted in response. "There would have been no other option."

He would *not* have had to shackle Galahad to keep him. Once he saw Trystan, Galahad would have been fighting to stay with him and Galahad never lost a fight.

"Maybe I would have refused to consent to your barbarous ways and you'd have to keep your hands to yourself." Galahad retorted, just to tease him. "Gryphons only take willing people to their villages, right? Didn't you tell me that?"

"Of course." Trystan agreed seriously. "We keep our captives until they are willing."

Galahad bit the inside of his cheek to suppress his laugh. "That's very fair."

Trystan obviously thought so, too. "Sometimes it takes a bit of adjustment, but in your case..." He shrugged, his hands continuing to caress Galahad's skin. "I am confident I could have won you over to the idea of easing me within a matter of hours."

"Yeah, I really do suck at playing hard-to-get, don't I?"

"I do not mind." His expression was filled with all kinds of beautiful emotions. "Tell me again you are in my care. I like to hear it."

"I'm in your care, Trystan. No one else's." Galahad's palm tightened on Trystan's hardness, ready to turn the tables. "Do you agree to be in my care, too?"

Trystan let out a hissing breath. His jaw clenched, instinctively thrusting deeper into Galahad's grip. "In *your* care? Lyrssa, you'd kill me within the week."

"Is that a yes?" Galahad traced the shape of Trystan through his pants, admiring his size. "Because, I can stop..." He pretended to draw his hand back.

"No." Trystan grabbed his wrist, holding it still. "I am in your care. I would have no other. I swear it."

Galahad grinned at him, triumphant and cocky. "You're such a pushover."

Trystan's expression went taut. "When you smile at me like that, I cannot think straight. You *know* this."

"I do know it." Galahad agreed in mock apology. "I'm a Bad guy, sometimes. I told you, it's in my nature. He shifted positions before Trystan understood what was happening. He slid sideways, twisting left, so he was on the other side of Trystan's body and spun him around. He pushed Trystan backward against the mural, satisfied the man was trapped and at his mercy.

"So, should we bet on who *really* would've been the captive during the War?" Galahad asked with an arch look.

Trystan stared down at him in surprise. "What are you doing?" He was used to being the aggressor. Having someone else in control seemed to confuse him. It also excited him, if the swelling of his erection was any indication.

"I'm taking you prisoner." Galahad unbuckled Trystan's belt and Trystan shifted his hips to let him. It was simple as hell to get the man naked, once you put your mind to it. "I really should tie you up, like you did to me. It's fun. But we can save that for next time."

"I am *your* prisoner? That is ridiculous." Trystan moved forward slightly, because it was his nature to always be in control. "I will be the one..." He stopped short when Galahad's hand flattened on the center of his chest and pushed him back against the wall, again.

"Warriors sometimes like to be taken, remember? You told me that, Trys."

Galahad wasn't using much strength to hold him. Trystan could have gotten free with no effort, at all.

...If he wanted to.

Instead of escaping, he seemed to become more interested in the game. "No one has ever taken me, knight. You think a virgin can do it?"

Galahad arched a brow. Using his foot, he nudged Trystan's legs farther apart, so he had full access to him. His body shifted into a more aggressive stance, pressing against Trystan's. "I think I've never failed at anything."

Trystan's breath shuddered out. "Prove it."

Galahad grinned at the dare, happy that Trystan was playing. His free hand found the fastenings of Trystan's pants. "I'm going to take your clothes off, now." He leaned up to kiss him. "If you're in my care, I need to take *very* good care of you." His lips slid across Trystan's in erotic intent. "Don't try to escape, while I'm busy down there. I'll just catch you, again."

Trystan didn't fight for freedom. He stood still, mesmerized, as Galahad knelt down to remove his boots and pants. Galahad had never undressed another person before and he found it far more arousing than he'd ever imagined it would be. His hands ran up the insides of Trystan's bare legs, astonished by the strength of them. His gaze lingered on the straining erection in front of him, proud that he was responsible for it. Wondering if he could...

"Don't." Trystan whispered. "Not yet. I won't last a minute, with your lips on me."

"Oh, you're not going to last long anyway." Galahad stood up and began working Trystan's jacket and shirt off of his wide shoulders. "I'm going to take you hard and fast." The man's body was so beautiful. Gryphon' clothes were designed to fit around their wings, so it was easy to pull the fabric free. Galahad's fingers still paused to caress the white feathers, unable to help himself. They were so soft and magical...

Trystan's patience snapped at the enthralled touch. "Enough." He automatically tried to move, like he was going to take control and hurry things along. "I cannot wait. I will have..."

Galahad cut him off. "Nope." He pushed him back, his hand in the center of his chest, again. "You're still my helpless captive, remember?"

Trystan's heart was pounding beneath Galahad's fingers. He glanced down at the restraining palm, a speculative look in his eye. "I might... *like* you holding me prisoner." He tried to shift away again, testing, and smiled when Galahad held him firmly against the wall. "Oh *yes*. I do like this. I understand your fondness for being the bound knight in that barbarous gryphon story."

"Both roles are starring ones, so they're equally fun to play. It just depends on the day."

"Today, I am your prisoner, yes?" Trystan was now fully engaged in the game. "Now that you've got me naked and subdued, make my body come for you." For a helpless captive, he still liked to give orders.

"In my hand?" Galahad's fingers slid downward, drawing it out. "Even though it's super intimate and kind of forbidden in your culture?"

"Please." Trystan sounded breathless now, like he still wasn't sure Galahad would go through with it. "I need it. Please. I need to see..." He broke off, like he didn't want to finish.

Galahad didn't want him holding back. "Tell me." His fingertips grazed along the full length of Trystan's arousal. "Tell me *exactly* what you want and it's yours."

Trystan groaned, whispering words in his own language.

"What's that mean?"

"Um..." Trystan's eyes were glazed. "Something that I would rather not explain in your dialect. It will lose the deeper meaning and I do not want to," he gave a sharp intake of breath, as Galahad's fingers grew bolder, "scare you away."

"I don't scare easy. I'm guessing it relates to deflowering my virginal palm, right?"

Trystan gave a ravenous snarl, as Galahad squeezed him tighter. "I want to see my seed all over your skin. I want you branded with it. I want others to see it, too, and know who you belong to. The words would roughly translate to this idea, but, in my culture, it does not sound so coarse. It has a less aggressive subtext."

"In this language it sounds like you're about to defile me." Galahad wasn't objecting to either interpretation. His hand on Trystan's chest traced the sharp lines of his abdomen, loving the rigid feel of them. "Are you about to defile me, Trys?"

"Gods, yes." His breathing was ragged. "I need to come in your grasp. Few gryphons would allow me to do such a thing. I have never even wanted to try it with another. But with you, the craving is so deep... Please. I need it."

"Anything you ask me, I'll say 'yes.'" Galahad leaned up to kiss him, soothing the man's worries. "Anything you want, I'll give you."

"If you had any idea of all the ways I want to despoil your body, you would not make such a vow. I have a vivid imagination and I have spent the past weeks thinking of little else."

"Now you're just getting my hopes up." Galahad gave him another grin. "This would be a good time to tell me you're crazy about me, by the way."

"You *make* me crazy. Does that count?"

"Partial credit." Galahad's palm finally encircled his hard, thick flesh. He'd never touched another man's naked member, so it was a revelation to feel Trystan's rock-hard desire. His gaze went up to Trystan's in surprise and pleasure. "Me or adrenaline?" He teased.

"*You.*" Trystan's fist clenched in Galahad's hair and he gave a choked sound that could only be called a chuckle. "Only you could reduce me to this state, knight. And I *truly* do not want to scare you, but your innocent expression of discovery does not help me stay in control."

"You're not in control." Galahad assured him. "This is *my* show, remember." He kissed the tense line of Trystan's jaw, his hand moving. "And I think you're going to like it more than my usual programs."

"I have wanted you since the second I saw that damn TV show." It was impossible to miss how far gone Trystan was. The man's massive shaft was fully engorged. "You were so beautiful and bright. That vivid gaze shone at me through the camera lens and I was... lost."

"You have nothing but complaints about my television show."

"Because it is fucking terrible. ...Aside from the magical glow of its star." He ground his teeth in ecstasy. "*P'don*, I have not touched another since I first watched you on screen."

Galahad beamed, thrilled to hear that. "Yeah?"

"I tried to find other companionship, but, compared to you, all others were lacking." He looked dazed, his body completely in Galahad's thrall. "Even when I thought you were a soulless monster, you caused me many frustratingly long and solitary nights."

"It's not breaking my heart to hear that." Galahad stroked

him harder, because Trystan deserved a reward for that revelation. "So, was I worth the wait?"

"You are worth any price." Trystan jerked like he'd been zapped by electricity. "I swear to Lyrssa, I will never recover from my need for you."

That was worth more than any award he'd ever won. "Poor Trys." His thumb brushed over the very tip of Trystan's desire. Moisture was beading there, because Trystan wanted *his* touch. This belonged to him. It was Galahad's greatest victory. "You didn't stand a chance."

"All who have seen us together would agree." Trystan panted, dipping his head to nuzzle against Galahad's temple. "Please, knight. Ease me. I am going out of my mind."

"That's my whole plan. I told you I was great at plans, right?" He twisted his wrist slightly. "This is the 'me-convincing-you-that-I'm-indispensable-to-have-around' plan."

Trystan groaned, his whole body quaking with need. He thrust against Galahad's palm, trying to find relief. "Oh gods..." He gasped. "It is a *Good* plan."

"I thought you'd like it." Galahad's fingers moved faster and the tendons in Trystan's neck stood out from his strain to hold on. "I'll do even better next time." He shrugged with false modesty. "I can be the best at anything, if I get a little practice.

Trystan looked down and their eyes locked. "You are already indispensable to me. You don't have to do anything but be Galahad and I am filled with light."

The unTrystan-like whimsy of that statement startled Galahad out of the game. "Really?"

Trystan's head tilted, like he was surprised by Galahad's surprise. "Really. Even if you *weren't* the best at this. Even if you weren't the best at *anything*. Even if you failed, as you claim to never do. I would still want you and no other."

Nobody had ever told Galahad that before. All his life, he'd pushed to be great at everything he tried. To compete at the highest level. To win every medal and every contest. Because excelling was the only way he ever got any acceptance. Being the best meant maybe people wouldn't leave him. The idea that Trystan wouldn't care if he failed... that he just wanted Galahad, because he was *Galahad*... was incredible. He wasn't sure what to make of it.

He blinked up at Trystan and felt suddenly vulnerable, even though he was supposed to be the one in control. "Really?" He repeated, just to be sure.

Trystan's expression softened at the question. "Really."

God, Galahad was just completely, irrevocably, mind-numbingly in love with this man. "I'm crazy about you, Trystan." He whispered and he knew his heart was in his eyes. "And luckily for you... I *am* the best at this." Galahad focused on proving it.

Trystan gave a wheezing gasp. "Just like that. Yes. Just like *that*. Lyrssa help me, I have never been so grateful for your myriad of talents. You are so gifted at all that you try."

He knew Trystan was about to come apart. "Ready to admit that I've taken you, yet?"

Trystan's brown gaze was illuminated with something deeper than desire. "You have taken *everything* in me. Everything. It's all yours."

Galahad pressed his palm harder against Trystan's chest, reminding him he was still a captive. At the same time, he leaned closer to Trystan's ear and lowered his voice. "You know how I sometimes get great ideas? Well, I just had my best one ever."

Trystan was struggling to breathe. "Is it the chocolate popcorn thing, again?"

"Pop-Chocolate is my *second* best idea. This new one just took the top slot and, since you're my prisoner, it seems like you should help me with it." Galahad's hand tugged with more pressure than he'd used before and he went in for the kill. "One of these times, when it's *your* turn to take *me*... I'd like to be flying."

Trystan was in complete support of that plan. He gave a bellow of release that echoed off the walls of the cave. "*Galahad!*" His eyes squeezed shut as he shouted out a reverent litany of gryphon words, helplessly pumping himself into Galahad's tight grip.

Galahad had never felt more powerful. He grinned, continuing to stroke him. "Being defiled is kinda nice, actually."

Trystan shook his head to clear it. "Let me see." He caught hold of Galahad's wrist, his breathing ragged. Galahad let him tilt his palm, so Trystan could study his own release thick on Galahad's skin. There was something primal and foreign about the small ritual.

Galahad liked it.

Apparently, Trystan was pleased, too. A shudder past through him, as he stared at Galahad's hand. His jaw tightening and his erection growing longer, again. This really was a new experience for him. Galahad could see his surprise and pleasure and still smoldering desire.

"What is the deeper meaning of this in your culture?" Galahad asked quietly.

"I did not release inside your body. My seed is covering your flesh in the open air. To gryphons, there is... ownership involved in that." Still gripping Galahad's hand, Trystan pressed it downward, sealing Galahad's fingers around him, again. "Do you feel owned, knight?"

"Yes." Galahad's palm squeezed. "Do you feel owned, Trys?"

Trystan's head went back as Galahad's hand resumed its work. "*Yes*." As promised, this time Galahad had learned enough to be even better at it. "My gods," Trystan breathed with a rapturous expression, "everything you do is art. Truly."

"You hate art, so I'm not sure that's a compliment."

"I no longer hate art." Trystan leaned down to kiss him with proprietary hunger. His lips parted to drink deep, relishing Galahad's eager response. "That should be obvious."

"Yeah?" Galahad nipped his bottom lip. "So, when did this 'obvious' change happen?"

"When I discovered that I'm crazy about violet-eyed artists."

Chapter Twenty-Two

The closest we ever came to the graal was in the third campaign. We had come across some half burned map in a library and Uther was insisting that it led to the Looking Glass Pool. Now this was *very* hush-hush stuff. Basically, just Uther and me and Kay, knew about it. Kay died at Mynyn, by the way. Another Good man lost to the hands of those winged devils.

Anyway, we couldn't figure the map out. Obviously. It was all but destroyed and covered in heathen pictures. But this Yellow Boot, named Marcus, says, "Hey, that looks like Fisher's signature on it!"

Turns out Fisher was this old gryphon bastard, so I'm like, "Great! We'll find this Fisher and make him tell us where the graal is, right?"

Wrong!

The asshole was already dead! We had captured him and he died in a goddamn fire. I swear to Christ, nothing is ever easy with those savages.

"Stopping the Savages" Podcast
Sir Dragonet of Camelot- Former Troubadour of King Uther and Host of the Program

St. Ives- The Siege Perilous Hotel and Casino

Trystan excelled at corrupting innocent knights.

Even he was impressed with his talent and he was used to excelling at everything he tried. He'd stroked Galahad to completion again and again on the trip to St. Ives. And the knight touched him, too. Each time Galahad found satisfaction against Trystan's palm or Trystan came against his, their eyes would lock. Then Galahad would lean up to kiss him and it was the closest Trystan had ever felt to anyone. He *felt* the intimacy and the connection.

It was beautiful.

The knight's body would soon belong solely to Trystan. That was his new goal and Trystan was ruthlessly efficient about reaching his goals. The key was to always have a plan for victory. Trystan still wasn't saying "yes" to the knight's continual requests that they have sex.

...Yet.

He had already bought a lubricant so he could take Galahad for the first time without hurting him, though. He was keeping it in his pocket, ready and waiting. As soon as he was confident that it wouldn't matter if his emotions weren't good enough, he was deflowering the man and nothing could stop him. Soon, all that would matter was how much Galahad's body craved his touch. Only time was needed to ensure his victory.

Trystan stood by the window of the hotel room he'd rented, staring down at the busy street six stories below. St. Ives was just about as bad as Trystan expected, only bigger. The knight had been right about his ability to get them inside the enspelled walls. He'd simply had to say that Mordy invited him and the guards had flung the gate open.

To Trystan, that was a sure indication of trouble. If Mordy's name engendered such respect from the rest of the assholes in St. Ives., he was most likely the biggest asshole of all. It only made sense. But the knight was immune to sense and refused to listen to that logic.

Mordy was currently near the Moaning Sea. When the guards had radioed him, on some mystio-powered channel, and informed him of Galahad's arrival, Mordy had excitedly assured them that he was headed back to town as fast as he possibly could. He planned to travel through the night to reach St. Ives (and Galahad) as quickly as possible. He insisted that Galahad join him for "brunch" the next day.

The entire exchange set Trystan's teeth on edge. Mordy wasn't willing to even wait a few hours for the dinner Galahad had predicted. No. They had to meet him at eleven o'clock in the morning. The knight had already agreed. It was apparently "only polite to stop by and say "hi" to a fan."

Trystan anticipated that polite "hi" would somehow lead to a bloodbath. With Galahad there, it seemed inevitable.

He brooded about it as he looked out at the bustling street. The large crowds were disconcerting, after so many days of traveling in virtual solitude. St. Ives was basically a full-sized city, without families or law. A city made up of transient, amoral, dickheads who were all addicted to easy, dirty money and Lyrssa only knew what else.

It was two in the morning, but St. Ives was still a hive of activity. The night sky glowed with aurora borealis and the streets glowed with neon signs. He missed the quiet of the desert. This part of the world was colder and louder and filled with disreputable men. Nobody came here looking to build lives. They just wanted to get drunk, get laid and spend their gold in dissipated ways. The town was eager to sell them any kind of debauchery they could dream up.

It was apparently a winning recipe for civic growth.

St. Ives was filled to the brims with criminals, rotten to the core with vice, and bloated on ill-gotten gains. Everywhere Trystan looked there were nothing but bars, casinos, night clubs, brothels, and sleazy hotels. Everything cost three times what it was supposed to cost. Every man he saw was a verified scumbag.

That was… troubling.

The knight didn't do well with scumbags. Philosophical differences tended to arise. Then, Trystan usually had to kill a bunch of people. He needed to get Galahad out of there, before Trystan was forced to take on the entire town. He had far more important things to focus on than wiping this hellhole off the face of the globe.

Like, for example, stealing Galahad away from his True Love.

If all went to plan, when that dickhead showed up, wanting his destined Love, he'd be shit out of luck. Trystan really *should* script television shows, because he knew *exactly* how the scene should go. He could picture the wingless dickhead approaching Galahad one day, spewing love, and joy, and fluffiness, and every other emotion under the sun.

And Trystan could picture himself coming up behind Galahad. His gaze would stay on the interloper, because he hated the man.

Hate was an emotion he could feel. He was sure of it.

Trystan would press against Galahad as he had in the hotel doorway in Ted-ville. The knight would lean against him, ignoring his True Love, who would probably weep with sorrow, but no one cared. Galahad would melt into Trystan's arms. Lavender eyes would turn up to Trystan with many warm feelings reflected in them. Unable to resist the care Trystan could provide. Not ever wanting to leave him.

Then Trystan would kill the dickhead True Love, because fuck that guy.

The end.

See? It was a marvelous story. There was no doubt Trystan had a staggering talent for fiction. The action practically wrote itself and the moral was clear to all:

Galahad was *his*.

The feeling that this man was his mate had been growing stronger each day. Trystan had not *fully* committed to the path, but he was no longer resisting its pull.

The wonderful part of corrupting an innocent knight -- besides having the fun of preforming the corruption itself, obviously-- was that you took the high ground. You were there *first*. You were able to dig in, preparing defenses. Trystan had been a warrior for many years. He knew how to push through and win against staggering odds. He knew how to evaluate his own weaknesses and plan around them. All other men would now have to invade Trystan's territory, if they wanted to steal Galahad away.

And Trystan knew how to guard his territory.

He glanced over to the gaudy bed, where the knight was sleeping. The room Trystan rented was designated as the hotel's "penthouse." Its overwrought, glitzy, sometimes blinking decorations were exactly what Midas would have selected, but they gave Trystan a migraine. Still, the suite was secure and that was all that mattered.

Given St. Ives was a lawless shithole, it seemed worth the investment to procure the best room in the best establishment he could find. All sorts of exotic weapons would be floating around a town like this one, mostly in the hands of idiots. Not even Trystan could keep up with the various technological advancements that the wingless made in the art of mechanized murder. The Siege Perilous Hotel and Casino might have had a menacing name, but it also had heavy security downstairs and multiple locks on the door to the room.

Since the most beautiful man on the planet was presently sprawled in Trystan's bed, he would take all the guards and locks he could get.

There wasn't a doubt in his mind that the knight was going to be a target in St. Ives. Women were in short supply, so even men who'd normally prefer females were going to be interested in him. Galahad was a lavender-eyed, kindhearted, unarmed magnet for Badness, even on the best of days. Surrounded by villains, he was going to be a goddamned nightmare to protect.

Trystan sighed, still gazing at the man.

Galahad had been fiddling with his rusty gun again and it was sitting on the dresser top. He'd cleaned it up to the point where it *wasn't* so rusty anymore, which seemed a minor miracle. Lately, he'd been working on inventing "non-lethal" bullets for it, which was an utterly pointless thing for a bullet to be. But it was still very adorable that Galahad thought to fashion them. The man's artistic mind was a constant source of delight.

Everything about Galahad brought delight.

Trystan's emotions were a confusing mass, most of the time. He was working on sorting them all out, but it was difficult. Trystan kept trying, though, because there was no other choice. If Trystan couldn't be Galahad's True Love, he needed to provide adequate sentiment to compensate or the man would still leave.

Luckily, Trystan's feelings seemed clearest when he focused on the knight.

They told him that he should keep Galahad safe, no matter what it took. That he would be lost forever if this moonlit creature slipped through his fingers. That everything else was *nothing* compared to holding him. Trystan wasn't sure what that emotion was called, but he trusted it the way he trusted his instincts.

He should lock Galahad in the hotel room for the duration of their stay in St. Ives. It would keep the knight far away from the assholes roaming this God-awful town. He could stay warm and safe, where no one else could touch him, while Trystan went off to kill his enemies.

Trystan's emotions told him it was a *great* idea.

Except Galahad was determined to have "brunch" with Mordy and nothing seemed likely to change the man's mind. Trystan also needed to find Marcus and kill him. Hopefully, both tasks could be finished by noon and then they could leave St. Ives. The city wasn't *that* big. A few questions downstairs had revealed that there were other gryphons in town.

One of them was apparently Konrad Redcrosse.

After Trystan left the zoo, Lunette's clan had been the ones to find him. He'd spent time with the Redcrosses, although he never became a part of their clan. He fought with them in the War and knew them well. Konrad had always been an amoral bastard with a lot of connections. It had taken very little effort to send word to him that Trystan wanted to talk. Konrad was probably already downstairs waiting to tell him everything he wanted to know about Marcus. But, Trystan was strangely reluctant to begin his hunt, so he was stalling.

That wasn't like him. He shook his head and forced himself to action.

"Knight?" Trystan headed over to the bed, crouching down beside it. His hand smoothed over Galahad's hair. It was still damp from his shower. For some reason, the man was even more attractive when he was wet. Trystan had the almost overwhelming desire to defile his perfect, clean, untouched body right then and there.

But he couldn't. He had to go meet Konrad, for many important reasons. …It was just hard to recall any of them, when he was touching the knight.

"Galahad," he cleared his throat, "I must go out for a moment." Without even thinking about it, his thumb traced down the center of the man's face from his forehead to the bridge of his nose. "You will stay here, yes?"

Those impossibly blue eyes snapped open with instant alertness. Warriors often awoke like that, because they were always braced for attack. The knight had been sleeping better ever since the night he'd told Trystan about Legion, but his past would always be with him.

Galahad's gaze locked on Trystan's face and he instantly seemed reassured. "Hi." He murmured, warmth and care in his expression. No one had ever looked at Trystan like that before.

He liked it.

"Hi." Trystan's fingers wound through Galahad's shimmery curls, awed, as always, by the silky texture of them. It was like touching moonlight. "I will be right back. All is well." He adjusted the garish silver-and-black blanket over him. St. Ives was cold and all Galahad wore was a hotel bathrobe. "I won't be long."

The knight smiled at him, relaxing again under Trystan's care and falling back to sleep.

Trystan's chest tightened in some way he didn't fully understand. It was like someone had ripped his heart in two and put half of it inside this man. Was feeling this way normal? Did it matter if it was normal? Either way, he would not seek to change it.

Even though it all felt so… messy.

Trystan's emotions were conflicted, now. A rising swell of

somethings was urging him to forget about Konrad. Urging him to just crawl into bed with Galahad and cover the man with his wings, resting easy for the night. That was how he'd been sleeping for the past week and it soothed Trystan in ways he never would have predicted. Lying beside Galahad, shielding him and holding him, gave Trystan peace. What was confronting Konrad going to give him? What did he need that he didn't already have?

    Vengeance.

    And that was what he'd dreamed of. What he wanted most. ...Wasn't it?

    Trystan shook his head, clearing away the *somethings* that were attempting to confuse him. Konrad could point his way to the men who'd betrayed him and then Trystan would finally have revenge. Of *course* he had to go.

    Determined now, he rose to his feet and headed out the door, checking the knob three times before he left. He wanted to ensure that the knight was safely locked away from the rest of St Ives. He skipped the elevator and took the stairs down to the casino level. It wasn't hard to spot Konrad by the bar. There were few gryphons left in the world and fewer still that had vivid red hair.

    "Hello, Konrad."

    Konrad looked up, as Trystan stopped in front of him. He was a handsome man, with brown wings and no moral compass. He had the same burning-out-too-fast glow in his eyes that he'd always possessed. Konrad would die young. There seemed little doubt about that. It was a miracle he'd lasted this long, considering he did everything at double the speed and twice the risk of more sensible men.

    Konrad was one of the few beings alive that Trystan would miss when he finally perished, though. The two of them had known each other longer than most anyone else alive. Even if Trystan did not exactly *like* the man, he was used to him. Used to his poor choices, and his reckless impatience, and his strange loyalty to their quasi-friendship. When Konrad finally exploded in some blaze of stupidity and bizarre choices, the world would lose some more of its light.

    "I began to think you weren't coming, Trystan. Do you have some hot pizza of ass upstairs, that you couldn't vault yourself away from?" Konrad swallowed some of his whiskey and nodded like all those words made sense. "I don't blanket you. Sex is as close as we can get to feeling, right?"

    Was it?

    Trystan occasionally saw flashes in others of his kind that

reminded him of the "somethings" that he felt inside himself. Perhaps Galahad had been right, when he said other gryphons might experience emotions. Even if gryphons were born emotionless, maybe as they grew, they could learn to feel. Or at least develop enough feelings to *miss* having feelings. There was nothing he could do about the gryphons' reality, either way. But, like many of Galahad's ideas, what seemed outlandish at first began to make more and more sense as you considered it.

Trystan shook his head again, focusing on his hunt. "I see you're still struggling to learn the wingless tongue, Konrad." Every third word was mispronounced, misused, or both.

"At least, I keep practacasing." Konrad raised his glass in a mock toast. "This buttery language is all anyone speaks around here. Itches the ears to hear it. This is the shit you have to deal with when you lose a war, I suppository."

Lyrssa help him... Trystan pinched the bridge of his nose and resigned himself to a very looooong conversation.

"My sainted mother says I waste my time to learn their language, of course. She believes the wingless words will die out, once we finally kill all the heathens. But their numbers seem too vast for us to wipse them completely out of existence, no matter how many she picks off." He winced. "But do not tell her I said so."

"Believe me, I won't." Trystan valued his own life too much to discuss politics with Caelia Redcrosse. It was safer not to speak with the woman, at all. The gryphons had no real art, but she took the torture of her enemies to such creative heights that it might just qualify.

"Mother always favored you, Trystan. Even with your wingless blood. She raided many prisons, after you were arrested. I believe that's why Uther moved you to the Four Kingdoms, just before he died. To hide you from her wrathy-ness." Konrad paused. "Though, to be fair, Mother does enjoy raiding prisons, simply for the sake of raiding prisons. I cannot be sure she was looking for *you*, so much as choosing easy targets."

"A thoughtful gesture, either way." Trystan leaned a shoulder against the bar, also speaking in the common dialect.

"What brings you to here?" Konrad asked. "It is not a smart time to visit St. Ives. There's been much consumer magic for sale recently. Powders and elixirs that I have never seen before can be easily bought. The wingless use them all for wicked purposes and it leads to wicked deeds." He hesitated, second-guessing the word choice. "Wicked *'porpoises?'*"

"'Purposes.'" Trystan assured him. "'Porpoises' are sea mammals, who rarely engage in evil." But, if they *were* up to some nefarious scheme, the knight would soon discover it as he 'decoded their secret language.' Trystan shook his head in exasperation. "You know, we really *can* speak in the gryphon dialect, Konrad. I do not mind."

"No, no. I am greatly improving-ish with the tongue." Konrad said easily. "Hey, how did you even get into this town? St. Ives only admits the Bad. I thought you were Good?"

"It depends on who you ask." Trystan had never excelled at small talk, especially when only half the words made sense, so he cut to the bottom line. "I am here looking for Marcus."

Konrad snorted. "Still? You always were a tenacious son of a chair."

Trystan smacked some gold onto the bar top and pushed it towards the man. "I am willing to pay." Konrad was interested in the wingless' money and all it could buy. He'd always been inexplicably loyal to Trystan, but most people were just paychecks to him.

"Why are you so determined to kill Marcus, after all this time?"

"He was leader of the Yellow Boots. I will hunt and kill all the Yellow Boots, no matter where they hide or how long it takes." Trystan dropped some more coins onto the counter. "Now, tell me where he is."

There was a bowl of bar snacks next to Trystan's elbow. It took him a moment to realize they were the knight's ridiculous Gala-Chips. Caramel-and-whey flavor.

The gold swiftly disappeared into Konrad's pocket. "Marcus is here. In St. Ives. He'll be at the race tomorrow, I'm sure. He always is."

Trystan very nearly smiled at the news that his quarry was so close. "Do you know a man named Mordy?"

"Sure. I know everybody and everybody knows Mordy Mordred."

"Good. Tomorrow, I'm having brunch with him at his establishment." Against his better judgement, Trystan carefully selected one of the Gala-Chips and took the smallest bite he possibly could, curious as to what Galahad had created. Instantly, incredible flavors burst across his tongue.

Shit.

It was delicious. Of *course* it was. Why was he even surprised? The man could do anything. Trystan snorted and ate three more, enjoying the crunchiness of them.

"What's a 'brunch?'" Konrad began rooting around in his pockets for a notepad, so he could write down the word. "I'm trying to build my vocabu-latary.

"It is a wingless breakfast with alcohol."

"Shit, I've been just calling that 'breakfast.'"

Trystan grunted, still munching on the chips. Galahad was completely wrong not to enjoy this flavor combination. Caramel-and-whey was apparently second only to kissing on the list of worthwhile wingless inventions. "So, can you get Marcus to Mordy's around eleven? I will just kill him there."

Whatever got them out of St. Ives the quickest.

Konrad forgot about his word-building lessons. "Marcus once lent me a scarf." He mused pointedly. "That is not something I easily disremember."

"Oh for Lyrssa's sake..." Trystan dumped some more money onto the bar. "Does this fog the memory of it?"

Konrad snatched up the gold. "It does seem to help." He agreed, cheerfully counting his coins. "Yeah, I can get Marcus to Mordy's place for you."

"Don't double-cross me." Trystan warned, pointing a finger at his face. "I won't die easily and I know how to hold a grudge."

"I wouldn't traitor-ing you. You're more interesting than most of the assholes left alive, so I prefer keeping you that way." He took a healthy drink from his glass. "Besides, my sainted mother considers you Aunt Lunette's child, even without a true adoption. Because Lunette died helping to save you in the zoo. Unafraid and strong to the last, with her mate beside her. You sharing this news of her end meant much to Mother."

"Lunette will always be my clan." Trystan agreed very formally and with the respect the woman deserved. "If Caelia considers me her sister's son, I am nothing but honored."

Konrad nodded, like that was only to be expected. "Mother --gods always be shielding her-- says you have an enspecial path and I should not disrupt it, no matter the gold at offer. I do much Badness, but I *never* go against my mother's wishes."

That was probably wise. Konrad's mother was the most bloodthirsty warrior Trystan had ever met. Lunette had been fearsome, but Caelia was close to a berserker in her rage. She once killed an entire legion of knights and then strung their bodies up in the trees along Camelot's boarder, just in time for the wingless' Christmas celebrations.

"Caelia spoke of my path?"

"Sure. Aunt Lunette probably told her about it. The old ones sometimes whispered to my mother, you know." Konrad touched the middle of his forehead. "Our family has a great destiny."

Trystan suppressed a shudder. Lyrssa help them all, if Caelia Redcrosse had a hand in reshaping the future.

"So anyway..." There was a new gleam in Konrad's eye now that business was out of the way. "It really is delightfully to see you, Trystan." He gestured for the bartender to bring Trystan a drink. "It's delightfully to see *any* of our kind, these days." He leaned forward, wanting to grab a Gala-Chip for himself.

Trystan moved the bowl out of the way, unwilling to share.

Konrad frowned, but retreated. "We're two gryphon warriors, with much history." He went on determinedly. "We should take advantage of this momentsitory day."

If Trystan wore a watch he would have impatiently checked it. "I wish to return to my room and the man I keep there. I do not have time to reminisce."

Konrad disregarded his lack of interest. "We can get wingless men anywhere... When's the last time you bedded a gryphon?"

"I don't know. I haven't been keeping track." Everyone other than the knight had faded from his mind forever.

"Well, for me, it's been *moths*. Bedding the wingless isn't the same. The women are scarce and breakable. And the men are," he looked Trystan up and down, "*much* too softer than gryphon men."

Trystan arched a brow. "You wish to have sex with me?" He translated. Konrad had never suggested that before. "Why?" The man must be bored.

"Because I am bored, Trystan." It was a whine. "This town is dullish and everyone in it is so... sentimental." He sighed. "Sometimes I wish Mount Feather was a real place and we could dwell there with the old clans. No wingless to deal with. It would all be far easier."

"The wingless are never the easy path." Trystan allowed. "But easy paths are never all that interesting to travel."

"Easy sex sounds *wonderful-ed* to me." Konrad scoffed. "Mother and I shared a wingless man in bed last week, who wished to hold hands with us afterwards. Can you picture it? Mother and I gripping his small wingless hands, after fucking his small, wingless body?"

"I would rather not."

"Exactly! It was preposterous-ish. With you, at least no one will cry." Konrad paused. "Oh, and I do not consider us cousins." He tacked on, like that might be a concern. "We share no blood."

"Rest assured, that fact is a constant relief to me."

"So, we will go have easy, boredom sex together, yes?"

"No."

"No?" He pouted. "Why not?"

"For starters, your eyes are not purple."

Konrad's head tilted in confusion. "What?"

"Your eyes are not purple. Your hair does not shimmer. You do not smile at me, or harass me into saving useless creatures, or claim me. You are not the man I want."

Konrad's eyebrows climbed higher and higher on his forehead, comprehension dawning. "You have a *ha'yan?*" He demanded, automatically switching to the gryphons' language. "And you *still* seek out Yellow Boots for longed-cooled grievances?"

Trystan hesitated. "I did not say this man was my *ha'yan.*" He muttered. But he also didn't say that he *wasn't*.

His Not-Cousin had known Trystan too long to miss that fact.

"If this vengeance costs you your life, your mate will be left alone, Trystan." Konrad shook his head, uncharacteristically serious. "This is not a world where I would leave my *ha'yan* alone. Were he mine, I would care for this man above all else."

Trystan's temper flashed, partly because Konrad's words made perfect goddamn sense. "Do not tell me how to care for my own…"

Galahad's hand slammed down on the bar between Trystan and Konrad, interrupting the argument. His body pushed forward, like he was ready for a fight, his back to Trystan and his eyes fixed on Konrad. Without saying a word, Galahad took the ground he wanted and then stood there daring someone to move him.

Konrad took a quick step back.

Trystan didn't blame him. The knight was suddenly the biggest badass in the room. Trystan couldn't imagine what had pissed him off, but he liked the reemergence of Galahad's aggressive stance. It always surprised him how much he really, *really* liked it. Trystan generally preferred being in control, but, every once in a while, it was exciting to have Galahad take the lead. You could never predict what he had planned.

"Didn't I request that you stay in the room, knight?"

"It occurred to me that you weren't just getting ice." Galahad flashed him a glare over his shoulder. He appeared to have haphazardly dragged on his clothing, and his damp hair was rumpled, and he was still half-asleep. Most everyone in the bar was looking at him with speculative lust, including Trystan. "It *didn't* occur to me that you were sneaking off to meet some other guy."

Trystan squinted at the utter lunacy of that statement. "I am not meeting another man. I am meeting Konrad." He flicked a hand towards Konrad. "This is Konrad."

"How is Konrad *not* another man?" Galahad shot back. "Explain it to me."

Trystan's eyebrows soared, realization dawning. The knight was jealous. Trystan identified the new feelings that filled him as... pleasure and amusement. Ridiculous as it was, Galahad's flash of possessiveness was oddly endearing.

"Are you honestly concerned that I plan to sleep with Konrad?" Trystan waved a disparaging hand at Konrad. "Is that honestly what this is about? *Honestly?*"

"I just heard him propositioning you as I walked over here!"

"And I turned him down, didn't I? Lyrssa, save me..." Trystan genuinely wanted to laugh. He ate another Gala-Chip, close to chuckling. "*No one in the universe* would prefer Konrad to you. Not even Konrad thinks that is a possibility, now that he has seen you." He looked at Konrad. "Do you think that is a possibility, now that you have seen my knight?"

Konrad slowly shook his head, his eyes on Galahad.

"You see?" Trystan demanded, his attention switching back to the knight. How could the man not understand what was clear as a crystal ball? "I would pick *no one* over you." His palm brushed over Galahad's hair, just because he could. "Your concern is ludicrous."

"Is it?" Galahad still wasn't satisfied, but much of his tension eased. "Because you're still down here for *some* reason that you don't want me to know about, aren't you?"

Trystan hesitated, his amusement fading.

"*This* is your mate?" Konrad interjected in the gryphon dialect, still gazing at Galahad with ravenous attention. He was clearly rethinking his stance on the wingless being undesirable. "And you would risk your future with *him*... for fucking *Marcus?*" He snorted. "I never took you for stupid, Trystan."

"You can leave, now." Trystan didn't like Konrad's opinion or the way he was undressing Galahad with his eyes.

Konrad's gaze lingered on the swatch of muscled abdomen that was revealed by the knight's misbuttoned clothes, and then slipped... downward. He made an appreciative sound that set Trystan's teeth on edge. "He's a dancer, right?"

Dancer?

"He is an *artist*." Trystan snapped, also in their language. The gryphon word for "artist" was very close to their word for "crazy." That wasn't a coincidence. "He is also a great warrior, when he remembers to be." He decided to fasten Galahad's shirt himself, before a riot broke out.

"Stop that." Galahad batted his hands away. "And why are you eating Gala-Chips? Especially the disgusting caramel-and-whey ones? I thought you hated junk food?"

"They have some nutritional value. Caramel is a fruit, yes?"

"No, it's not a fruit!"

"Most dancers call themselves 'artists,' ya know." Konrad interjected in their native tongue, ignoring the byplay. "Mother would approve if I brought home a dancer. She enjoys the pretty ones, even if they are wingless."

"Caelia will not come near my knight." Trystan warned. Holy gods, it would lead to another war. "He is spoken for. By *me*."

"He agrees to be in your care?" Konrad's stare left slimy trails all over Galahad as he ogled him. "I've not heard of a wingless being receptive to our care in many years. How did you accomplish this, Trystan? It's... extraordinary."

Trystan hesitated, because it *was* extraordinary. His eyes flicked to Galahad, considering the impossible odds he'd beaten in finding this man. Hardly any of his kind possessed what he now did. There were few gryphons left. And the War had split the wingless and remaining gryphons to such an extent that they rarely forged real bonds.

The inability to have children would cripple the gryphons in the long run, but the lack of mates would doom them far sooner. Even generally emotionless races needed partners in life. If you took that hope away, what did they have left?

Without dreams, people became ghosts.

"My mate is extraordinary." He told Konrad in their dialect, not even hesitating over the word, now. There was no sense in denying who Galahad was to him. The truth was obvious.. "I did nothing. *He* is the one who claimed *me*. I believe the gods sent him to me, but I do not know why I deserved the gift."

"I had given up on finding *ha'na*." Konrad seemed entranced by Galahad and the new possibilities he offered. "But you have found it? It's still possible for us? This man has entered into the bond with you?"

Galahad hadn't entered into anything with Trystan, but there wasn't a chance in hell he was telling Konrad that. "He is mine." Trystan said instead. The words were deadly cold.

"Does he do *more* than dance?" Konrad asked eagerly. "Because, I will pay whatever price you ask to bed a man who's genuinely attracted to our kind. If you're willing to share him..."

Trystan leveled a flat look in his direction and the other gryphon stopped talking mid-sentence.

"Quit arguing with Konrad in another language, and tell me why you're sneaking out of our room." Galahad ordered. "Maybe it's not for sex, but it's for something shady."

Trystan switched back to the wingless dialect. "I did not sneak. I told you I was leaving and that I would be back. Your annoyance over this is ridiculous."

"Reverse our positions, Trys. Would it be ridiculous for *you* to complain if *I* was the one who slipped off to meet some strange, propositioning guy at two in the morning?"

Trystan's jaw ticked. Shit.

Galahad arched a brow, sensing he'd just made his point.

"You do things like this all the time." Trystan muttered, not willing to admit defeat. "Not rendezvous at hotel bars, perhaps. But I turn my back for a moment and you are inside a tomb or riding a hippocamp or engaged in a gunfight without a working gun."

"That's completely different!"

"It is the same. This is about hunting the man I plan to kill. I am well within the parameters of our deal to keep you far from it."

"We agreed to be allies."

"Allies on *your* mission. Not on mine."

Galahad stopped arguing so fast he literally blinked. He stared at Trystan, saying nothing for a long moment.

Trystan frowned, expecting him to continue quarreling over this nonsense.

Instead, the knight let out a long breath and looked away. "Yeah." His eyes landed on the slot machines against the wall, thoughts reflected in them that Trystan couldn't read. "Alright." His voice was calm. "That's a fair point."

Trystan hesitated. "It is?" It was his point and even he saw the flaws in it.

"Sure. You've been very clear from the beginning on wanting to keep your mission your own. I got confused on the alliance thing, but I think you're technically right. You never agreed to make me a part of anything, did you?"

"Not yet." Trystan allowed, uneasy with the man's quiet

tone. "I am considering many options."

"Yeah, that's probably the smartest way." Galahad nodded, his expression thoughtful. "You always were better at strategy, than me." He took a step back, away from Trystan.

He had *never* done that before.

Trystan felt a chill.

"Trystan has wrotten list of people he's going to kill." Konrad interjected, unhelpful to the last. "It'll take him *years* of traveling around remote kingdoms to get them all dead. He just told me this. Did he tell you this?"

"No." Galahad said very evenly. "He didn't tell me that."

P'don.

Chapter Twenty-Three

Long ago, an evil spell befell the ancient land, slowly sinking it. Year by year, the territory around the first gryphon temple seemed to shrink and waters seemed to rise. Most people fled the forsaken kingdom and moved into Lyonesse.

But, the Looking Glass Pool could not be moved.

It would have been destroyed by the rising waters and the graal would have been lost.

For the Good of the world, that could not happen. To protect the future, the gryphons built a wall around Listeneise, higher and higher.

Until it nearly touched the sky.

How the Wingless War Happened
Skylyn Welkyn- Gryphon Storyteller

St. Ives- The Siege Perilous Hotel and Casino

Trystan sent Konrad a look that should have ignited his wings. Stupid chattering *asshole*. Telling Galahad about Trystan's plans to leave Camelot indefinitely was going to do nothing to ease this deteriorating situation. If it wouldn't have further distressed the knight, he would have slain the blabbering dickhead right there in the casino.

Sensing his life was in peril, Konrad edged back another step.

Trystan ignored him and moved closer to Galahad, closing the distance the knight had created between them. "I can explain this."

"You don't have to. I get it." Galahad's body shifted away again, almost like it was instinctive. "I'm Galahad, by the way." He extended his hand to Konrad. "I'm traveling with Trystan, for the moment."

Trystan scowled. "For the moment?" What did that mean?

"I'm really sorry for causing a scene." Galahad continued, his attention on Konrad. "I hate causing scenes. I hope you didn't feel uncomfortable."

Seizing the knight's hand, Konrad gave it a vigorous shake. "No, no, I was comfortable a lot." He rushed out, in some broken version of the common tongue. Galahad's presence seemed to excite him and make him forget what little he knew of the language. "I am not Trystan's cousin. We grew up golfing much."

Golfing?

Trystan arched a brow. Whatever word Konrad was searching for, that wasn't it. Trystan would bet that the man couldn't tell a golf club from a spinning wheel.

"You like... golfing?" Galahad seemed understandably baffled by that remark, but he was too polite to say so. "Sure. Okay. Me, too. Last time I played on Camelot's Greens, I was fifty-three under par. I'd like to see if I could shave another point off."

Now, Konrad looked confused by *Galahad's* response, possibly because he had no idea what he'd even said in the first place. "Yes. Par is under." He said vaguely.

Trystan did some mental math. From what he grasped of that pointless game's scoring system... "You achieved eighteen hole-in-ones, knight? All in a row?"

"Seventeen. One shot took two swings. I got distracted by a new breed of butterfly I discovered. Really unique. Doctors think its DNA might be a breakthrough cure for hangnails."

Trystan didn't care about breakthrough bugs. He cared that Galahad hadn't met his eyes when he answered. As if he was uncomfortably looking for somewhere else to be and someone else to talk to. Trystan didn't like that.

At all.

Konrad pushed onward, showcasing his doomed conversational skills in their full glory. "My mother wishes me to find a mate. Not just a man who holds hands and cries much, after a proper bedding. This is horrible, yes?"

Galahad floundered for an answer to that gibberish. "Well, I'm sure most mothers want their children to find happiness, don't they?"

"With my mother, it depends greatly on the child. Some she has ill wishes for." Konrad nodded. "But me she favors! She would *much* like it, if I brought you home to share."

"You're not bringing my knight *anywhere*." Trystan interjected flatly. "Especially, not to 'share' with Caelia." It would be a literal virgin sacrifice.

"Yeah, I'm sorry, but I need to stay here." Galahad told Konrad. "It's always nice to meet fans, though. I can give your mom an autograph, if you'd like."

Konrad didn't seem surprised by the refusal, but he also didn't let go of Galahad's hand. "You are the best Galahad I have ever seen. I'm sure mother would agree." His eyes glowed with earnest sincerity. "I mean that."

Galahad squinted at him.

So did Trystan.

"Uh… thank you?" Galahad offered cautiously and tugged on his palm, trying to retrieve it.

Konrad still didn't let go. "If you ever tire of traveling with Trystan's moment, I am welcoming." He assured Galahad, hungrily. "If you are receptive to our kind, mother and I would offer to care for you *well*."

A film of red coated Trystan's vision.

Galahad seemed mystified by what Konrad's suggestion meant. It was abundantly clear how he'd remained untouched. A thousand prurient thoughts were reflected in Konrad's devouring gaze, but the man somehow missed them all. "Well, that's very kind."

Trystan didn't think so. He jerked Galahad away from Konrad's grasp. "If you offer to care for my knight again, I *will* kill you." He warned in the gryphons' language, so there could be no misunderstanding. "We have much history, Konrad. But for this man, I will kill *anyone*."

Konrad arched a brow and relented. "Not so stupid after all, huh?"

"Bring Marcus tomorrow." Trystan snarled. "And do not speak to my mate." Done with this whole debacle, he looked down at the knight. "We will talk alone." He started for the elevator, dragging Galahad along with him and leaving Konrad with the bar tab.

"Why are you so upset?" Galahad walked with him, but he also freed himself with some practiced twist of his arm.

The move was meant to seem casual, but it had been very deliberately executed. No one else in the world could have gotten free of Trystan's hold so easily. Galahad wasn't of this world, though, and misty creatures were impossible to catch. If the knight decided to pull away, nothing would stop him. He could literally slip right through Trystan's fingers, at any time.

Gryphons did not worry often, but Trystan began to worry.

"I am not upset." Trystan muttered. "I just do not like that *you're* upset. My meeting Konrad alone was not a diminishment of my...." *P'don*, now he was the one hunting for wingless words. "My *respect* for you as a warrior. I just do not want you involved in the tracking of my enemies."

"I get that." The knight reached the elevator panel and pushed the up button. "It's not a big deal."

"You still seem upset."

"No. I just feel a little left out. But I'll recover." Galahad shrugged. "It's completely understandable why you wouldn't want to be allies on this mission. This is your thing. And I don't even carry a sword, right?"

Galahad smiled, like all was well, but he stood several inches farther away than he usually did. At the beginning of their journey, he'd arranged himself like that. Ever since the snake tomb, he'd been slowly moving closer. Trystan hadn't really noticed the slight, almost imperceptible changes, but now he saw them happening rapidly in reverse. The physical and mental distance grew, as Galahad cautiously pulled back from him. That mysterious core of him was locked tighter than ever.

Thus far, most of their disagreements had been about the chaos Galahad caused and which of them was the *ya'lah*. The knight refused to stop helping idiots or acknowledge the truth about his heroic destiny, so conflict was inevitable. But he did not become distant from Trystan when they quarreled about it.

This wasn't right.

Trystan was unsure how to fix the new wariness in the man. He tried to use his feelings to navigate, but they were all screaming different things and impossible to understand. In desperation, he fell back on Elaine's stories. Whenever he asked, she'd explained that the moonlit creatures could not be caught. (And he'd asked *often*. The tale had been his obsession.) If you saw one, you should never grab at it and scare it away. It would just vanish from your grasp. Instead, you needed to let *it* come to *you*. Show it that you meant no harm and it would drift towards you of its own accord.

Misty beings would only get closer, if you proved yourself safe.

"The Yellow Boots killed two of my clans." Trystan said abruptly. "I will kill their leader tomorrow."

Galahad's head snapped up to look at him, shocked by that news and that Trystan was volunteering it. It was the first time that Trystan had ever seen him truly speechless.

The elevator door *bing*-ed open. Rather than hustling Galahad where he wanted him, Trystan stepped inside and waited. No ropes binding him. No pulling him along. He took a deep breath and forced himself to do nothing.

The knight followed him into the lift and stood slightly closer than he had before.

Trystan cleared his throat, more thankful than ever for Elaine. "I have a list of men to kill. Who deserve to die for their actions during the War." He told Galahad, pressing onward since this tactic seemed to be working. "Marcus is at the top."

"Sounds like a very organized way to assassinate people." Galahad punched the button for the top floor, his voice calm. "Shouldn't I be on the list?"

"No!" Trystan protested indignantly and then hesitated for a beat. "Well, you *were*, but I crossed you out, long ago, for Gwen and Avi's sake."

"That's thoughtful." The knight watched the numbers light up over the door.

"The Yellow Boots helped Uther find my village, when I was a boy. This is how my parents and grandparents died. Years later, they destroyed the zoo. Marcus was there that night. I will kill him for what he took from me and from the world. Then, I will hunt down all the other Yellow Boots and kill them, too."

"Alright." Galahad said quietly.

"You see why I am on this mission, yes?" Trystan prompted when Galahad said nothing else. "Do you see why I am doing all this?"

Galahad looked right at him. That was a promising sign. His eyes traveled over Trystan's face and studied him for a beat. "I see that you're as trapped in the past as I am."

Trystan's brief moment of optimism faded. "I do not dwell on the past. I fought on the right side, regardless of the outcome. I have no regrets."

"You dwell on your enemies, though. Maybe I'm broken in a lot of ways since the War, but so are you. Do you really plan to track down and slaughter a whole list full of people? Even if they deserve it?"

"Of course. Why else would I make the list?"

"How many people are *on* the list, though? A lot? Because Konrad said it could take years to search the various kingdoms and find them all."

"I have time."

"And nothing better to do with it?"

Trystan frowned, wanting him to understand. "My enemies must die." Planning their deaths had kept him alive in the Wicked, Ugly and Bad Mental Health Treatment Center and Maximum Security Prison. "Marcus helped Uther capture me, as well. I spent three years in a jail cell, because of him. I understand that you now reject killing..."

"I don't reject killing this Marcus bastard." Galahad interrupted seriously. "I would happily kill him myself, if you couldn't do it just fine on your own. When people hurt you, I *always* want them dead. You saw my reaction in Ayren's village about the zookeeper. My desire to live in peace means *nothing* compared to your safety."

Trystan warmed. "You do not need to kill Marcus for me. I am looking forward to doing it myself."

"I can see that. Honestly, I don't think Marcus is the biggest threat to you, right now, so I'm not focused on him. He'll be dead in a few hours. At the moment, I only care about protecting you."

"The man poses no threat to me..."

Galahad cut him off, again. "*No one* poses a threat to you... Except *you*. And my protecting you also means protecting you from yourself, when you're about to make a mistake. None of the men on your list are more important than your family."

Trystan's frown deepened. "I never said they were more important than my clan."

"But you're going to leave Camelot to hunt Yellow Boots, right?"

"Only because I *must* leave..."

"Why?" Galahad interrupted again. "Are these jackasses really worth more of your time than Avi? Playing with her? Being with her as she grows up?"

"I give all that I am to Avalon." Trystan shot back. "*Everything* in me, I give to her without reservation. You are twisting this around."

"Am I? Trust me, Trys. I've been exiled for over a year and it sucks. I have missed time with my goddaughter and with Gwen that I will *never* get back. Avi will barely remember me, now. Do you want that?"

No. Being forgotten by Avalon and his clan was the stuff of nightmares. Trystan cleared his throat, unsettled by the turn of the conversation. "The child did not forget you. She told me she loves you and that you are her third best friend." He paused. "I am her *second* best friend, obviously."

"Obviously." Galahad's voice contained humor now, but his gaze was still clouded. "Because you were there with her when she needed you and I was far away. The way *you* will be far away, if you go looking for men to kill, instead of staying in Camelot to watch over her. You lost two clans to Yellow Boots and now you want to give them another?"

The logic of that was inescapable and Trystan didn't like it.

He shook his head. "My enemies *must* die. The Yellow Boots are traitors to their own people. There is nothing worse."

"I know you hate traitors, but..."

"*Everyone* hates traitors. They are the scum of existence."

Galahad sighed and rubbed at his eyes.

It suddenly occurred to Trystan that the knight had been banished for treason.

P'don.

He quickly tried to fix this new mess. "I was not calling *you* a traitor. Why are you even thinking that?"

"Because, I am a traitor. Literally. I was exiled for betraying the crown."

"Yes, but the crown in question was worn by that dickhead *Arthur*." To Trystan's way of thinking, the *real* traitors were the knights who took vows of honor and then served the king in the face of his cruelty. "Arthur was a staggering moron who only staggering morons would follow."

"The court-martial didn't agree."

"No lives were lost with your actions. You *saved* lives, unlike the Yellow Boots."

Silence.

"Look, none of my shit matters, now." Galahad finally decided. "Just... think about what I've said about your revenge mission. Okay? Think about what your parents would *want* for your future. A clan who loves you ...or an endless mission to kill pointless assholes?"

Trystan scowled. "I can have both."

"Can you? For every choice you make, you give up something else. Be sure what you're surrendering isn't worth more than what you'll gain."

"I am surrendering *nothing*." Trystan reiterated firmly. "In the end, I will have *all* that I desire."

"I hope so." The elevator door opened on their floor and Galahad stepped out. "Is this why you haven't slept with me, yet? Because, you thought I would try to stop you from leaving Camelot?"

"No." His reasons were far more selfish and revolved around stealing Galahad from his True Love.

Galahad nodded, but he didn't look convinced. He went inside the room, apparently still willing to share it with Trystan. That was *something*, anyway. "Do you still want to look for Atlantis with me?"

Trystan was startled by the question. "Of course. We agreed to be allies in the quest, did we not?"

"In *that* quest? Yeah." Far from continuing his campaign to dissuade Trystan from leaving Camelot, Galahad began undressing, like he planned to return to bed. "If you need to do your own thing, I get it. But you should do it *after* we find the graal."

Trystan frowned, irritated at how often the knight was saying "I get it" when he clearly didn't. "I am just going to kill Marcus tomorrow. I will obviously not search out *more* of my enemies until after we find Atlantis." He snapped, offended that was even in question.

"Good. Because, I really think you're the only one who can find the graal, Trystan. Really. It has to be you who breaks the curse."

"I am not the *ya'lah*, knight." He bolted the door, engaging every lock and then testing them. "You are the *ya'lah* and so *you* will break the curse."

"No. That's *your* job. You're the *ya'lah*. Think about it logically and you'll see I'm right."

Trystan was not going to get sidetracked with this nonsense. They'd been going round and round with the arguments since the fire cave, both of them insisting that the other was wrong. At the moment, he had bigger problems. "You are done haranguing me about my mission, then?"

"Pretty much." Galahad tossed his shirt onto a chair.

The ease with which he let the matter drop irritated Trystan even more. Only a complete imbecile would find fault in the knight's realistic and supportive response to all of this, but it was pissing Trystan off. "And you are not angry about this plan?"

"I told you, I don't like to get angry. I'm just... bothered."

"Bothered?" What the hell emotion was that?

"Yeah. I'm concerned that you're going to get lost in your vengeance and not find your way back out. You could waste your whole life and never get to live it. Like a ghost."

Trystan stilled, remembering Fisher's warning to make better choices than he had. To never be like him. To not roam the world without bright hopes or a true path. Trystan shook memories of the old man away.

"But you seem sure of your plan, so it's probably better to skip the fighting, right?" Galahad went on, like he wanted to stop talking about it. He did not seem to consider any of Trystan's plans worth an argument.

Trystan didn't like that.

"I had thought you'd continue your attempts to dissuade me, knight." He prodded, trying to provoke a more satisfactory response.

Galahad tilted his head. "Nothing I say will change your mind, will it?" He didn't even wait for an answer. "No one's ever changed their plans for me. Don't worry. I won't push you about becoming the first."

Trystan didn't appreciate being lumped in with others, especially when those others were colossally stupid. Galahad excelled at harassing him into doing all sorts of ridiculous things. Why did he not care to even try this time? Trystan felt... *hurt* by the lack of effort the man was putting into keeping them together. If their situations were reversed, Trystan would have had the knight tied up again by now, if that's what it took to ensure Galahad remained beside him.

Trystan cleared his throat, again. "I am the first man who promised to care for you, so it would seem logical that you'd have concerns about my absence. That you would wish to complain about my plans to leave, even temporarily."

"What would be the point?" Galahad asked, as if he'd already surveyed the terrain, calculated the inevitable outcome of the skirmish, and decided to cede the ground.

Trystan's lips thinned in irritation.

That was *exactly* what Galahad had done during the War. He'd never lost a battle, in part, because he fought only the ones that he knew he'd win. The rest of the time, he was willing to wait out his enemies, take smaller losses, and retreat. Sunk cost meant nothing to him. He'd stop advancing on a dime, if he thought one more step was too many. That unpredictable, egoless, patient approach to warfare had driven Trystan crazy then and it drove him crazy now.

"Fine." He ground out.

Galahad's head tilted, as if sensing that Trystan wasn't pleased with his reactions. "No one could talk me out of my mission and you're way more stubborn than I am. That's all I'm saying. I would never try to get in your way."

"*Nothing* will get in my way." Trystan made it a challenge. "More than anything, I want to kill my enemies. I told you this was my dream, yes?"

It *was* still his dream, right? It had to be. He'd been planning it for years.

Galahad shrugged. "That's what you said, alright."

Instead of reassuring Trystan, his acceptance just made it seem like the man had already given up on him. Trystan did not like being seen as a lost cause. The alleged "best knight ever" should not just *give up* on people so easily. He should berate Trystan about his wrongheaded ideas. He should try to give Trystan a *new* dream.

"Fine." Trystan said again. What else were you supposed to say to someone who was agreeing with you, even when you were wrong?

There was a long moment of uneasy silence.

The knight frowned, like he was hunting for a less charged topic. "So, uh, the guy downstairs seemed a little… troubled." He said as if Konrad's part in this tale vaguely interested him. "I think he wanted me to meet his mom, right?"

"It's hard to know what inhabits Konrad's mind." Trystan didn't consider that a lie. Konrad was a fucking idiot. "It's best to think of him as a pathetic simpleton." He paused. "And also a eunuch."

Galahad nodded. "Should we do something to help him?"

"He fought with me in many battles. It left scars, I'm sure." Trystan touched the side of his head, indicating the many and varied psychological issues that possibly plagued Konrad. "Konrad is assisting me in Marcus' death, but do not be alone with him. Or his mother. It would lead to… Bad things."

"You think I could stir up traumatizing memories for the poor guy? Because I was a knight and he's a gryphon?"

"Oh, I think he would be traumatized. Yes." Trystan would slaughter that son of a bitch if he came near Galahad. That would no doubt be very traumatizing for poor Konrad.

"Well, I'll avoid him, then. I wouldn't want to give him a setback." Galahad sighed, distracted by some do-Gooding he could do.

"There really should be more mental health programs for veterans on both sides."

Trystan made an "umm" sound of agreement. "I'm sure you will start a few." The Camelot's Wounded Knights Association had already appointed Galahad an honorary board member for life, after he invented a device that helped blind soldiers "feel colors." Whatever the hell that meant.

There was another beat of silence.

"You know," Galahad said suddenly, in the faraway tone he always used when something new and strange occurred to him, "Marcus stole three years of your life, but..." He trailed off again, like he wasn't sure he should finish that thought.

"Yes?" Trystan prompted, eager for the knight to continue lecturing him. If he stopped caring what Trystan did, it was one step closer to Galahad disappearing back into his own world and leaving him grasping at air. "Tell me."

Galahad hesitated. "Well, I was just thinking..." He turned and met Trystan's eyes. "If your path sent you to prison, wasn't it *always* your path to go to prison? Like, you were supposed to be there, so events would unfold in a certain way?

"Paths are not linear. The choices we made guide them."

"Well, if you hadn't been in prison, you would've been fighting in the War. *That* would have been your choice."

"Yes."

"And you are a *great* warrior, Trystan. The greatest in the world. But not even you could have won the whole thing, by yourself. It still would've come down to Legion, only this time you could have been there with the other gryphon fighters. You would've done all you could to stop the destruction of the town."

"I would like to think so." Trystan agreed quietly. But he was not the greatest warrior in the world. *One* of them, yes. But there was a lavender-eyed knight who could match him.

"I *was* there." Galahad continued. "I saw my men shoot that village with the Rath, a weapon that never should have been invented. I saw your warriors fall from the sky and hit the burning ground. If you had been there, you'd be dead. I would have killed you."

Trystan said nothing, because that was probably true.

"And if you were dead, Midas would have died in prison, right? And without him and you to help them, Gwen and Avi would've died at the Scarecrows hands. You told me all about that." Galahad's head tilted. "So, if you look at it a certain way... Marcus *saved* all of you."

"I do not look at it that way." Trystan scoffed.

"Kill Marcus tomorrow." Galahad went on. "He deserves it. Anyone who hurts you should be wiped off the face of the world. I believe that with everything in me. But, don't *ever* regret what happened to you, because this path was the right one. It led you to the people who needed you most."

Trystan considered that. "You also would have died without me saving you from smoke inhalation with the pigs. And at the snake tomb. And with Solomon Grundy. And many *other* times, had I not been there."

Galahad rolled his eyes, much like his normal self. "Nah." He sat on the edge of the bed to take off his shoes. "I would've been okay on my own. I always am."

"You would have died." Trystan repeated. "And I would have lost all of my clan, without even knowing you."

The knight seemed surprised. "You consider me part of your clan?"

Did Galahad not understand that? How could he miss it? It wasn't as if Trystan had been subtle. Everyone in Lyonesse had noticed that Galahad was his and St. Ives was going to find out real damn quick. The first person who looked at the man wrong would go through a goddamn wall. It was absolute lunacy that Trystan now had to explain what was already so blatantly obvious.

"Of *course* you are part of my clan." Trystan crossed to stand in front of him. "You are in my care. I have told you this." If he gave Galahad some clearer reassurances, perhaps it would ease the knight's mind and bring him closer, again. "You are an indispensable part of my life, now and forever."

Some of the distance faded from Galahad's gaze. "I consider you my family, too, Trys. No matter what happens between us, that won't change."

Galahad had never had a real family. For him to say such a thing was important. Still the phrasing of his pledge seemed wrong. Why would anything change between them? "I am content with our..." Shit, what was the wingless word for "mating?" "With our *relationship*, just as it is." Trystan decided. "Are *you* content?"

"Yes."

"Good." Relief filled him. "So, do not forge *another* 'relationship' while I go off to kill my enemies and all will be well." He ran a hand over Galahad's shimmery hair and was pleased when the man didn't move away. "Once I return, I would only have to kill that male, too. And his grisly death would no doubt trouble you."

He said that ridiculous idea lightly, but Galahad seemed to take it in a serious way.

"Well, hang on... Hypothetically, if I met another man, you couldn't just breeze back into town and hurt him, Trys."

Trystan blinked at him, trying to catch up. "...What?" Galahad had never once indicated an interest in anyone else. Until this moment, he'd claimed that only Trystan would do for him. Fireworks of panic, and possession, and fury detonated inside of Trystan's skull, all at once, making it hard to think. "Wait, *what?*"

"It wouldn't be right for you to target a totally innocent guy, just because I'm sleeping with him." Galahad reiterated, sounding perturbed by the suggestion. "I mean, if you left, we'd have to rethink the idea that we're dating exclusively. We'd obviously agree to see other people..."

"I would not agree to that! Why would I agree to that?"

Galahad kept talking. "...So, you couldn't *then* return to Camelot and kill whatever poor guy I chose. It wouldn't be fair"

What the fuck...? Trystan gave his head a clearing shake. It didn't help. "Fair?"

"Theoretically, if I cared for someone enough to sleep with him..."

Trystan cut him off, again. "You cannot care for another male, when you have already claimed *me!*" Was Trystan losing his mind? How was that not the most sensible thing in the world?

"Isn't there a gryphon rule for this situation?" Galahad asked, because he was always asking the most insightful goddamn questions at the worst possible times. "There must be. When a gryphon leaves the person who's claimed them, the one who's been abandoned must be allowed to move on, right?"

Certainly, there was such a rule, but Trystan didn't give a troll's ass. "I will not be abandoning you, so what does it matter?"

Galahad's eyes narrowed slightly. "If you left me for who-knows-how-long to do who-knows-what, technically I'd be free to find somebody else." He wasn't willing to fight about Trystan's mission, but he would stand firm on his philosophical right to seduce strange men. It was infuriating. "It's hard for me to imagine finding anybody else, obviously. But, for arguments sake, if I *did*, it wouldn't be cheating."

It wasn't hard for Trystan to imagine Galahad finding another man, at all. Within moments of Trystan's departure any number of wingless, do-Gooding artists would be lining up for the knight to choose from. One might even be Galahad's True Love, who he would share his deepest thoughts with, and rely on without reservation, and willingly fight for.

P'don. P'don. P'don.

"I mean, the same freedoms would apply to you, obviously." Galahad went on, like that made any kind of difference. "Historically speaking, the odds are a lot higher that *you'd* meet someone, than I would. Once you were out in the world, you'd probably thank me for making this easier on you." He gave a contemptuous snort. "But that's really not helping me make my point, so we won't dwell on it."

Trystan tried to translate that bullshit. "You believe I'll *thank you* for bedding another male behind my back?"

"I'm not *actually* going to meet anyone else." Galahad said tiredly, like Trystan was the one being irrational. "I wouldn't even *want* to. You don't just start dating other men, once you've found your..." He broke off and waved a hand. "Forget it. We're way out in the weeds here, because, as usual, you want to get bogged down in semantics."

"How is it semantics that you plan to bed other men? You literally said these words."

"I did not say that! Jesus, it's an *abstract* debate, Trystan."

"Abstract?" Trystan echoed suspiciously.

"Yes." Galahad ran a hand through his hair. "Focus on the cause-and-effect relationships of this plan, because I'm trying to make it clear what you're *really* suggesting here. I'm using hyperbolic examples of how events *might* play out, if we followed this path you're advocating. Understand?"

"Believe me. I am very clear on how events will play out."

If another male touched Galahad, Trystan would kill the son of a bitch. That was clear as a cloudless sky. Trystan had already claimed this man. That had been clear since nearly the first day they met. Galahad was his mate, given to him by the gods and secure in Trystan's care. No one was stealing his goddamn mate, while Trystan still breathed.

Very. Fucking. Clear.

Bellowing any of those extremely clear facts would do nothing to achieve his goals, though. The knight was already on the verge of vanishing. One clumsy grab would send him dissipating into the mist forever.

"I would have your promise that you'll wait for me." He got out in a semi-normal tone. It might have been an "abstract" discussion in the knight's mind, but Trystan needed some concrete reassurances. "*Now*, Galahad."

He sighed. "It'd be better if we don't have any promises like that. When people promise to come back and don't... It leads to hard feelings. I would never want that between us, Trys."

Galahad's mother and father were to blame for this.

Trystan saw that suddenly. They were why the knight was so hard to get close to. His parents had dropped him at the door of the Knights' Academy and never looked back. That experience left Galahad with the deep certainty that no one else could be depended on. Galahad always expected to be unwanted, in the end. It was why he obsessively excelled at everything he tried. To be worthy.

To be loved.

With that thought, a new light dawned.

Maybe Galahad doubted that Trystan could love him. That must be why he was pulling back. Because he already suspected that Trystan's feelings weren't good enough.

Shit... Trystan closed his eyes, momentarily overcome with the scope of his problem. Love was the biggest emotion. It had to be. He had no idea how he was going to hold even a sliver of it. Love was gigantic and all-encompassing, while his abilities to feel *anything* were next to worthless. He struggled to even identify his emotions, let alone offer them to someone who deserved nothing but the best.

But, if Trystan didn't give Galahad what he needed, the man would never be his. He would just show Trystan pieces of himself, as he did with most people. Trystan didn't want pieces. He wanted *everything.* If he was going to get it, he needed to be calm and reasonable and show Galahad that he had control over all the confusing feelings that swamped him.

Trystan took a deep breath. "I will not touch another, while I am gone." He spoke as evenly as he could, considering nameless emotions were ricocheting in every direction. "I give you my word on the matter, even if you do not give me yours."

Unreadable purple eyes met his.

Trystan stared back, his gaze level. "I want you to feel... *trust* in my emotions for you. You spoke of trust to me, in Ted-ville, remember? You said that we should have faith in each other. Well, I want you to have faith that I will return to you, as soon as I am able. You understand this?"

"I understand that you intend to return."

That was one of his patented "life of truth" evasions, where he pretended to agree without outright lying.

Trystan tried again, attempting to get past the unreasonable reasonableness of the man. "It is not just an 'intention,' it is a fact. I have no thought of choosing another or staying away indefinitely. I would *always* come for you, Galahad. I feel very…" he struggled to identify his desperate, all-consuming need for the man, "*attached* to you."

"You're 'attached' to me?" Galahad's eyebrows climbed. "Is that what you're calling this emotion between us?"

"Yes." He scowled. "This is not correct?"

The knight studied him for a long beat. "You're the one who's always telling me what words really mean, Trys." He shrugged. "I think it's up to you to figure it out for yourself."

Chapter Twenty-Four

So, after we realized that this old Fisher guy who drew the map was dead, we started thinking maybe he told someone. A little digging and it turns out he was in a zoo cage with this kid, right? Well, the kid's older now, but maybe he still remembers something useful.

Marcus-the-Yellow-Boot helps us catch this guy in a trap, using some old gryphons as bait. Now, this zoo-kid is a *big* guy, so we drug him with angelycall to get him under control. The drug knocked him out some.

Then, we started asking him some *hard* questions about Fisher. Real hard. But no matter what we do, the son of a bitch won't talk. We didn't even bother telling him about the map, because he's not saying a *word*.

A part of me respected that. A bigger part of me spit on him when we dumped his ass in prison.

Uther died not long after that, so we never did figure it all out. It was probably just a dirty gryphon trick.

"Stopping the Savages" Podcast
Sir Dragonet of Camelot- Former Troubadour of King Uther and Host of the Program

St. Ives- Kit-Cat-Sack Street

"This isn't my fault." Galahad declared. "I see on your face that you're thinking this is somehow my fault, but this *isn't* my fault."

Trystan didn't seem convinced.

"It's not my fault!" Galahad gestured to the neon sign with an emphatic wave of his hand. "I had no idea that Mordy owned a strip club!"

The Seven Husbands was written out in cursive neon all along the front of the building. Mordy's establishment was a glittering, gaudy, architectural-disaster of a building situated on St. Ives busiest thoroughfare. Several thousand flashing lights and semi-indecent pictures were plastered all over it, adding to the overall sleaze of the place.

Trystan arched a brow. "It's a surety that you will cause some new type of chaos each day, knight. I wake up resigned to it, at this point. But the variety and unpredictability of the disasters is truly remarkable."

"This isn't funny."

"I am not laughing. Believe me."

"I didn't know this place was a strip club." Galahad repeated, scowling up at the building. Kit-Cat-Sack Street seemed to be nothing but bars and brothels. Even in that dis-illustrious company the Seven Husbands stood out in its tackiness. "I would never have agreed to meet at a strip club, if I *knew* it was a strip club. A lot of my fans are children, for God's sake. I can't be associated with anything tawdry."

Trystan shook his head in exasperation. "You are missing the bigger issue here."

Galahad paused. "Good point. This is even worse than setting a poor example for kids." He nodded, infused with new certainty. "This is about the exploitation of women."

"Lyrssa save me... It's a *male* strip club."

"Really?" Galahad's eyebrows shot up and he glanced Trystan's way. "How can you tell?"

"Because it's advertising *men*." Trystan pointed at the huge sign looming above them. It depicted a badly painted knight, nude except for a strategically placed broadsword and a come-hither smile.

Galahad processed it for a beat. "Oh."

Trystan grunted, seeing he'd convinced him. "Told you so."

Galahad ignored that, but it was hard. And was he imagining things or did that sign kind of look like... him?

"I am not a fan of art, but even I appreciate that imagery." Trystan mused.

"Still not funny."

"Still not laughing."

Galahad shook his head in aggravation. "You know, exploiting men is wrong, too."

Trystan continued to squint up at the gaudy advertisement. "That sign kind of looks like *you*, yes?"

Galahad ignored that opinion and started down the street, towards the entrance of the club. "Most of the people who work in these kinds of places are young, and broke, and have no other options. They need *help*, not someone profiting off of their desperation. Mordy needs to understand that this is a real problem."

Trystan dragged his gaze from the sign. "What?" He headed after Galahad. "Wait, you cannot still think to meet with this man."

"Of course, I'm going to meet with him. How else can I explain all the inequities that he's perpetuating? Either he makes changes or he's out of my fan club. I mean it."

Trystan hesitated, clearly wanting to throw a fit about Galahad entering The Seven Husbands. Since their argument the night before, though, he'd been making an effort to be agreeable. All morning he'd been biting back his normal complaints and straining to stay calm.

God only knew what he hoped to accomplish with the act. Galahad had spent twenty-four hours a day with the man for weeks, now. He knew that Trystan was anything but easygoing. But, it was kind of fun to watch him take deep breaths to refrain from bellowing every ten seconds. Galahad was curious to see how long he could keep it up before he cracked.

"I feel... *apprehensive* about the idea of you having brunch with this person." Trystan said very carefully.

"Nothing Bad's going to happen. I'm just going to reason with him."

Trystan literally cringed at that news. "I would feel more... *comfortable* if you reconsidered."

"I can't reconsider. You're supposed to meet Marcus here to kill him, remember? And I'd like to discuss shutting down this den of iniquity. So that means we're stuck with this..."

A goat-legged satyr gave an appreciative whistle, interrupting the retort. He was leaning against the corner of a building that sold discount sex spells, idly passing out pornographic advertisements to everyone who walked by. "Hey there, Gal-la-had." He sing-songed. "Looking *good*, boy."

Galahad automatically glanced at the guy with a frown. Sometimes people recognized him and made passes, but they were rarely so blatant. "Whoever you are, I'm not interested." He said as politely as he could.

"Well, *I'm* interested." The satyr reached up to rub at his curved horns suggestively. "You at Mordy's? I can stop by later and -- uh-- you can perform some heroics on my cock, yeah?"

Trystan's head angled in an eerily homicidal way.

Shit.

Galahad ignored the weirdo and grabbed hold of Trystan's arm. "He's probably drunk." He dragged Trystan away before the stranger's blood was splattered all over the sidewalk. "Just let it go."

Trystan watched the satyr over his shoulder, his eyes burning with fury. "*Fine*." He snarled, still pretending to be zen. He grabbed a wide-brimmed hat off the head of a random passerby. The guy turned to protest the theft... Then took one look at Trystan's size and kept walking. Trystan snorted in satisfaction and plopped the hat on Galahad's head. "Wear this." He tugged the brim down to hide Galahad's features. "That son of a bitch is the bigger issue, I spoke of. You see this, now?"

"That satyr is one random nut. You're overreacting." Galahad pushed the hat out of his eyes. "Why am I wearing this? I don't get sunburned and, even if I did, there *is* no sun in this place."

"So you are less noticeable and so I will be called on to slaughter fewer men."

Galahad sighed. "I don't like hats. I always lose them."

"I don't care." He jerked up the collar of Galahad's jacket, obscuring the line of his jaw. The man also refused to accept that Galahad didn't need a coat, no matter how many times Galahad told him that he was impervious to cold. Trystan was obsessed with his clothing choices. It was cute, in an exasperating kind of way. "There are several thousand dickheads in this town just like that satyr, waiting to pounce."

"That's not true. That kind of thing doesn't usually happen to me." He turned to frown back in the direction of the weirdo. "It was really strange, right? There could be something --like-- mentally wrong with him. Maybe we should call someone."

Trystan caught hold of his chin, turning Galahad's head so their gazes connected. Trystan's eyes were such a beautiful deep brown that Galahad found himself forgetting how *bothered* he was at the man.

"I can kill many people for you." Trystan said seriously. "But I cannot kill thousands, all at once."

Galahad blinked. "I can handle whatever happens, so you don't have to kill anyone *at all* for me. I don't want that."

"That will be welcomed news to all the dead man I've left in your wake, so far. They can unbury themselves and return to breathing."

Galahad frowned at the sarcasm.

"Anyway, those bastards are not the issue." Trystan waved them aside. "It is my right and duty to protect you. I do it gladly. But there are many men in this town who will want you for themselves. For your own safety, you need to keep a low profile. Understand?"

"Most guys here probably like women, so I don't think..."

Trystan cut him off. "Look around. This town has minimal women and many criminal assholes. Even if they typically prefer females, the criminal assholes must fulfil their desires somehow. So the criminal assholes will turn to *men*. This is simple biology." His palm found the back of Galahad's neck and Galahad's insides took the same pleasurable dip they always did when Trystan touched him. "You must be careful. Please. I would feel... *sad* if you were hurt."

Galahad's heart warmed. "You would?"

"The depth of my desolation would be matched only by the abject suffering I inflict on those who harmed you." Trystan assured him. "This emotion is 'sad,' yes?"

"Close enough." Galahad gave him a genuine smile. Bothered as he was at the man, he was still impressed by his abilities. "It's amazing how fast you're recognizing your feelings."

Trystan's beautiful eyes brightened. "You see my efforts to succeed in this area?"

"Of course. You're doing great." It was true. Trystan had been pushing to categorize and explain his feelings ever since Ted-ville. Very few people, of any species, would put that kind of effort into their emotional growth. "I'm so proud of you."

...Even if Trystan *was* struggling to figure out the whole "attached" thing.

Trystan watched him intently. "I will feel all that you need me to feel. I give you my word. I just need more time to learn how."

Galahad frowned, a little confused. Trystan already felt the same things that everybody else did. That had been obvious to Galahad, after just a few days in his company. It would take Trystan some time to learn how to identify all his emotions, but he'd *always* felt them.

"Okay." He said anyway, because it seemed important to Trystan that he agree.

"Fine." Trystan nodded in something like relief. "This is good. You are not so distant from me today. Have you given more thought to our discussion from last night?"

Galahad's smiled dimmed, remembering to be bothered. "The discussion where you told me you were leaving Camelot and there was nothing I could do to stop you? But I should wait at home and--like-- pine for you, while celibate? That discussion? Yeah, I thought about it."

And he'd come to the conclusion that he was going to keep his True Love, even though his True Love was a gigantic dimwit.

Trystan's gaze narrowed. "Interestingly enough, *I* remember it as the discussion where you passionately argued your right to sleep with other males."

Of course, he'd focus on the theoretical bullshit instead of anything that mattered. "I'm not going to sleep with anyone else. Jesus! Why do we keep going over this? It was a *hypothetical, abstract, philosophical discussion*."

"In which you said you would sleep with other men."

"I was just making the point that a long distance relationship would be difficult for us, given the lack of trust."

"And I was making the point that our 'relationship' is unbreakable, no matter the distance. If any other man touches you, I will rip off his head and *put* it on a very sharp point. Literally. That will happen."

Galahad had seen the suitable-for-framing pictures in Trystan's war file that proved that wasn't an empty threat. He arched a brow. "Have I mentioned you're really possessive?"

"And I have so little reason to think that strange males will try to lure you away." Trystan waved a sardonic hand back towards the weirdo satyr who'd propositioned Galahad.

"Hey, I had nothing to do with some guy trying to pick me up..."

"I am not blaming *you*." Trystan interrupted. "You cannot help being perfect." He paused. "Although if you wore more hats, you could perhaps disguise some of your perfection. This would help."

"You're out of your mind."

"I am *right*." Trystan insisted, because he always thought he was right. "You attract horrible people. They are lurking everywhere and you will not even fight them when they attack. And when I am gone, hunting my enemies, they will be swarming around you like rabid glatisant lizards." He laid a hand on his chest, the soul of compromise and rational thought. "This is why I simply want you to avoid all men who aren't me. Why is this so difficult to understand?"

"Oh, I understand it. I just think it's insane."

"You are deliberately seeking to complicate things that are..."

"Let's just not rehash this, alright?" Galahad held up his palms to cut Trystan off, before he kept talking and Galahad kept getting progressively more bothered. "I don't want to argue."

"You never want to argue. In an argument, you might reveal more than you wish to reveal. This makes you uneasy."

Galahad's jaw ticked. "Or I just don't want to argue."

"I tell *you* what *I* am feeling." Trystan crossed his arms over his chest. "I would like to hear what *your* emotions are. What do you feel towards me?"

"Right now, I'm feeling mostly pissed off." Galahad snapped, before he could stop himself.

Trystan looked encouraged. "You are angry with me? Why?"

Galahad opened his mouth to begin listing off reasons and then closed it, again. "I don't like to get angry." He repeated, instead. "I told you, I'm worried about what might happen if I get out of control. So, I'm being *not* angry."

"You comprehend that 'angry' and 'pissed off' are synonyms in your language, yes?"

Galahad wasn't going to rise to that bait. He *wasn't.* "I already have a plan to fix everything that you're screwing up, so it doesn't even matter." He ground out.

Trystan's brows came together, like he was frustrated that Galahad restrained from bellowing at him. "You have a plan?" He repeated skeptically. "I swear to the gods, each time you say that, all the hair on my arms stands straight up."

Galahad arched a brow at the sarcasm. Trystan was back to being his normal confrontational self, it seemed. Clearly, he wasn't ready to hear Galahad's very simple resolution to this problem. Alright. Well, if he wanted to keep fighting, he could figure things out the hard way.

"I'll let *you* think of the obvious solution to our problem, then. In the meantime, I'm late for brunch." Galahad started for the strip club, again.

Behind him, Trystan muttered off a bunch of gryphon words

that Galahad didn't understand. Yet. After last night in the bar, listening to Trystan and Konrad go back-and-forth in the gryphons' language, Galahad had decided he'd better learn it, too. It was the only way he was going to be able to keep up. Besides, now that he knew that the dead gryphons weren't just figments of his imagination, it made sense to figure out *exactly* what they were saying to him. If they were trying to guide him, he might as well understand the guidance.

Fortunately, St. Ives was a melting pot of different cultures and a hotbed of capitalism. The gift shop at the Siege Perilous Hotel and Casino sold beginners' guides to the gryphon dialect. Galahad had already started reading the book, but he'd never been great at learning languages. It would take him at least a couple days to master it.

"What is the obvious solution to our problem?" Trystan shouted after him.

"You don't want to hear my plans, remember? You want to do everything yourself. Speaking of which…" He pointed upward. "When did Konrad say this race starts, again? Because, it seems like you missed it by about three hours."

Above his head, a banner was stretched between lamp posts advertising a "HUGE RACE TODAY!" Konrad hadn't been lying about that part, although Kit-Cat-Sack Street wasn't exactly lined with spectators. Possibly, because the sign said the race was supposed to begin at eight and it was almost eleven.

Trystan glowered at the time printed on the banner. "Shit." He muttered.

"Maybe they mean eight *p.m.*" Galahad suggested sarcastically. "Just stand here until tonight and hope for the best. I'll be in the club."

Trystan sure didn't need *his* help. Of course not. He was doing *super* on his own.

Jackass.

Galahad might love the man, but he'd spent the entire night fighting the urge to smother him in his sleep. When Trystan had told him he planned to leave Camelot, Galahad's first instinct was to react the same way he'd reacted when his parents had called, year after year, to explain that they didn't have time to visit. To be composed and logical and as detached as possible, because it would be pointless to get upset over something that wouldn't change.

But that plan wasn't really working this time.

Galahad was trying hard to be understanding, but he was *bothered* that Trystan planned to skip out on him.

Really. Incredibly. Bothered.

Still, Galahad wasn't about to lose his True Love, even if the man was a colossal dickhead. Side note: If Trystan just had sex with him, *he'd* know they were True Loves, only he still didn't want to consummate their relationship. But Galahad wasn't angry about that, either. Nope. He was A-Okay with Trystan "considering many options," while Galahad fell deeper and deeper in love. Galahad would just deal with that, too, because *clearly* he was the only person in their relationship capable of rational thought.

There was one obvious way out of this mess: Galahad was just going to tag along on the revenge mission. Since he wasn't a moron (like some big, oblivious gryphons) he'd already figured it out. It was settled and *done*.

Trystan just needed to not be a moron and figure it out, too.

Galahad's eyes skimmed over a hot cross buns vendor as he neared the entrance of Mordy's club. Then his gaze snapped back, as his brain registered what he was actually looking at. The hot cross buns were being heated on a high-powered heat lamp. In order to ensure they were all kept at the same temperature, they were being turned over that lamp on a rotisserie. And in order to spin the rotisserie, a tiny pixie was being forced to walk in endless circles on a hamster wheel.

It was a Rube Goldberg design of sticky dough and enslavement.

The tiny pixie was staggering with exhaustion, trying to keep the whole mechanism going. A teeny chain was around her neck, locking her in place. Her wings drooped with malnutrition, her short blonde hair was unwashed, and her clothes were rags. Pixies were often subjugated by larger beings, so she looked resigned to the servitude.

God, Galahad was sick of all the unfairness in the world.

Trystan caught up with him. "Knight, *stop.* We are not finished with this discussion."

"Do you see that?" Galahad demanded, nodding towards the hot cross bun cart.

Trystan frowned, momentarily distracted. "Not even you are reckless enough to eat food from that filthy vendor. It is probably dosed with every wicked spell imaginable. I have told you this land is filled with Bad magic, yes? Powders, elixirs, incantations..."

"Yes, you've mentioned it *a lot*."

"Well Konrad told me that this epidemic is even worse in St. Ives, of late. Dark spells that no one has ever heard of before are for sale, now. You must be careful."

"I'm always careful." Galahad kept his eyes on the poor pixie. "Relax. You just focus on your big race. You only have nine more hours to prepare for it."

"I will deal with the race later. Right now, I am talking to you."

"I don't want to talk, anymore."

Trystan wasn't in the mood to respect his boundaries. "We do not have a lack of trust." He snapped, backtracking to Galahad's earlier remark. "*You* have a lack of trust. You do not trust my feelings for you. This is why you keep most of yourself hidden."

Unbelievable... Galahad dragged his gaze off the food cart. "So this is *my* doing, now?"

"Yes! I have more faith in you than I have ever had in anyone, but you give me minimal trust in return." Trystan challenged, like he wanted Galahad to get mad. "You give me as little as possible of yourself. Pieces, when I want the whole."

"You really want to talk about reciprocity, Trys?" He challenged. "Which of us keeps saying 'not yet' when I ask if you're ready to sleep with me?"

"That is not because of distrust..."

"Which of us didn't make me an ally on *his* mission, even though I made him an ally on *my* mission days ago?"

"You are deliberately missing the..."

"Which of us claimed *you* and which of us has *not* claimed me?"

"I *have* claimed you!" Trystan bellowed, like he was the aggrieved party.

Passersby were now crossing the street to avoid their shouting match. The entire citizenry of the town was Bad, engaging in all sorts of criminal activities, but Trystan and Galahad were the ones making a scene. Ordinarily, Galahad disliked making a scene. At the moment, though, he barely noticed. All his attention was on Trystan.

"You claimed me?" He repeated, his heart pounding. "When? I didn't hear it." And he'd been listening closely.

"I should not have to say it aloud." Through some kind of mental gymnastics Trystan had convinced himself that Galahad was the one being difficult. It was amazing. "I have proven my devotion, again and again, with my actions."

That sounded like a cop-out to Galahad. "You have to actually say the words to claim someone. I'm pretty sure that's how it works, according to the gryphons' rules."

Trystan cursed under his breath, which meant Galahad was right. "My commitment to you is already apparent to every living thing who's seen us together." He began ticking them off on his fingers. "Ayren and her men. The fifty thousand helpless beings you made me save. All the random scumbags in this town, and uneaten leprechauns in the desert, and the whole population of goddamn Ted-ville... *Trees and bushes* have no doubt noticed my feelings."

"You need to say the words." Galahad reiterated. "Aren't you the one always going on about the importance of language?"

"Then give me words, too." Trystan moved so he was directly in front of him. "Explain why you are so "bothered" *in words*."

Galahad's jaw clenched. "Can we do this later?" Without waiting for a reply, he turned back to the hot cross bun vendor. The man was a troll, with a round stomach and a scraggly ponytail. "Hey!" He shouted, drawing the bastard's attention. "Are you paying that pixie a fair wage?" He seriously doubted it.

The man flicked him off without answering.

Galahad's jaw ticked.

"Are you bothered because I am leaving Camelot?" Trystan stayed laser-focused on the topic at hand. "Do you still fear that I will not return? I said that I would. Again, this is you not trusting me."

"I don't want to do this. Why do you want to do this?" Galahad shook his head, *very* fucking bothered, now. "I can't do this. I have to go deal with this guy, right now."

Trystan spared the hot cross bun vendor a dismissive look. "I will slay that asshole for you, in a second." He promised distractedly. "Right now, you need to explain this discrepancy to me. Last night you said you *weren't* upset over my mission and now you are upset. Why?"

"Last night, I said that I wanted to be supportive and...."

"Was it a *lie* that you are not angry?" Trystan interrupted. "Just tell me the truth."

"I live *a life of fucking truth!*" Galahad shouted. All his suppressed "bother" suddenly boiled over into white-hot rage at the colossal moron he planned to marry. "I told you I wasn't upset and I'm *not* upset. That word doesn't even *begin* to fucking cover it. I'm *fucking furious* at you."

Perversely, Trystan seemed hopeful at that revelation. "Yes?"

"*Yes*. You think you can fucking walk out on me? You think I will fucking let that happen?" He jabbed a finger into Trystan's chest. "Rewind every goddamn thing you know about me. Think it all through, in your goddamn head, and try to figure out what kind of man you're *actually* dealing with here."

Trystan's gaze gleamed, enjoying all the swearing, but he didn't comment on it. "Tell me, then. Give me the core of you."

"You won't fucking like the core of me." Galahad snarled, attempting to calm down before it was too late. "Just stop trying to..."

"You're really handsome when you're angry. Has anyone ever told you that?"

That was *exactly* what Galahad had said to him back at the waterfall and it produced *exactly* the same reaction in Galahad that it had in Trystan.

His temper detonated.

Spending his whole life in the military had given Galahad an amazing vocabulary of vulgarities. He didn't like to use them, but he knew them all. (Some of the worst ones he'd actually invented, although he didn't love seeing his name next to them in various dictionaries.) Now, every curse word in existence was leveled at Trystan, in such volcanic, impressive, and creative ways that even the hot cross bun vendor's eyebrows shot up in shock.

Trystan's mouth curved as Galahad let loose on him. "Now, I've caught hold of you." He murmured.

"This is *really* what you want to do? *Really?*" Galahad seethed, trying to reign back. "Have this discussion, when I am so fucking angry? Because, it's a lousy fucking idea, Trystan."

"Is it?"

"Yes! Killing people is your fucking dream? Well, it's a *shit* dream. And it sure as fuck isn't mine. *My* dream is *you*. And I'm going to *have* my dream, with or without your fucking cooperation. I ran a fucking army. You think I got that job because I'm such a nice fucking guy, all the time? Or do you think maybe I got it because I'm the most determined son of a bitch you will ever fucking meet?"

Trystan looked mesmerized.

"We are already on a path, you and I." Galahad continued. "Nothing you do will change that. I won't *let* you change it. Try and get rid of me and see what fucking happens. I am fifty times Badder and a hundred times darker than you will *ever* be."

"I believe you." Trystan didn't seem worried about it, though.

He should've been.

"Even in our battles, I always played fair with you, Trystan. But, if you push me far enough and it matters to me deep enough, I will break rules that you would *never* break. I will go farther than you *ever* will. I will flatten civilization itself to keep what's mine."

Brown eyes glowed. "You think I am yours?"

"I *know* you're mine."

Trystan didn't argue. How could he? It was the truth. "And you don't fear that I lack adequate emotions to give you these feelings back?"

"I fear you lack adequate fucking brain cells. Jesus Christ! When have you *ever* not felt 'adequate emotions' towards something? Ever? *I'm* the fucking calm one in our relationship. *You're* the one who's always freaking out about something."

"This is you being the calm one?"

"This is me telling you that you aren't dumping me."

"You will fight to keep me, then?"

"The fight is *over*. I've already *won*. I don't need a sword, or threats, or an army to get what's rightfully mine." Galahad leaned closer to him. "I just fucking *took* you."

Trystan's eyes gleamed. "Yes." He agreed quietly. "You did."

"I've never lost a battle. Even the battles I *wish* I'd lost." Galahad went on, too far gone to even process the agreement. "I sure as hell didn't lose the most important one of my life. You might be the *ya'lah*… but I'm a fucking *knight*."

"I am not the *ya'lah*." Trystan was going along with everything else, but that part he wanted to dispute. "*You* are the *ya'lah*. Why must we continually debate this?"

"Because you're continually wrong!"

"I do not wish to argue about it." Trystan waved a dismissive hand, stealing Galahad's former position for his own. "I wish to argue about you keeping me for yourself, instead. Although I am not actually arguing about that, either, as I greatly like this conversation."

"I'm so glad you're fucking entertained."

"Yes, you should yell at me more often, because you say many interesting things when you are mad. In between the swearing and wrongly believing I am the *ya'lah*, anyway."

"You are so goddamn…" Galahad let out a long hissing breath of frustration. "*Fuck!*" His gaze fell on the hot cross bun vendor, again. "And you…" He snapped, finding another outlet for his wrath. "Let that pixie go. *Now*." He jabbed a finger at the man, more than ready to march over there and do it himself. "Or I will shove *you* into that goddamn wheel, *head fucking first!*"

Trystan seemed absolutely delighted with that threat. "My knight is only bothered, at the moment." He sent the troll an amused look. "I would not make him angry, if I were you. The man perfected his own form of martial arts, which is currently being taught in fifty-eight lands."

The troll was apparently smarter than his hair style suggested. He raced to unchain the pixie. The beleaguered creature paused to incline her head a Galahad and then flew off into the gray sky. Hopefully, she was escaping to a better world. The troll's small eyes stayed fixed on Galahad, like he was afraid what might come next.

"*Thank* you." Galahad bit off. "And try to be a nicer fucking person in the future."

The troll frantically bobbed his head.

Trystan's mouth twitched upward.

Galahad took a deep breath and turned back to him, starting over. "Look, this is all very reasonable, Trystan: I will never let you go. Understand it now, because it'll save us a lot of trouble later on. You are *not* leaving me, no matter what I have to do." That was reasonable, right? "Now, we can walk down this path together at any speed you want. But if you try to go wandering off on some *new* path without me…" His eyes narrowed. "I will fucking *stop* you."

"Alright." Trystan said as if they'd just settled on pizza for dinner. "I agree to this."

He did? Galahad's eyebrows slammed together. "You do?"

"Yes."

"Oh." Galahad blinked. "Good. *Finally*, you're making some fucking sense."

"For once, your use of 'reason' is persuasive. Even the bun man seems to think so." He looked over at the troll. "Don't you think so, bun man?"

The troll was too busy wheeling his cart away to answer that. He dashed off as quickly as he could, hot cross buns flying every which way.

Great. Now, the jerkoff was littering.

"I'm *always* persuasive." Galahad told Trystan testily, ignoring the mess. "It's just that no one ever listens."

Trystan stared down at him, a hungry glint in his eyes. "Well, you were wrong about at least one thing: I *very* much like the core of you, knight. And I am considering *many* interesting options on how to deal with the whole man I am seeing."

"That is certainly my favorite option, but you are also involved."

Konrad appeared before Galahad could respond to that.

336

Except for a pair of mirrored sunglasses, the other gryphon was dressed in the exact outfit he'd worn the night before, like he hadn't slept. St. Ives was a town where daytime was just a late night for most of the residents.

"Excellent, you are here, Trystan. Marcus is nearly arriving. He's following the race."

"The race started three hours ago." Trystan shot him a glare, annoyed by the interruption. "That sign says so." He pointed up at the banner.

"I can't read their scribble-ish language." Konrad scoffed. "I just know the race will be here soon. We should get preparation-ed." He glanced at Galahad and then did a double take. "Wow..." He looked him up and down over the tops of his aviators. "Looking like this, you will make much gold this day."

Galahad had no idea what that meant.

Trystan seemed equally clueless. "What the hell are you talking about? More importantly: Why are you talking to my knight, at all? I told you to *not* talk to him."

"I was just talking that he looks fantastic! I much like that hat."

Galahad squinted upward at the hideous brim of his hideous hat. He'd forgotten he was even wearing it. "If you like this hat, you can have it." He offered testily.

"Do not take off that hat." Trystan muttered in an absent tone, still glowering at Conrad. "The knight and I are having a conversation here, so you need to go away until..."

"Oh no, we're *done* the conversation." Galahad assured him. "*Marcus* is on his way, after all. He's *way* more important." He stalked over to yanked open the door of the strip club. "Far be it from me to stand in the way of your glorious dream."

"You don't want to stay and watch me get my revenge?"

"What's to watch? You'll have Marcus dead within two minutes." Galahad had never been less worried about anything. The outcome of the fight wasn't even a question. "Besides, I'm not your *ally* in this, right? So, I'd just be in the way."

"You have not made him your ally?" Konrad scoffed. "If asked, I will make him *my* ally. The man would not be in my way. I can think of many places where he will nicely fit."

"You shut up." Trystan warned. "And knight, you come back here."

Galahad kept walking.

"You can struggle, but there's no more escaping back to your realm." Trystan called after him. "All the pieces of you are in my grasp. I can see into the very heart of you, now."

"The very heart of me is *you*, dipshit. *Everyone* sees that." Galahad slammed the door behind him.

A sign taped to the glass read "Closed for Private Brunch," so Mordy was obviously expecting him. There was no one in the Seven Husbands small foyer to greet him, though, so Galahad headed down a darkened corridor towards the main bar area.

He always did his best to not get angry. It was dangerous for someone with so much Badness in him to risk losing control. He knew that. But, now that Galahad was calming down and taking stock, everything seemed to be kind of... okay. Galahad hadn't felt the darkness swirling inside of him. Trystan had never been endangered. No one else was hurt. Even the pixie was free.

It was all okay.

If anything, talking about all his feelings had been cleansing for Galahad. Instead of repressing everything until he couldn't contain it, he'd dealt with it in a (loud, but) rational conversation. Minus some cursing, it felt safe and clean and not entirely terrible to say everything he thought. And Trystan had seemed bizarrely thrilled and kind of turned on by the whole thing, so that was an unexpected plus.

Galahad absently took off the stupid hat, running a hand through his hair.

Maybe he should try to look on the positive side of his inadvertent detour into screaming rage. He'd learned something about himself and that was always important. Galahad embraced self-growth. Maybe Trystan was right. Maybe Galahad needed to channel the Badness within him, instead of pressing it down. Like a pressure valve, maybe it was healthy to release some of his darker emotions. Maybe from now on, he should worry less about losing control and more about being true to his feelings, as they arose. It would be better to...

Galahad's introspective thoughts stopped short as he rounded a corner and the interior of the club came into full view. For one second, he was so astonished that his mind magnet-wiped of everything else. His eyes widened, horrified for a variety of reasons, by what he saw.

"Holy *shit!* Llamrai, is that you?"

Chapter Twenty-Five

Battle of Pen Rhionydd
Start of the Second Looking Glass Campaign

Trystan disobeyed the other gryphons.

After escaping the cage, he didn't immediately fly away from the fight. Instead, he ran down the twisting paths of the zoo, his heart pounding. Electricity in the city was out and would stay out for months, but fire was lighting his way. The sounds of the battle still echoed all around him, the screaming of the combatants so close than some of them had to be within the confines of the zoo itself.

But, to Trystan, the animals seemed a much realer threat.

Bombs had decimated most of the enclosures, killing or freeing their inhabitants. All the polar bears were dead, their white bodies burnt black. The vulture-monkeys were loose and shrieking from the trees. A cyclops sat in the remnants of his cage, both hands covering his eye, as if he did not want to see anything more. Jackalopes ran every which way, panicked by the chaos. Like Trystan they weren't sure where to go next.

The blue tiger cage was empty.

Trystan hesitated for a step, afraid that the deadly cat might be free and lurking nearby. Blue tigers were some of the most deadly predators in the world. His father had been a great hunter, so he'd told Trystan of many animals. Trystan remembered all the stories. He remembered everything his clans told him. His father had said you had to be very still, if you ever encountered a blue tiger, because the creatures would devour anything that moved before their sapphire eyes.

But Trystan's clan needed him, so he *couldn't* stay still.

Holding his breath, he snuck past the eerily silent cage. Nothing stirred. Perhaps the blue tiger had already fled. Trystan let out a relieved breath and continued his search. He needed to find the zookeeper. *Had* to find him. His bare feet thudded against the pavement, as he looked up and down the pathways, growing increasingly desperate. It had been four years since Trystan was free to run. The outside world seemed huge to him and he'd never been alone in it before. His whole life, adult gryphons had protected him.

Now, he would protect them.

Trystan found the zookeeper by the giraffe pen. The man was leaning over one of the slender animals, trying to stop the blood that was pouring from its wounds. It looked like shrapnel from one of the bombs had shredded much of its body. The giraffe was dying. Bleating, humming sounds of pain emanated from its long neck.

Trystan skidded to a halt next to it, panting for breath. "I need the key." He got out in the wingless dialect.

The zookeeper looked up, tears in his eyes. "Are you out of your cage? Good. Help me save him."

There was no saving the giraffe.

The zookeeper already seemed to know that. He broke down sobbing as the creature's life slipped away, blood coating his hands. For all his faults, the old man cared for the animals in his charge.

Unlike many of the wingless workers who oversaw the gryphons, the zookeeper wasn't cruel. Trystan didn't fear or despise him. The man just saw the gryphons as... beasts. He gave them the same regard that he gave the lions and the barghest. It never occurred to him that they were his equals in thought and in humanity.

Occasionally, though, the zookeeper snuck Trystan apples through the bars of the cage. In a world where no other wingless had ever showed him any kindness, Trystan counted that as something of note. The zookeeper was the only person he could think to turn to for help. Trystan was willing to risk being punished or recaptured, if it meant saving his clan.

"I need the keys to the gryphons' cage." He repeated, sounding out the words clearly in the common tongue. He knew the language, but rarely used it. Who among the wingless would he want to talk to? "My clan is trapped."

The zookeeper blinked, trying to focus. "Shit." He wiped at his damp cheek with his shirt sleeve. He seemed too frazzled to even be surprised that Trystan was talking to him, although none of the gryphons had before. "Yes. Of course." He fumbled with his belt for a moment, unclasping the keyring. "Here." He tossed it to Trystan. "Set them free. Set all the animals free."

Trystan caught the heavy keys. "We were never animals." He said, although he knew the zookeeper wouldn't understand that.

Still, in that moment of desperation, the old man gave Trystan a chance to save his clan. Because of that, Trystan would never add him to his list of people to kill. He would never hate the man. He would always heed Elaine's final instructions and judge the zookeeper on his best day, instead of on his blind stupidity.

Turning, Trystan raced back towards the Primitive People's Exhibit. He could see the dome of the enclosure peeking over the smoldering trees. It wasn't so far away. He kept his eyes on it, rather than looking at any of the dangerous animals running loose around him. He could do this! It was going to work. He'd use the keys to open the cage and then his clan would be safe. They could all leave this horrible land and...

Boom!

The explosion was massive. The shock wave of power tossed Trystan to the ground, nearly knocking him senseless. His vision blurred, his ears ringing. For one dazed moment, he had no idea what had happened. He lifted himself into a sitting position, fingering the new cut on his forehead.

And saw the gryphons' enclosure burning.

"*NO!*" He was on his feet and sprinting for the cage again before he even realized that he was moving. The entire building was burning, flames jumping high into the sky. A bomb must have fallen on the enclosure, aimed at higher value targets in the battle, but inadvertently destroying Trystan's whole world.

"No! Elaine! Ban! *No!*"

He raced for the Primitive People's Exhibit, refusing to believe that it was too late. Maybe they were still alive. Maybe he could still get them out. Maybe he...

"Who the hell is this, now?" Large hands grabbed Trystan as he dashed by, lifting him right off his feet.

"No!" He struggled against the stranger's hold, his eyes still on the cage. "Stop! I have to go back. I *promised* them I'd be back!"

"Shut up." The man snapped, not letting him go. "Gods, where did you even come from? Marcus!" He raised his voice to a shout. "There's a child over here!"

Trystan twisted in the man's grasp and bit down on his wrist. The man gave a shout of pain and surprise, loosening his hold enough that Trystan could squiggle away. He hit the ground at the man's feet, his eyes falling on the pair of boots that he wore.

Bright yellow boots.

Trystan's gaze slammed upward. The stranger was a gryphon. He'd been too panicked to notice the man's features before, but now his brain was processing more details. Yes. He was a gryphon, with dark hair, a large nose, and silver-tipped wings. Even if he was a hated Yellow Boot, he was still one of Trystan's kind. He might be able to help.

"My clan is in the cage." He said in the gryphons' language. "The wingless had us locked in there."

The dark-haired man glanced towards the enclosure, his expression unreadable. "Gryphons were exhibited in a *zoo?*"

"What's the holdup, Horatio?" A new Yellow Boot demanded, striding over to them. He looked so much like the first man that they must have been related and he spoke in a tone that suggested he was used to giving orders. His cheap wingless "uniform" was covered in cheap meaningless medals. "A child? What race?"

"One of ours. He says there are gryphons trapped in that building over there." The first man, who must have been Horatio, nodded towards it. "He wants us to let them out."

"I can do it. I have the keys." Trystan staggered to his feet and lifted the keyring up for them to see. "Please. I have to save them."

Horatio actually paused, like he was considering the idea.

"Save them?" The one called Marcus scoffed. "Why the hell would we do that?" He snatched the keys from Trystan's hands. "If they die now, it's less gryphons that we'll have to fight later."

"No!" Trystan jumped at him, trying to get the keys back. Marcus held them out of his reach. "They'll burn to death, if we don't help them!"

Already, the building was beginning to fail. He could hear the dome cracking, even at a distance. They were running out of time!

"The whole Sunchase Clan territory burned when I was a boy." Marcus retorted bitterly. "None of the other clans came to save us, when we had nowhere to go. Why should I save them?"

The Sunchase Clan had always been apart from the other gryphons. They lived in harsher conditions and under their own brutal rules. They had no permanent home, now. Perhaps, that was why they were one of the few clans who'd sided with Uther in the War. Their lives were so miserable that even his false promises were better than no promises, at all.

"Fuck Lyrssa." Marcus shoved Trystan away. "I'll take my chances with the wingless." He declared and looked over at Horatio. "Tie him up. We'll take him back to the King's Men."

Horatio glanced down at Trystan, obviously torn. "It would not take much effort to check the cage. Perhaps some of the gryphons are still alive and..."

"Perhaps you should follow orders." Marcus interrupted. "Uther put *me* in command, because he knows I'll get shit done. The sooner all the savage clans are wiped out, the sooner we can ascend to our rightful place, *j'ah*. When this war is over, Uther will place *us* in charge of Lyonesse, as the Sunchase Clan always should've been. That is what matters."

"Uther wants to kill *all* the gryphons." Trystan snapped. He knew that firsthand, his earliest memories filled with fighting and death. "If he favored the Sunchase, why has he not lifted the curse for *your* clan? Why do you suffer with the rest of us?"

"Uther will lift the curse, once we prove ourselves." Marcus insisted. Did he really believe it or was he trying to convince himself? Trystan was never sure. "The wingless king is the only one who can stop our people's extinction." He looked back at Horatio. "Even if it costs some gryphon lives now, more will be saved in the long run."

Horatio nodded, his hesitancy gone. "You're right, brother. We work towards a greater good." He reached down, intending to grab Trystan and ship him off to another wingless jail.

And that's when the Primitive People's Exhibit fell.

The glass dome toppled down in a waterfall of jagged shards and the walls caved in, burying everything inside. The rush of oxygen had the fire increasing like a furnace. The Yellow Boots stepped back, shielding their eyes from the sudden spike of heat. The animals around them all screamed out in terror.

And Trystan had no more clan.

Whoever had been left alive inside the cage after the bomb dropped, died in the final collapse. The strength left Trystan's legs and he sank to the sidewalk, staring at the fire with stunned eyes. He was too frozen to even cry. To shout out. To run.

He just... stared.

"Well, that ends the debate, does it not?" Marcus said dismissively. "Gryphons like that are better off dead, anyway. They live in the past. You adjust to the wingless ways or you die like animals."

Trystan looked up at him, still sitting on the ground. His heart was beating in his ears so loudly that he could barely hear anything else. "I'm going to kill you, one day." He said very seriously.

Marcus didn't look impressed. "Well, that day is not today. *Today* you're going back into chains and Uther can decide what to do with you. Now, tie him up, Horatio." He snapped his fingers impatiently. "Let's go. We have more enemies of Camelot to round up tonight."

Horatio sighed, moving towards Trystan, again. "It is a shame that a gryphon this young will die. Children are getting rarer..."

He never got to finish that lament.

A sudden blur crashed into him, knocking Horatio off his feet. The man gave an agonized bellow, instinctively trying to fight off his attacker. But it was no use. No one could defeat an eight hundred pound cat with their bare hands.

The blue tiger had gotten hold of Horatio and seemed intent on devouring him whole. Whether it was hungry or crazed by the noise or if maybe something else was guiding it, Trystan never knew. He just knew the cat saved him.

It was hard to see what was happening in the darkness, but Trystan's other senses told the grisly story. There was an earthshattering roar. Bones crunched. Blood splashed out, splattering across Trystan's tattered clothes.

And Horatio stopped screaming.

Marcus didn't try to help *him*, either. Still clutching the keys to the other cages, he took off into the sky. Cursing and terrified, he left his brother to die. He flew away like he was afraid that the tiger might evolve wings and pursue him, not even looking back. Trystan didn't see any more of Marcus that night. He didn't see anyone else in the zoo, at all.

He just saw the tiger.

The blue cat's eyes flicked to Trystan, still crouching over Horatio's body. It was gigantic and wild, the color of deepest midnight. Trystan didn't move, just like his father had told him. The raw power of the creature was overwhelming. Hypnotizing. He was close enough to touch its darkly striped coat. Close enough to see the red staining its teeth.

But the tiger didn't attack him.

With an arrogant shake of its head, the huge blue cat began dragging Horatio's corpse away. It must have decided that Trystan wasn't appetizing, because it didn't pay him any attention. It left him alone.

All alone.

Trystan sat there and watched the tiger disappear into the

bushes with its meal. He sat there for hours, mindlessly rocking and listening to his mother's voice singing to him in his head. Sat there until the fire in the Primitive People's Exhibit went out and the first hints of daylight began to appear.

Awareness slowly began to break through his shock and despair. A desire to keep his word to Ban. Somehow, Trystan managed to rouse himself from his stupor and crawl into the hedges, hiding until it was dark, again. The next evening, he began his trek westwards, towards the lavender hues of twilight.

Purple was his path.

In his mind forever, he would recall the sound of the glass dome shattering before the enclosure fell. He would replay all that happened again and again, trying to find a way he could have saved his clan. He would eternally blame Marcus Sunchase and the Yellow Boots for letting them die. At odd moments, he would hear that song his mother sang to him, giving him comfort and guidance.

And he would always have a deep respect for tigers.

Chapter Twenty-Six

Who is the *ya'lah*?
How can one single person hope to undo all the evil Uther rained down on the world?

I do not know. No one does.

Not yet.

But, the gryphons' time runs short. Our people will become extinct within decades. The *ya'lah* might already be alive. This generation could well see the graal itself, held in the *ya'lah's* hand.

Then we will know the answers to questions that stretch far back into history.

I just hope we are smart enough to listen.

How the Wingless War Happened
Skylyn Welkyn- Gryphon Storyteller

St. Ives- Kit-Cat-Sack Street

Trystan had accomplished the impossible: He was holding a creature made of moonlight.

He stood on the street, gazing at the door to the club that Galahad had disappeared through, and the world rearranged itself around him.

Everything he'd ever wanted was in his grasp.

The knight was furious at him, but he was also giving Trystan all of himself. He was sharing pieces that he never shared with anyone else. He wasn't fighting to get free and disappear back into his own realm. He was fighting to keep Trystan with him. If Trystan didn't fuck this up, he could have... everything.

What could *possibly* be worth losing everything?

Vengeance?

Suddenly, he didn't think that was worth much, at all. He'd spent his entire time in prison dreaming about revenge. But now that dream felt pointless. Leaving Camelot to hunt his enemies could cost Trystan *everything*. The men he planned to kill mattered little to the world at large and were nothing at all when you compared them to Galahad.

Why in the hell was he risking everything on nothing?

The more he considered it, the less sense it made.

"If I had a mate who looks at me, as your mate looks at you, I would not let him out of my sight." Konrad volunteered in the gryphons' language, as if he was reading Trystan's mind. "My sainted mother always says the best way to hold onto something valuable is to never let it go."

Trystan glanced at him in surprise. "Caelia said that?"

"Well, it's kind of the *second* part of her advice." Konrad allowed with a shrug. "In part *one*, she mentions that it's a smart idea to preemptively kill anybody who might want to steal from you, in the first place. Cuts way down on the risk."

Yeah. That sounded a lot more like Caelia.

"You should do all you can to keep that man." Konrad nodded wisely, the neon lights of St. Ives reflecting off the lens of his mirrored sunglasses. "Watching you together... I see a *brightness* in you that was not there before. He gives you a spark of life, Trystan. Do not lose it."

"I won't." He had no intention of losing the knight or the light the man brought him.

Trystan's plan to leave Galahad in Camelot, while he went hunting his enemies, would never work. It was so obvious. He'd been a moron to even consider it.

Assuming the knight pledged to patiently wait for him (which was doubtful) Trystan would still not see him each day. Would not be able to listen to his insane ideas, or protect him from his numerous enemies, or touch his shimmery hair. It would be torturous. Weeks and months without the person he liked best in the world? Weeks and months where Galahad might forget him?

No.

That was *not* acceptable.

Trystan could not stand to be indefinitely parted from the knight. It would be like returning to prison. Worse, because now he'd know what he was truly missing. He needed Galahad with him.

...So Galahad would just have to come with him.

That seemed like the simplest solution. Now that he thought about it, it was no doubt the plan that Galahad had been claiming was so obvious. It *did* seem obvious. The knight could just accompany Trystan on his mission. Yes. That was the only thing that made sense.

So why was he still so unsettled by the plan?

"Where the hell is Marcus?" Trystan glanced down at Konrad, impatient to kill the man and get back to his mate.

"I told you, he's following the race."

"What race? You keep speaking of one, but I do not see it." As far as Trystan could tell, no one in St. Ives was racing by foot, horse, or wing. "All I see are banners with the incorrect time on them." He waved at the cheaply printed sign over his head. "It says eight o'clock, not eleven. Are you *sure* we didn't miss this damn thing?"

"The time's not wrong. The race started at eight and it's still going."

"Started from where? Oz?" It had to be somewhere far distant, if it took three hours to get to the finish line.

"No. It started just around the block. Sometimes it can take a while to get here, because it's a tortoise and hare race." His eyebrows went up, seeing Trystan's look of incomprehension. "Backwards, ya know?"

"Backwards?"

"Right. The slowest one wins." Konrad nodded. "Spectators sort of stroll along side of the runners, talking and drinking and placing bets. But everyone will come right by here." He paused. "Eventually."

"Lyrssa save me..." Trystan didn't have time for this shit. "Marcus must die *now*. I am not about to leave this Mordy person alone with my knight over an intimate goddamn brunch, while I stand here waiting for a fucking turtle."

"Probably smart." Konrad nodded. "Mordy's got seven mates, but yours would be the crown jewel of his collection, so..."

"Seven mates?" Trystan interrupted, glancing at the club's neon sign. It seemed as if everything in the whole damn town was constantly blinking. "Wait, he *literally* has seven husbands?"

"Yes. I think that's the word. Whatever the wingless call their *ha'yan*, he has seven of them." Konrad switched to the common dialect to guess at the proper vocabulary. "Wives? Husbands? I cannot keep the gender titles straight. They make much confusion."

"Is it legal in their culture to have seven mates?" Trystan wasn't sure, but he doubted it.

Konrad switched back to the gryphon tongue. "Mordy and his riches run this town. Everything he wants to do is legal, the moment he decides to do it."

"My knight will not approve of that judicial philosophy." Trystan shook his head. "He is already upset with Mordy for owning a strip club and possibly exploiting the downtrodden. If he decides that Mordy is oppressing people into unwanted matings, it will lead to many deaths."

Hopefully, one of them would be Mordy's. Trystan didn't look forward to making over a half-dozen men widowers, but he just didn't like the guy.

"Why is your mate upset about the strip club, when he works at the strip club?"

"He does not work at a strip club! Why do you...?"

Trystan broke off mid-word, his gaze falling on a group of people slooooooowly rounding the corner and making their way towards the club. They were moving down the center of Kit-Cat-Sack Street at approximately the same speed that lead tuned to gold.

Lyrssa save him...

Trystan pinched the bridge of his nose. "This is the race?" He guessed with a sigh.

"Yeah, that's it." Konrad craned his neck to gauge which creature was in the lead. "I got some money on the hare to win, so try not to screw up the results for me. The tortoise has been on fire lately, but he can't keep up the streak forever, right?" He paused, like something new occurred to him. "Only he has to *lose* in order to win in a backwards race, so maybe I should have bet against him. But it's also backwards *day*, which reverses the rules if..." He trailed off with a puzzled look. "Shit. Who was I supposed to put money on?"

"Do not speak to me." Trystan warned, frustrated at the world. He had pictured hunting down his enemies many times, but it had always been more grand and less ridiculous.

Fuck it.

He pulled his axe and stalked into the street, directly into the path of the race. Spectators were clustered around the tortoise and hare in a loose circle. The men constantly adjusted their positions, so as not to get left behind. Not that there was much chance of that.

This was *literally* a bunny and turtle race.

Literally.

The two animals were the regular, non-humanoid kind. The ordinary hare was taking a break to chew on its own foot, while the ordinary tortoise waddled steadily along. The gambling men surrounding the small creatures didn't seem concerned about the glacial pace. They chatted and laughed, easily keeping out of the race's direct path. Moving forward, inch by painful inch. They expected that Trystan would move forward, too.

Trystan didn't move.

The tortoise ran right into his foot. Stymied by the obstacle, perhaps blinded by its lust for victory, it tried to climb right over his boot. ...Which resulted in the creature helplessly toppling over onto its back, stubby legs waving in the air as it rolled around on its shell.

The hare did not even try to get past Trystan. It huddled down in a puffy ball of trepidation, nose twitching and with no passion for competition in its pink eyes. The animal gave up too easily. It would never win. Konrad had been a fool to bet on it in any capacity.

"Damn bunny." Konrad muttered from somewhere behind him, realizing the same thing.

Trystan kept his gaze on the men who led lives pathetic enough to consider this race a worthy use of their time. "I am only here for Marcus Sunchase." He warned. "Do not interfere and you will not die alongside him."

St. Ives wasn't a place where you got mixed up in other people's vendettas. In unison the spectators' eyes seemed to ping-pong from Trystan, to his axe, and then to a man at the back of the crowd. After a moment of tense murmuring, they shifted apart and Trystan had a clear view of a familiar figure in yellow boots.

"Hello, Marcus." He said. "I've been looking for you."

Marcus had aged, but he was still tall, with a large nose and silvering wings. And still dressed in the second-rate "uniform" that Uther had given him when Marcus vowed to betray his people. Marcus put his hands in the pockets, like he wanted to puff out his chest and display the cheap medals jangling upon it. He was so proud of something that forever marked him as the trained pet of the wingless king.

"I knew you'd show up sooner or later." He told Trystan snidely. "Most of our kind are driven by primitive impulses, instead of logic. And you've always been particularly stupid."

Trystan didn't blink. "I promised to kill you one day. The day has arrived."

The races' spectators all edged backwards a few steps.

"I was the only gryphon who ever used his brain." Marcus went on, believing in his choices to the bitter end. "If we had given into Uther's demands, he would have lifted the curse. Instead, that bitch Lyrssa killed him, we *still* lost the War, and our future is doomed, as well. Which of us was *truly* in the wrong, Airbourne? Me or the foolish gryphons who fought against the inevitable?"

"You." Trystan didn't even hesitate with the answer. "I will give you thirty seconds to find a weapon. Then I will kill you, armed or not."

"I'm not going to fight you, boy." Even as he promised that, though, Marcus was surreptitiously easing a gun out of his pocket. "We're past our grievances, now. It's time for all gryphons to come together, again. We are too few in number to kill each other over events we cannot change."

"You have fifteen seconds." Trystan told him flatly.

"I remember the first time I ever saw you, skinny and dirty and screaming for your clan. I remember how my brother hesitated about turning you over to Uther." Marcus's eyes narrowed. "And I remember how that fucking tiger killed *him* and not you." He yanked the gun free, hoping to catch Trystan off guard.

Trystan wasn't caught off guard.

He threw the axe at Marcus's forehead before the man even got off a bullet. The axe spun, end over end, and slammed into Marcus' forehead, the weight of it propelling him backwards. The blade imbedded itself into his skull, bisecting his face and killing him instantly. His body fell into an uncoordinated heap in the street. Dead.

Marcus Sunchase was finally dead.

Trystan blinked at the anticlimactic finish to so many of his daydreams.

For a moment, there was silence.

"Shit." Konrad lamented. "That was the least exciting fight I've ever seen."

"Um…" Some brave soul cleared his throat and looked at Trystan. "Can we get back to the race, now?"

Oh.

Right.

Trystan stepped out of the tortoise's path, using the toe of his boot to flip it right-side-up, again. The turtle scrambled for purchase for a beat and then continued on its waddling way. It truly was a competitive beast. Inspired by that confident example, the hare and the men joined it, as well. All of them resumed their lives like nothing had happened.

Trystan went back to staring at Marcus's body. He didn't know what he'd expected to "feel" after killing the man, but, now that it was over, all he felt was... hollow. It hadn't felt satisfying or like the fulfilment of something important. It just felt like a total waste of time and effort.

"So, I was looking into it, and I can probably find some more Yellow Boots for you to kill. Perhaps the next fight will be more thrilling." Konrad came up beside him and spared Marcus' corpse a dismissive look over the tops of his sunglasses. "You still want to kill more Yellow Boots, right?"

Trystan kept staring at Marcus' body.

So many people had died trying to keep Trystan safe as a child, believing that he was worth the sacrifice. Was this what they had hoped he'd do with the gift? (Well, perhaps Lunette. She would be pleased that any Yellow Boot was dead.) But would any of his clans have been truly *proud* of his mission?

No.

They would want him to go forward, not dwell in the past. That was what he'd want Avi to do, in his place. To keep going forward, carrying his stories and finding peace.

Trystan suddenly found the idea of tracking down all the other Yellow Boots pointless.

Galahad had been right, the night before. Being away from Camelot would mean giving up time with his clan that Trystan would never get back. The very first feeling Trystan had ever identified in himself was the unhappiness he felt when he was away from them. Now he wished to make himself unhappy for years? How could he watch Avi grow, if he wasn't in Camelot to watch her grow? How could he teach Midas how to rule a kingdom, or spend his afternoons bickering with Gwen over nonsense, if he was thousands of miles from them? He couldn't. He would miss all of that in favor of killing assholes and feeling hollow.

This entire revenge mission was *pointless*.

What did he want most? What was his dream?

Galahad had asked him that, after they left Ayren's village, and suddenly Trystan knew the answer wasn't to kill his enemies. He wanted his clan. He wanted to wake each morning with happiness and hope for the day. He wanted his mate and possibly some young to raise and a future.

He dreamed of Galahad. That was the true answer.

More than anything he wanted the knight beside him and content in his care. Even if Trystan took the man with him on his mission, Galahad did not wish for that life. He wished to be in his homeland, making terribly written TV shows, and playing games with Avi, and building a school for pitiful artists. It would make Galahad so much happier if Trystan did not leave on the mission, at all.

Trystan's mate wished for him to change his plans.

So, Trystan changed his plans.

Once he realized how easy the choice was to make, it seemed ridiculous that he hadn't made it before. Galahad would prefer to stay in Camelot and so they should stay in Camelot. Of course they should! Hell, *Trystan* would prefer to stay in Camelot. A future with his clan surrounding him and his perfect, irritating mate smiling up at him was worth all the days of Trystan's past combined. *That* was the path he wanted.

Why would he obsess over darkness, when he had moonlight?

The War was over for Trystan. All of it. He chose to let it go. He would not linger in the shadows, with hatred and hopeless memories. He would not dedicate even a moment more to vengeance. He would never kill all the men on his list. (Some, but not all.) And he would live his life in the kingdom he'd once hated above all others. In Camelot. He knew all of that suddenly, although he should have seen it long before. He would *always* choose Camelot. He would stay in that strange foreign land forever, because Camelot held every dream that mattered to him.

Trystan took a deep breath and felt... *better*.

His eyes flicked over to Konrad. "I have no need to track down any more Yellow Boots." He said with utter certainty. "I already hold what I want."

Konrad studied Trystan for a beat and then nodded. "This is the better path." He agreed, quietly. "The one I would make, if I were lucky enough to find a mate. When you are handed a gift, you do not squander it on insignificant dickheads."

Konrad was often smarter than he seemed.

Trystan extended his palm to him and they clasped hands in the way of gryphon warriors. "Farewell, Konrad. If you wish to settle in a more peaceful land, Camelot is open to all gryphons and the Redcrosse Clan is especially welcome." He paused. "So long as Caelia does not kill any wingless."

Konrad's eyebrow arched. "Have you *met* my sainted

mother?" He slapped Trystan's shoulder. "Now, hurry and retrieve your knight, before Mordy steals him away." He went strolling after the tortoise and hare. "I need to go figure out how much money that bunny is going to cost me. Shit man... Never gamble while drunk on a magical elixir. All I can remember is karaoke and being invisible for half the night."

Like with so many things Konrad said, there was no possible response to that remark, so Trystan didn't even try to think of one. He just headed into the Seven Husbands, eager to find Galahad and tell him everything that had happened in the short time they'd been apart. He barely processed his surroundings as he marched through the club's entrance and down the hallway towards the main room. He would hold the man, and breathe in the scent of his shimmery hair, and look into his violet eyes, and tell him...

Trystan's thought skidded to a halt as he suddenly found himself face-to-face with a horse.

A taxidermy palomino was preserved under glass, a museum-like sign affixed to the huge case. It read: Llamrai- Beloved Childhood Horse of Sir Galahad.

Trystan blinked and looked around the club's interior, growing increasingly more confused. At first glance, it appeared like any other tacky bar, with poles for strippers and garish décor. ...Except, there were pictures of Galahad *everywhere*. Clips from his TV shows played on overhead screens. Replicas of his armor were displayed against the walls. The curtains of the raised stage were color-matched to the exact shade of his eyes.

What the hell was *this* about?

He would've asked someone to explain it, but no one was really around. Just a couple making out at one of the booths. Two men seemed to be seconds away from ripping each other's clothes off. Their mouths were suction-cupped together, they're bodies graphically gyrating and their hands tugging at their clothes. Trystan's eyes flicked over them without much interest, scanning for Galahad.

It took him a full second to realize that he'd found him. His gaze jerked back to the passionate couple, belatedly processing the reality of the situation.

Galahad was kissing another man

Chapter Twenty-Seven

The gryphons know where the graal is! They've known they whole time. I don't buy any of the sob stories about it being lost or inaccessible. How could you lose a fucking graal?

Give me a break.

No, they're just biding their time, waiting for the perfect moment to use it against us. Half of our kind is in on it *with* them, too. Trust me. This is all like a puzzle that only the *true* knights among us can see.

"Stopping the Savages" Podcast
Sir Dragonet of Camelot- Former Troubadour of King Uther and Host of the Program

St. Ives- The Seven Husbands Strip Club

Trystan was genuinely too stunned to even be angry. He froze, trying to process what was happening. "Galahad?" He barely recognized his own voice. It sounded like it was coming from far away.

"Shit!" Galahad jumped away from the stranger he'd been kissing, startled to see Trystan standing in the club. "Wow! I totally didn't hear you come in." He stood up and ran a hand through his hair, smoothing it down. "Sorry. I guess I was lost in the moment with Eric."

Trystan didn't move. "Eric?" He repeated blankly.
"Yeah, this is Eric." Galahad waved a careless hand in the

other man's direction. Eric looked to be barely out of his teens and wore an overly-designed flannel shirt. "He works in the kitchen here."

"Yo!" Eric gave Trystan a casual salute. "How you doin', dude? Cool wings."

Trystan very slowly blinked at him, then swiveled his attention back to Galahad. "What is going on here?" He asked in the calmest voice he'd ever used. "Explain it to me. *Now.*"

"Right, well, the thing is..." Galahad shrugged. "We've had a lot of fun together, but I think it's time we move on. Eric and I just had this instant chemistry. Honestly, I feel like I owe it to myself to see where this thing goes with him."

"Instant chemistry." Trystan repeated, trying to make sense of the words. "With Eric."

"Yo!" Eric said again, nodding at his name. He lounged in his tacky silver seat, looking only vaguely aware of the world beyond his nose ring. "I usually bang chicks, but what the hell, ya know?" He ate a Gala-Chip from the bowl sitting in the middle of the table. "I support equality in all forms of fucking."

Was he going crazy?

Trystan thought maybe he was going crazy.

"Galahad," Trystan let out a controlled breath, trying to stay in control, "is this due to our argument? Because you were very clear on the idea of dating other men being abstract and hypothetical, yes? Are you now trying to strike out at me, because you were so... *bothered* outside?" He shook his head, grappling for a foothold. "I assure you, there is no need to go so far."

Galahad looked confused. "Um..." He floundered for a beat and then gave his hair a toss. "No. Shit. This isn't about that... thing... before. This is about *now*. About me and Eric pursuing something *real* that's sprung up between us. Right, Eric?"

"Yo!" Eric agreed, momentarily distracted by picking at his black nail polish.

Trystan was beginning to break free of his shock and feel the stirrings of many, *many* somethings inside of him. "This realness sprang up in the fifteen minutes I was outside killing Marcus?" He demanded. "This is what you're claiming?"

Eric's head snapped up, forgetting about his manicure. "Wait... Hang on, everybody chill for a sec. He *kills* people?" Eric frowned over at Galahad. "I agreed to help you, dude, but you didn't say this winged-guy *kills* people."

"Do you wish me to kill Eric?" Trystan kept his eyes on Galahad. "Is that your aim here? Is this a test of some kind?"

"No, it's not his aim!" Eric yelped, his bugged-out eyes flashing to Galahad. "Yo, man, tell him that's not your aim!"

"Maybe Eric is my True Love." Galahad shouted, sounding a little desperate. "Maybe *that's* why I'm so drawn to him. Stop standing in the way of my happiness and accept the fact that I don't want you anymore!"

Trystan hesitated, his emotions screaming at him now. Eric was Galahad's True Love? The knight had recognized him and now felt compelled to be with him? Was that possible? He wasn't sure but the idea triggered every insecurity he had about their relationship.

Galahad saw him pause to consider the idea and seemed pleased. "Now, I'm *super* sorry about this, but what can I do, right?" He ate one of Eric's Gala-Chips, like he wanted to show how unaffected he was by all of this. "The heart wants what it wants." He shrugged. "If gryphons had emotions, you'd totally get that."

Trystan barely heard him, his mind racing. Shit, how was he going to fix this? He couldn't kill Galahad's True Love. On the surface, it was a marvelous plan, but the knight would never forgive him. In the end, it would gain Trystan nothing. He gazed at the tabletop, thinking it all through and not seeing any obvious solution. If this was real, how could he convince the knight to forsake Eric and...?

The Gala-Chips were caramel-and-whey flavored.

Trystan suddenly processed that fact, recognizing their golden-colored sugar-sprinkles from the night before. They were *definitely* caramel-and-whey and the knight hated caramel-and-whey. Why was he eating caramel-and-whey?

His eyes slowly traveled back up to Galahad's face, new thoughts occurring to him. "Are you and Eric going back to Camelot, then?" He asked, carefully studying the man's reaction.

"Who knows? We have a lot of traveling to do, getting to know each other." The man smirked a smirk that was not Galahad's smirk. It lacked the magic and mischief and joy. "You probably won't see us again for a while."

Trystan's head tilted. This man's eyes did not glow with Galahad's exact twilight-sky combination of blue and purple. There was no light in him, brightening the world by simply being in it. None of the thoughtful pauses that came from peering into misty realms that no one else could see.

As his initial shock and panic and confusion and fury and heartbreak receded, Trystan began to see things clearer. Now, he added up all the pieces and found them... wrong. No. This man was *wrong*. Whatever was happening, it was all very, very wrong. Every instinct told him so and Trystan trusted his instincts. The memory of Avalon's voice sounded in his head, the last words she'd shouted at him during their phone call in Ted-ville.

Be careful of the wrong Galahad.

"We have to get going, actually." Wrong-Galahad tugged at Eric's arm. "Let's go." He hissed.

"What about the cash you offered....?"

"*Now*, you hipster idiot." Wrong-Galahad hauled him from his chair and shoved him towards the door.

Trystan's eyes narrowed, silently watching this unGalahad-ish Galahad... Watching as he turned away from Trystan with no hesitation... Watching as he prepared to leave for parts unknown with no goodbye for Avi or Gwen. ...Watching as he deliberately picked up a *hat* from the chair beside him and pulled it on over his not-quite-shimmery-enough hair.

Nope.

Trystan lunged forward, his hand clamping down on the Fake-Galahad's neck.

"Stop!" The unidentified man squealed as he was lifted off the ground and slammed into the wall. "What the hell are you doing?"

Eric took off running, sprinting out of the building, too scared to even look back.

"Whoever you are, you have made a mistake." Trystan told the imposter flatly. "The real Galahad cannot be duplicated, replicated, or replaced. And he is not someone I will *ever* walk away from." He leaned forward so their noses nearly touched. "*Ever.*"

"I have no idea what you're talking about, you psycho!" The stranger tried to fight back and it was pathetic. The actual knight would have been free by now. "You can't attack me, just because we're breaking up! Why are you acting so crazy...?"

Trystan interrupted the wailed protests by crashing the stranger into the wall again, so hard that the building rattled. "Galahad is my *mate*." He snarled. "I would recognize him blindfolded and he is *not* you."

Faux-Galahad froze and Trystan could see his mind working.

"Return my knight to me *now*," Trystan warned, "or I will level this whole fucking town." It was a wrathful promise. "I will kill anyone and everyone who stands between me and the *true* Galahad of Camelot. ...And I will start with you."

The duplicate swallowed hard. "Gryphons don't have feelings." He ventured, looking pale. "You can't be sure about any of this."

"I am sure of that man, as I am sure of nothing else in creation. I *know* Galahad, inside and out. He is a part of me." Trystan arched a brow, his fingers tightening on the charlatan's throat. "And he does not like hats."

Imitation-Galahad clawed at the hand crushing his windpipe, trying to breathe. "Upstairs." He gestured towards the ceiling with his eyes.

"He is upstairs?"

"No, *Mordy* is upstairs!" Not-exactly-violet eyes filled with tears. "My husband. They took him prisoner!" The pretend-knight started bawling. "They said that if I didn't convince you to go away, they'd kill him and all my other husbands. What else could I do? They're my family! I *love* them!"

P'don.

Trystan loosened his grip on the man, letting his feet touch the ground. "Someone came in here and captured Mordy? Why? Where is *my* Galahad?"

The look-(kind-of)-alike was bawling too hard to answer. He sank to the floor, weeping about saving his family.

Since there was no getting a straight answer out of the man, Trystan turned his attention upstairs. He was in too much of a hurry to take the winding steps. Using his wings, he launched himself upward, flying onto the balcony above. His heart slamming in his chest, he began opening doors. Each one led to a different bedroom and each bedroom was decorated with photos of one of Galahad's body parts. His shapely backside. His muscular chest. His wide shoulders. But, Trystan didn't find any sign of the *actual*, fully-assembled Galahad.

In the seventh room he checked, he did find Mordy, though.

The man was tied to a bed, trying to shout for help through the gag in his mouth. Rotund and bearded, he resembled Santa Claus more closely than a strip club owner. He was also a monopod, a race born with one leg, which was centered in the middle of their body. Usually, they were content to lazy away their days in warmer climates, lying on their backs in the heat of the afternoons, using their one huge foot as shade from the sun. Trystan had no idea what one of their kind was doing in the cold of St. Ives.

Still, Trystan had little doubt that this man was Mordy Mordred. He was wearing a t-shirt that read "My Ideal Weight is Galahad on Top of Me." His eyes widened when he saw Trystan in the doorway and desperately thrashed around to indicate he was in trouble.

As if that wasn't already fucking obvious.

Trystan stalked over to the bed and yanked the gag from his mouth. The room was wallpapered in pictures of the knight's perfectly-shaped lips and lush mouth, which did nothing to soothe his temper. "Where is Galahad?" He bellowed.

"Closet." Mordy gave a cough. "Please."

Trystan leapt over the mattress and yanked open the room's only other door. Inside were six blond men, all huddled together. His eyes desperately scanned over their terrified faces. Holy *shit*... All of the half-naked guys were made-up and/or enspelled to look like the knight. They resembled Galahad in the way a counterfeit painting resembled a genuine masterpiece.

Close, but... wrong.

None of them were *his* knight, but Trystan *was* beginning to understand why Konrad had believed that Galahad was a dancer. And why the entire club was decorated with artifacts from the knights' life and career. And why Mordy's name engendered such respect among the horny assholes of this town. And why that dickhead satyr on the street had propositioned the knight for just walking past.

The Seven Husbands was a Galahad-themed brothel.

Muttering curses under his breath Trystan quickly untied the bootleg versions of Galahad. "Where is the *real* Galahad of Camelot?" He demanded to the room at large.

"Who are you?" One of the Galahad-copies cried, refusing to answer the very simple goddamn question. "Are you one of them?"

"I am Galahad's *mate*."

"Oh!" Mordy exclaimed from the bed. "Galahad told those guys that a gryphon would be coming after him. He didn't mention you were his mate, but he warned them that you'd be pissed."

Trystan glanced at him sharply. "*What* guys?"

"The ones who came in here and took him, of course." Mordy jerked his chin towards the window. "They dosed him with some kind of compliance powder and took him out the fire escape."

Trystan automatically looked towards the large opening, his stomach sinking. Oh gods... This was *way* beyond the scope of Galahad's usual catastrophes. Compliance powder was rare and powerful. It temporarily confused the mind and left people easy to manipulate. At its worst, it was used by rapists to force victims into sexual situations they'd never agree to willingly. Konrad had been right. The magic for sale in St. Ives was strange and incredibly destructive.

And now Galahad was right in the middle of it.

Trystan's insides churned, imagining what might happen to

the knight.

"The villains didn't believe you'd be a problem. My husband downstairs is incredible at impersonating Galahad. They thought you'd fall for his act and go away." Mordy paused with a worried frown. "Is he okay, by the way? You didn't hurt him, did you?"

"Your husband is fine." Trystan muttered distractedly. "And he looks *nothing* like the real knight."

Mordy took offense at that. "What do you mean? Benny is a perfect duplicate. *All* my husbands are enspelled to look like Galahad. The black market glamour potions available in this town are incredible. They can even make their clothes look like Galahad's outfits. But Benny had his spell cast by a professional witch."

"It must have been the worst fucking witch in the world, then." Trystan didn't have time for this shit. "Tell me *exactly* what happened here."

"A group of men just barged in and took us prisoner, early this morning. Then they waited. When Galahad arrived, they dumped the powder on him and told him he had to go with them. He was drugged, so he listened."

"*P'don!*" Trystan raged. While he was wasting time with goddamn Marcus, someone had stolen his mate. ...And that "someone" was going to die screaming.

"Galahad was *so* brave, though." Mordy gushed. "Really. Even though he was compelled by the compliance powder, he fought it and said he'd only leave with the villains, if they didn't hurt me or my husbands." Mordy sighed dreamily. "He was *exactly* as heroic as I always pictured him."

It would serve no greater purpose to kill Mordy, but Trystan was sorely tempted, anyway. Only the fact that he'd then have to deal with the useless man's even more useless husbands stayed his hand.

Once Trystan had them free, the six phony-Galahads ran for the mattress to see Mordy. They clambered all over him, checking him for injuries, pulling him free of the ropes, sobbing against his chest. The knight needn't worry that the gaggle of husbands were being oppressed by Mordy. They clearly loved the asshole and he clearly loved them. He was blotting their tears, petting their heads, and assuring them he was safe.

Trystan wasn't particularly touched by the reunion. "Who were the men who stole Galahad?" He snapped, ready to take his wrath out on any handy target. Especially one who was selling facsimiles of his mate to any scumbag looking for a blowjob. "Friends of yours?"

"Of course not."

"Then how did they know Galahad would be here?"

"Well, I mean, I told a few people, but..."

"Give me their names or I will kill *you* and then find them myself."

"I don't know who they are! I swear it. They wore masks, but I didn't recognize their voices." Mordy massaged his single thick ankle, which had been bruised from the ropes. "Whoever they are, I don't think you need to worry. Galahad is the best knight ever! He'll escape those criminals in no time."

All six of his husbands loyally nodded.

"This is not some damn puppet show, where the happy ending is assured!" Trystan jabbed a finger at Mordy. "My mate has been *kidnapped*. You will help me find him or I'll toss *you* out the window!"

Mordy frowned. "Well there's no need to be testy." He looked around at his husbands. "Why is he being so testy? Galahad should have a sweet-tempered mate, don't you think?"

Trystan made a frustrated sound and started for the bed, ready to carry out his threat.

"The men were working for knights." One of the Galahad-doubles piped up quickly, wanting to stop the brewing violence. "The ones who took him, I mean. They talked a lot, while they were waiting for you and Galahad to show up. I listened."

Trystan's head tilted. "Knights are behind this? From Camelot?"

"I guess. I just overheard that some group of knights had hired these Bad guys to come into town and snatch your Galahad. They've been following you since you got to St. Ives, they said. They must've known you'd come here."

Trystan processed all that, his mind whirling. "Did they say *why* these knights wanted Galahad?"

"Something about a treasure map, I think?"

Trystan expelled a hissing breath of frustration. Those goddamn ex-knights, who had tried to kill Galahad before he met Trystan, must've finally caught up with him. Trystan had *told* the man this would happen. Why did he never listen?

"Galahad is always looking for treasure on his TV show." Mordy interjected, pleased with this new detail he could add to the story. "I *knew* he would be the same in real life. You can see his authenticity right through the screen. That's why his fans love him so much." He made a cutesy kissing sound at his closest husband. "Isn't it, my brave little knight?"

"It's not the *only* reason." The man cooed back, cuddling closer.

Trystan ignored them and scraped a hand through his hair, trying to think. "Does anyone know where these men were going next?"

All seven of them shook their heads.

"Fine." It didn't matter. Trystan would catch up with them, no matter where they went. They didn't have that much of a head start. He just needed to find their trail. He marched for the door, only to stop and turn back to Mordy. "Be glad I do not have time to discuss this establishment with you. ... Because I have *much* to fucking say about this establishment."

"Oh, Galahad already said it." Mordy assured him, blithely. "Before they dragged him away, he told me that he doesn't approve of selling sex, even if both parties are willing. He's going to invest in my reality show, instead."

"...A reality show?" Trystan echoed. Yes. That was *precisely* what this god-awful situation needed to reach the pinnacle of lunacy.

"Sure. About St. Ives! Everyone's interested in seeing inside this town. Having a TV series has always been my dream." Mordy looked choked up just thinking about it finally coming true. "All Galahad asked in return was that I closed the club and give his taxidermied horse a respectful burial. Isn't that amazing? In my whole life no one has ever taken a chance on me, like he is."

Trystan was completely unsurprised that Galahad had managed to solve Mordy's problems in the midst of his own abduction. "That is why you can never duplicate the man, no matter how many witches you employ." He shook his head, resolve filling him. "My mate is one of a kind. ...And I will have him back."

Chapter Twenty-Eight

What is the graal? How does it work? What does it look like?

These are questions that all who seek it ask. But no one knows for sure.

Perhaps we are not meant to know. Not until the moment is right and the graal reveals itself to the *ya'lah*.

How the Wingless War Happened
Skylyn Welkyn- Gryphon Storyteller

Beach of Ultima Thule- Edge of the Moaning Sea

Galahad had a slight immunity to consumer magic.

He wasn't sure why. He'd just been born that way, the same way he'd been born with eyelashes so thick and admired that his fans had built them their own webpage. (Sir-Gala-Lash.com.) Potions, powders, and hexes from naturally magical beings worked on him, of course. But, any effects that secondhand spells had on him were muted and over with quickly.

On Galahad, bought-and-sold magic was like wearing a cheap cologne. It dissipated quickly and kind of gave him a headache.

His resistance to the compliance powder hadn't been *total*, unfortunately. He'd still found himself leaving St. Ives with the men, helpless to resist their orders. But the compulsion faded by sunset, because of the way his system metabolized the spell. By the time his head felt clear, again, he was alone with one of the large goons who'd kidnapped him.

It was *not* where he wanted to be.

Galahad tried hard to be optimistic, but it was difficult to see the upside in his current situation. The men had made camp on the beach, by the edge of the Moaning Sea, waiting for "Those Damn Knights" to meet up with them and trade Galahad for gold.

It didn't take a genius to know who "Those Damn Knights" were.

Maybe Trystan was right and it was time to reconsider his not-killing-people rule. The world would be so much easier if Galahad went back to killing people.

"Those Damn Knights say they're after a map." The kidnapper muttered at Galahad, pacing around the makeshift campsite. The other two were off gathering dry fire wood, so he'd been left in charge and the responsibility didn't rest easy on his shoulders. And they were *big* shoulders. He was a massive guy, with a shaved head and a rod that connected his nose to his pointed ear. "Where's it lead to?"

"Atlantis." Galahad said honestly.

The kidnappers had chained him to a wishing tree stump and Galahad was working on freeing himself. He'd actually invented the style of padlock they'd used to secure the heavy links, so he knew how to get around the mechanism. It just took a while when it was fastened behind you and in the dark.

"What's Atlantis?"

"It used to be the land out there." He nodded towards the water at his back. It was black in the moonlight and shimmering with frosted magic. "Before it all sank."

The guy snorted. "Well, I guess you're shit outta luck then. Can't exactly go scuba-diving in the Moaning Sea. You'd freeze solid. Pretty much anything that touches the water freezes, except enspelled boats and icen jellyfish. The whole ocean is cursed. Whatever is down there, you ain't gonna find it."

"My True Love and I are both pretty creative." Galahad finally felt the lock click open behind him. "I'm confident we can figure it out."

"The gryphon guy?" The kidnapper scoffed. "I told you, we took care of him with that Galahad lookalike. Your boyfriend is gonna think that you dumped him and walk away."

"I'll betcha five gold pieces he doesn't."

In the hotel room, the night before, Trystan had said that he wanted Galahad to trust him. To know that Trystan would *always* come for him. Well, Galahad was giving him that faith, now. It was so simple to do, that he wasn't sure why he'd ever hesitated. Of *course* Trystan would always come for him. He'd *never* just forget Galahad existed and move on with his plans. He needed Galahad as much as Galahad needed him.

Galahad believed that completely.

Trystan would see through the imposter. Their connection was too deep for some jackass in a magical Galahad mask to fool him for long. Trystan would figure out the ruse and find Galahad, even if it killed him...

Which was Galahad's only real concern, actually. Without his supervision, something might have happened to Trystan. The man averaged about three dead bodies a day. Galahad needed to escape and find the quickest route back to St. Ives, so that he could make sure Trystan was okay. It was his job to protect his True Love.

Speaking of which, it was about time the man noticed that he was Galahad's True Love.

Galahad had spent the last few hours planning lots of new ways to convince him, actually. He was tired of waiting for Trystan to come around to the idea on his own. It was time for a new strategy. Galahad was pretty pleased with all the graphic sexual details he'd brainstormed for when he finally had Trystan back. Not even the gryphon was going to be able to resist him for much longer. Galahad had a real good feeling that unzipping Trystan's pants and then sucking the straining length of him into his mouth would work *great* as a seduction hint.

In the meantime, though, he needed to escape.

Galahad slipped his hands free of the chains, opening and closing his fingers so that the blood flowed back. "So." He looked up at the kidnapper. "When are those ex-knights coming to pick me up?"

"Couple hours." The guy stopped pacing in front of Galahad. "Since we're stuck together 'til then and you're still in a *compliant* mood, maybe we should --uh-- find a way to pass the time, huh?" His hand moved to the front of his pants, pantomiming what he wanted.

Galahad frowned. "Really? *That's* where we're going with this, now?" He shook his head in disgust. "Given the fact that I'm a hostage and you're a kidnapper, there's an imbalanced power-dynamic between us. You see that, right? Even if you *hadn't* tied me up and drugged me, I could never actually give consent in this situation. There would always be an element of coercion involved."

The guy hesitated, a strikingly dumb look on his face. "Huh?"

Galahad gave up trying to explain it to him. "The answer is

no." His hand snaked out and grabbed the pouch of compliance powder off the guy's belt.

"Hey, what the hell...?!"

The guy jumped back in surprise and panic, but Galahad was already dousing him with the stuff. A glaze look entered the man's eyes as the powder worked it spell on him, opening his mind to any suggestion that Galahad wished to give.

"Sit down." Galahad told him, rising to his feet.

The guy sat.

"Now, I want you to stay here and think about all the terrible choices you've made." Galahad instructed. "Go over *alllll* the horrible things you've done and really *think* about your actions. Consider how they made other people feel."

The guy nodded, his eyes already welling with tears as he recalled his multitude of crimes.

"Good." Galahad headed back towards St. Ives and his True Love. "And I'm going to take one of your horses. I feel like the least you can do is loan it to me, after all the trouble you caused."

The kidnapper was crying too hard to answer that. "When I was six..." He swiped a hand under his nose. "I dumped all my little brother's Christmas gifts into the fire. Just because I was jealous that he got the bicycle *I* wanted." He bent over sobbing. "No wonder he never answers my calls."

Galahad actually felt slightly guilty about the man's heartbroken wails. Maybe he should tell the kidnapper it was okay to forgive himself at the end of his...

Voices sounded off to Galahad's right, interrupting his thoughts. Shit. The other two guys were coming back. *Shit*. He didn't want to kill them and he couldn't escape without them noticing, so he was going to need another plan. Galahad thought for a beat and then improvised. He untied all the horses from the wishing trees and then smacked their rumps to get them running. The horses crashed through the trees and brushes that grew at the sea's edge, stampeding straight at the men.

That should distract them.

"Goddamn it!" One of the abductors bellowed. "The horses is loose! Larry! Come help us catch the damn things."

The crying kidnapper went lumbering off to help, the compliance powder making it impossible for him to refuse. He went dashing off into the thick undergrowth, not sparing Galahad a second look.

Galahad sighed. Well, now he didn't have a horse, but at

least he was free. That was certainly a positive. If he could just...

A palm slammed down over his mouth, dragging him deeper into the bushes.

***

"I have you. You're safe."

Trystan shifted in the darkness, pulling Galahad into the shadows. "Are you alright?" His wings came up to shield him. They *always* wanted to be wrapped around the knight, holding him tight, but now the need was so deep that Trystan couldn't have stopped his feathers from encircling his mate, even if he wanted to. And he didn't want to. All his protective instincts were aroused. "Are you hurt?"

Relief flashed across Galahad's face when he realized who'd grabbed him. "No, I'm fine. I'm kind of immune to consumer magic. Did I ever tell you that? The effects of the compliance powder faded pretty quickly, so I escaped."

Trystan's mouth curved, much of his tension easing. "I would expect no less from you." He ran a hand over Galahad's hair, basking in the man's specialness. "No one else is so skilled."

"Most people think I skate by on luck."

"Most people do not know you, as I do."

"*No one* knows me, as you do." Galahad smiled and his voice brightened. "So, how'd killing Marcus go?" He asked, like they were catching up on each other's day.

"He is dead and it felt hollow. I only wished to be with you and then I found out you'd been stolen. Also, Mordy says we are now bankrolling his new TV show. It has been a very trying afternoon on many levels."

"But you didn't fall for that other Galahad." Galahad leaned against him, looking smug. "I knew you wouldn't. I bet five gold pieces on you seeing through him."

"A wise bet." Trystan closed his eyes, his chin rubbing against the man's hair. "You realize that you do feel trust in me, then?"

Galahad shifted even closer to him, which was *exactly* how it should be. "I have total faith in you."

Trystan grunted. "As you should." But it was gratifying to hear.

Galahad looked amused, but he nodded. "You're right. No matter what, you would always come back to me. I should never have doubted it. I'm in your care, after all." He leaned up to kiss Trystan's jawline.

"I told you so." Trystan's wings surrounded the man even tighter. "But everything else I said last night was stupid. Leaving you in Camelot is not an option for me. It never could be. I cannot bear to be apart from you."

"I can't bear to be apart from you, either. I was worried you might have gotten into trouble without me, though." Galahad's mouth trailed down Trystan's throat, pressing his lips to Trystan's pulse and causing it to jump. "I was just coming to look for you, but you arrived to rescue me first."

Trystan arched a brow. "You can rescue me next time, yes?"

"Deal." Galahad sighed in satisfaction and rested his head against Trystan's shoulder. "And I'm sorry I cursed so much at you before."

"I'm not." Trystan's hands slid down the man's back, relishing the smoothness of his muscles. The lack of wings would always be exotic to him. "I liked seeing all sides of you. They are all beautiful to me. I truly would have searched forever to have you back." That was the stark truth. "I said I was 'attached' to you before. But, I do not think that is the correct name for this emotion. What I feel is so much… bigger."

Galahad's fingers caressed the feathers that cocooned him, tunneling deep and grazing the delicate skin beneath in *just* the way Trystan enjoyed. "You're so good with defining things, Trys. I know you'll think of the right word." He grinned, safe and content in Trystan's care.

And Trystan knew what it was to fully belong to your mate, heart and soul.

"I would do anything for you, Galahad." He said simply. Meaning it. "Whatever that emotion is, it is already yours."

Galahad's head tilted at the pledge, as if a new idea lit up in his mind. "Anything?" That incredible smirk danced at the edges of his lips.

"Anything at all." Trystan felt it with every *something* inside of him. "Whatever, whenever, and whyever you wish it, it's yours."

Galahad brightened. "Awesome." Half a second later he was on his knees, yanking open Trystan's pants. "I'll take this then. I didn't anticipate talking you into it so soon, but I'm not going to give you a chance to change your mind."

"What?" Trystan blinked, his brain trying to keep up with Galahad's rapid turns. "Knight, that is not…"

"Please. I need it. And you promised me anything."

Trystan jolted at the feel of his fingers, growing aroused despite himself. "Let me go kill those kidnappers, first. Then, I will happily be seduced. Believe me. *Happily* is the emotion I will feel all over my body."

"Now. I need you, *now*. They can wait and I can't."

Trystan's jaw clenched as Galahad's palm coaxed him into readiness. His body didn't give a shit about logic. It just wanted the knight. Despite his best efforts, Trystan went rigid with need.

"This is not strategically sound." He tried desperately. "It would be better to ensure our enemies are... *Fuck*."

Galahad sucked him into his mouth.

Trystan's chest heaved with the effort to get oxygen. Oh, this wasn't going to last long. Galahad's tongue learned the shape of him and Trystan stopped arguing against the idea. He needed Galahad, too. The knight was new at this, but he possessed a natural gift. His lips traced the length of Trystan and it was like being reborn.

P'don.

Trystan's eyes flickered closed for a heartbeat, wishing he could savor the experience. He needed to stay focused on the kidnappers still running around this area, though. Make sure they didn't threaten his mate.

Galahad licked the tip of him and gave a low groan of desire. Trystan's teeth ground together, his hooded gaze fixed on the campfire. Trying to stay alert. Every god in the heavens should be rewarding him for his restraint. He really was an angel where this man was concerned.

"How did the horses even get loose?" One of the kidnappers was bellowing from off in the distance. "Damn it, Larry, why do you always have to screw up everything? And why the hell are you crying?"

"It wasn't my fault!" Larry sobbed. "I keep thinking about the time I shoplifted that six-pack in tenth grade and it's *breaking my heart*." His voice rose in a wail of anguish.

Trystan had no clue what that craziness was about, but the knight was surely behind it.

Galahad's teeth grazed, growing bolder. Trystan's hand came down to rest on his head, tangling in the soft curls of his shimmery hair. Everything about Galahad was so beautiful. Everything he did.

Trystan's breathing grew rougher. "Deeper." He whispered. "Let me all the way in."

Galahad wasn't sure how to make that work, but he was

willing to give it a try.

Trystan's teeth ground together, as the man's swallowed more of him. "That's it. Take all of me." He ran the golden strands through his fingers and gently rocked into Galahad's eager mouth. "I won't hurt you. I would never hurt you. You are the brightest part of my world."

The knight shifted, trusting Trystan to guide him. Learning what pleased him.

Oh *gods* yes.

The wonderful part of having a mate who was good at everything...? He was good at *everything*. Natural talent and the desire to excel meant that Galahad didn't mind practicing until he was the very best at whatever he chose to do. Over and over, no matter how long it took.

It was inspiring.

"Just like that." Trystan's hands tightened in Galahad's hair, trying to hang on. "Just like *that*. Fucking perfect. You're such an artist, in all that you do."

So many emotions were flooding through Trystan that he couldn't even feel them all. He was out of control and powerful at the same time. No one else could make him feel this way. No one else in the world.

Just Galahad.

"I would die for you." Trystan wasn't sure what language he was speaking in, but it didn't seem to matter. Galahad's mouth kept up its glorious work and Trystan was helpless. Shudders wracked his body, needing to come and dreading when it would be over. "I would die *without* you. Don't ever leave me, again. I would become a ghost."

Those beautiful lips were stretched over Trystan, just as he'd been imagining for weeks, and his instincts took over. His hips drove forward. Harder. Faster. Deeper.

Galahad quickened his pace, sensing Trystan was getting close. Very close.

"Look at me, knight."

That perfect lavender gaze rose to his and Trystan could see the hunger in the man's eyes. The need. Galahad *liked* this. His body eagerly responded whenever Trystan touched him. He was a sensual creature and no one had been caring for him until Trystan arrived. No one else ever would.

"I'm going to come." Trystan kept his voice low, but even he could hear the thick lust in his words. "Do you wish to pull back?"

Galahad shook his head, drawing Trystan's girth even deeper

into his mouth. He wanted all of Trystan, but he was going to instinctively retreat when he finally got it. He was inexperienced. Innocent. No man had ever touched him but Trystan. The big blue eyes and perfect lips and heroic heart belonged only to Trystan.

His mate.

Sure enough, the knight gave a start of surprise as he felt the first jolt of Trystan's release. Trystan gently kept him in place, murmuring reassurances as best he could through his clenched teeth. He wasn't sure what he said or if the knight understood the words. He just wanted to soothe Galahad, even as his body began to surge.

It seemed to work. After the initial burst, Galahad relaxed again. He gave a hum of delight, like he wanted more. Trystan's palm stayed clenched in his hair, unable to help himself. Wanting to dominate. To possess. Some drumbeat in his head insisted that he mark the man in the most primal way possible.

Teeth nipped, demanding now, and Trystan was beyond talking in any language, he just pumped himself into the knight's mouth. Nothing had ever felt so perfect. Trystan nearly blacked out from pleasure. His head went back, the tendons in his neck standing out with strain as he fought to hold back his roar. It was better than flying.

In that instant, he saw... everything.

Galahad finally lagged against him, spent. His arms wrapped around Trystan's waist, hugging tight, and Trystan's heart flipped in his chest.

Lyrssa, he knew now what Midas endured when he first looked at Gwen. He fully identified with his brother's wonder, and fear, and protectiveness, and lack of rational decision-making skills during their courtship. It all made perfect sense.

His hand gently smoothed over Galahad's hair, trying to breathe. Trystan still wasn't sure what to call the emotion that filled him, but he knew it was far deeper than the other feelings. It felt like it was everywhere within him. Every cell of his body and drop of his blood.

Everything.

"Thank you." Galahad whispered.

Trystan arched a brow, wanting to make him smile. "Thank *you*, knight."

Galahad gave a grin and Trystan's world was perfect. "You know, this is exactly like my favorite part of *Corrupted by the Winged Devil*."

"I have never seen the film, but it is my favorite scene, as well. Believe me. You will be reenacting it again soon." He helped Galahad to his feet, dusting him off, because he wanted to keep touching him. "You're sure you're alright?"

"I'm great. Are you okay?" Galahad scanned Trystan up and down, as if perhaps he'd injured him somehow. "I kinda pushed you into that."

"I forgive you." Trystan assured him dryly and refastened his pants.

"No, I'm serious. I should have waited to seduce you, until we were in a better spot, but I saw you and I just..." He shrugged helplessly. "Needed you. I needed you so much, Trys."

Trystan liked that admission. "As you should." He said again and leaned down to find Galahad's lips with his own. "I am yours, knight. Your needs are my own."

Galahad shifted closer to him, his mouth parting to accept Trystan's proprietary kiss. "I am yours, Trys." He breathed. "Forever."

"Forever." He pulled back and ran his thumb over Galahad's face without even thinking about it. A tender touch down the center, from his forehead to the bridge of his nose.

Galahad blinked rapidly, like the gesture startled him. "Why did you do that? What does it mean?"

"It is a pledge of..." Trystan hunted for some way to explain it. "Affection. Devotion. Respect. Caring." His head tilted, taking in Galahad's strange expression. "Wait... Someone *else* has used this caress with you?"

Galahad stayed quiet, which meant yes.

P'don.

Trystan was in possibly the best mood of his life and now some unknown asshole was trying to spoil it. "Who?" The stranger was about to die. *No one* gave Trystan's mate that touch except Trystan. The stroke of the thumb wasn't sexual. It was even more important.

It was as close as gryphons had for an expression of love.

The knight shook his head. "It doesn't..."

"Where the hell is Galahad, now!" An angry man shouted from the campfire. "What are we gonna tell Those Damn Knights when they show up to pay us for him and he's run away, Larry!"

"I should never have cheated on Rhonda." The other man wept noisily. "Not on her birthday. Not in her hot tub. Not with her wicked stepmother."

"We will need to go kill those men." Trystan muttered, distracted by their annoying voices. "Especially the crying one. Even you see the logic in this, yes?"

"I'd rather just leave. I don't want either of us to kill anyone." Galahad paused. "Unless these guys had hurt you, Avi, or Gwen. Then they can die in the street, like Marcus did."

Trystan melted at the sweet words. "These men hurt *you*." He stressed. "And I will see them dead for it. No one will threaten my clan and then continue on their path unanswered. Stopping evil men is *just*. It's what warriors do to keep the whole world safer. I could kill half of St. Ives and feel nothing but satisfaction."

"It's different for you." Galahad shook his head, again. "You never have to worry about the darkness, because you're Good straight down to your soul. I'm not. I'm so much more ruthless. One day, I could go too far."

"That is not true…"

Galahad cut him off. "I've already done things that you would *never* do. Things that you'd never forgive me for, if you knew about them."

Trystan's hand found the back of his neck. "There is nothing you could *ever* do that I wouldn't forgive. I promise you." He leaned forward so his forehead rested on Galahad's, keeping their eyes linked. "Tell me something you don't want me to know and I will prove it. You have promise to give me your trust, yes?"

Silence.

"I'm a traitor." Galahad finally said in a soft voice. "You hate traitors and I am one."

It was hard not to roll his eyes at that claim. "Because of that nonsense when you were banished? We have been over this. Freeing Ayren and helping Gwen was in no way traitorous, regardless of what the ridiculous laws…"

"Because I'm the one who let Lyrssa Highstorm out of her cage at Legion."

Trystan's hand stopped moving on the back of Galahad's neck. "You released Lyrssa from her captivity?" He repeated, unsure he'd heard that correctly.

"Yes."

"You let Camelot's greatest enemy go free?" Trystan tried to wrap his mind around that revelation.

"Lyrssa was the one who did the thumb thing on my face." Galahad pulled away. "I just wanted to stop innocent people from dying, but I was losing myself to the darkness. I think she understood that. She told me to choose light and she touched my face."

Holy gods.

Trystan stared at him, dazed. "Lyrssa killed Uther. You loved Uther."

"I couldn't let him fire the Rath, again. You didn't see it, Trys. It was evil. *He* was evil. I couldn't let evil loose on innocent people. I know that it was a betrayal of Camelot. But there were no Good choices that day."

Trystan let out a shaky breath. "No. *You* made Good choices that day."

Galahad met his eyes, like the response confused him. "I stood against my king."

"You stood against a monster to protect children." Trystan closed the distance between them and pulled him close, again. He truly was holding the *ya'lah*. It was all true. "Gods... I am forever in awe of you."

"I took an oath to protect the innocent." Galahad reiterated, like Trystan still might not get it. "I *had* to do what I did. I didn't want to. I just... didn't have a choice."

Neither did Trystan. "I claim you, knight."

Galahad blinked at the non sequitur. "What?"

"You said you needed words. These are the words: I claim you and you are fucking *mine*. In my care and no one else's." Claiming him wasn't even a question. Had it ever been a question? Galahad already owned so much of him that Trystan couldn't remember what it was like before he'd found him. The world must have been a wasteland. "Tell me you accept my claim."

The knight looked confused. "Are you sure you want to do this?"

"Tell me you accept my claim." Trystan's stance became more aggressive, impatient with the hesitation. "*Now.*"

"You *know* I accept it! I just want you to be sure of what you want."

"I have been sure of what I want for weeks."

"Really? Because, this morning you were planning to leave Camelot and..."

Trystan cut him off. "You do not like this plan. So, I have changed it."

Galahad froze. "You've changed your plans?" He blinked. "For me?

"Also for me." Trystan shrugged. "I have abandoned my ideas for revenge. I do not wish to track down all those men on my list and be separated from my clan for years. That is not my dream. *You* are my dream."

Galahad looked mesmerized. "I could just travel with you on your mission." His hand came up to rest on Trystan's chest. "We could be together, no matter where you want to go."

"I want to go to Camelot. Come home with me and be my ally in all things."

Galahad's expression turned open and warm. "God, I am so crazy about you."

"Fine." It was all settled. "Now, tell me you still claim me and that I am still in your care."

The knight instantly complied. "I claim you and you are in my care. Forever."

Trystan made a sound of satisfaction at the quick reply. "You are *everything* to me, knight." He slid his palm under Galahad's, so they were holding hands against his chest. Konrad had been wrong. It was not horrible, at all. "Am I everything to you, as well?"

Galahad's fingers curled around Trystan's, holding on tight. "Yes." He whispered.

"Good." To Trystan, that exchange was the equivalent of wedding vows. Gryphon culture didn't give a shit about fancy ceremonies. If mates pledged themselves to each other, it was done. "Now, I respect that you wish to live a life of peace and so I will pressure you no more about slaying these assholes who kidnapped you."

Galahad looked genuinely touched. "Thank you, Trys."

"I will just kill them *for* you." It was no great hardship. Trystan pressed his lips to the side of Galahad's obstinate head. "Wait here." He went stalking towards the campfire.

"Trys! That's not what I... *Damn it*."

"Who the hell are you?" The biggest man demanded as Trystan drew closer. He scrubbed at his tearstained cheeks and braced his feet, ready for conflict. "What do you think...?"

He never got to finish that angry demand.

Trystan slammed his sword through the man's chin, upward so it came out the top of his skull. For an endless second, he held him there, somewhere between life and death, standing like a puppet in the firelight.

"You tried to steal my knight." He leaned forward holding the man's shocked gaze as he perished. "I don't like that."

He yanked the sword out again and the dead man fell in an uncoordinated heap in the dirt.

The other two were even easier to kill. They swung weapons at him so clumsily even Avalon could have avoided the blows. Morons.

They were dead instantly. Trystan stepped over their carcasses, unwilling to waste his energy digging graves for such men. Let the animals have them. At least they would have some use.

"That's the guy who owed me five gold pieces." Galahad said, moving into the firelight. "I seriously doubt he's going to pay up, now."

"He would not have honored the debt, anyway. He does not seem the sort."

Galahad sighed and looked around with a shake of his head. "I can't believe you killed all three of them in twelve seconds. They were dead before I even got over here."

Trystan made a face. "I know." God, it was so unsatisfying to fight talentless men. "Stores shouldn't sell swords to those who cannot use them. It gives idiots confidence they do not deserve." Given that this part of the world was filled with new and exotic weapons, he supposed he should be grateful that the imbeciles weren't armed with something more dangerous. They wouldn't have been able to use those weapons either, but they might have actually inflicted some damage.

"No, I mean… You are such an artist, Trys. When you fight, it's just beautiful."

Trystan grunted. Of course Galahad liked to watch him fight. He liked to watch Galahad fight. It was completely understandable. They were both warriors. Both the same. The only two men in the world who could rival each other in battle.

Trystan hesitated, a new idea occurring to him. A way to return a sword to the knight's hand without upsetting him with violence. A way to help him overcome his phobia of the blade and leave the dark memories behind. "You think I am a talented warrior, then?"

"Of course." The words were earnest, surprised that he'd even asked. "If you had been born in Camelot, you'd be called the best knight ever."

Trystan smiled at that. "No." He said truthfully. "I believe there is only one of those."

Galahad shook his head, missing the point. "You are the greatest warrior in the world, Trys. Not just because your skills are beyond compare, but because your whole life embodies the Knights' Code. No one else even comes close to you."

Picturing himself as a King's Man was not exactly thrilling, but Trystan still accepted the compliment. "Thank you for the reassurance." He intoned, in what he hoped was a suitably grave tone.

"It is helpful. I sometimes feel... *worry* than I am slipping."

It was not a *real* lie. Just a small bit of theater. Enacting countless doll adventures with Avi gave Trystan some background in pretending and he called on all of his skills. It was hard for a gryphon to play act. Everyone knew they were too direct for it. But luckily, since everyone knew they were too direct for it, it didn't take much to fool someone when you gave it a shot.

"Slipping?" Galahad's eyebrows compressed. "What do you mean slipping?"

"Well, it's difficult to find partners to practice my swordsmanship with, these days. Midas sometimes tries, but he was never trained in combat. He's better at street fighting." Trystan sighed, as if it was all terribly vexing. "Without practice, I fear my skills will diminish and one day it will not be so easy for me to win."

No, he didn't fear that, at all. But Galahad loved worrying about nonsense. Planting this new concern in the knight's head was all it took to have him frowning with adorable alarm.

"Well, you *have* to practice, Trystan. It could be dangerous, if you don't. Men attack you all the time. I've seen it. You need to be ready."

Actually, Trystan had been the one attacking in every battle Galahad had witnessed, but it was adorable that he thought otherwise.

"Oh, I'm sure I will be fine." He waved a palm, as if his possible death at the hands of unstoppable assassins was a small thing. "How many more people could *possibly* be plotting vengeance against me? I am very likable, yes?"

Galahad literally paled.

It was all Trystan could do not to smirk. He'd never smirked before, but now it was right there tugging at the edges of his mouth. Perhaps he should be on a TV show, after all. He was clearly as skilled at acting as he was at all things. He could see the knight's mind working, counting up the unfathomable number of enemies Trystan had collected over the years. He waited...

"I'll practice with you." Galahad blurted out, right on cue. "I'll do it."

"Oh no." Trystan firmly shook his head. "I would not want you to break your vow to never touch a sword on my account. I will be *fine*. There is no need to feel anxiety over more practiced men slaying me as I innocently walk down the street. My lifeless eyes staring up at the sky for the last time, as my blood pours..."

"*Practicing* with a sword wouldn't be breaking my vow." Galahad interjected. "No one would be hurt, so it would be okay.

Alright? You'll practice with me." He nodded like it was all settled. "We can spar every day."

"Well…" Trystan drew out the word, like he was thinking it over. "I suppose, that would be alright. If you truly think it's best."

"I do. I really, *really* do. I will protect you. I promise."

The emotion that filled him was… pleasure. Trystan's primary drive was caring for others. It gave him a path. But, he hadn't realized that he also liked being cared *for* until his knight arrived. He liked the feeling of warmth it gave him when Galahad promised to protect him. True he had manipulated the man into the pledge with ridiculous fear-tactics, but it was still very pleasant that they worked so easily. His innocent, heroic, Good-hearted mate was watching out for him. That made life so much *better*.

"Thank you, knight. You have relieved my mind…" Trystan began.

The next heartbeat of time was filled with overlapping events. Trystan saw Galahad's expression change in the firelight. Read the sudden panic on his face. Heard a strange sound behind him. Turned to see what it was.

And then the world went black.

Chapter Twenty-Nine

Yes, crybabies. We all know that the gryphons are nearly extinct and it's a shame that it had to happen.
But it *had to happen*, okay?

Evolution, folks: Get with the damn program or get out of the way.

Just last week, I heard about these portable rabbit hole devices, right? Like some kind of amazing mix of science and magic that open short-range, but *controlled* dimensional portals.

The military applications for these things are off the charts! *That's* what our society can build. We have weapons and tech that could blow up the world. Meanwhile, what have the gryphons ever invented? Goddamn leprechaun stew?

"Stopping the Savages" Podcast
Sir Dragonet of Camelot- Former Troubadour of King

Uther and Host of the Program

Beach of Ultima Thule- Edge of the Moaning Sea

Sir Bedivere, Martyr of Legion, glowered at the slain kidnappers on the beach and then at Galahad. "I should have known you'd find a way to fuck this up for me."

Galahad's jaw tightened.

Why had all the assholes survived the war?

His eyes flicked to Trystan's unconscious body, afraid to move for fear of setting Bedivere off. The ex-knight was standing over him, a strange looking gun pointed at Trystan. "What did you do to him?" Galahad asked in the calmest voice he could muster.

Bedivere was silhouetted against the swirling surface of a dimensional portal. It didn't look like a normal, naturally occurring rabbit hole, which probably meant that it was some kind of manufactured one. Wherever it had come from, it had brought Bedivere right to the kidnappers' campsite.

...Which meant Galahad's guess had been right. Bedivere was *definitely* leading the group of knights who'd hired the kidnappers to grab him from St. Ives.

Huge surprise.

There was no one else it could be. Bedivere was the ex-knight under Galahad's command, who'd tried to kill Galahad in the desert, before the pig village. Now he was back to finish the job. He wanted the map and he'd hated Galahad since the War.

That wasn't a combination that led to Good things.

"I shot the gryphon up with angelycall." Bedivere's dissipated lifestyle had aged him, so he now looked far older than his years. His cheeks were sunken, his dark hair lank around his sallow face. "It's the same shit we used to knock out Lyrssa, when we captured her before Legion." Bedivere poked the cylindrical gun at Trystan's neck and tilted his head at a mocking angle. "You remember Legion, right, Captain?"

"I remember everything about that day." Galahad's mind was racing. In that moment, he could have killed Bedivere without hesitation, but he couldn't reach the ex-knight before the man shot Trystan. He was too far away. "And I remember you tried to murder me, a couple weeks ago, because you still blame me for what happened."

"Because you're to blame!" Bedivere roared. "I couldn't believe it, when I came back to camp and saw you sitting with my men in the desert. I knew then that God had sent you to me. So I could finally make you pay. So I can make up for my failure to stop you at

Legion and be the hero I was always *supposed* to be."

Galahad didn't argue. He wasn't going to do a damn thing to set the asshole off.

Instead, he dug deep within himself, suppressing his fury and reaching for some kind of reasoning that might work. "And you wanted the map, right?" He very slowly reached into the pocket of the coat Trystan had bought him. "Here." He extracted the folded piece of paper. "I will give it to you. Just step away from Trystan."

"Why are you traveling with this demon, anyway?" Bedivere demanded, not coming any closer to Galahad. He was probably afraid. "Are you fucking him? Is that what you do now? Fuck monsters?" He made a scoffing sound. "It's a good thing Uther isn't here to see this."

"Yes, it's a *very* Good thing Uther is gone from the world." Galahad agreed quietly.

Bedivere didn't appreciate that opinion. "I saw what you did that day." He seethed. "I saw it *all*. And I vowed right then that I would kill you, if it's the last thing I ever do!"

"Fight me then." Galahad challenged. "Move away from Trystan and you and I will settle this like knights."

"I'm *not* a knight anymore thanks to you! And I'm not stupid enough to challenge you to a duel. You'd win. You *always* win." Bedivere shook his head. "No. The only way to beat you is to cheat and so *that's* what I'm going to do." He gave Trystan's prone body a kick. "As long as I have him, you'll give me whatever I want, won't you?"

Galahad's jaw ticked. "Yes." It wasn't even a choice for him. "But the reverse is also true. Right now the only thing keeping me from ripping your spinal cord out through your chest is Trystan. As long as he's safe, I'm cooperating. As soon as he's *not* safe... We're doing all this differently."

Bedivere hesitated.

"You've seen what happens when I let the darkness out." Galahad went on, in a hard tone. "You've seen how far I'll go. And that is *nothing* compared to what will happen to you, if you harm that man on the ground. Don't fucking try me, Bedivere. I will make you *wish* you'd died in the fires of Legion."

Bedivere swallowed.

Three more ex-knights stepped through the portal, behind Bedivere. They were Bedivere's asshole friends, who Galahad had thoughtfully not killed last time they fought. None of them looked grateful about his consideration.

"About time you got here." Bedivere snapped at the men,

recovering from his terror now that he had backup. "Galahad's killed everyone."

"Son of a bitch." Sir Urien grumbled, scanning all the dead guys scattered on the sand. His custom-made armor was covered in ravens eating a writhing figure alive. It perfectly summed up his tender feelings for his fellow man. "Well, at least we don't have to pay them, now, right?"

"I still don't understand why Galahad is even here." Sir Lamorak snapped. He was blond and twitchy, with a nervous habit of tugging at his eyebrows. "How do you still remember enough to get all the way to St. Ives?" He demanded, tugging at his eyebrows and scowling at Galahad. "We doused you with amnesia potion, before you escaped. You should have forgotten all about the map." He looked at the biggest man present. "Did you not use enough?"

Sir Segwarides took offense at that. He'd always been touchy. "Bullshit! I used more than enough to get the job done." He was a gigantic man, who insisted on wearing armor that was too small for his frame. "It must have been a crap product."

"All my spells are flawless!" Bedivere shouted. His voice echoed, even over the sound of the icy waves crashing against the shore.

"If they're so great, why does Galahad still have his memory?" Lamorak shot back, still tugging at his brows. "Why is it so hard to steal this damn map from him? I think the guy's --like-- blessed or something. Protected."

"Either that or everyone else is cursed with stupidity." Urien muttered with typical cheeriness. "Maybe a spell's been cast on the whole world to just *love* the asshole."

Segwarides seized on that idea, nodding enthusiastically. "I thought of that, too! My mom has a shitty calendar of his watercolors hanging in our kitchen. His annoying little pictures stare at me when I eat my morning cereal. How else do you explain it, if not an evil spell?"

Fairly easily. That calendar had been Camelot's number one Christmas gift five years running. People kept buying it, even after the dates changed, because they loved Galahad's paintings so much. Everyone in the kingdom owned one.

Galahad kept his eyes on Bedivere, rising above the insults about his interpretive landscapes. "You're the one selling all the dangerous magic in St. Ives?"

"I have to make money somehow, don't I? It's how I buy fun toys like this." He gave the strange gun a jerk. "You remember the

Rath, don't you? Well, I paid a guy to rig-up a mini version of it. For home defense." He snickered. "Shall we see what it can do to your boyfriend's face?"

That gun was a smaller version of the Rath?

Jesus, no... Galahad had seen what the twisted magic it fired did at Legion. Seen the burning and screaming and death. He'd thought the technology behind it was gone forever. Seeing it now, aimed at Trystan, was like reliving every nightmare in his head. "Don't." He warned Bedivere quietly.

Bedivere continued to taunt him. "At this range, I think it'll blast the gryphon's skull right apart. It'll be like the War, when I was fighting beside Sir Perceval and we had to wring their heathen blood from our clothes after the battles."

"The War's over." Galahad said, his pulse thudding in his ears. Having this asshole threaten his True Love was making him crazy and he couldn't afford to go crazy. "Whatever you did back then, it has nothing to do with Trystan."

"It has everything to do with *you*, though!"

"You're the one who ran and never came back to Camelot."

"What did I have to come back to?! Everything I believed in was dead!" He pressed down harder with the evil gun, its long muzzle digging into Trystan's flesh. "I should kill this winged devil right here and let you see how it feels to watch..."

"You need him to get the treasure." Galahad interrupted.

That caught Bedivere off guard. "What?"

"It's a *gryphon* treasure." He nodded to the map. "Trystan's people drew this. Only he can reach the end of it." Segwarides stepped forward to snatch the map from Galahad's hand. Galahad let him have it, all his attention on keeping Trystan alive. "You need him"

"You're lying. You always did care more about the gryphons than your own kind." Bedivere snapped at him, eyes blazing with hate. "You always were on their side, weren't you?"

"I don't lie." Galahad glanced at Lamorak. "Tell him."

"He doesn't lie." Lamorak reluctantly agreed. "The rest of us spent days with him, out in the desert. Galahad lives a life of truth. He said it like a thousand times. He wouldn't even tell Segwarides that he looked skinny in his new armor."

Segwarides sent Galahad a vicious glower, still angry about the perceived fat-shaming.

"Commenting on someone's weight, either way, sends the wrong message." Galahad told him honestly. "That's not what we should be celebrating about you, as a person."

Segwarides flicked him off and looked towards Bedivere. "The writing on this map is in the gryphons' language." He grudgingly admitted.

Bedivere grunted, somewhat accepting that Galahad was telling the truth. "So *that's* why you're with this monster?" He demanded, nudging Trystan with the toe of his boot. "Because of the gold?"

"We're working together." Galahad wasn't about to tell him that there *was* no gold. Bedivere needed an incentive to keep Trystan alive. "Trys grew up with the man who drew the map. He is the key to *everything*."

Despite his earlier words, Galahad would have lied without hesitation to save Trystan's life, but he didn't have to. All of that was a hundred percent true. Not just because Trystan was the *ya'lah* and the only one who could find the graal, but because he was *Trystan*. Without him, the whole world would be empty.

Bedivere tilted his head. "This guy is the key to everything? He is the only one who can get the treasure?"

"Yes."

"You're *sure* about that?"

"Yes. I swear it on my life."

"Well, then what the hell do I need you for?" Bedivere lifted the Rath-gun and fired it right into Galahad's chest.

The blast hit Galahad like a wrecking ball.

He went flying into the air, knocked right off his feet. The twisted magic it fired should've killed him, but somehow his coat shielded him from the worst of the blast, almost like a bulletproof vest. Trystan claimed the jacket was "enspelled with protective magic" and Galahad suddenly believed the hype. Whatever spells were woven into the threads, they were stronger than Bedivere's gun. They blocked the destructive energy from incinerating him.

But they didn't stop the sheer force of it.

The percussive power sent Galahad careening backwards and then splashing down into the Moaning Sea. He had no idea how far the magical-weapon had launched him, but the water was deep enough to suck him under into inky blackness.

Shit.

Why did he always seem to end up underwater? Thanks to that helpful yeti he'd met in his travels, Galahad was impervious to freezing. He could still feel the frosty magic of the ocean, though. The power of it clawed at him, wanting to entomb him in its frigid depths. He fought against the pull, trying to figure out which way was up. It was so hard to tell in the dark.

As his eyes adjusted, Galahad attempted to orient himself. Delicate beings of illuminated blues swam all around him, giving him the help he needed. Icen jellyfish. Some of the only creatures who could survive the curse of the Moaning Sea. He could see them everywhere, lighting the undersea world. They were beautiful. ...And they showed him the way to the surface. Using their eerie glow as a guide, Galahad swam upward. Animals truly were a blessing.

He surfaced, more than a dozen yards from shore, and looked back towards the beach. The ex-knights weren't taking the time to bury any of the abductors Trystan had killed earlier. No, Bedivere and his gang were already disappearing through the portal, dragging Trystan's unconscious body with them.

God*damn* it.

Galahad swam towards them as fast as he could, but he already knew he was too late. Trystan and the ex-knights were gone, by the time he reached land.

Bedivere had just kidnapped his True Love.

Galahad staggered onto the sand, palms braced on his knees, breathing hard. Trying not to panic. Trying not to give into rage. There wasn't time for it. He needed to focus. He needed to save Trystan. He needed to come up with a plan.

Fast.

Galahad closed his eyes and let out a slow breath.

The ex-knights thought he was dead, frozen into an ice cube and lost in the waves. That was an advantage. And he knew where they'd be going. They had the map, so they'd get a boat and head for the lost gryphon temple. Galahad needed to get there before the other men realized there was no gold to find and so they didn't need Trystan to find it. He had no idea how he was going to locate the island without the map, but he needed to think of a way.

Improvise.

That was how he'd won all his toughest battles. It was the only way he'd win, now. He needed to come up with a strategy, one step at a time.

Step one: How was he going to cross the water? He couldn't fly and he had no boat, but maybe he could... Wait. Galahad's eyes popped open. No. He *could* fly. Thanks to Avi, he had a flying carpet! The damn thing was turning out to be incredibly useful. Knowing his goddaughter, that was probably why she'd prompted him to buy it in the first place. The child knew everything.

Straightening, Galahad headed up the beach, looking for

where Trystan might have left their horses. Trystan wouldn't have come to save him without a way to bring him back to St. Ives and he probably would have brought their stuff along. That only made sense.

As he walked, Galahad absently rubbed at his ribs. He was pretty sure they were cracked, but he'd still gotten away lucky. The coat really was quite a find, for a sale rack. Trystan would be I-told-you-so-ing about making Galahad wear it, for years to come.

Hopefully.

Galahad found the horses and quickly untied the magic carpet. Okay. Excellent. He had a way across the water. Step two of his improvised plan was finding the damn island. He wasn't sure how to do that except to fly out there and look for it. ...So he was going to fly out there and look for it.

Great. Moving on to step three. Rescuing Trystan.

That meant getting to that island and then stopping everyone who threatened his True Love. It probably meant killing them. He didn't want to. He'd try other, less-permanent avenues first. But if they had to die to save Trystan...

So be it.

Galahad's jaw tightened and he began tearing through the saddlebags. He pulled one of Trystan's many, *many* spare swords free and looped the scabbard around his shoulder. Then, he found the antique gun he'd fixed and he shoved it into his waistband. There was a ruthless side to Galahad. He'd warned Trystan about that and it was true. No matter what he had to do, Galahad was saving his True Love. He'd burn down the whole world to get him back. There was no other option.

The man was *everything*.

He ignored the unsettling weight of the sword on his body and pushed forward. The power wasn't in the weapon. That was what Trystan told him and he was right. Galahad hated the sensation of the blade touching him, but he could deal with it. The darkness wasn't swirling within him. He didn't feel out of control. Inside of him there was just unbreakable determination.

He *would* have Trystan back in his arms.

Within two minutes, he was on the magic carpet and flying over the ocean. Looking for an island that could be anywhere in a vast swath of open water. Wherever the gryphon temple was, it had to be far enough from land that no one had ever seen it. That made sense, right? It had to be *way* out in the sea, where few people ever ventured. Otherwise, it would have been found, even in this remote spot.

Since he didn't have a better idea, he flew towards the horizon.

After hours of fruitless searching, though, he was beginning to question his theory. The Moaning Sea was so much bigger than he'd imagined. When it submerged Atlantis, it had spread outward for a hundred miles in any direction. How the hell was he supposed to stumble across one tiny island in so much space?

What of the island wasn't there, at all?

What if Trystan had been right and the gryphon temple had sunk with the rest of Atlantis? Maybe it was at the bottom of the ocean now, forever hidden from view. Galahad's mind went to movies. Where undersea labs existed in huge, magical bubbles, dry and protected. Could something like that actually happen? With strong enough magic, pretty much *anything* could happen.

Maybe he needed to change strategies.

Could any species of mermaids survive the Moaning Sea? Galahad had a great working relationship with mermaids. He'd raised a lot of money for their retirement homes. If he could speak to one who lived here, he was pretty sure he could convince them to help. He could ask them if they'd seen any sunken temples under the water. That would really narrow his search.

Except it would also take time and he didn't *have* time. It was already early afternoon. He needed to find Trystan *now*, before Bedivere killed him and everything was lost.

Galahad paused the carpet, trying to decide which way to go next. The thick floral weave was drenched with sea spray, soaking his already soaked clothes. He rested his forehead in his hands, desperate and needing help.

He needed help.

For the first time ever, he reached for the dead gryphons who sometimes spoke in his head. He concentrated on contacting them. On getting some guidance.

Help me. Please.

For a long moment, there was silence. Then whispers drifted through his mind and Galahad heard Fisher. He knew it was Fisher, even though he had never met the man. And he understood the words, even though he didn't speak the gryphons' language. He didn't have to speak it. If he listened, he just *knew* what the man was saying.

He listened to the instructions that Fisher had given Trystan, long ago in the zoo, like he was sitting right there with them. The same instructions that Trystan had repeated to Galahad in the Fire Cave of Corbenic, his finger gesturing towards the ground.

Find a dream and follow it, boy. And when you're lost and your dream follows you...? Tell it not to look at the horizon. Look straight down.

Galahad looked straight down. ...And saw a hole in the ocean.

He blinked, trying to make sense of it. There was a hole in the ocean, round and deep and about an acre in circumference. All the water around it was being held at bay by a massive, and undoubtedly enspelled, wall. A wall that stretched from the seabed, up and up, to a point just over the highest crests of the waves. If you weren't directly above it, you never would have seen the top of the wall. You would have no idea that it was even there, hidden by the constant movement of the Moaning Sea.

But Galahad had listened to Fisher and looked down.

The ocean rolled beneath him, but the land inside the walls stayed mostly dry. Galahad craned his neck to look into the hole. *Allllll* the way down, far below sea level, was a perfect circle of golden sand with a building sitting right at the middle of it.

An island, sunken in the sea.

The flying carpet dropped without Galahad even having to think about it. He dove the rug downward, finally landing it on the marshy sand. Sea spray rained down on him from high above, as the waves crashed against the magical stones that surrounded him, getting him even wetter. Stepping off the carpet, Galahad's astonished gaze went up to the towering walls.

It was like being a ship in a bottle.

Galahad wiped the moisture from his face and turned his attention to the listing structure in front of him. Hidden from view from the modern world, covered in barnacles and algae, the building took up almost every square inch of sand. Aside from skittering periwinkle crabs, it didn't seem like any living creature had visited it in countless years. The constant mist of the ocean kept it forever damp, but it wasn't submerged.

The lost gryphon temple still sat on dry ground.

The sinking of Atlantis had not been kind to Listeneise. It was a shipwreck of a building, crumbling in places. The columns on its front had toppled and were half-covered in sand. Part of the steeply-pitched roof had fallen in, giving it a lopsided appearance. It was smaller than he'd thought it would be and looked like it might fall down with a gentle push.

But it was *there* and that was all that mattered. Galahad had found the *exact* spot that he needed to find, using the *exact* tools he needed to find it, at the *exact* moment his True Love had needed him most.

There was no way that happened by chance.

Trystan's clans were still protecting their son.

"Thank you." He told the dead gryphons who'd helped him. Who'd seen his struggle to repent after Legion and who had given him this chance to prove himself. Who had sent him a gift that he didn't deserve, when they put Trystan in his care. "*Thank you*. I won't let you down."

Chapter Thirty

Only the *ya'lah* can break Uther's curse and they must be from wingless blood.

Some despair that this is impossible.

But I believe the gods are far smarter than the king and his sorceress.

I believe that the curse is why the old ones were entrusted with the graal, in the first place.

The gods saw all of this coming to pass. The graal's power was *always* intended to save the gryphons in our hour of most desperate need.

That hour is now.

How the Wingless War Happened
Skylyn Welkyn- Gryphon Storyteller

Atlantis- Listeneise

Trystan awoke with a metallic taste in his mouth. It was strange, but familiar. He'd experienced it before, when Marcus and Uther had dosed him with angelycall and dumped him in prison. Who the hell had drugged him this time?

And where was Galahad?

He opened his eyes, scanning for his mate and not spotting him.

He did see that he was in some sort of underground room, though. It was dark and damp and periwinkle crabs were skittering around. Frigid water was dripping onto his head, from somewhere up above. It was hard to see in the dim light, but the chamber appeared... big. Really big and irregularly-shaped. Like maybe it was carved right into the bedrock.

Trystan pulled himself into a sitting position. Whoever had drugged him also tied his hands in front of his body, which he didn't appreciate. Trystan had gotten pretty skilled at freeing himself from his captors, over the years, so he wasn't *too* upset about that. The ropes seemed flimsy. If he needed to, he could escape and kill whoever had done it, within a few minutes.

Right now, he had way bigger problems to focus on.

Where the hell was Galahad?

A group of knights appeared to be digging random holes in the ground, which was a typical show of intelligence for their kind. There were six wingless men, in total. Trystan wasn't sure who they were, but it didn't matter. At the moment, only one thing in the world truly mattered to Trystan.

"Where is Galahad?" He demanded.

The knight closest to him had sunken cheeks and a bored expression on his face. He had to be the leader of the group, since he was the only one of the six not working. "You're awake." He told Trystan, like maybe Trystan hadn't noticed. "Good. I was beginning to think you'd be out all day. We need to know where the treasure..."

Trystan cut him off, not giving a shit about any of that. "*Where is Galahad?*" He repeated harshly.

"Dead." The man crowed, rising to his feet. There was a strange cylindrical gun in his hand. "I killed him myself."

Trystan felt the world stop. "Dead?" He echoed blankly.

Oh gods... Howling emptiness screamed in his mind, threatening to destroy him. For just a second, he waivered. Wanting to give into it and die himself. Without Galahad he would have no reason to go on. His path would end. He would have nothing at all to...

No.

Trystan's instincts kicked in, cutting through the panic. *No.* This man was lying. He had to be. Were instincts and emotions the same things? Is that why Trystan had always felt them? He wasn't sure. He just knew he trusted them and they told him the knight still lived. Trystan would know if Galahad was dead. He would *feel* it.

"How did Galahad die?" He demanded, his heart pounding.

"I knocked his ass into the Moaning Sea."

Trystan's head tilted. "You froze him?"

"Yep. I imagine he's nothing but a knight-icle, by now."

Relief rushed through Trystan, leaving him slightly dizzy. The knight was immune to freezing and gods-only-knew what else. That would not kill him. Trystan was half-convinced that *nothing* could kill the man. The gods protected their miracles.

Satisfied that Galahad was safe, for the moment, Trystan took closer stock of his own situation. "I know you." He told the knight, staring up at the stranger and finally processing his features. "You're dead. I've seen your ugly memorial statue."

"I'm *not* dead." Bedivere the Brave snapped, looking insulted. "And that damn statue looks nothing like me. Arthur deliberately picked the worst likeness he could find. He always was an asshole."

Trystan couldn't argue with that assessment. "You are the one who tried to kill Galahad in the desert? The ex-soldier who served under him in the War, but blamed him for some Bad memories?"

"Bad memories?" Bedivere scoffed. "Is that what he told you? *Bad memories?* My whole life was ruined because of Legion!"

"Many lives were ruined because of Legion."

Bedivere ignored that truth, focused only on his own petty complaints. "That day, I lost *everything* I believed in." He rose to his feet, agitated and pacing around the damp floor. "I wanted to tell the truth about it, but I knew that no one would ever believe me. Not over *him*. I *had* to run." He'd clearly repeated that excuse for his cowardice so many times that he'd even convinced himself.

"In the meantime, Camelot has made you into a martyr." Trystan arched a sardonic brow. "I suppose this enshrined legacy had nothing to do with your choosing to stay dead. Your ego was not involved, at all."

"You don't know what you're talking about." Bedivere stabbed a finger at him, outraged by the sarcasm. "If I had told everything that happened that day, I would have been painting a target on my back. Galahad was too popular to stand against. Everyone would have sided with him and I'd probably be in jail!"

"Also, returning to Camelot would have revealed you to be a deserter, rather than a man who heroically died saving children from a fire. Then, you would *definitely* be in jail, yes?"

"Shut up!" Bedivere shouted. "You're only alive to help me find the treasure. Once I have that, I can buy my way back into the real world. I'll be *twice* the hero, they think I am." He pulled out Galahad's map, holding it up for Trystan to see. "This led us here, but this damn temple is a maze. We've been circling around for hours. Where do we go next?"

Trystan's eyebrows shot up, distracted from arguing with the moron. Holy shit! Had they truly found the last gryphon temple?

He looked around the damp cellar and realized it was the lower level of an ancient structure. No. This was *not* the temple, but it was no doubt close. As his eyes adjusted to the darkness, he could see the stone ceiling above his head was crumbling in spots. Through the holes, he could see the remnants of columns carved with gryphon words. Off to his right, there were stairs leading upward, grooves worn into the center of them by centuries of feet.

...And directly in front of him, there was the steep drop-off of a cliff face.

"What is that?" He asked quietly, even though he already knew. He could feel the power radiating from it.

"You tell me." Bedivere grabbed Trystan's arm, trying to drag him to his feet.

Since Trystan topped the man by a foot, he mostly just got in the way. Trystan shouldered the dickhead aside, walking to the cliff's edge himself. Transfixed by the strange silver light glowing from far below. Every childhood story Elaine had ever told him flickered through his head. He was beholding something straight out of legend.

The Looking Glass Pool.

Trystan stared down at it, awed. A hundred feet below, the glittering surface of the Looking Glass Pool moved like liquid mercury. It was like seeing magic for the first time. His brain tried to make sense of it, even when he knew it was impossible to explain with logic.

"My gods..." He breathed in awe.

What *was* the pool? It was like nothing else he'd ever beheld. Rabbit holes had mirrored surfaces, so that was the most likely guess. But rabbit holes were usually small and the Looking Glass Pool was the size of a lake. The rippling funhouse mirror surface shielded whatever hid below and reflected a distorted image back.

Was it just a regular pool of water, disguised by some glamour to keep people away?

Trystan frowned. That was certainly a possibility. A dimensional vortex would transport anyone who passed through it to parts unknown, so only a crazy person would just jump into a rabbit hole. Esmeralda, the wicked witch, had fallen through one and she hadn't been heard from since. It could be the ancient gryphons knew that people feared rabbit holes and had used some spell to make intruders think the Looking Glass Pool was too dangerous to enter.

On the other hand, it could also be *worse* than a rabbit hole. It could lead to plain old death.

It was possible that his ancestors could have rigged a dozen deadly ploys to stop trespassers from stealing the graal. The mural on the wall of the cave flashed through Trystan's mind. The final step on that emerald trail had led *up*. Not down. He'd seen it himself. So was it wrong ...or was the Looking Glass Pool some kind of elaborate trick? Generally, gryphons did not swim, so this could be a trap targeting the wingless. To lure them into a quicksand of liquid mirror that would never let them escape.

Anyone who went into that "water" might never come back out.

Standing high above the pool, it was impossible to know for sure. Therefore, the smart play was to send a camera into the mysterious liquid and scan for hidden dangers before going any farther. The graal was supposed to be down there, and while every other part of the tale had proved to be true, Trystan still wasn't eager to risk his life on a plan with so many blind corners.

And he *especially* wasn't ready to risk Galahad's.

As soon as he saw this place, the knight would be bubbling with excitement to press forward. Trystan had always been more methodical when it came to strategy, though. He wasn't ready to dive right into the pool based on nothing but hope and enthusiasm.

He wanted *facts.*

Trystan stepped back, away from the edge. "That's the Looking Glass Pool." He reported unnecessarily.

"I know it's the fucking Looking Glass Pool!" Bedivere snapped. He came up next to Trystan, staying safely out of range and keeping the odd gun pointed right at him. "Are the gold and gems beneath it? Is that it? Is that why Uther was *really* searching for it?"

"I am not the one to ask about Uther's thoughts." Trystan lifted a shoulder in a shrug, not really answering the question. "I have never understood their darkness."

"Don't try that shit with me, demon." Bedivere glowered up at him. "Galahad said you knew where the treasure is. It's the only reason that I didn't kill *you*, when I killed *him*."

Trystan arched a brow at that news. "Galahad told you I alone could find this treasure?" He repeated in exasperation.

Yes. That sounded *exactly* like a Galahad plan. To ensure that Bedivere kept Trystan alive, the knight would spin any number of creative tales. Of course, Galahad could have claimed that *Galahad* was the key to understanding the map. That would have been the best way to ensure his own survival and it would have been what Trystan would've *wanted* him to say. But, instead he'd protected Trystan, at the risk of his own safety.

Trystan sighed, not even bothering to get upset. As maddening and unnecessary as it all was, he felt... *touched* by Galahad's vigilant protection. No one since the zoo had put so much effort into Trystan's care. It was very adorable.

"You're damn right, he told me that!" Bedivere insisted. "Galahad told me you were the key to *everything*. He said that you..." The man hesitated, as if suddenly realizing how conveniently the claim aligned with Galahad's wishes. His eyes widened, rage reflected in their beady depths as he saw he'd been played. "*Shit!*"

In a blind rage, Bedivere fired the strange gun at the Looking Glass Pool. A colossal amount of pressurized magic and vivid green fire slammed into the mirrored "water." Rather than passing through, the fiery blast ricocheted off the surface, like it was a solid mass of ice or metal. The tremendous bolt of energy bounced back, sheering off part of the rock wall of the cliff, before finally dissipating into a shower of sparks.

Trystan blinked, surprised by the gun's power. How did a jackass like Bedivere get such a weapon? Where did he find it?

"If I hadn't already killed Galahad, I would kill Galahad!" Bedivere stomped around, enraged. "I have to get into that pool! There *must* be a way!"

Trystan considered the impossible physics of what he'd just seen. He was *definitely* not diving into that silver lake without more investigation. The magic guarding it was like nothing he'd ever felt. The Looking Glass Pool was powerful beyond known limits. They would need to do more testing before he or Galahad ventured down there.

"Whatever my knight said to you, I'm sure it was not a lie." He told Bedivere absently, considering many options. "Galahad lives a life of truth."

"I'm so sick of hearing that."

"And yet it's true."

Galahad did not have to lie to achieve victory. He could convince you of any insane thing he wished, without ever uttering a false syllable. During the War, his ability to misdirect had been maddening. Now, Trystan found he enjoyed watching the man's artistic mind at work.

...When he was directing his deceptive skills at some *other* poor bastard, anyway.

Bedivere ran a hand through his hair, his mouth nearly foaming with frustration. Trystan knew that feeling well. "Look, is the gold inside the Looking Glass Pool or not? If you can't tell me what I want to know, then I have no use for you."

Trystan felt many emotions, at the moment. "Intimidated" was not one of them. Even with that imposing gun, Bedivere was weak. The power was in the warrior, not the weapon. "And if I help you, you will let me go?" He challenged, just to see what the other man would say.

"Sure, I will. You have my word on it."

Bedivere did *not* live a life of truth.

Trystan grunted. No matter. He planned to kill all these men, either way. Still Bedivere might as well make himself useful, before his inevitable death. Maybe they did not *need* a camera to know more about the Looking Glass Pool.

"Something beyond price lies hidden within that pond." Trystan allowed. "But I do not know if we can safely pass through the pool to find it. There could be booby-traps."

"Booby-traps? Bullshit. You're stalling."

"You saw the blast from your gun fail to penetrate its surface and it seems very powerful." Trystan retorted. "What makes you think a living being will fare better?"

"This gun *is* very powerful." Bedivere boasted. "It's a handheld Rath."

This was a small version of the Rath? No wonder Legion had been laid to waste. Trystan's jaw tightened, imagining his *ha'yan* facing down a scaled-up version of the weapon's destructive energy. Somehow standing against the cannon to save the gryphon survivors. "Riding before it, with blood dripping from his hands," according to the witnesses. Gods... Galahad seriously needed to tone down on his heroics.

Trystan had always wanted a hero, but he also wanted his mate *alive*.

"My ancestors built this place with the express purpose of keeping others out." Trystan told Bedivere tightly, resisting the urge to get sidetracked with visions of Galahad being blasted into microscopic particles. "We will have to test for hidden dangers, before we go any further."

"Test?" Bedivere still seemed skeptical. "How?"

Trystan shot Bedivere a sideways glance and then pointedly turned to look over at the other five knights. They were still randomly digging and bickering over the pros and cons of low-carb diets. "Do you have any strong favorite among these men?"

Bedivere followed his line of thinking. "Nope." He said

easily. "Lamorak is always tugging on his eyebrows and it drives me nuts, though."

Trystan lifted his shoulder in another shrug, happy to thin the heard and also further understand the Looking Glass Pool. Two birds. One stone. "If there is gold down there," (which there wasn't) "the fewer men you have to share it with the better, yes?"

"I couldn't agree more." Bedivere raised his voice. "Lamorak! Come here for a minute!"

A twitchy looking knight reluctantly slid closer to them, nervously plucking at his brows. Bedivere was right. It was an annoying habit. "Something wrong, boss?"

"We're not sure, yet." Bedivere slapped him on the back. "We need you to test it for us."

He gave Lamorak a shove, sending the other knight careening off the edge of the cliff. Trystan and Bedivere craned their necks to watch him fall. Lamorak screamed all the way down and hit the mirrored surface of the pool like a bug on a windshield.

Trystan and Bedivere winced in perfect unison as the other knight smashed every bone in his body. His horribly twisted carcass lay there for a long moment, blood spreading out all around him. Then the shiny, deadly "water" finally parted beneath his corpse. It swallowed him up, dragging him into the mysterious depths of the pool.

Huh.

Trystan frowned in consideration. "You see? *That* is a booby-trap."

"Did you just kill Lamorak?!" Another knight yelled at Bedivere. "Are you out of your mind?! He was one of us!"

"He slipped!" Bedivere roared back. "What did you want me to do, Wain? Jump in after him?"

"You pushed him!" The one called Wain insisted, his pox-marked face flushed. "I saw you do it!"

Bedivere leveled the Rath-gun at the man's chest. "Did you?" He challenged.

Wain took a step backwards and stopped talking.

"That's what I thought." Bedivere sniffed. "Get back to work."

The other knights began whispering fiercely amongst themselves, but none of them approached the edge of the cliff to confront Bedivere further. They truly were a weak bunch.

"No one understands what it takes to get ahead in this world. Sometimes you have to kill the goose to get the golden egg, right?" Bedivere's shook his head in irritation, his attention flicking back to Trystan. "So, *now* what are we going to do? If that big-ass pool is blocking me, how can I get the treasure?"

"You *can't* get the treasure. Obviously. This is not your path." Trystan pointed down to where Lamorak had met his gory end. "Did you not see the test?"

"Maybe I should have *you* go down there and test again." Bedivere swung the gun up to point at Trystan's face. "You can fly down and land on it, looking for a way through. If it kills you... Well, one more dead gryphon won't matter to anyone."

"It would matter to Galahad." Trystan smirked. "And he is already going to be pissed when he gets here, so I would not do anything else to make this situation even worse for yourself. The man has a temper."

"Galahad's not coming, you winged idiot. Galahad is *dead.*"

"I'll bet you five gold pieces he's not." Trystan drawled, paraphrasing his very-much-alive mate.

Galahad was going to show up to rescue him. They had made a deal and it was Galahad's turn to do the saving. Until then, Trystan was content to sit back and wait. He'd never been rescued before, so he was quite looking forward to the event.

Trystan would have to be the one who eventually killed these men, of course. Galahad would no doubt want to rehabilitate them with chocolate brownies. Then he'd argue that his plan was somehow *not* a failure when it inevitably failed. But Trystan didn't mind. He just wanted to see Galahad riding to his rescue. The man's creativity was unrivaled. It would be fascinating to behold what ludicrous plan he'd somehow weave into reality.

Bedivere waved a dismissive hand. "You think I'm scared of Galahad. Even if he *was* somehow still alive... So what? I'm poised to be a bigger hero than he'll *ever* be! Once I get this treasure, I'll be able to buy my share of all the glory he's been hogging. I'll have my *own* coloring books, and action figures, and video streaming service!"

Trystan hesitated. "Galahad owns a video streaming service?"

"Yeah. The damn thing only shows puppet shows and it *still* makes a fortune."

Trystan's mouth twitched. "Do you truly think you can best Galahad of Camelot?" He asked and almost felt... *pity* for the man's hopeless quest. "In anything? My knight has never lost a battle."

"He lost the War!" Bedivere screamed. "He lost *Legion!*"

Trystan rolled his eyes. "Camelot won Legion. Did you miss

the ending, as you fled?"

"Because of Galahad, the gryphon race escaped extermination." Bedivere raged, distracted from the treasure hunt by the festering of old wounds. "Uther would have wiped out the very last of your kind, but Galahad made sure that didn't happen. He ended the War before it was *really* over. He stole Camelot's ultimate victory! He made sure our side *lost!*"

"Queen Lyrssa was the one who killed Uther. If you must blame someone..."

"Lyrssa didn't kill Uther!" Bedivere interrupted harshly. "Is that what Galahad told you? Because it's a fucking lie."

"My knight lives a life of truth. I explained this, yes? He does not lie."

"Are you really that blind?" Bedivere stared at Trystan, an amazed expression on his face. "My God... He's fooled you, too, hasn't he? He's convinced you it was all that bitch Lyrssa's fault."

What the hell was Bedivere talking about?

"People who were there saw Lyrssa flying off with Uther's bleeding body." Trystan had read reports of it himself. "Your kind makes movies of the event. Galahad did not invent this story."

...But, now that Trystan thought about it, Galahad hadn't *exactly* told him that Lyrssa killed Uther when he described the battle. He'd just let Trystan assume what everyone already assumed. Shit. The man's ability to confuse and obfuscate was truly second to none.

What was he trying to hide?

"I don't need to watch movies about Legion." Bedivere sneered. "I was *there* and I saw what he did. Maybe I'm the *only* one who saw it. I should have stopped it, but I was too frozen by Galahad's legend to stand up to him. I just... watched it all happen."

He sounded very, very sure if his recollections.

P'don.

"Watched what happen?" Trystan reluctantly asked, bracing himself for some new Galahad-created disaster. "My knight letting Lyrssa out of her cage? I know this occurred..."

Bedivere cut him off again. "Galahad set Lyrssa free, but only *after* Uther was dead."

"That's impossible. Uther valued his own skin too highly to engage in battle. He would have been safe from the gryphons, well away from the fighting."

"The King was *already dead* when Lyrssa got to him." Bedivere repeated, hissing out the words. "Or close to it. But he didn't die in battle. Oh no... He wasn't even armed that day."

Everything inside of Trystan went still. "Uther was unarmed?"

"He was always unarmed! He was the king. But he still wound up with a broadsword slammed through his goddamn torso." Bedivere smiled spitefully. "Guess who's blade it was?"

Trystan's lips parted, pieces suddenly fitting together in his brain. Galahad's deep aversion to swords... His reluctance to talk about Legion... His worry that Trystan hated traitors... His claim to have killed an unarmed man...

"Come on. Guess." Bedivere taunted, seeing he had Trystan's undivided attention. "It shouldn't be hard to figure out, even for one of your primitive kind. Who's the only knight crazy enough to suddenly side with his enemies *on the last fucking day of the War?*"

A knight whose blinders had just been ripped off by the true brutality of Uther's campaign. A knight who would always do what he deemed right, even if he had to walk the path alone. A knight who believed in his vow to protect the innocent so completely that he would condemn himself to years of nightmares and a possible execution to fulfil his oath.

The best knight ever.

Bedivere leaned closer to Trystan, his eyes glowing with hatred. "Now you see, don't you? You see who *really* murdered King Uther and doomed his glorious cause forever."

"Galahad." Trystan whispered.

Chapter Thirty-One

Battle of Legion
End of the Third Looking Glass Campaign

"Kill every one of the little bastards!" Uther screamed at the knights. "Fire the Rath, again!" Men began reloading the magical cannon, as Legion burned. Readying it to kill the last of the children and elderly gryphons trying to flee. "Don't let any of them escape! Don't let them get to the mountains!"

And that's when Galahad took the best and worst action of his life.

That's when Galahad murdered his own king.

He reached up to pull Uther from his horse, dragging him to the ground. There was only one way to stop more of his hideous orders from being carried out. Only one way to save the remaining gryphons from slaughter. Galahad's sword was in his hand without him even reaching for it. Slamming through the stomach of his unarmed commander. The man he had vowed to follow and obey and protect. The man he had loved like a father. Slaying Uther right there in that horrible place to spare the lives of their enemies.

Hot blood sprayed across Galahad's face as he screamed out his anguish. The king bellowed, too, in pain and surprise and fury. The horse reared, startled by the cries and the fight. It all happened, at once. But, very slowly.

For an endless moment, Galahad's eyes locked with Uther's.
...And then he let the man fall.

Uther hit the grass, still alive but already dead.

Galahad gave a sob, broken by what he'd done and what he hadn't. For what he'd become, through his actions and inactions. Something within him was shattered.

"Traitor." Uther whispered, blood leaking from his lips. "Traitor to your own kind, Galahad. To your race. To your king. You'll be damned for this forever."

Galahad staggered backwards, turning away from his old life. Away from everything. Everything he'd ever believed in was gone. *He* was gone. He fell to his knees, rage and violence and grief filling him. Consuming him. Nothing anchored him, now. Darkness like he'd never known grew within his mind.

He would kill everyone.

Kill all the knights who had participated in this massacre. Kill the scientist who'd built the Rath and the men who started the fires and the spy who'd told him how to find the village. He would kill them *all*, so they would no longer pollute the world with...

Something touched his face.

Galahad's head snapped up and he realized he was kneeling by Lyrssa's cage. She had reached between the bars to run her thumb down his forehead to the bridge of his nose. He had no idea why, but it snapped him out of his spiraling breakdown.

"Don't let him win, knight." She said softly. "Don't follow him down that path."

Tears traced down his face, through the drying blood on his cheeks.

"Fight for something *better*." Her eyes were so dark and so deep that they looked like ebony pools. "There is a far greater path for someone who does what you just did. *Fight* for it. Fight against the darkness."

Galahad swallowed. "I can't. It's too late. I have to..."

"Darkness is not the answer." Lyrssa cut him off and her voice held all the wisdom in the world. "Only light protects the innocent. Only light can save us. Choose the light."

Galahad released a shuddering breath.

Somehow his fracturing mind found a foothold with her words. Only light. He desperately clawed for purchase and seized onto the core belief of his being. The simple code that defined him. It held him fast, when he would have tumbled into the abyss.

A knight protects those weaker than himself.

He had faltered this day, but the truth of the Knights' Code was still real and solid beneath his feet. It was the light that guided him. No matter the cost to himself. No matter what anyone else thought. No matter the consequences. A knight *always* protects the innocent.

No matter what.

Galahad swallowed again, staggering to his feet. "Go." He opened the enspelled gate of her cage. "Leave now."

Later, he would have trouble remembering *exactly* how he'd unlocked the door. He must've gotten the key from Uther, but he'd blocked that part from his head. He simply did not want to recall returning to the king's side and pulling the keyring from his dying body. His mind thankfully shielded Galahad from details of that moment. But the wet blood coating his hands afterwards told enough of the story.

Lyrssa blinked as he set her free. "You release me?"

"Yes." Galahad still didn't trust her, but, in that moment, it didn't matter. "You need to go far from here." He swiped a hand under his nose. "Hurry."

Lyrssa climbed down, her eyes still on his, not quite trusting him, either. "You are either the greatest knight ever born or a complete lunatic. Either way, I do not work with your kind. I must search for a path that no wingless can follow."

"We're not working together." He might be a lunatic, but, in his brainwashed mind, the idea of working with a gryphon was still ludicrous. It would take years for him to think clearly. "I'm freeing you and then I'll save however many of your people are left in the town. That's it."

"*You* will save my people? I should trust a knight with their lives?"

Galahad met her eyes. "I will save the gryphons or I will die trying. You have my word on it."

For whatever reason, she believed his vow. "I will leave my people in your hands, then. But, I am taking your king."

"What?" Galahad automatically shook his head, most of his attention on planning a way to stop his men. No genius ideas were coming to mind. "No, you can't..."

Lyrssa cut him off. "The wingless will see it was your sword that cut him down, otherwise, and know what happened here. He is dead, anyway, even if he still breathes for another few moments. I can do him no more harm."

"I did this to him. I will take the blame."

"There is no blame, only credit." She insisted. "And it is mine. You have a mission beyond this place, knight. Focus on that and do not tell what happened here. No one will believe you, anyway. Regardless of your words, Uther's demise will rest on me in everyone's mind. And both of us will be the better for it."

Later, Galahad would never lie about what happened to the king. ...But he'd never dissuade people from believing that Lyrssa had killed him, either. For her part, Lyrssa seemed to relish taking all the credit. Some said she ritualistically displayed Uther's mangled corpse as a trophy before disposing of it, but Galahad would never want to know about that. A part of him would always love the man he hated. He had no desire to seek out information on the body's ignominious end. His last memory of Uther would always be here.

He gave a reluctant nod. The Rath was being readied, again. There was no time for debate. "Take him."

Lyrssa's head tilted at an odd angle, like she was seeing something both far away and deep inside of him. "You're not a lunatic, knight. It would be easier for you, if you were." She whispered. "I see your path, like I see my own. I see the *ya'lah*. I see Atlantis."

He could barely think. "What?"

"Find Atlantis and you will find a future for us all. A treasure beyond price. A way back to the light. *That* is your mission, now."

Galahad wasn't sure what she was talking about and he couldn't wait around to figure it out. "*Go.*" He said again and headed for King Uther's horse, because he had no idea where his own was. When had he even dismounted? Everything was a blur. "Do not come back to this land. It is not safe here."

"Oh, I *will* return." Lyrssa grabbed Uther, who gurgled in the last gasps of life. If he knew what was happening he gave no sign of it. Death was already upon him. "And I will meet you, again, knight. In a better world."

With that, she took off into the sky.

Galahad let her escape. Allowed Camelot's greatest foe to leave with its dying king. To vanish into the clouds. He wasn't sure where she went after that, but he knew she was alive and that her side had been the right one. That was all that mattered.

It was then that his reddened gaze fell on a soldier, standing a few feet away. Bedivere, again. The boy was staring right at him, an extinguished torch in his hands, his eyes full of disbelief and hatred.

...And Galahad knew that Bedivere had seen everything. Seen Galahad kill the king and free Lyrssa. Seen him betray Camelot to stay true to himself. Did it matter that the boy knew?

No.

"This is my path." He told Bedivere simply, unconsciously echoing Lyrssa's words. "You can turn me in for treason later. I don't care. But, now is the moment to decide what *your* path will be. Is it killing children? Are you a monster, after all? ...Or are you a *knight?*"

Bedivere's mouth thinned, conflict evident on his young face.

"You *know* this is wrong." Galahad pressed, swinging a

desperate hand around the carnage. "Help me stop this slaughter and protect the innocent. Follow the code!"

Bedivere dropped the torch and raised his gun, pointing it at Galahad. The muzzle was shaking.

"Do it, then." Galahad opened his arms, ready to die. "But don't miss, because I'm not stopping, even if I have to go right through you."

Bedivere hesitated for a second and then made his choice. Without saying a word, he dropped the gun too and took off running. He ran from the fighting and from Galahad and from his own demons. On the official rolls, he would be listed as presumed KIA. The youngest knight to die that day. The Martyr of Legion.

Galahad let him go. Mounting Uther's horse, he wheeled towards the Rath.

"Stop!" He bellowed. "Stop shooting!"

But they weren't going to stop. He knew it, even as he shouted. They would keep up the deadly assault until everyone was dead or they were forced to cease. So he improvised.

Galahad rode the horse into the path of the cannon, halting directly before the barrel of the weapon. Uncaring what the unnatural magic would do to him if they fired. The knights would have to shoot him before the fleeing gryphon. Before any more innocents died.

He sat there, Uther's blood still staining his hands, and blocked the Rath. "Let them go!"

The King's Men paused in their terrible work, unsure of what to do. Not wanting to blast their commander into dust.

"The next soldier who raises a gun, I will kill myself!" Galahad meant it with everything in him. "I will kill *every fucking one of you* before I let you murder another child."

His furious words seemed to lessen the bloodlust. To bring back sanity to some of the men. Weapons slowly lowered, no one looking each other in the eye.

"The king said to destroy all the heathens!" Sir Perceval shouted back. His bigotry towards the gryphons ran the deepest. His sense of righteousness the most twisted. "The king's orders..."

"Uther is dead." Galahad interrupted, ignoring the shocked gasps and cries at the news. "His orders died with him. I am in command and I'm telling you to let the gryphon go."

Perceval hesitated.

Galahad stared him down. "If you want to disobey me, get out... your fucking... sword." It was a direct challenge, every word a snarl of repressed violence.

Perceval's lips tightened, but he wasn't stupid enough to want to fight Galahad. He backed away without reaching for his weapon.

And then the Battle of Legion was over.

In all, it took fifteen minutes --perhaps less-- to rip apart the world.

Afterwards, Galahad did what he could to protect the few survivors who were left. To give them safe passage to the mountains. But, it wasn't enough. It could never be enough. Nothing would ever atone for this day.

At the end of the chaos, when everything beautiful was dead and his honor was gone, Galahad watched the swirling black smoke for a long time. Watched it blot out the sunlight and darken the bright summer sky. Wishing he could run away like Bedivere had. Just run and run and never stop. How could Galahad ever go home to Gwen and Avi with so much blood on his hands?

In that moment, at his lowest point, he nearly succumbed to the sorrow. He was damned for what happened at Legion. He knew that. He should die right there with the others. What possible purpose did he have in the world, now? He should take his own life and be done with it.

Except, just then, a rocking-horsefly flittered by Galahad's face. Its translucent wings shimmered like magic and, for no real reason, he thought of Lyrssa Highstorm giving him that bizarre mission. Speaking of a way back to the light. Promising a better world.

Telling him to find Atlantis.

Chapter Thirty-Two

So the results of last week's poll are in.
Remember we asked: What do you think the graal looks like?

Fifty-six percent of you said "gun or sword." Totally agree. Glad to see some of you are using your heads

Thirty percent of you said a "cup or bowl." Idiots. All of ya. That's obviously what the gryphons *want* you to think. Eleven percent said "book or scroll." God save me from intellectuals. You people are as vile as the winged devils. And three percent of you answered "not sure." Way to commit, folks.

Anyway, interesting stuff. For next week's poll we're asking another head-scratcher about the graal:

Do you think it will ever be found?

"Stopping the Savages" Podcast
Sir Dragonet of Camelot- Former Troubadour of King Uther and Host of the Program

Atlantis- Listeneise

Trystan burst out laughing.

It was the wrong reaction. He knew that even as the laughter overcame him. Killing Uther had surely been difficult for Galahad. The knight had loved Camelot's king like a father, so it would've been distressing for him to gut the asshole on Legion's battlefield. When Trystan eventually spoke to Galahad about the delightful slaughter of that sadistic madman, he would have to attempt to show empathy for the conflict the knight must have endured.

But Galahad wasn't there, at the moment. And since hearing about Uther's delightful slaughter was really, *really* delightful, Trystan gave into his emotions and laughed. He had never laughed before. At least not that he could recall.

It felt... *freeing*.

Bedivere blinked, shocked by Trystan's reaction. Whether it was because gryphons weren't supposed to have emotions or because he thought Uther's demise needed to be regarded with more reverence was anyone's guess.

"Do you understand what I'm saying?" He demanded. "Galahad *murdered* King Uther. That bitch Lyrssa helped him cover up his crimes. She told Galahad he was super-goddamn-special and then flew away with Uther's corpse. His boots fell off his body, as she dragged him through the air!"

Trystan laughed harder.

Of *course* it had all happened that way. Uther really should have seen it coming, lost boots and all. When Galahad got involved, nothing ever went to plan. If he didn't hate the dead king so deeply, Trystan would almost feel... *sorry* for old Uther's final moments. The sheer *frustration* the man must have felt! All his crazed scheming for power... All the heartless deaths... All the countless hours he'd wasted strategizing a flawless victory... *Finally,* Uther's vicious tactics had paid off and he'd been poised to win.

And then Galahad went and fucked it all up for him.

Trystan's shoulders shook with the force of his mirth, his bound hands wiping at his cheeks. It was hilarious. It would never *not* be hilarious. He now understood the appeal of "jokes," because humor truly did lighten the soul.

"It's not funny!" Bedivere screamed. "I was traumatized!" He pointed a finger at his own chest. "Just for a second, I almost bought into his lies. I almost helped him stand against my own kind.

Galahad said, 'Be a knight!' and I almost believed..." He stopped and shook his head. "But, it was a trick. Uther's plan to wipe out your monstrous race was *right*. Everything Galahad's ever said is a lie."

"I live a life of truth, dickhead." Galahad snapped, walking down the stone steps and into Listeneise's cellar. "So believe me when I tell you, I'm about to kick your ass."

Trystan's heart soared. He twisted his wrists, breaking the ropes binding him, eager to get on with his rescue. Having a knight in shining armor show up to save you was really quite exhilarating. He should let Galahad do it more often.

Bedivere paled, backing away from Galahad like he'd seen a ghost. "How the hell are you here?!" He jerked the Rath-gun up, frantically aiming it at the knight. "You're not going to ruin this for me, too!"

Trystan grabbed hold of the cylindrical barrel, wrenching the weapon out of the other man's hand before Bedivere had a chance to harm his mate. The moron would no doubt have failed anyway, but why take a chance? Trystan had seen what that weapon could do and it had no place in this world.

"I told you my *ha'yan* lived." He murmured and tossed the gun off the edge of the cliff. It crashed against the rock-hard surface of the Looking Glass Pool shattering into pieces. "Perhaps you should run." He arched a brow at the seething man. "You excel at that, yes?"

That was good advice. Bedivere didn't take it.

"Kill him!" Bedivere screamed at his minions, ducking behind Trystan's large body for safety. "Stop him, before he slaughters us all!"

The other men rushed forward, following Bedivere's orders. They headed for Galahad, five against one. Trystan made a "tsk" sound. Terrible odds. The men were doomed.

Galahad ignored their approach, his attention on Trystan. "Are you okay?"

"I am fine, now that you are here to save me." He scanned the knight up and down, admiring the water beading on Galahad's muscular flesh and dripping from his shimmery hair. "You have come to ensure my liberation while wet?" He arched a suggestive brow. "I approve of this."

The other men warily circled the knight, swords drawn.

Galahad barely noticed, still focused on Trystan. He looked both relieved and exasperated. "I'm wet, because we're on an undersea island, Trys. Literally. There are walls of sea water all around us, drenching this whole place. It took me an hour to wind my way through the ruins and get down here, so I'm soaked to the skin."

"I deeply appreciate that image. *Deeply*."

Galahad rolled his eyes. "Hang on for a sec..."

The five men came at him en masse and the knight ducked out of the way. He pulled the ogre girl's revolver from the waistband of his pants and ducked under the first attacker's wide swing. It was all one, smooth, perfect movement, which was gratifying to watch. Still...

Trystan made a face at the weapon choice. "Knight, there is a sword on your back, yes?" Trystan was surprised and pleased to see it there, as a matter of fact. "You should use that and not that damn gun."

"It's my turn to do the rescuing, right? Let me try it my way, before I resort to killing them."

Trystan was warmed by that idea. "You would kill these men to rescue me?"

"Of course, I would..." Galahad pointed the revolver at the first attacker's face and fired. The guy was dressed in armor covered in devouring ravens. A mist of golden dust enveloped his features and he collapsed to the ground.

Snoring.

Everyone in the room froze, like they were trying to make sense of what happened.

"...But hopefully I can find a more peaceful way." Galahad finished.

Trystan pursed his lips and studied the unconscious man for a beat. "The sleeping sand from Ted-ville?" He guessed.

"Yeah, I invented a non-lethal bullet. I told you that, right?" Galahad shifted out of the way as two knights recovered enough to swing their swords at him simultaneously. Not even Trystan was sure how Galahad managed it, but he somehow slipped from between both blades, like it was a dance he'd practiced a thousand times before.

Trystan tilted his head, mesmerized. No longer feeling the need to backseat-drive this fight. The knight had characteristically underplayed his talents. Galahad didn't just "know a little about guns," as he'd claimed. When he fought, he could turn the firearm into an extension of himself. He knew exactly how to use it so that each movement of his body became art.

To hell with swords, Galahad should continue carrying that gun with him wherever he went. It was magical watching him work with it.

Galahad shifted to one side, the revolver coming up like he didn't even have to think about using it. Like he could foresee every move of the fight, before it even happened. The man wasn't even out of breath. Sleeping sand exploded in his opponents' faces and they hit the stone floor, side-by-side and already asleep.

Galahad glanced at Trystan. "See?" He said calmly. "They're incapacitated, but alive. That's totally within my not-killing-people rules."

Trystan nodded. "Fine."

He was through with encouraging Galahad to slay his enemies. That was not in the knight's nature and Trystan had been a fool to try and change it. You did not ask moonbeams to change how they shined. You just trusted in their light. So long as the man could defend himself, Trystan was satisfied.

…And he was satisfied the man could defend himself.

He was also fairly certain that the "non-lethal" bullets were going to keep Bedivere's accomplices unconscious for a very, very, very long time. Galahad was using *a lot* of sleeping sand in this assault. They might never awaken, which would be no great loss for the world.

The last two men rushed at him and Galahad made a face. "You gonna help me with these guys anytime soon, Trys?"

"No." Trystan shrugged. "I will watch you save me. I find it… stimulating."

Galahad's mouth curved. He spun the gun in his hand and casually shot both men. Not even looking at them. Dead center of their faces. His eyes staying on Trystan's the whole time.

It was so beautiful.

"Let me guess: You are the greatest marksman in Camelot?" Trystan ventured, his thoughts hot and lustful.

"Of course not." Galahad smirked his incredible, wicked, sure-of-himself smirk. "Not to sound arrogant… But I'm the greatest marksman in the world."

Trystan's intention not to have sex with the man "yet" vanished into thin air.

"Yet" was fucking *now*.

His mate truly was the best knight ever. Better than all the other fighters, in all the other lands. Better than the craftiest hired killers money could buy. Better than battle-hardened soldiers who only survived on brute strength. Better than decorated generals commanding vast armies to victory. Better than everyone, Good or Bad.

Nobody could match Galahad of Camelot. …Except maybe Trystan.

His arousal redlined at the thought. Gods, regardless of who won the match, every sparring session they held was going to end in

Trystan ripping the man's clothes off. There wasn't a doubt in his mind. He would never be able to watch Galahad fight and stay in control of his need for long.

Galahad arched a brow, seeing Trystan's smoldering desire. "Give me two minutes." He promised and stalked towards Bedivere, who was still cowering behind Trystan. "Get out here, you little punk."

"Blow me!" Bedivere screamed back, fumbling in his pockets. "I'm not going to fight you! I could *never* win."

Trystan grunted. It was a fair assessment.

"I know that I can't beat you!" Bedivere slammed something sharp into Trystan's arm. "Maybe *you* can beat him, though, gryphon."

A needle.

Trystan made a frustrated sound. Bedivere had just sent more magic coursing through his system. Of *course* he did. Gods, so many of the wingless could just never fight fair. They were always jabbing Trystan with needles, or drugging him, or...

The world spun and Trystan blinked rapidly. It didn't help to fix his vision. Everything was already doubled and getting worse.

"Trys?" Galahad's voice rose in alarm. "Are you alright?"

"I am fine." He said automatically, trying to push through the magic.

"Amnesia potion!" Bedivere crowed. "It didn't work on you, but I'll bet it works on the gryphon. In about two minutes, he'll think he's back in the War." He laughed nastily. "Then we'll see how far your love for the winged-devils really goes."

Shit.

This was an amnesia potion? Trystan's mind frantically worked as the magic began to take hold. If Bedivere was right... If he thought this was still the War... If he did not remember who the knight was to him...

"Trystan will know who I am, even under a spell." Galahad scoffed.

Would he?

Trystan couldn't be sure. The knight seemed unconcerned, even scornful, about Bedivere's plan. But, Trystan was... *scared*. His head was already beginning to fog. He had asked Galahad for trust, but the knight now seemed to be giving him *too much* trust.

"He'll *murder* you, you idiot!" Bedivere shrieked, like he was disappointed in Galahad's calm reaction to his big plan. "He'll only remember that he's a gryphon and you're a knight. Either you'll kill him or he'll kill you. And either way, you'll fail! For once, you'll finally *fail!*"

"Maybe I *will* fail one day. And maybe that'll even be okay, because everyone fails sometimes. ...But, right now," Galahad shrugged, "I'm still on a winning streak, asshole."

Galahad fired the gun directly into Bedivere's chest, the force of it inadvertently knocking the man backwards a step. Bedivere balanced on the cliff's edge for a timeless moment, grasping at air. Then, he tumbled backwards, slamming onto the solid surface of the Looking Glass Pool far below.

"Whoops." Galahad muttered.

Trystan glanced downward and saw Bedivere's carcass lying on the unforgiving silver mirror. Indisputably dead. He'd probably been in a coma from the sleeping sand before he made impact, which was a better end than he'd deserved. The Looking Glass Pool slowly shifted beneath his body, sucking him under like it was devouring him and entombing his corpse forever.

"That wasn't my fault." Galahad defended, like Trystan had been arguing the fact. "That was gravity. It doesn't count as me killing him."

Despite everything, Trystan nearly smiled at that passionate assertion. The knight was coming around to his way of tallying dead bodies. "Fine."

Galahad nodded, taking that as agreement. "So... is that the Looking Glass Pool." He asked, peering over the cliff. "I didn't expect it to look like that. Is it a rabbit hole, do you think?"

"I do not know." And at the moment, he did not care. He was fast losing consciousness, still trying to fight the spell.

Galahad slowly shook his head, still looking down at the pool. "I think it's enspelled water." He decided. "Keeping out people who come looking for the graal for the wrong reasons. I think we could get through it. I think it would let us pass. The gryphons in my head think so, too."

"No! Do not jump into that..." A sudden spasm overtook him and Trystan staggered to his knees. "*P'don.*"

"Trystan!" Galahad rushed to his side, seeing his genuine distress for the first time and forgetting about everything else. "Shit. Don't struggle against the magic, you'll just hurt yourself. Here. Let me help you up."

"No." Trystan tried to push him away, even as he collapsed to the ground. "Leave me in this place." He ordered, weakly. "Hurry. The magic is strong and I cannot risk harming you."

"You would never harm me." Galahad reiterated with total faith. "I'm in your care, remember?" He knelt down beside him, refusing to flee. "You're going to be okay. This spell is a pain in the ass, but it isn't dangerous to either of us. It'll fade. Don't worry."

Trystan was worried. Deeply, frantically worried. Under the very best of circumstances, he wasn't sure that Galahad could defeat him in combat. They were too evenly matched. Under *these* circumstances, though, Trystan was positive that he'd triumph. There wasn't even a doubt. Galahad would let him win, if that's what it took to keep Trystan safe.

"If I think we are back in the War, I will not know any of my emotions for you." He told Galahad, trying to make him see reality. "Whatever it takes, you *must* protect yourself from me. Even if it means killing me, you *must* do it."

"I'm not going to kill you, Trystan. You know that."

He did know it.

Shit.

"And you won't kill me, even if you forget who I am." Galahad soothed, seeing his panic. He ran a hand over Trystan's hair. "You told me that yourself, back in the Fire Cave. You said that even if you'd captured me during the War, you would never have been able to torture me to death. You said you would have met me and been lost."

"That is what I believe, but I cannot take a chance on..."

Galahad cut him off. "It's going to be alright, then. If you're confused for a minute, I'll just reason with you."

Trystan was more horrified than ever. "You will use *reason?*"

"Yeah. Once I talk to you, you'll recognize me." He sounded supremely confident in his plan, as he always did just before disaster struck. "The spell will be broken."

"We do not know how this amnesia potion works. We do not know how deep it might go." Trystan would *never* take such a risk with his *ha'yan's* safety. "You must kill me *now*, before the magic fully takes hold." He meant it with everything inside of him. His body was now too weak to move or he'd have done it himself. "I would always choose your life over mine, Galahad. Always."

"I know you would. But I wouldn't choose that life." Galahad shook his head, his expression resolute and serene. Filled with unbreakable conviction in Trystan's ability to know and protect him, even through a haze of magic. "I wouldn't want a life, at all, without you."

Trystan met Galahad's trusting purple gaze, fear deeper then he'd felt since the zoo chilling him. It was no use. Galahad would never raise a sword against him, no matter what Trystan said or did. Trystan was going to chop the man in half within seconds, the way he had with countless knights during the War, and Galahad would just let him do it.

Trystan was about to murder his own mate.

"At least, shoot me with the sleeping sand gun." He whispered, still trying to get through to him. "Please, knight. I do not care if it sends me into a coma. *Please*. I cannot lose you."

"You won't." Galahad soothed. His lips brushed Trystan's in a reassuring kiss. "I'll think of something to get through to you and fix all of this. I promise. I'm great at improvising."

Lyrssa fucking save them...

And after that, Trystan remembered no more.

***

"Trys?"

A voice filtered through his consciousness. A voice with a wingless accent.

"Trystan, can you hear me?"

Trystan opened his eyes and had no idea where he was. It looked like a basement of some sort. He blinked, pushing himself into a sitting position. How had he gotten here? The last thing he remembered was the Battle of Flags. Yes. That had been yesterday.

Hadn't it?

He held his hands to his temples, trying to think through the pounding in his head. He wasn't sure what was happening. He needed to... Trystan's gaze fell on the knight, sitting a foot away from him. A man with shimmery hair and no wings.

His enemy.

"What the fuck...?" He was on his feet in less than a heartbeat, angry and confused. The gryphon battle mask descended on his face, obscuring his features with the misty profile of an eagle. "Do you think to capture me?" He reached for his axe and found it wasn't there. Why was he unarmed, unless he'd been taken prisoner?

"No." The man held up his palms, slowly getting to his feet. "I just want to talk to you." There was a gun in his hand and the man deliberately tossed it over the edge of the cliff next to them. "I'm Galahad. Do you know me?"

Trystan frowned. This was Galahad of Camelot? Holy *shit*. He'd had no idea his greatest foe on the battlefield was so beautiful. "Yes, I know you." He snapped, irritated that he'd even noticed. "You're the imbecile who let us escape at Flags."

Galahad smiled, as if the answer amused him. The

brightness of it was like moonbeams shining down on a dark night. "That's me." He agreed. "I was demoted for what happened at Flags. That was a long time ago."

"It was yesterday." Why was the man lying?

And why had he tossed the gun away? It shot sleeping sand. Trystan wasn't sure why he knew that, but he knew that. The knight could have used it on Trystan. Why hadn't he?

It had to be a trick.

Suspicious and ready to fight, Trystan grabbed one of the spare swords lying on the floor of the cellar. It had apparently belonged to an immense knight in too-small armor, who was currently sleeping on the ground. Galahad's handiwork. Why had the man incapacitated his own kind?

Not willing to give him the benefit of the doubt, Trystan swung the sword at Galahad, driving him back. "I don't know what you're plotting, but it will not work."

Galahad stepped away, his hands still up. "You always think I'm plotting." He complained, but he didn't try to strike back with a weapon of his own, although a sword was strapped to his back. He also didn't call for reinforcements or try to flee the room. He didn't do *anything* a trained warrior would do. He was just trying to stay alive.

No one ever won a fight by just trying to stay alive. Surely the man knew that.

"You're not going to survive this way." Trystan warned. "I have been planning to kill you for a long time and I will take the opportunity now. Arm yourself."

"No." The knight said calmly.

Did he *want* to die? It made no sense. But then little the man did in combat ever made sense to Trystan. Galahad of Camelot was the only wingless man Trystan had respect for as an opponent. He was unpredictable, but he did not cheat. He won through cunning and skill, not through slaughter. As much as he detested the knight, even Trystan saw his skill as a warrior. He could do far better than this showing, if he tried.

"Fight *back*." Trystan ordered.

The asshole still didn't make a single offensive move. "I'm not going to fight you." He said, half-heartedly dodging a blow. "And you don't want to fight me. You and I are on the same side."

"Bullshit." When had knights and gryphons ever been on the same side?

"It's true." The knight insisted. "Stop for a second and *think*. Try and see through the magic. You know who I *really* am, Trys."

The shortening of his name triggered something in his head. A vision flashed through his mind of this man in firelight. Galahad's hair shimmering gold, and his eyes sparkling blue, and he was laughing at something that Trystan had said. Laughing like he was having a good time, and wanted to be there, and cared for Trystan.

Also, he was naked.

P'don.

Trystan instinctively jerked back on his sword's next swing. The blow went wide. Too wide. Just wide enough that another trained warrior *should* have been able to take advantage of the opening he left. This was the knight's chance to win.

...Except Galahad didn't move.

Trystan stood there, breathing hard, and met the man's violet eyes. In his head, he suddenly heard voices whispering. *Ban's* voice. Clear as it had been the last night he was alive, telling Trystan how to get home.

Purple is the path.

As insane as it was, the tip of Trystan's sword dipped towards the ground.

"Let's look at this reasonably." Galahad suggested, like there wasn't a life-and-death struggle happening between them. Like Trystan hadn't just nearly beheaded him. Like this was all going to be easy to resolve, if they just talked it out and hugged or some shit. "I'm *great* at using reason."

"You are?" He doubted that.

"Not usually, no." The knight said honestly. "But I know it'll work this time."

"Why's that?"

Galahad smiled at him again and it was so... beautiful. "Because I know *you*."

Looking at the knight made Trystan's brain pound in his skull. Why did his head hurt so badly? He pressed a hand to his aching temple again, trying to concentrate through the pain.

"There are three things you need to understand here." Galahad went on, in what must have been his "reasonable" tone. His voice was soothing and soft like he was trying to calm a horse. "One," he held up a finger, "you are under a spell."

"No." Trystan shook his splitting head, instinctively denying it. "No, I am..."

Galahad cut him off. "You think this is still the War. Only the War is over. It has been for a long time. You and I are different people, now."

"*No.*" That wasn't true. He knew it. It couldn't be.

This was all some sort of wingless charade. That was the only explanation. The knight was somehow making images appear in his mind, when they weren't real. If he got rid of the man, they would all go away, and his skull would stop throbbing.

He lifted his sword, again, determined to push through this madness. "If I were you, I would stop talking and start trying to kill me, knight. Because I'm about to kill *you*."

Galahad very slowly reached behind him and pulled the sword from his scabbard. Trystan grunted in satisfaction. Yes. *That* was more like it. Now things would begin to make sense. For a second, the world was right again and the knight held the weapon extended out in front of him. ...Then he dropped it to the ground.

The blade hit the stone floor with a defiant *clang*.

Trystan's mouth parted in shock. "What the hell are you doing?" He blurted out. "We are enemies. You can't just *not* kill your enemies."

"You will *never* be my enemy." Galahad said quietly. "I don't kill anymore. Not ever, again."

Something about that claim was oddly and irritatingly familiar. "What about those guys?" He gestured to the dead bodies around them.

The knight frowned and it was... adorable. Shit. Why was it so adorable? "They're asleep, not dead." He said in an irritatingly adorable tone. "I used sleeping sand."

"They're *permanently* fucking asleep, by the looks of it. That's the same thing."

"No, it's not." Galahad insisted. "Their hearts are still beating. They're alive. Some big, winged jackass told me that's the way it works."

Did the knight mean *him?* Trystan thought maybe he did and it warmed something within his chest.

He made an aggravated sound, unsure if he was angry at himself or Galahad. "You are the best knight ever." He snapped. The words popped into his mind and he knew they were true. "I *know* of your success in battle. I *know* you are a fearsome opponent. What the hell is happening here, that you will not fight me?"

Galahad missed the point. "You think I'm the best knight ever?" He looked genuinely touched. "Thank you, Trys. My God, that is so..."

"Focus!" Trystan jabbed his blade at the man and any normal person would have either run or armed themselves. "You have no choice but to fight me, now."

"Of course I have a choice. I will die right here and right now, before I hurt you. *That's* my choice."

Trystan blinked. "But, I'm going to kill you." He repeated, confused and almost... concerned by the man's refusal to defend himself.

"No, you're not." Galahad said with utter confidence. "You're the *ya'lah*. And I don't think the greatest warrior in the world is going to kill an unarmed man."

Trystan's eyes widened. "I am the *ya'lah*? This is the craziest thing you've claimed yet!" How did the knight even know the term?

"I say you're the *ya'lah*... You say I'm the *ya'lah*... I think maybe neither of us is right, because both of us are right." Galahad shrugged. "I think the graal can only be found by *both* of us. I think we're allies in being the *ya'lah* and *that's* what's going to break Igraine's curse. A gryphon and a knight, working together."

Fisher's words echoed in Trystan's memory. His claim that no one was the *ya'lah*. *"One is not enough. Count higher."*

All these years, Trystan had been thinking about it wrong. That statement wasn't a denial that the *ya'lah* existed, at all. It was a number. "No one" didn't mean not anybody. It meant no singular *ya'lah* was enough for this mission. No *one*. Because there were supposed to be *two*.

He blinked.

"I know you feel the truth of our connection." The knight pressed, looking irritatingly attractive in the blue coat he wore. "That's why you don't really want to kill me."

Trystan tried to concentrate. "Yes, I *really* do." Was the man an idiot? "I just told you I was going to slay you where you stand. Why aren't you picking up your sword?"

"Because, second thing you need to know:" Galahad held up another finger, continuing his countdown of nonsense. "I am crazy in love with you, Trys." He gave a casual sort of shrug. "And you are crazy in love with me."

Trystan stared at him.

"Granted, you haven't exactly said the words to me, yet." The knight went on. "But somewhere inside, you feel it. I know you do, because you're standing there with a sword and I'm still alive. If you *really* wanted me dead, I'd be dead."

Trystan kept staring.

The knight's "reasoning" was insane. ...Except Trystan still wasn't killing him. Why wasn't he killing him? And why did he have to look so appealing when he was wet?

"You're out of your mind." Trystan told him hoarsely.

"Stab me, if I'm so nuts." The knight spread his arms, lavender eyes level. "I'm not going to stop you. Go ahead and do it, if you want."

Trystan's jaw tightened. None of this made a damn bit of sense, and Trystan's head was going to explode, and the knight's face was goddamn perfect, and the dickhead still wasn't picking up his sword. Of everything, his stubborn refusal to protect his own life was pissing Trystan off the most.

He took a threatening step closer to the knight. "If I spare you, it would only to be to torture you for information on your murderous king. You know this, yes? You would do better to fight me now and die standing, before I have you tied up and at my mercy."

"I don't know. Being at your mercy doesn't sound *so* horrible." Galahad mused, unconcerned with the threat. "We can find another cave and you can do all kinds of barbarous things to my willing body. It could be fun."

Another flash in Trystan's head. The knight pressing him to the wall of a cavern, stroking Trystan with his hand in a way that denoted intimacy. Kissing him, as Trystan's seed coated his skin. Unafraid of the possession. Unafraid of *Trystan*.

Trystan couldn't even think through the blinding headache. "I don't... I can't..." He couldn't get the words out. He couldn't even process what words he wanted to say.

"I love you, Trystan. I claimed you. I would die for you, without a second thought."

Another flash. This one of the knight stepping between Trystan and a bullet, shielding him with a saddle, of all crazy things. A memory of sheer terror as he pulled Galahad back, sure he'd been injured. Furious that he'd done something so stupid. Desperate to save him.

The sword fell from Trystan's hand and he barely noticed.

More images played in his head. All of the knight. Times and places that Trystan did not remember. Logic told him it was all a wingless charade and he should just slaughter the man, but something deeper was telling him to stop. He heard voices from both his clans, now. Whispering to him. Trying to protect Trystan from making a catastrophic mistake. Assuring him that his life was linked to Galahad of Camelot, now and forever.

Was he going crazy or was this real?

"Trys, this is just a spell. You can beat it. You can do

anything."

Trystan slowly crouched down, his body wracked with pain. The battle mask faded from his features. As he often did in moments of crisis, he reached into himself, listening for the song his mother sang. Focusing on it, rather than all the distractions in his own mind.

And he slowly felt the truth take hold.

Standing against the knight was... wrong. Doing anything except caring for the blond moron was wrong. A world without Galahad in it would be *wrong*. Trystan's instincts were screaming at him and he trusted his instincts. He trusted the flashes of memory, and the voices of his clans, and the clarity that his mother's song brought him.

Most of all, he trusted the knight.

Galahad's questionable "reasoning" skills *actually* worked. His words *actually* made sense. Trystan *actually* believed him.

He was under a spell.

There was no other explanation. There was some kind of fog in Trystan's head and it wasn't natural. The desire to hurt Galahad was not coming from him. Trystan tried to clear it away, but it was like looking directly into a strobe light. Piercing brightness and then overwhelming darkness, leaving him disoriented. He squeezed his eyes shut, struggling to see reality through the haze in his mind.

"Do you remember me, yet?"

"I don't know." He didn't know anything for sure, except his skull was about to fracture open. And that he still *really* wanted to kill this man. And that he would sooner die himself than kill this man.

"Okay, then the third thing you need to know." The knight went on softly. "I hold Camelot's record for free diving. Over three hundred meters deep. It's how I got the Princess of the Salamanders her ball back, when it fell in that wishing well. I can hold my breath for ages. I don't like to brag, but..." he shrugged, "I'm *really* awesome at it."

Trystan squinted, that bizarre claim cutting through his confusion and misery and pain. "Why do I need to know *that?*"

"I'm about to do some shock therapy and I don't want you to freak out... too much."

Then, the knight smirked at him. A slow, slanty, "gotcha" sort of grin with a hint of Badness, and the gleam of unconventional ideas, and a shit-ton of personal magic. It was clever, and cocky, and utterly beautiful.

Trystan *knew* that smirk. He would know it anywhere, anytime, and through any goddamn spell. There was only one person in the universe who could smile like that:

His fucking lunatic mate.

Galahad.

Trystan drew in a deep breath, his dazed eyes sharpening on Galahad's face. Feelings for the knight swamped him and, for once, he had genuine names for all of them. Passion. Delight. Admiration. Frustration. Amazement. Fury. Amusement. Possession. Tenderness. Need.

Attachment.

Love.

He felt... *love*.

Felt it so deep and so true that he wondered why he'd ever questioned his ability to experience the emotion. It was so clear. The whole world changed around Trystan, like a greasy filter was pulled back, revealing the bright image beneath. Until all he saw was Galahad.

His head tilted to one side, memories coming faster now. This was the man who helped every helpless dimwit he passed on the street. Who'd killed his sadistic king to protect his enemies. Who'd taught Trystan how to kiss. Trystan had claimed this man. For him, there would never be another.

This was Galahad of Camelot and this man was *everything*.

Trystan opened his mouth to say something. Beg forgiveness, or shout at the jackass for risking his life, or express total shock that his "reasoning" skills weren't so terrible after all, or at least utter some halfway intelligent word.

Before he could say any of that, though, Galahad stepped backwards off the edge of the cliff. Freefalling towards the solid surface of the Looking Glass Pool.

...And Trystan's entire existence imploded.

Chapter Thirty-Three

Once the *ya'lah* arrives, can they fix all the evil in the world?

I think it is impossible. None of us can do it alone, even if we are the *ya'lah*. I think that the champions who are born among us are meant to inspire and set things aright. But, not to solve our problems forever.

No, everyone must play a part in writing a better future. That is the story of us all.

How the Wingless War Happened
Skylyn Welkyn- Gryphon Storyteller

Atlantis- Listeneise

Any trace of the amnesia spell that remained in Trystan's head was obliterated in less than a heartbeat. Galahad went over the cliff and Trystan's insides dropped right along with him. It was like a bomb went off at the center of his mind, wiping away everything false in a shockwave of pure, unadulterated panic.

"*NO!*" The bellow came from every piece of him.

Trystan didn't consciously jump over the ledge after Galahad. He was just suddenly in the air. His wings came out to slow his descent, scanning for the place where Galahad landed. Looking for his broken body, desperate to somehow save him.

Instead, he saw one spot in the pool rippling outward in

concentric circles of silver.

Galahad hadn't been smashed to death, like Lamorak and Bedivere. He'd gone right through the Looking Glass Pool's shining barrier and into whatever lay on the other side. The magical pond had opened for him, like a gate with a key.

It had opened for the *ya'lah*.

Trystan plunged after him, not caring that he might crash headfirst into the surface. In his mind, he recited the gryphons' death prayer, because he was about to follow his mate or die trying. Luckily, the Looking Glass Pool let him pass through. The silver surface gave way, as if Trystan was diving into a lake.

The crazy idea of two *ya'lahs* must have been right, because there was not even a moment's resistance to Trystan's entry and then he was suddenly on the other side. At the moment, he didn't care that he'd somehow been chosen as a champion of his people. All he cared about was protecting his *ha'yan*.

The Looking Glass Pool was not a dimensional portal. He deduced that fairly quickly, because rabbit holes were rarely so wet.

Trystan was plunged into a bottomless abyss of freezing water. That was almost worse than being dumped in some other dimension. It wasn't the cursed waves of the Moaning Sea, so he didn't die from touching it, but it was still pretty goddamn cold. Gryphons weren't swimmers, by nature. They were born and bred for the sky. It took Trystan a moment to orient his body and figure out how to keep his wings from drowning him.

P'don.

He hadn't been in water since his grandfather taught him to swim, over thirty years before. It took a long minute for the skill to return to him.

He scanned for the knight, who'd better be alive, because Trystan was plotting to kill him, again. Fully cognizant and free of magic, he was even more pissed than he'd been before. Galahad had just jumped off a cliff as some kind of "shock therapy" to jolt him free of the spell. What the hell was he supposed to do with a man like that?

Fortunately, it wasn't as dark as Trystan would have expected under the water. There seemed to be a light coming from somewhere far below. And in the eerie silver illumination, he saw Galahad swimming beneath him. Swimming, not up towards the oxygen, but *down* towards the weird light.

Yeah. Trystan was definitely going to kill him.

He dove after Galahad, using his wings to push himself

through the water, trying to catch up with him. No small feat, considering the man had been one hundred percent honest about his freediving skills. Trystan's lungs were cramping from a lack of air, while the knight was zipping along like a dolphin. Maybe he'd learned swimming skills from them, when he was "decoding their secret language."

Just as Trystan was convinced that he was going to die forty feet underwater, Galahad vanished from his sight. Just *vanished* right into a hole in the rock wall. It seemed to be where the silver light was coming from. A normal person would have been wary about barging through the glowy opening without knowing what was on the other side.

But Galahad was not a normal person.

Trystan forgot about breathing. Forgot about everything except reaching his lunatic mate. He lunged forward with all his strength, propelling himself straight through the opening, as well.

...And landed in another room.

The hole in the wall led to a completely dry chamber that was thankfully full of oxygen. Trystan collapsed onto the stone floor, soaking wet and wheezing for breath. What the hell just happened? He looked over his shoulder, trying to figure out why he wasn't underwater anymore. The hole must have been protected by magic, because all ten million gallons of the Looking Glass Pool were being held back by some invisible force. It was bizarre. Like looking into an aquarium without glass. The ancient gryphons must have enspelled this entire room and...

Fuck it. Who cared?

He coughed and staggered to his feet, focused on way more important things. "Galahad, I need..."

The knight excitedly cut him off. "You remember me?"

"How could I forget you for long? You're a goddamn maniac." Trystan retorted, pushing his dripping braid back from his shoulder. "But that's not..."

"Yep, that sounds like you, again." Galahad grinned at him, happy and wet, which was *not* helping Trystan calm down. "Hey, guess what? It's not just gryphons who can guide us. I heard your wingless grandfather, while I was up there. He said you absolutely *could* swim, no matter what you said before. So, I knew this plan would work."

Of *course* his grandfather would be with the gryphons. He was part of the Airbourne clan. Trystan was not surprised in the least. "I said gryphons *generally* couldn't swim. Not that *I* couldn't swim. Your grasp of your own language is..."

Galahad wasn't listening. "I wasn't expecting *this* to be here, when I hit the water, though." He swept a hand around, indicating the large room. It was empty, except for benches and a long table and some old pottery strewn around. It seemed to have been some kind of dining hall. "I just saw the light and I thought maybe this is where the graal was hidden."

Trystan gave it all a disinterested glance. No. The graal would not be kept in a place like this. It would be inside the temple. "Knight, focus. I need…"

"But, this seems like a dead end." Galahad went on, looking troubled, now. He scanned around the windowless, doorless, completely unremarkable space. "Do you think the graal is gone? Do you think we're too late? Or that someone else found it?"

"*Knight*."

"I don't even know what the graal is supposed to look like." Galahad ran a hand through his dripping hair and Trystan's whole body throbbed. "In my head, it's a goblet. Right? Maybe one of these broken things is secretly it." He squinted at the shattered earthenware mugs on the ground. "None of them look particularly special, but…"

Trystan grabbed him. His hand fisted around the fabric of Galahad's coat, dragging him backwards. Doing this the civilized way was taking too long. He shoved the man against the nearest wall, nearly out of his mind now. Both palms slammed against the stone wall on either side of Galahad's head and he stared down at him, breathing hard.

"Hey, you look flushed." Galahad could have pushed Trystan away. Anyone else would have at least tried. Instead, he touched Trystan's face, like he was checking for a fever. "You okay?"

His mind and body were both on fire. "Yes." The word was dark and filled with lust.

Galahad didn't seem to notice. "'Yes' you're okay? You sure?"

"Yes, I agree to your proposition. You ask me forty times a day if I'm ready to have sex with you, yet. *Yes.* I'm ready."

The knight's eyebrows soared, suddenly noticing Trystan's out of control desire. Lyrssa, the man's innocence was going to be the death of him one day. "Oh!" He blinked. "Great! Look, I'm all for that idea. But, maybe you should wait until…"

"Now." Trystan interrupted. He borrowed Galahad's words from the beach, trying to express the overwhelming feeling swamping him. "I need you, *now*."

Galahad stared up at him for a beat, finally realizing how far gone he was. "Alright." He agreed and started taking off his coat. "I'm yours. You know that."

Trystan exhaled, pleased by the easy capitulation. It actually calmed him, somewhat. "Three things you need to understand, first." He held up three fingers and Galahad's mouth kicked up at the corners. "One: If I'm ever under another spell and trying to kill you... *fucking defend yourself*. Understand?"

"You weren't going to hurt me, Trys." Galahad leaned forward to kiss the base of his throat and Trystan's eyes drifted shut.

"You have no way of knowing that for certain."

"Sure I do." He grinned. "You're kind of a pushover for me."

That was true.

Trystan grunted. "Point two." He continued in the most serious tone he could muster, under the circumstances. "You *are* the best knight ever."

"Thanks." Galahad was barely listening, all his attention on his shirt. "Shit. One of the buttons is stuck. Just..."

Trystan took hold of his chin and met his eyes, forcing him to pay attention. "You freed the queen of my people, even though she was your enemy. You stood before the Rath to protect children, even though it could have killed you just as easily as them. You struck Uther down, even though it nearly broke you."

Galahad hesitated. "I thought you might be upset about that last part."

"Why in the hell would you think something so stupid?"

The knight's mouth twitched again at the phrasing. "Well, you do go on a lot about loyalty and honor. And I did stab my own king, so..." He trailed off with a shrug.

"I know every warrior's tale there is to tell. And *none* are as heroic as what you did that day." His head tilted. "Have I ever mentioned that I am extremely attracted to heroes?"

Guileless lavender eyes blinked up at Trystan. "Really?"

"*Extremely*." Trystan held his gaze. "So, the next time I try to tell you how to be a warrior, you tell me to shut the hell up. Okay? Because you were born the best."

"You were just lecturing me about fighting you when you're enspelled like fifteen seconds ago."

"Well, that time I was right."

Galahad smiled like he found that answer humorous. "I really am crazy in love with you, Trystan."

"Good." Trystan solved Galahad's button problem by just ripping the wet fabric apart. The stupid buttons went flying. "That brings us to point three: I am your *ha'yan*."

Galahad swallowed. "That's the marriage thing, right? Is this --like-- your version of a proposal?"

"No." His hands went to the knight's belt, because Galahad's eagerness was now making him fumble with the buckle.

Galahad let him yank it free. "No?"

"No, I am not 'proposing' anything. It is *done*." Trystan sank to his knees before him, jerking Galahad's boots off. "I do not need one of your people's hollow mating rituals to give me what I already possess. Even through an amnesia spell, I recognized that you are my mate. Right now and forever."

Galahad bobbed his head, his breath coming in shallow pants. "I know. I've known this whole time. *You're* the one who needed to consider many options."

"You are the *only* option. Everything else is darkness."

"About time you noticed that."

Trystan arched a brow, wanting to be clear. "There will be no others for you. Ever." The knight's pants were yanked off, revealing just what Trystan wanted to see. Galahad's freed erection was already weeping with need. "There will only be *me*."

"Of course only you. God, don't get distracted with hypothetical men, again." Galahad paused for a beat, like he was trying to think. "I want a wedding, though. It's how my people commit themselves to each other."

Trystan rolled his eyes. "You commit yourself to your mate by caring for your mate, and guarding your mate, and pleasing your mate, and working hard for your mate, and being with your mate each day. A ceremony filled with words is pointless."

"Don't worry. I'll talk you into it later." His body was shuddering with need. "Much, much later."

Trystan liked the man's eagerness. His tongue stroked the tip of Galahad's shaft, nearly smiling as the knight's body helplessly jerked.

Now that he considered it, a wedding might not be a *complete* waste of time. The ritual would tie Galahad to Trystan more strongly in the man's own head. In *everyone's* head. The kingdom's laws and customs would say they were mates. All of Camelot would have to agree that Galahad was his. Really, there was no downside to that idea, at all.

"We'll have a ceremony if it makes you feel more secure. And afterwards, you will take the name of my clan." This entire plan was growing on him, by the second. "That's how it typically works in your culture. Yes?"

Galahad's breath was choppy. "Either that or you would take my name. Which would be a title, since I'm a knight. Well, *was* a knight. But, either way, you probably wouldn't want to be 'Trystan of Camelot.'"

Trystan fixed him with a flat look.

Galahad laughed at his expression. The sound was full of happiness. Shit… Trystan would call himself whatever this man asked. Luckily, the knight was already agreeing to exactly what Trystan wanted.

"Galahad Airbourne sounds awesome to me, Trys."

"It sounds 'awesome' to me, too."

"So you're going to marry me, then?"

"Fine." He sealed their deal by sucking Galahad's staff deep into his mouth.

"*Trystan!*" The shout echoed loudly in the room. "Oh God…" Galahad's head went back in bliss. "Oh my *God!*"

No one had ever pleasured him this way before. Even if Trystan hadn't already known that, he would've been able to tell from Galahad's genuine shock and delight. It made him want to make the experience perfect for his mate. When Trystan set his mind to something, no one could best him. His mouth did things that had the knight crying out in pleasure. The torment went on and on, no matter how the other man begged for release. He refused to finish it until he was sure Galahad was his completely.

It was glorious.

Trystan's teeth nipped Galahad's delicate flesh and the knight gave a snarl of passion, realizing that Trystan wasn't going to make this quick. A primitive warning. Trystan *liked* that sound. Warriors took what they wanted, but they also liked to be taken sometimes. He wanted to make Galahad lose all his inhibitions and *take*.

Trystan made his movements slower. Deliberately withholding the friction Galahad needed to come. Enjoying the game.

"Trys?" Galahad's tone was deeper. Right on the edge. "I need it harder. You know I need it harder."

Of course he knew. Trystan looked up at him and arched a brow. It was a dare.

"Are you taunting me?" Galahad's staying power was impressive, but even he had his limits. "Wonderful time for you to develop a sense of humor."

Trystan pulled back a bit. "In your youth, you wanted to be

taken by a gryphon? I wanted to be taken by a hero. Take me like you did in the Fire Cave, only this time harder and come deep in my mouth. This is what we both want, yes?"

Galahad's eyes were glazed. "I'm not totally in control, right now. I'm afraid I will be *too* hard."

"You would never harm me." Trystan said with total surety and went back to his not-quite-strong-enough suckling. "You know, in gryphon culture, when heroes win great victories, they are rewarded with whatever they want." He lapped up a drop of moisture. "Well, you've won today. You saved me from those men."

"You could have beaten them yourself." Galahad was barely hanging on. "Easily. You just wanted to watch me fight, because it turns you on. In fact, I don't think you're "slipping" in your fighting skills, at all. I think you totally tricked me into agreeing to spar with you."

That was true. Trystan shrugged. "You were still victorious." His tongue licked down the entire length of the man. "So, what do you want to take as your prize, knight?"

Galahad snapped. "You." He pushed forward, farther into Trystan's mouth. "I want *you*." It was a groan of surrender and lust. "Now. Take *all* of me. Every inch."

Trystan swallowed, taking him deeper. The knight's hand wrapped around his hair, guiding his movements. Trystan tried to keep his original pace, just to tease him, but Galahad wouldn't let him. His hips pistoned, claiming more and more territory. Trystan's own manhood tightened painfully, turned on by the knight's orders and the sensation of being dominated.

"That's it. God, you're beautiful." Galahad's face was taut as he watched Trystan's lips stretching around him. "If we were living in one of your people's villages, and I'd won some great victory, I could just pick anybody I wanted and they'd agree?"

Of course. So long as they were unmated. It was an honor to be chosen by a hero. To be the one thing he or she wanted after an epic battle. It was how his mother had first taken his father, as a matter of fact. She'd wanted him and she'd been a great warrior. He'd been proud to serve her. Trystan had always aspired to their example.

Trystan glanced up at him and Galahad must have seen the answer in his eyes.

"Damn." His violet gaze glowed even hotter. "I would have been the most victorious son of a bitch in the world, just so I could take you like this, again and again."

Trystan liked that idea. On the occasions where he triumphed, he would choose the knight. And on the occasions when Galahad triumphed, he would choose Trystan. That would pretty much be *all* the occasions, because who else could even compete with them? And after each inevitable victory they achieved, Galahad's body would only respond to Trystan's touch. He would only need Trystan to ease his desire.

Because his heart belonged only to Trystan.

"You are my goddamn soul, Trys." Galahad whispered, as if reading his mind. He gave a rapturous groan, his hand tightening on Trystan's braid, like he was afraid to let him get away. "God, yes... Just like that. Don't stop until I tell you."

It pleased him to push his *ha'yan* beyond his controls. To drive him mad for a bit. To be the one person that he was desperate for. He obligingly allowed Galahad to thrust into his mouth unrestrained, giving him the suction he was demanding, using his hand to help him along.

"*Trystan!*" Galahad bellowed his name as he erupted, still holding his head in place. Not that Trystan was trying to get away. This man's pleasure belonged to him. It was his right to enjoy it.

His mate. Only his.

"Oh shit." Galahad whispered when he was spent. He ran a palm over his face and reality slowly seemed to return. "Shit." He said in a more alert tone and he met Trystan's eyes, looking worried. "Did I hurt you?"

Trystan grinned and rose to his feet. The man was adorable. "No."

"I'm serious." Galahad insisted, scanning him for injuries. "I was too rough. Are you okay? I'm sorry. I just..."

"I am always eager for you." Trystan took hold of his arm, drawing him towards the table. "I asked you to take me and you did. I liked it."

Violet eyes met his, hot and needful. "I think you're right about warriors needing to take and be taken. I like both, too. *A lot*."

"Told you so." Trystan spun Galahad around, gently urging him to bend over the edge of the wooden surface. "Are you now ready to be taken, then?"

"Yes." The answer was immediate.

"Such a Good knight." Trystan pulled off his own clothing, his eyes never leaving Galahad's perfect body. The man was built like a warrior, but he never resisted Trystan's demands. His foot touched the inside of Galahad's ankle, wanting his legs to part. "I was victorious today, too. I will claim my prize. Open for me. I need to be inside of you."

Galahad gave a shuddering breath and complied. He was already hardening, again. "Please." He leaned against the table, always eager even when something was new for him. Always craving Trystan's touch. Always trusting that Trystan would care for him. It was humbling. "Now, Trys."

"Now." Trystan agreed. He had waited long enough to claim his mate.

***

Galahad would never get enough of this man.

"I like that you have no wings." Trystan leaned over him, running a hand down his back and it was like being branded. "I like that I can watch your face as I take you. I like that I can get so close."

"Get closer." Galahad urged. "Get closer, Trys..." He let out a hissing breath as he felt Trystan's massive heat brush is thigh. "Okay." He gave a breathless smile of anticipation. "So, it feels like one *hell* of an adrenaline rush is hitting you."

Trystan laughed. Honest to God *laughed*. "A violet-eyed knight has hit me, like a bat to the head. I cannot think of anything but you." He kissed Galahad's hair, his voice a rumble of sound. "Deflowering you is going to be a fucking joy. We will go slowly, though, yes? I am large and you will be very tight. I must use care, so I do not injure you, as you become mine."

"I'm already yours." He was going to lose his mind if he didn't hurry. "You need to take me, now."

Trystan's mouth was at his ear. "I claim you." He repeated, like he wanted to be sure there could be no going back. "Forever." From somewhere or other, he'd produced a lubricant and spread it on Galahad's flesh. Slick fingers slipped deep within his body, readying him. "Anyone who seeks to take you from me, I will brutally kill and then burn their corpses as a warning to others."

The man said the sweetest things.

Galahad ground his teeth together, struggling to hold on. Trystan's possessive words were like kerosene on an already raging fire. The erotic touch, and his surety in their connection, and the submissive position he was laying in. It was too much. "Please..." He ground out.

"This is *ha'na*." Trystan went on, his tone rough with desire. He continued to work, stretching Galahad's flesh until he was satisfied.

Then, his fingers moved away and his erection was right at the entrance to Galahad's body. "I see the bond whenever I look at you. I see my future and it is *you*. You will know this too and tell me so. *Now*."

"I know it, too." Galahad reached back to hook a hand behind Trystan's head, pulling him in for a kiss. "I love you, Trystan."

Trystan surged forward.

Galahad let out a roar of approval, his palms coming down to grip the edge of the table. It was better then he'd thought it would be. *More*. Pieces of him fit against pieces of Trystan like they were meant to go together. Of course they did.

The man was his True Love.

Above him Trystan had gone still, breathing hard.

Galahad turned his head to look at him. "You feel it, too." It wasn't a question. He could already tell.

"I feel it." It was a whisper of reverence. "You're my True Love."

Good folk always felt the True Love bond when they slept with their other half for the first time. Even some gryphons apparently, at least when they had wingless blood. Trystan had finally realized the bond was there and he seemed shocked. The man was adorable.

Galahad found himself grinning. "Surprise!" He got out, happier than he'd ever been.

"You knew this?" Trystan demanded, his breath coming in pants.

"Of course." Galahad's body rocked against his, needing Trystan to fill him completely. "I'm not as Good as you are. I felt the connection, even though I couldn't explain it. I've been crazy about you since the second I saw you coming through the smoke to rescue me. It *had* to be True Love."

"And you didn't announce this theory, right away?" Trystan was arrogantly amused.

"Would you have believed me?"

"By the time we left Ayren's village, I would have believed it." Trystan began to move within him, claiming territory no one else had ever touched. "I believe everything you tell me. Even the things that are impossible."

Galahad groaned, thrusting backwards, wanting even more.

"Slowly." Trystan ground out like he was in pain. "Give it a moment. Allow your body to adjust to me." He eased in another few inches, stretching Galahad's flesh. "Gods, you're so *tight*..."

The invasion was relentless and all-consuming. Galahad let Trystan set the pace, but it was hard not to instinctively rock beneath him and hurry things along. The need was building to unbearable levels.

"That's it." Trystan's hand ran over Galahad's hair, fingers tangling in the blond curls. "Nice and slow. I will take care of you. I promise."

"Please, Trys. I need all of you."

"All of me is yours." Trystan kept talking, like he wanted to soothe Galahad, even as he pushed in deeper and deeper. "It must have been torturous for you to stay quiet about our bond, knight, given how difficult it is for you to play hard-to-get. I would expect you to proclaim you were my destined mate, as soon as you bid me 'hello.'"

"It took me a while to be certain..." Galahad swallowed, trying to focus through the incredible sensation of Trystan's thick girth inside of him. "And then I thought... Maybe you wouldn't feel it back."

"How could I not feel it? It's everywhere. Everything."

"Or at least... resist the idea, then. I thought I'd... let you figure it out for yourself."

"And I *have* figured it out, *ha'yan*."

Galahad gave a gasp as Trystan sank in as far as he could go, filling him completely. He was so big. So hot. He felt so good. Galahad made a broken sound of need, so close to the edge he could see it shimmering before him.

"Fuck yes." Trystan muttered in lustful satisfaction, holding himself still as if he was reveling in his complete possession. "Like you were made for me."

He *had* been made for him.

Trystan's beautiful wings came forward, brushing Galahad's arms. Trystan instinctively wanting to shield him from the world. "I like that you have wings." Galahad breathed, turning around Trystan's earlier compliment. "I like when they touch me. I feel safe."

Teeth grazed the back of his neck in a small show of dominance and Galahad shivered. "You are safe." It was a vow. "You are in my care. Always."

"I know. And you're in my care."

"I know." Trystan kissed his shoulder, right where he'd bitten him. "You are tight and warm and welcoming, knight. Just as I knew you would be." Hands ran over his body, touching him. "I didn't know of our True Love bond, when we first met. But I knew that I felt a need for you that was beyond anything I've ever experienced. I looked at you and I was... lost."

"I love you." Galahad whispered, his mind a fog of need and pleasure and sensation. It was the very heart of him and the only thing he could concentrate on long enough to say. "I love you, Trys."

Trystan's palm came around to stroke him in time with his thrusts. "I like it when you pledge yourself to me in the words of your people." His voice was intent now, his body more demanding. "I like it *a lot.* You will say it often. Understand?"

"Yes." Galahad bobbed his head. That was seriously not going to be a problem.

"You will tell me again, now." Trystan did something miraculous with his hand. "Right now, *ha'yan*."

"I love you." Galahad was going to come. He couldn't stop it. "I love you, Trystan. I love you *so much*." He exploded, chanting Trystan's name and words of soul-deep devotion.

Trystan liked that.

He found his own release with a series of hard thrusts that ended in a roar that shook the room. "*Galahad!*" He shuddered for an endless moment in triumphant possession. Then, his drained body collapsed against Galahad, like all the strength had left it. "My gods..." His lips brushed the nape of his neck. "You truly are everything."

Galahad smiled, out of breath and energized. "You still feel 'attached' to me?"

Trystan's fingers moved to caress Galahad's hair, not wanting to break contact. "The emotion is called 'love.'" He murmured, as if awed by the whole experience. "I have finally defined it."

"See? I knew you'd figure it out."

"It was not difficult. Uther locked me in a prison for three years and I didn't break, but I would die begging on my knees before I lost you. This fact drastically narrowed the field of possible emotions." Trystan snorted, sounding more like his normal self. "In fact, my love for you is so obvious that I should not even have to say it aloud. You know how I feel. *Everyone* knows it."

"I do know it." Galahad shifted beneath Trystan, so they were face-to-face. "But, say the words, anyway."

Trystan's mouth curved. "I love you, Galahad." His hand cupped his cheek. "You are my light."

"Good." Galahad leaned up to give him a smacking kiss. "I love you, too." He paused for a beat. "Hey, who do you think invented sex?" He asked randomly. "Like the first person who had the idea? How did the conversation go, when they tried to talk someone else into it?"

Trystan laughed again and the sound was beautiful. He rested his forehead against Galahad's, letting out a contented sigh. "I think some crazy, artistic virgin got the idea." He theorized. "And I think it was *very easy* for him to convince his mate that the plan was the height of creative genius."

"Oh, it wasn't that easy to convince you. Trust me."

Trystan looked smug and tender, at the same time. "I apologize for the hold up. It was a doomed and very stupid choice on my part to try and resist your seduction."

"No kidding."

"But, I thought perhaps you had some wingless True Love, waiting for you." Trystan ran a thumb down the center of Galahad's face. "I did not wish to give you a reason to reject me for him, if we had sex and you did not feel a connection."

"The connection between us is because you're *Trystan*. I would always feel it. Even if you weren't my True Love, I would claim you over all other men."

"This is pleasant to hear." Trystan arched a brow. "It would *also* have been pleasant to hear it a week ago."

"Is this why you kept harping on imaginary guys? Because you thought I might one day want someone else?" Galahad chuckled at the idea of another man even comparing to this one. "Jesus, you *never* have to worry about that, Trys. I have my hands on a hero and I'm keeping him."

"Gryphons do not often worry. Only when the moonlit creatures we need to survive threaten to slip away."

"I need you to survive, too, so I'm not going anywhere." He smirked. "I built a working satellite for my sophomore science fair project, by the way. It's still the foundation of Camelot's telecommunications network. Pretty sure I can figure out a way to track you down, if you ever change your mind and decide to wander off to kill people without me. Just saying."

"I am pleased with my hero, as well." Trystan gave him a kiss. "I have no intention of wandering anywhere without you."

"Good thinking." Galahad grinned at him. "So, wanna have sex, again?" He asked eagerly. "I can do it even better next time."

"You will kill me, if you do it any better." Trystan reluctantly straightened up. "But… yes. I do wish to do that, again. Give me a chance to find a way out of here and then we will go test how long I survive your insatiable appetite."

"We can swim out, just like we came in." Galahad dragged his clothes back on and hoisted himself up to sit on the edge of the table. "But we can't just *leave*, Trys. Not yet."

"Why, you wish to honeymoon here?" He scoffed. "No. I fully intend to take you in a bed, next time. This is the care that any proper *ha'yan* would show their new mate."

"You have shown me *excellent* care." Galahad's shirt no longer had buttons, so he left it hanging open. "As your new mate, I am very satisfied having sex with you lots of places."

Trystan grunted and pulled his pants back on. "Good, because you will be having sex with me in lots of places."

"But we can't leave, yet." Galahad went on. "We have to try pushing on all the stones in the wall to see if there's a secret passage or something."

"Why in the hell would we do that?"

"Because this room is what the Looking Glass Pool was shielding. Why would it be doing that, if there wasn't something valuable down here? The gryphons built a whole temple around it."

"This stone building is not the temple." Trystan scoffed. "Listeneise is a covering intended to *guard* the temple."

Galahad blinked. "What?"

"All of this?" He gestured around to indicate the entirety of the crumbling edifice. "Is not what we are searching for, knight. This is just the shell. The graal would be in our most sacred space. Inside the temple itself. At the core of gryphon culture. *That* is what we must find. The heart."

"So... this isn't really the temple?" Galahad repeated blankly. "Even though you said it *was* the temple."

"I do not recall saying such a thing. Why would I say such a thing? It isn't true."

"You definitely said Listeneise was the temple, Trys!"

"I said the temple was *in* Listeneise. Not that the temple *was* Listeneise." Trystan rolled his eyes skyward. "You do not listen. That is the issue..." He stopped his lecture on Galahad's inability to pay attention, his focus suddenly fixed on the ceiling.

"What?" Galahad automatically looked up, too. "You see something?"

"The mural on the wall of the Corbenic Fire Cave... The maze of rooms that Fisher drew." Trystan kept his gaze on the roof. "The last step in the graal journey was depicted as *upward*."

Galahad hopped down off the table and hurried over to join him. "Fisher never got this far. You said he didn't even try to go through the Looking Glass Pool."

"Fisher heard my ancestors, when he found this place. He

knew what was down here." Trystan's head tilted, his gaze scanning every crack in the ceiling. "Hold onto me."

Galahad wrapped his arms around Trystan, excitement filling him. "You think it's up there?"

"I think if it is, we will both need to be present to reach it."

"Two *ya'lahs*." Galahad agreed. "A gryphon and a knight needed to come together to complete this mission. That's destiny, Trys. You see that, right?"

"Either that or we are about to crash our skulls into stone blocks." Trystan flew them up towards the ceiling.

Flew them *through* the ceiling.

What looked like stone blocks was really just air disguised with a glamor. It had been put in place to hide a circular room with a domed roof and a low stone altar made of coral.

Galahad's lips parted in wonder. Trystan was wrong to think that all gryphons hated art. Every surface of the rounded space was covered in a painting of sky. White clouds and a brilliant blue expanse, and small, flying figures soaring free.

The ancient power of the place made the hairs on the back of his neck stand up.

Trystan landed them on a small ledge, a mesmerized expression on his face. "*This* is the first gryphon temple." He whispered. "We found it."

Galahad nodded, feeling the energy all around him. It felt like thousands of years of prayers had soaked into the walls. This whole mission was like nesting dolls. Find Atlantis, to find Listeneise, to find the Looking Glass Pool, to find the temple, to find the graal. He hadn't understood that when he began, but now it was so clear. Like with any worthwhile venture, you had to keep digging until you saw... *everything*. You had to look past your preconceptions and prejudices, if you wanted to see the treasure that was hidden deep inside. At the very heart.

"Do you hear the voices, knight? Do you hear them, too?"

"I hear them."

The voices were singing. Hundreds of them, all overlapping each other.

"My mother used to sing me this song." Trystan swallowed hard. "When I heard you whistling it at the hotel in Ted-ville, I knew it was a sign. I knew you must be able to hear my ancestors." He gave his head a dazed shake. "I felt the shadow of fate, as I always do when I look at you, and I knew you were given into my care for a great purpose."

"I think the same thing about you, Trys. That you're a gift. The very heart of me."

Trystan kissed his forehead. "I claim you again, here in the oldest site of my people. Now and for all time, Galahad Airbourne. Never leave me. I would be lost." He gave a wry paused. "...And I would track you down, too."

"Yeah?"

"Yeah. Unlike you, though, I would not need a satellite to accomplish my search. I can easily locate you, wherever you are. I just follow my path."

"I like being found by you." Galahad teased in a quiet tone. The holiness of the room made you want to speak in a respectfully lowered voice, even when you were flirting with your fiancé. "Hey, what's that thing over there? It looks like a soap bubble."

Trystan's head snapped around. "A bubble?"

"Yeah." Galahad gestured to the coral alter and the iridescent orb sitting on its rough top. It was about the size of a bowling ball and appeared to be made of very old glass, a rainbow of colors dancing across its surface, even in the dim light. "See?"

Trystan gave a low chuckle, his gaze falling on the shiny orb. "*That* is the big glass bubble that Avalon's been nagging me to find."

"Avi told you to find that ball?" Galahad's eyebrows climbed.

"Yes. She asked me to bring it back to her." Trystan explained quietly. "She told me to bring *you* back, too. To be nice to you. That I would love you." He lifted a shoulder. "The child is always right."

Galahad beamed at him. "So, all those times you complained at me, and tied me to stuff, and threatened to feed me to tigers you were being *nice*?"

"Of course. Even when I did not have the word for the true feeling, I wished for you to become as *attached* to me as I was to you. I have therefore been on my best behavior, since we met. How is that not obvious?"

"Fine." Galahad shook his head in amused exasperation, borrowing Trystan's favorite word. "Well, if Avi sent you after me and that bubble, you know what it means, don't you?"

"It means she knew you were my True Love. My heart, and my future, and my dream. So I probably shouldn't strangle you, no matter how irritating you became."

"And?" Galahad prompted, his eyes shining.

A victorious smirk played around the corners of Trystan's mouth, his gaze flicking back to the magical orb. "And it means we just found the graal."

Epilogue

So, this is my final broadcast.

It turns out that this podcast only has twenty-six subscribers.

I guess no one else cares about the gryphon menace, these days.

I guess everyone just wants to move on from the Looking Glass Campaigns and live in peace, now.

What a crazy goddamn idea...

"Stopping the Savages" Podcast
Sir Dragonet of Camelot- Former Troubadour of King Uther and Host of the Program

Camelot

Three Months Later

"There's no way we're filming this." Galahad took a red pen and crossed out the whole page. "You kill seven pig-guys in the first paragraph! Parents' groups will be writing us hate mail for months."

"Those pigs in Wilbur's village were all terrible people. Their deaths will teach an important lesson to children, about not being assholes." Trystan frowned down at his own copy of the script. "Certainly, more valuable than this shit you've added to the scene where Medusa's tomb collapses. You describe every single rock in those cairns for pages on end."

Galahad's head snapped up. "Oh no, we need that part. Rocks are super interesting." He'd studied them extensively, when he'd created a machine to stop earthquakes. "One of the reasons I've always wanted to go to the moon, is to collect some cool space rocks."

Trystan fixed him with an exasperated look. "We're not going to the moon, Galahad."

"Well, no. Of course not!" He paused. "...Not right *now*."

Trystan sighed loudly and ate some more caramel-and-whey Pop-Chocolate.

The chocolate and popcorn snack was just as delicious as Galahad had imagined it would be. At least, in its original formula. Its success had led to new flavors being developed, including the disgusting caramel-and-whey version that Trystan couldn't get enough of. As much as he loved the man, Galahad was baffled by his lack of good judgement sometimes.

"I like rocks." Avi piped up from the third seat at the table. She couldn't actually read the script for the pilot episode of Galahad and Trystan's new TV show, because she was too young to read. Instead, she was drawing pictures of rocking-horseflies all over her copy. "They's pretty."

The three of them were sitting in the courtyard of Camelot's Palace, shaded by a large umbrella and drinking lemonade. Everyone agreed that the small picnic area was much more useful than Bedivere's hideous statue had been.

Galahad looked at Trystan. "See? Avi likes rocks."

"I like pig fighting, too." Avalon continued cheerily. "They both is fun."

Galahad frowned.

Trystan arched a brow at her. "This is why you are here, Avi. To force the knight to compromise with my superior taste. That is what it means to have a true partnership, yes?"

Galahad wouldn't have phrased it quite that way, but he supposed Trystan had a point. That *was* the moral of the new show they were creating, after all. Kind of. The idea was to adapt bits and pieces of their actual lives into a children's program, featuring a knight and a gryphon learning to be allies. All the proceeds would go to rebuilding Lyonesse.

Galahad's goal was to show that the War really was over forever. To model to children that it was okay to be friends with people, who were once your enemies. To show that each culture was special and deserving of respect. To teach love, and compassion, and forgiveness, and maybe a little something about interesting rocks.

Trystan's goal was to drill kids on battle tactics.

Between the two of them, Galahad was pretty sure they were going to wind up with a program approaching art. How could it be anything else? Every word of it would be true.

He nodded at Trystan. "Okay. You can wound some pigs. You can't chop them into bacon, though. And, as a compromise, I'll only talk about rocks for two minutes. Three max."

Trystan grunted. "Fine." Galahad could translate all the man's "fines" now and that one indicated contented agreement.

"We have to add some puppets, though." Galahad tacked on, because every show needed a few puppets.

"Lyrssa save me..." Trystan shook his head, not even bothering to argue.

Galahad smiled at him. The man truly was an angel.

Across the courtyard, Amelia, the ogre girl, was practicing her sword-handling techniques against a straw dummy. Trystan was teaching her fighting skills and the child was dedicated to memorizing every word he said. Living in Camelot's palace had done wonders for Amelia. Her blue fur was healthy and combed. Her eyes shone brightly. She was eating well, and sleeping safely in her bed, and always had a thousand questions about everything around her.

Soon she would be ready to go to school. Amelia no longer wanted to be a great highwaywoman. Now, she wanted to be a knight. Luckily, the new and improved Knights' Academy would be opening again in the fall and she would be one of the first students admitted. If that was her dream, Galahad would make sure she reached it.

As Trystan always said: Without dreams people became ghosts.

"While we're making changes, I want to rewrite part of the Knights' Code." Galahad decided. "It really should be, 'Knights protect those weaker than *themselves*.'" He glanced at Avi. "That's way more inclusive. *Everyone* can be a knight, right?"

She nodded happily.

Trystan reached over and ruffled her hair. He was so wonderful with children and there were so many orphans from the War who needed a loving home. When was the curse on the gryphons going to be lifted? It had been months since they found the graal and there was still no sign of Lyrssa. Avi assured them that the queen was on her way, but Galahad was beginning to wonder if he should do something to hurry her along.

The next day, he and Trystan were getting married. Gwen and Galahad had planned the whole wedding, given Trystan's tendency to scare away all the vendors. (The caterer was going to need therapy after Trystan's insistence on ordering leprechaun hors d'oeuvres.) Still, the reception would be pretty damn awesome, if Galahad did say so himself. After the wedding, though, he was really going to hone in on making sure the gryphons' future was assured, even if it took another mission or two.

"Trystan!" Gwen shouted, marching across the lawn towards them. "Your wedding guests just set the royal portrait gallery on fire. All the paintings of Camelot's former kings are now ash."

Trystan gave an unconcerned shrug. "Caelia is not a fan of Camelot's former kings or of art. It was only to be expected."

Gwen crossed her arms over her chest. "She set the pictures on fire while they were still hanging on the wall. Half the castle could have gone up."

"Caelia does not like castles, either. That is why I upgraded the sprinkler system before she arrived. Do not worry, *j'aha*."

"Queens don't worry." Gwen mocked and arched a brow at him. "That's what we have our brothers for."

Trystan was the world's most impressive sigher and he liked to regularly demonstrate it. "Fine. I will speak to the Redcrosse Clan. If I am murdered the day before my wedding, though, it will be on your head."

"I'll take my chances." Gwen sat on the arm of Galahad's chair and ate some of Trystan's Pop-Chocolate. "So what are you doing out here, when you're *supposed* to be finalizing the seating charts? Still arguing over your new show?"

"Trystan wants to kill all the other characters." Galahad told her, continually thrilled to be reunited with his family. "I've just talked him out of it."

"The knight wishes to dedicate the show to rock-hunting." Trystan retorted. "I have just talked *him* out of it."

"I'm sure Avi talked you *both* out of it." Gwen winked over at her daughter. "And whatever program you two come up with, it *has* to be better than that God-awful reality show you talked Midas into airing on his TV network." She wrinkled her nose. "For real. *Inside St. Ives* is utter trash."

"It's the highest rated show on TV." Galahad defended, although she had a small point about its overall quality. The program was nothing but naked bungee jumping with Eric, Konrad touring endless sleazy bars, and the Galahad-duplicates trying to turn their former strip club into a modeling agency. "Everyone loves Mordy." He was the host.

"I don't love Mordy." Trystan and Gwen chorused. The two of them were usually in synch.

Galahad tried a diversion. "Hey... Since marbles are glass and not marble, why do you think they're called marbles?" He asked, partly to distract them and partly because it was an interesting question.

"I imagine because the game was played with small rocks, before they invented the glass toys." Trystan guessed without missing a beat. He always followed along when Galahad's mind wandered now, rarely even blinking at the strange tangents.

Galahad made an "ummm" sound of thought. "Yeah, that makes sense."

"Focus." Trystan urged, eager to quickly return to the topic of murdering people who annoyed him. "I know you feel some *kindness* towards Mordy, as you do towards all pitiful idiots. But the man is a stalking menace, who is lucky he still breathes."

"Agreed." Gwen chimed in. "I can't *believe* you invited him to the wedding, Gal. He'll probably try to kidnap you, again."

"He never tried to kidnap me..."

Trystan cut him off. "Mordy's coming to my wedding?!" He repeated in outrage, sitting up straighter in his chair. "When the fuck did *that* happen?"

"Cursing is a no-no." Avi interjected, still coloring all over the script pages. It looked like she was drawing bubbles, now.

"Sorry." Trystan muttered, his gaze still on Galahad. "When the *heck* did we agree to invite that dickhead?"

Gwen made a face, unimpressed at his efforts to clean up his language.

"This wedding is *so* important to Mordy." Galahad nodded earnestly. "He feels like he helped bring us together. I think it would have broken his heart to be excluded, Trys."

"This is how you rationalized inviting half of Ted-ville. I am already building them a factory and tomorrow I must feed them cake, as well. And now *Mordy* is coming?"

"He's going to do a very special episode on our wedding." Galahad defended. "He has it all planned. He won't get in the way. I promise."

Trystan made an aggravated sound. "Fine." He jabbed a finger at Galahad. "But, he did *not* help bring us together. He gets no credit for the fact that I looked at you and was lost. It was all me being a pushover for crazy ideas and violet eyes."

"That *is* pretty much how it happened." Galahad agreed cheerfully. "You were head-over-heals 'attached' to me, right from the get go."

Trystan's mouth curved. "Yes." He murmured. "That is pretty much how it happened."

"Hey, *I'm* the real matchmaker here." Gwen declared, eating more Pop-Chocolate. "It was my idea to send Trystan after you, Gal." She glanced at Trystan. "Speaking of which, we still need to find that wicked witch who got lost in the rabbit hole. Midas made a deal with her family. You can look for her next, since you're so amazing at tracking people down." She paused. "…But you don't have to marry her, at the end."

Trystan fixed her with a put upon look.

Galahad laughed, loving his life and the people in it.

"Uh… Galahad?" Midas came up to them, walking very slowly across the lawn. The graal was carefully balanced in his hands, like he was afraid he might drop it. "I looked up and this thing was blinking. Is it supposed to be blinking?"

Sure enough, the glass orb seemed to be slowly shifting colors. Pink, green, blue, red… one after another in a never-ending rainbow of lights.

Trystan and Galahad exchanged a quick look, rising to their feet. They had carried the graal all the way back to Camelot and it had never blinked. It was as if it had somehow been activated, now. That was Good, right?

Yeah. That was Good. Galahad could feel it.

Trystan wasn't nearly so optimistic. Huge surprise. "Midas, put it down." He warned, moving towards his brother. "If it explodes or releases some toxic substance, I do not want you harmed."

"Why would it explode and release a toxic substance?" Midas demanded. "Shit, you brought this thing home and it might release a *toxic substance?* We've been keeping it on the goddamn mantle, Trystan!"

"I'm not sure what it does!" Trystan roared back, snatching the graal away from him. "Which is why I don't want you touching it. Especially, when it begins blinking for gods-only-knows what reason."

"So much cursing." Avi lamented, setting down her crayons. "I'm going to tell Lyrssa as soon as she gets…." She stopped short and glanced towards the sky. "Yay! She is coming, now!"

All four adults looked up.

A gryphon was flying above them, with massive wings and a

patch covering her eye. Galahad recognized her instantly. There was only one person in the world who looked like the gryphon queen. His mouth curved.

Gwen and Midas seemed astonished.

"My gods..." Trystan breathed in awe.

"Hi, Lyrssa! Hi, Lyrssa!" Avalon ran right to her as she landed in the courtyard, throwing her arms around Lyrssa's waist. "I'm Avi! I saw-ed you in my head!" She lowered her voice to a dramatic whisper. "Guess what? Daddy and Trystan was cursing before. But, I told them to stop and they did, so it's okay."

The Queen of the Gryphon ran her thumb down the center of Avalon's face. "I've seen you, too, child." She murmured. "You could never be mistaken for another. My ancestors say you will one day light the future for us all."

"Yeah, the gone-away gryphons like me a lot." Avi beamed at her. "Everybody likes me!"

Lyrssa came as close as most gryphons could get to smiling. "I am unsurprised. Corrah Skycast would have only the best for a granddaughter." Her eyes flicked over to Midas. "And a son. The Skycast Clan ruled with strong principles and kindness. You are living up to your mother's example, yes?"

Midas still looked stunned. "Corrah was the very best." He said quietly. "I always try to make her proud."

Gwen's hand slipped into his, squeezing tight.

Lyrssa seemed to appreciate the answer. Her one-eyed gaze flicked over to Galahad. "Hello again, knight. You look much improved."

"My *ha'yan* has helped me find the light, again." Galahad told her in the gryphon dialect. He was now fluent at the language, even though Trystan continued to nitpick the exact definitions of words. He did that with *all* languages, though, so Galahad wasn't discouraged. He inclined his head at Lyrssa. "You look well, too, your majesty. It appears we have both reached a better world."

"At last we have." She agreed. "This is your mate, yes?" She looked at Trystan. "I am pleased you claimed this knight. His path is a bright one. And the Airbourne Clan should not end. There is so much more for you to do."

Trystan seemed to rouse himself from his shock. "Where the hell have you been?" He demanded, in a typical show of tact. He'd never even met the queen before, but that wasn't stopping him from expressing his displeasure. The more Trystan got in touch with his emotions, the more everyone got to hear about them. "The whole world thinks you're dead, Lyrssa. Why did you allow that? Our people needed you *here*."

Midas winced a bit at his tone.

Gwen nodded like Trystan was making some great points.

Avi went happily skipping over to play with Amelia.

Galahad kept right on smiling. "We're getting married tomorrow." He told Lyrssa calmly. "Would you like to come?"

"Yes." Lyrssa decided, but she kept her gaze on Trystan. "I saw the path the knight would take. I knew there would need to be two *ya'lahs* to find the graal. I am not even one. I had to wait."

"And what? Vacation for five years?"

"Gryphons do not take vacations." She waved a dismissive hand, missing the sarcasm. "No, I was hunting for Mount Feather. Where the clans of old still survive."

Trystan hesitated. "You found Mount Feather?"

"I found it." She repeated, her eyes bright. "I found more of our people, Trystan Airbourne. The old clans. Enough gryphons that we can start a new chapter. Tell a new story." She nodded towards the graal in his hand. "And with *that* to heal the curse, we can finally begin again."

"I hope so." Trystan forgot about being angry and handed her the blinking orb. "But, this is my home and I do not wish to leave. Not even to reside on Mount Feather, with the other gryphons. I will stay with my clan." He gestured to the people in the courtyard. "Always."

Gwen beamed up at him. "*Finally*, you see reason."

Midas clapped a hand on Galahad's shoulder. "Thank you." He said quietly, crediting him with convincing Trystan to give up on his revenge mission.

Galahad smiled at him. "It was Trystan's decision. Without him micromanaging our lives, he thinks we'll all die following breadcrumb trails into evil forests."

"You will." Trystan grunted.

"I do not blame you for choosing this path." Lyrssa told Trystan sincerely. "Many gryphons live with the wingless, now. Many will wish to stay, I'm sure. That is a Good thing for our race. For *all* races. Knowing each other better and learning from one another will make us less likely to war again in the future." She held the graal over her head and closed her eyes for a beat. "And *all* of us deserve a future."

Lyrssa dropped the graal.

Galahad cringed as the ancient glass shattered on the

flagstones. For a second nothing happened and he wondered if they'd screwed something up. Then iridescent bubbles began to rise upward. Millions of them. Small and powerful. Twirling around Lyrssa. Curing her of Igraine's spell. Carried on the wind, the bubbles then drifted outward. Shimmering in the air.

Spreading their healing magic everywhere.

Beside him, Trystan drew in a deep breath. "You did it, knight." He looked down at Galahad, in something like reverence. "I felt it. Your mission has lifted the curse."

"It really wasn't me who..." Galahad began.

"Did you see what he did?" Trystan interrupted, looking over at Lyrssa with pride. "Do you see what my mate accomplished? No one else could have completed this mission. No one else had the heart and the strength and the *ideas* to carry it off. Just Galahad Airbourne. When you tell the others this tale, you remember to credit him as the best knight ever, yes?"

"We did all this together, Trys." Galahad put in, honestly. "It'll be a great last episode for the show, right?"

Lyrssa flexed her hands like she could feel the graal's energy cleansing her whole system. "Both of you have done much to help the world. And you will do much more. I see that path stretching far into the future. Your children will be warriors."

"And artists." Galahad stipulated.

He knew now that he had the strength inside of himself to keep the darkness at bay. But he still didn't want to focus on battles. There were too many other beautiful things in the world.

Galahad was sparring with Trystan each day and it was easing his phobia about swords. Holding one wasn't nearly as traumatic as it had once been. Psychologically speaking, it helped that after every sparring session Trystan made love to him. A lot. Often, he took Galahad in the shower, his hands running all over his wet body, murmuring words of love and praise, and licking the water from his skin. It was hard to feel anything but *awesome* after that.

Sometimes Trystan won the sparring match. Sometimes Galahad won the sparring match. But in the end they *both* won.

"All Airbournes are artists." Trystan told Lyrssa, like it was common knowledge. "It is a rule of our clan."

"It is?" Galahad arched an amused brow at that confident assertion. "Since when?"

"Since I realized that only artists can combine reason and imagination to make impossible things into reality. This is a great skill. It is why Airbournes are the best at all we attempt." He leaned down to kiss Galahad with satisfied possession. "You are right. We *must* build an art school, knight. Children of all races would only benefit from these ideas."

Galahad leaned against his mate, happy and safe in his care. "Told you so."

Author's Note

If you were one of the people who wrote me and asked if Trystan and Galahad were going to get a story and I responded with something like, "I think it's a really cool idea and I do have stuff in the *Kingpin of Camelot* that supports it, but I'm not sure yet who their True Loves are" rest assured I was not lying to you. I never have any idea what a book will be until it's published. Until the very last second, I am making changes and deciding whether or not to even publish. This is because I am picky about an idea being right and also because sometimes what I *think* is right just doesn't work out.

Case in point: Why are Nia and Sullivan not a couple in the Elemental-Phases series? I planned for them to be. I had thousands of words of a book starring them completed. And yet, I could tell it was wrong as the book progressed. So I scrapped it and started over with *Warrior of the Shadowlands*. I don't regret that, at all. Sometimes, you have to wait and see what the characters want to do, before you can be sure of a concept. So I try not to be definite in any of my answers to you, until I am definite myself. And I am rarely definite about anything until I stand back and look at the finished product.

Galahad himself was not a character I was a hundred percent definite on, when he first appeared. I needed another contender for Avi's father in *The Kingpin of Camelot*, so the book had some tension. Galahad started out as a necessity of the plot to annoy Midas and keep the story moving. I had no real plans for him, beyond that. Quickly, though, he became more interesting to me, as Gwen began listing all his insane achievements. He wasn't even in the book, except for flashbacks, and I still saw him so clearly as a character. By the end of that novel, I knew I wanted him to have his own happily-ever-after.

When you are setting out to write a story featuring well-known fairytale or fantasy characters, I recommend looking at the source material for your initial inspiration. It wouldn't make any sense to me if I used famous characters in my stories, only to take away the stuff that made them that famous character to begin with. To me, the important characteristics about Galahad needed to be included or he would just be a generic knight.

Luckily, I had centuries of source material, as Sir Galahad has been around for about eight hundred years. In my research, I looked for what really differentiated Galahad from the other knights in the King Arthur tales. What made him unique? I finally narrowed in on, what I thought, were the simple, fundamental, *essential* ingredients to making Galahad Galahad:

1) He's on a quest for a grail
2) He's a virgin
3) He's chosen by destiny to achieve great things
4) He's the best knight in the world
5) Everybody *knows* he's the best knight in the world

It seems like this guy would be... perfect. Which would be incredibly annoying to the un-perfect people around him and also sets an impossibly high bar for Galahad to live up to. If you're destined for flawless nobility, how can you possibly reach it? The Battle of Legion chapters were the first ones I wrote, which I think helped me to understand my version of Galahad and shape his character. In the end, I feel like Galahad's struggles made him more interesting than if it all came easy for him. ...Although I did enjoy coming up with all of his incredible, impossible, utterly insane achievements. My personal favorite is Galahad decoding the secret language of the dolphins.

In the Kinda Fairytale series, I try to use a mix of references from fairytales, mythology, legends, nursery rhymes, etc... from various cultures. For *Best Knight Ever*, I of course drew on all of that again. (The 2802 model number of Galahad's gun comes from a possible solution to the riddle of how many people were traveling to St. Ives, for instance.) But, I leaned heaviest on the King Arthur tales for inspiration in this book. They had so many weird details, just dying to be mined for ideas. There is a "hand of fire" protecting a castle in some iterations of Sir Galahad's story. How could I not include *that*? Ditto with the glatisant lizard. I mean, if the Arthurian Legend wants to give me something like "barking lizards" to play with, I feel almost obligated to have Trystan eat them. There is also a subtext of infertility in the grail legend, with lands being reduced to wastelands and various "thigh wounds." This fits with the gryphons being cursed and Uther being unable to have more children. It all just seemed to come together in my head.

Whenever possible, I also tried to use place and character names from the King Arthur tales, even though I doubt I could pronounce some of them correctly. (Mynyw???) For instance, the

Fisher King helps to guide the grail-questers on their way in many versions, which is how Fisher Welkyn got his name in my book. "Siege Perilous," the name of the casino in *Best Knight Ever*, is my favorite borrowed phrase. In the Arthurian legends, it is the vacant seat reserved for the knight who finds the grail. Not only does that kind of fit with the theme of the book, it also just sounds cool. I thank all the authors who added and told these amazing stories for the past thousand years. They gave me a lot of material to draw from, as I built this world.

Trystan is one aspect of this book who did not relate to the King Arthur stories, though. He appeared almost by accident in *The Kingpin of Camelot*. His entire character sprang from the very small part of *Alice in Wonderland* featuring griffins. I had originally slated him for Esmeralda's story, but that version of her book faded away pretty quick and Trystan migrated to Camelot. For this book, I lifted some names from the Tristan and Isolda legend, which does connect to the Camelot tales, but I don't really consider that Tristan and my Trystan to be the same character. In the Arthurian Legend, Lyonesse is the homeland of Tristan, though, and it sinks beneath the sea. This reminded me of Atlantis, so it fits perfectly in my story. And in keeping with the idea of a sunken island, I made sure to dunk poor Galahad in water as much as possible. Trystan appreciated my efforts.

I see this book as more of an Adventure Romance story than a Medieval Romance story, so searching for Atlantis also helped to give the characters some adventure-y things to do. (If you've read Linda Howard's "Heart of Fire" or seen *The Mummy* movie from 1999 that's the genre I was going for here. A treasure hunt through a dangerous land, while falling for your partner on the quest.) I also mixed in some Western elements, because Westerns often have themes of post-war societies trying to rebuild. I feel like the time Galahad and Trystan spend in Ted-ville is especially drawing from that idea.

Since Trystan has no real fairytale/legendary counterpart for me to acknowledge, he was wide open for me to write however I saw fit. Which basically means he talked and I wrote it down. Fortunately, Trystan is very easy to write... which sometimes makes him hard to write. He almost always knows what he wants to do. If I need him to do X and he doesn't feel like doing X, then X doesn't happen. On the plus side, this means that is character stays consistent and his voice always comes through to me. On the down side, this means he can be stubborn about what storylines he will accept.

Fortunately, he liked Galahad. A lot. Writing them together was never difficult, because Trystan would always think of something to say. Usually it was something sarcastic, but I could tell he was interested in Galahad pretty quick. Writers shouldn't play favorites with their characters, but I love Trystan. He's one of my favorites. I wanted to give him the True Love he wanted and I feel like I did.

For the purposes of literary authenticity, my sister, Elizabeth, and I selflessly investigated the soundness of Galahad's Pop-Chocolate idea. (You're welcome.) The research was arduous. We popped a bag of extra-butter microwave popcorn and scientifically sprinkled some semi-sweet chocolate chips over it. The combination only occurred to me because we keep chocolate chips and popcorn in the same kitchen cabinet, so I wasn't sure it would actually work. (Somewhere, someone else has no doubt tried it first, but this is the highly sophisticated way that I got the idea.) Anyway, I am happy to report the success of the experiment. Even Liz was impressed and she was skeptical about the entire concept. We both highly recommend the melty goodness of this super-complicated recipe. I have no idea how to make potato chips with candy coating, so I'm unsure how Gala-Chips would taste. I'm guessing pretty good, though. Well, maybe not a caramel-and-whey flavor...

With regards to the next book in the A Kinda Fairytale series, I am still writing Esmeralda's story. (I do not blame anyone who is rolling their eyes as they read that, given my well-documented troubles with the book.) However, I have recently been working on it from a new angle and I feel more encouraged. I also have written several chapters of a new Elemental-Phases book, which makes me pretty happy. My hope is to keep up the momentum and get books out quicker. Please stay tuned!

On a sadder and more serious note, there have been real instances of people being put in zoos. In the early part of the twentieth century, an African man named Ota Benga was exhibited in the Bronx Zoo in New York. Public outcry about his treatment eventually led the zoo to stop Ota Benga's exploitation, but his life continued to be a tragic one. There have been several books written and films made about Ota Benga. It is worth learning more about him and about this very sad moment in American history, if only to help insure that this type of inhumanity can't happen, again.

Please drop me a line if you have any questions or comments about this book or any other at: starturtlepublishing@gmail.com. The same email address can be used to sign up for our mailing list for news about our upcoming books. We also have a Facebook page, which we update fairly regularly, and a new and improved website at www.starturtlepublishing.com. I hope to see you there!

Sneak Peek!

Please enjoy the previous book in the "Kinda Fairytale" series, *The Kingpin of Camelot*.

Winner of the Romantic Times award for best Fantasy Romance of the Year!

In a world where fairytale characters are real, there are laws in place that attempt to keep the wicked witches, ugly stepsisters, and big, bad, wolves under control. But now, the bad guys are fighting for their rights...

The Queen: Guinevere must save Camelot. Ever since Arthur died, the evil Scarecrow has been trying to marry her and gain the crown. Unfortunately, the only man strong enough to help her is Kingpin Midas, a flashy, uneducated mobster dealing with a curse. Gwen is a logical, rational woman, though, and she can draft one hell of a contract. She's pretty sure she can come up with an offer not even the kingdom's greatest villain can refuse.

The Kingpin: Anything Midas touches turns to gold. Literally. The curse has helped him to rule Camelot's underworld with an iron fist. He's convinced there's nothing he can't buy. One look at Gwen and Midas knows that he's about to make his most brilliant purchase, yet. He's about to own the one woman in the world he would give anything to possess. All he has to do to claim her is somehow win a war against the smartest man in Camelot, hide his growing feelings from Gwen, and adjust to a five year old demanding bedtime stories from a gangster. Simple, right?

Can their "fake marriage" become more real than either of them ever imagined?

"To summarize (The Kingpin of Camelot), crazy worldbuilding, a huge fierce marshmallow of a hero disguised as a terrible monster, a queen who assures everyone that she is not a violent person after shooting people threatening her child, funnies, and a surprisingly sweet romance. ….I don't want to ruin it, because you have to discover

Midas."- Ilona Andrews, #1 New York Times Bestselling author

Buy *The Kingpin of Camelot*, now available on Kindle and in paperback!

Printed in Great Britain
by Amazon